WONDER of SMALL THINGS

POEMS OF PEACE & RENEWAL

Edited by
James Crews

Foreword by
Nikita Gill

Storey Publishing

The mission of Storey Publishing is to serve our customers by publishing practical information that encourages personal independence in harmony with the environment.

Edited by Liz Bevilacqua
Art direction and book design by Alethea Morrison
Text production by Jennifer Jepson Smith
Illustrations by © Vicki Turner

Text © 2023 by James Crews, except as shown on pages 207–211

Foreword © 2023 by Nikita Gill

All rights reserved. Hachette Book Group supports the right to free expression and the value of copyright. The purpose of copyright is to encourage writers and artists to produce the creative works that enrich our culture. The scanning, uploading, and distribution of this book without permission is a theft of the author's intellectual property. If you would like permission to use material from the book (other than for review purposes), please contact permissions@hbgusa.com. Thank you for your support of the author's rights.

The information in this book is true and complete to the best of our knowledge. All recommendations are made without guarantee on the part of the author or Storey Publishing. The author and publisher disclaim any liability in connection with the use of this information.

The publisher is not responsible for websites (or their content) that are not owned by the publisher.

> Storey books are available at special discounts when purchased in bulk for premiums and sales promotions as well as for fund-raising or educational use. Special editions or book excerpts can also be created to specification. For details, please send an email to special.markets@hbgusa.com.

Storey Publishing
210 MASS MoCA Way
North Adams, MA 01247
storey.com

Storey Publishing is an imprint of Workman Publishing, a division of Hachette Book Group, Inc., 1290 Avenue of the Americas, New York, NY 10104. The Storey Publishing name and logo are registered trademarks of Hachette Book Group, Inc.

ISBNs: 978-1-63586-644-5 (paperback); 978-1-63586-645-2 (ebook);
978-1-66863-263-5 (downloadable audio)

Printed in the United States by Lakeside Book Company (interior and bind) and
PC (cover) on paper from responsible sources
10 9 8 7 6 5 4 3 2

Library of Congress Cataloging-in-Publication Data on file

What if wonder was the ground of our gathering?
Ross Gay

Sometimes, love looks like small things.
Tracy K. Smith

CONTENTS

Foreword, Nikita Gill xi

What Brings Us Alive, James Crews 1

Wendell Berry, The Peace of Wild Things 5

Ted Kooser, In Early April.. 6

Paula Gordon Lepp, Can You Hear It? 7

Ellen Rowland, What Branches Hold 8

James Crews, Awe 9

Albert Garcia, Ice 10

Andrea Potos, Crocheting in December 11

James Armstrong, First Snow 12

Diana Whitney, Cathedral 13

Joseph Bruchac, Tutuwas 14

Reflective Pause: Let Wonder Guide You 15

Rita Dove, Horse and Tree 16

Michael Kleber-Diggs, The Grove 17

Toi Derricotte, Cherry Blossoms 18

Julia Alvarez, Locust 20

Laure-Anne Bosselaar, Lately, ... 22

Maggie Smith, First Fall 23

Nikita Gill, The Forest 24

Kai Coggin, Essence 25

January Gill O'Neil, For Ella 26

Ross Gay, Sorrow Is Not My Name 27

Reflective Pause: A Time for Everything	28
Mark Nepo, Under the Temple	29
Marjorie Saiser, Crane Migration, Platte River	30
Ellen Rowland, The Way the Sky Might Taste	32
Lorna Crozier, First Kiss	33
Alison Prine, Long Love	34
James Crews, Here with You	35
Alison Luterman, Heavenly Bodies	36
Jacqueline Jules, The Honeybee	38
Reflective Pause: Choosing Peace	39
AE Hines, What Did You Imagine Would Grow?	40
Rachel Michaud, Crossing Over	41
Mark Nepo, Stopped Again by the Sea	42
Carolyn Chilton Casas, Ocean Love	43
Angela Narciso Torres, Self-Portrait as Water	44
George Bilgere, Swim Lessons	46
Rudy Francisco, Water	47
Rosemerry Wahtola Trommer, Belonging	48
Danusha Laméris, Dust	49
Li-Young Lee, To Hold	50
Holly Wren Spaulding, Primitive Objects	51
Donna Hilbert, Ribollita	52
Ada Limón, Joint Custody	53
Lucy Griffith, Attention	54

Reflective Pause: The Place of Attention 55
Peg Edera, Harbors of Miracle 56
Natalie Goldberg, Home 58
Rebecca Baggett, Chestnut 59
Zeina Azzam, Hugging the Tree 60
Linda Hogan, Home in the Woods 61
Danusha Laméris, Nothing Wants to Suffer 62
Reflective Pause: The Awe of Aliveness 63
Kimberly Blaeser, The Way We Love Something Small 64
Brooke McNamara, Listen Back 65
Michelle Wiegers, Slow Down 66
Joshua Michael Stewart, November Praise 68
Susan Varon, The Gentle Dark 69
Jacqueline Suskin, Sunrise, Sunset 70
Joanne Durham, Sunrise Sonnet for My Son 71
Meghan Dunn, Ode to Butter 72
Robbi Nester, Rot 73
Naomi Shihab Nye, Little Farmer 74
James Crews, Tomatoes 76
Sarah Wolfson, What I Like About Beans 77
Susan Musgrave, Tomatoes on the Windowsill
    After Rain 78
Mary Jo LoBello Jerome, Tomato Intuition 79
Leah Naomi Green, Carrot 80

Reflective Pause: Nothing for Granted 81
Jessica Gigot, Amends 82
Lahab Assef Al-Jundi, What the Roses Said to Me 83
Rage Hezekiah, Layers 84
Dorianne Laux, My Mother's Colander 85
Sue Ann Gleason, Ask Me 86
Paola Bruni, The Lesson 88
Meghan Sterling, Chickadee 89
Faith Shearin, My Daughter Describes the Tarantula 90
Laura Foley, Lost and Found 91
Joy Harjo, Redbird Love 92
Kim Stafford, Wren's Nest in a Shed near Aurora 94
Sharon Corcoran, Encounter 95
José A. Alcántara, Archilochus Colubris 96
Emilie Lygren, Meditation 97
Margaret Hasse, Art 98
Mark Nepo, Art Lesson 99
Cristina M. R. Norcross, Breathing Peace 100
Caroline Webster, Expecting 102
Mark Nepo, The Clearing 103
Laura Foley, What Stillness 104
Reflective Pause: The Gift of Stillness 105
Lisa Zimmerman, Lake at Night 106
Joseph Bruchac, Birdfoot's Grampa 107

Heather Swan, Boy	108
Nikita Gill, Your Soft Heart	109
Joyce Sutphen, From Out the Cave	110
Marilyn McCabe, Web	112
Anne Evans, A New Variant	114
Barbara Crooker, This Summer Day	115
Ted Kooser, A Glint	116
Derek Sheffield, For Those Who Would See	117
Reflective Pause: Winks of Calm	118
Sally Bliumis-Dunn, Aubade	119
Kim Stafford, Advice from a Raindrop	120
Danusha Laméris, Let Rain Be Rain	121
Nina Bagley, Gathering	122
Stuart Kestenbaum, Holding the Light	123
Alberto Ríos, The Broken	124
Alfred K. LaMotte, Gentle	125
Patricia Clark, Creed	126
Michael Simms, Sometimes I Wake Early	127
Marjorie Moorhead, Head in the Clouds	128
Joseph Fasano, Letter	129
Penny Harter, Just Grapefruit	130
Jane Kenyon, In Several Colors	131
Kathryn Petruccelli, Instinct	132
Terri Kirby Erickson, Goldfinch	134

Ada Limón, It's the Season I Often Mistake............................ 136

Katherine J. Williams, Late August, Lake Champlain...........137

Laura Ann Reed, Fortitude 138

Nathan Spoon, Poem of Thankfulness.. 139

Annie Lighthart, Let This Day 140

Reflective Pause: Let It Change..141

Laura Grace Weldon, Common Ground.................................... 142

Rena Priest, Tour of a Salmonberry 143

Rosalie Sanara Petrouske, True North 144

Connie Wanek, Talking to Dad 146

Tyler Mortensen-Hayes, After the Heartbreak 147

Ingrid Goff-Maidoff, The Listening Bridge................................ 149

Brad Peacock, A Morning in Thailand 150

Julia Fehrenbacher, The Only Way I Know
to Love the World.. 151

Jacqueline Suskin, How to Fall in Love with Yourself 152

Brad Aaron Modlin, One Candle Now, Then
Seven More 153

Judith Chalmer, Pocket 155

Adele Kenny, Survivor..157

Lois Lorimer, Rescue Dog... 158

Yvonne Zipter, Seeds 159

David Mook, Milkweed..160

Bradford Tice, Milkweed 161

Jane Hirshfield, Solstice 162

Julie Cadwallader Staub, Reverence 163

Jennifer G. Lai, In My Mind's Coral,
 Mother Still Calls Us from Inside 164

Reflective Pause: Worlds of Wonder 165

Rosemerry Wahtola Trommer, Latent 166

Charles Rossiter, Transformation 167

Tony Hoagland, Field Guide 168

Rage Hezekiah, Lake Sunapee 169

January Gill O'Neil, How to Love 172

Reading Group Questions and Topics for Discussion 173
Poet Biographies 178
Credits 207
Acknowledgments 212

FOREWORD

My grandmother once told me that where there is wonder, there also lives poetry. She told me this on a golden spring day at her home in the countryside while we finally picked the ruby-red strawberries she had planted months ago. She held one up to the dazzling Indian sun and said, "To a poet, even a little strawberry like this is a poem." Something about that moment burns so brightly in my mind, I see it in vibrant Technicolor even though I couldn't have been more than six years old when it happened.

This treasured memory is what I think of when I read this gorgeous anthology. What my grandmother gave to me that day was a sense of wonder that the world around us holds magic in what might be considered small and ordinary. The bird that sings outside your window every morning, or as Maggie Smith says in her gorgeous poem "First Fall," "the leaves rusting and crisping at the edges." All you need to do is see it through the enchanted lens that turns the everyday into the extraordinary. This is precisely what poets do so well. Consider these words by Kai Coggin: "did you know these tiny sprouts these little leaves and baby greens already hold the heavy flavors of their final selves?" This revelation tells us that there is so much we do not know about nature, about what we plant in our own gardens, about the trees and the rivers and towns that surround us.

In the introduction to this anthology, James Crews powerfully reminds us about our natural sense of curiosity, of the quiet adventure that is found even on a peaceful walk. Every poem in this collection is filled with such awe and reminds us of the duty of the poet: to collect that awe and write it down. I consider each of these poems to be a lighthouse that beckons others toward its light, giving them hope and safety. Here, Ross Gay reminds us of how little pieces of wonder become a lifeline, a reason to say, "But look; my niece is running through a field calling my name. My neighbor sings like an angel and at the end of my block is a basketball court."

Mary Oliver once said that it is the job of a poet to stand still and learn to be astonished by the world. If there were ever an anthology that proves her thesis, it would be this one. I hope you read this book and delight in these poems as I have. Read them on a sunny day in the garden or in the safety of your bedroom as the rain falls heavily from the sky. Read them when your heart is heavy and your mind feels fraught. Find in these pages your little moments of peace, nourishment for your soul.

As my grandmother said, where there is wonder, there are poets. And where there are poets, there are also the words you never knew you needed, exactly when you need them most.

Nikita Gill

WHAT BRINGS US ALIVE

My husband, Brad, and I were walking the forest trail near our house one autumn afternoon. I found myself feeling bored and more than a little annoyed, however, with the monotony of our usual walk—the same trees starting to shed their leaves, the same rocky path, and same patches of sunlight breaking through the thinned-out canopy. Then Brad gasped and fell to his knees. I thought something was wrong at first, but no—he had spotted a neon-orange caterpillar inching across the crisp leaves that lined the trail, making its slow way across to the other side. "Have you ever seen anything like this?" Brad asked. I told him I had not. He then pulled out his phone and began to film its movements from every angle while I crouched beside him, not only amazed by this creature but also in awe of Brad's awe for the world around us. In just a moment, our so-called boring walk had transformed into one I would never forget, and I was learning once again how to be more present to the everyday wonders that so often occur right at my feet, right in my own backyard. I thought of all the times I had heard Brad give an audible gasp when he saw the white head of a bald eagle coasting above the Battenkill River, or a baby painted turtle swimming in a stream in the abandoned gravel quarry down the road. "I've never seen this before," Brad said as we stared down at that tiny turtle, the reverence evident in his voice.

That same deep love for the world is present in every one of the poems gathered in this book. Wonder calls us back to the curiosity we are each born with, and it makes us want to move closer to what sparks our attention. Wonder opens our senses and helps us stay in touch with a humbling sense of our own human smallness in the face of unexpected beauty and the delicious mysteries of life on this planet. No matter how we name these sensations, we have all felt some version of awe as we were lifted out of the thinking mind, even if for an instant, and brought more fully back into our bodies. In this way, like mindfulness, wonder and awe root us in the moment, and when we create the space in our lives to feel them, the inevitable result is a deep sense of rest, renewal, and peace. The poet and philosopher Mark Nepo has written: "Wonder is the rush of life saturating us with its aliveness, the way sudden rain makes us smile, the way sudden wind opens our face. And while wonder can surprise us, our daily work is to cultivate wonder in ourselves and in each other." In other words, we don't need to wait for amazement to find us, and we don't have to search for it outside of ourselves either. Like the qualities of kindness and gratitude, which have been the subjects of my previous poetry anthologies, wonder and peace can be cultivated and practiced daily with the people, places, and things we encounter.

Poetry often originates in potent bursts of insight, so it is the perfect medium for deepening our practice of reverence for the world. As you'll see, these poems often shun the sublime in favor of the more ordinary blessings we find immediately at hand. In "It's the Season I Often Mistake," for example, the US Poet Laureate Ada Limón describes mistaking birds for leaves and leaves for birds in early winter: "The tawny yellow mulberry leaves are always goldfinches tumbling across the lawn like extreme elation." You'll find many more moments like this throughout the collection, focusing on wonders and insights so slight, we might be inclined to ignore them. Yet these small joys are what most of us can access, and they are the riches of an attentive, mindful life. In order to hold on to such moments, I have also included reflective pauses throughout the book. These sections welcome you to slow down, reflect on a particular poem, and then practice doing some writing of your own, if you wish. I recommend keeping a journal or notebook nearby as you read each poem, since any piece of good writing can transport you more deeply into your own experience.

You'll come across many poems that find the ready-made awe always available in the natural world. It's become clear to us that our planet is in peril, and while we must work to preserve the beauties of this world, we must also remind ourselves, and the generations to come, of all the small wonders they are fighting to save. As the Nebraska poet Marjorie Saiser writes in "Crane Migration, Platte River," "I am in danger of forgetting the cranes . . . how they came as if from the past, how they came of one mind." We sometimes risk forgetting the wonders held in ourselves and in each other, too. In "Talking to Dad," Connie Wanek confesses that she can still speak with her late father no matter where she is: "I need only the faintest signal like a single thread of what used to be his tennis shirt. Like an empty chair at our table into which a grandchild climbs." In her luminous poem "Nothing Wants to Suffer," Danusha Laméris calls us back to radical empathy with each other, animals, and even objects we often consider inanimate, which also deserve our kindness and wonder. "The chair mourns an angry sitter. The lamp, a scalded moth," she writes. "A table, the weight of years of argument. We know this, though we forget."

These poems call us back to our original creative selves, who were never ashamed to give time and attention to something as simple as moss clinging to a fallen log, or a perfect carrot grown in the garden. As Nikita Gill tenderly reminds us, we always have the capacity to practice peace: "You are still the child who gently places fallen baby birds back in their nests." We might rightly feel harmed by the difficult parts of our lives, and alarmed at the state of our world, the endless appetite of the powerful for war and destruction. But to dwell in the brokenness and worry of our lives would be a disservice to ourselves and future generations, who need permission to cultivate wonder, awe, and delight in the middle of a life that's busy, frightening, and amazing all at the same time. As poets and lovers of poetry, we can share the wonders gathered here far and wide. We can use these poems, reflective pauses, and discussion questions to remember what brings us alive, what helps us all find our own moments worthy of savoring.

James Crews

Wendell Berry

THE PEACE OF WILD THINGS

When despair for the world grows in me
and I wake in the night at the least sound
in fear of what my life and my children's lives may be,
I go and lie down where the wood drake
rests in his beauty on the water, and the great heron feeds.
I come into the peace of wild things
who do not tax their lives with forethought
of grief. I come into the presence of still water.
And I feel above me the day-blind stars
waiting with their light. For a time
I rest in the grace of the world, and am free.

Ted Kooser

IN EARLY APRIL

A tree in blossom is a passing cloud
that floats from some warmer place
then slows and snows itself away,
a blizzard of petals that will take
your breath away if you are there,
aware of what's about you, petals
in drifts on the sidewalk, each
with a delicate fragrance that sticks
to the toe of your shoe as you scuff
your way along. All this can occur
in the space of a day, even an hour.
Can you be present when it happens
or will your thoughts have skipped off
into summer and the life beyond?

Paula Gordon Lepp

CAN YOU HEAR IT?

There are days when,
although I try to open myself
to wonder, wonder just
won't be found. Or perhaps,
it is more accurate to say
on those days I am simply
blind to what the world
has to offer

until I look down, and there,
beside the sidewalk,
are blades of grass completely
enrobed in ice, shimmering
in the glow of the setting sun,
and as they sway and move
into each other, if I listen,
really listen,
even they are singing
faint little bell-notes of joy.

Ellen Rowland

WHAT BRANCHES HOLD

This is the hush you've been seeking
isn't it? Silence lush with listening.
Yes, it's cold, so cold and so?
Haven't you come dressed just for this?
And so you pull the soft wool closer, push
the fleeced collar higher, part
the snow-laden branches
and step in, knowing full well
you will be baptized. Allow yourself
to be called deeper and deeper
into this dense huddle
of gentle bark and quiet drape. Did you
ever think you could be so lost and so found
in the same visible breath?

James Crews

AWE

It's a shiver that climbs the trellis
of the spine, each tingle a bright white
morning glory breaking into blossom
beneath the skin. It can happen anywhere,
anytime, even finding this sleeve of ice
worn by a branch all morning, now fallen
on a bed of snow. You can choose to pause,
pick it up, hold the cold thing in your hand
or not. Few tell us that wonder and awe
are decisions we make daily, hourly,
minute by minute in the tiny offices
of the heart—tilting the head to look up
at every tree turned into a chandelier
by light striking ice in just the right way.

Albert Garcia

ICE

In this California valley, ice on a puddle
is a novelty for children
who stand awkward in their jackets
waiting for the school bus.
They lift off thin slabs
to hold up in the early light
like pieces of stained glass.
They run around,
throw them at each other,
lick them, laughing as their pink tongues stick
to the cold, their breath fogging
the morning gray.
       Between the Sierras
in the distance and a faint film
of clouds, the sun rises
red like the gills of a salmon.
From your porch, watching the kids,
you love this morning more
than any you remember. You hear
the bus rumbling down the road
like the future, hear the squealing
voices, feel your own blood warm
in your body as the kids sing
like winter herons, Ice, ice, ice.

Andrea Potos

CROCHETING IN DECEMBER

We live to learn new ways to hold
summer sun through winter cold.
—Robert Francis

I'm wandering the craft store aisles—
yarn bins to the ceiling of blackberry dusk,
lime sherbet, heather bloom,
grape gala and so much more.
I pass them all to find
what will carry me through
the cruel months to come: the softest acrylic
sunny day—a slight sheen on its surface
as if dusted with air of high June.

I fill my arms with skeins.
I will take them home, use what I need
for the warmth of winter gold.

James Armstrong

FIRST SNOW

As you lie in bed,
you can tell it has snowed
by the radiance in the window—
light comes from the ground and not the sky
as if you suddenly lived on the moon.
In that moment, you are back to childhood
when any change of the exterior world
is a change of heart, when the light
tells you what to feel, when you need the sky
and its endless changes.
When that first snow fell,
each snowflake whispered
a secret so intimate
it took the rest of your life to un-believe.
Here it is again.
Your chance to repent.

Diana Whitney

CATHEDRAL

Aquarian sun blazes off the snowpack
blinding me with birdsong,
blue skies and change.

Every year I make a pact
with darkness.

I surrender to the season,
bed down with animals,
eat red meat and chocolate

clad in layers of wool.
But here it is again—sunlight

on my face in the windless
meadow. Actual heat,

not the polar queen's bitter gaze.
A flock of wild turkeys
scores its three-pronged tracks

like runes for me to trace
into the forest. I didn't know
I was waiting for a sign.

In the cathedral of pines
a rough arch, a gold shadow,
the red walls of my heart

expanding in snow.

Joseph Bruchac

TUTUWAS

I know the names
on this land
have been changed,
printed on maps
made by those
who claim their ownership.

Some say nothing survives.

But the wind
still sings
the same song
of our breath.

The hilltop trees
still bend like dancers
in ceremonies
that never ended.

And the little pines,
tutuwas, tutuwas,
lift up, protected
from the weight of snow
by the held-out arms
of their elders.

REFLECTIVE PAUSE

Let Wonder Guide You

"Tutuwas" finds delight in the simple winter scene of little pines, or tutuwas, as they were once called by Indigenous people of eastern North America, covered in snow. Joseph Bruchac explains that, "'Tutuwas' is the name of a song that is also called 'Little Pines,' which can be heard in various Wabanaki nations throughout New England from Vermont to the Canadian Maritimes, Western Abenaki, Penobscot, Passamaquoddy, Malecite, and Miq'mac. It's usually sung by children and danced by their mothers. The words ask the dancers to move toward each of the four directions, and spin around. The title 'Tutuwas' refers to human babies as well as the small pine trees that are protected by the outstretched arms of their elders." By using a word that applies to the young of both humans and trees, Bruchac reminds us that we are elements of the natural world. We can feel protected by the "held-out arms" of elders who were rooted here.

Invitation for Writing and Reflection

Focus on some plant or animal that draws your attention and describe it in specific detail. Let it speak to your creative, intuitive self, allowing curiosity and wonder to guide you in your exploration.

Rita Dove

HORSE AND TREE

Everybody who's anybody longs to be a tree—
or ride one, hair blown to froth.
That's why horses were invented, and saddles
tooled with singular stars.

This is why we braid their harsh manes
as if they were children, why children
might fear a carousel at first for the way
it insists that life is round. No,

we reply, there is music and then it stops;
the beautiful is always rising and falling.
We call and the children sing back *one more time*.
In the tree the luminous sap ascends.

Michael Kleber-Diggs

THE GROVE

Planted here as we are, see how we want
to bow and sway with the motion of earth
in sky. Feel how desire vibrates within us
as our branches fan out, promise entanglements,
rarely touch. Here, our sweet rustlings. If only
we could know how twisted up our roots
are, we might make vast shelter together—cooler
places, verdant spaces, more sustaining air.
But we are strange trees, reluctant in this
forest—we oak and ash, we pine—
the same the same, not different. All of us
reach toward star and cloud, all of us want
our share of light, just enough rainfall.

Toi Derricotte

CHERRY BLOSSOMS

I went down to
mingle my breath
with the breath
of the cherry blossoms.

There were photographers:
Mothers arranging their
children against
gnarled old trees;
a couple, hugging,
asks a passerby
to snap them
like that,
so that their love
will always be caught
between two friendships:
ours & the friendship
of the cherry trees.

Oh Cherry,
why can't my poems
be as beautiful?

A young woman in a fur-trimmed
coat sets a card table
with linens, candles,
a picnic basket & wine.
A father tips
a boy's wheelchair back
so he can gaze
up at a branched
heaven.
          All around us
the blossoms
flurry down
whispering,

Be patient
you have an ancient beauty.

          Be patient,
             you have an ancient beauty.

Julia Alvarez

LOCUST

Weybridge 1998

Happiness surprised me in middle age:
just in the nick of forty I found love,
a steady job, a publisher, a home,
ten acres and a sky-reflecting pond—
a better ending than I'd expected.
We built our own house on a bare hillside
and started planting trees: elm, maples, oak.
Under my second-story writing room
(which was all windows on the southeast side)
we put in locusts for their "instant shade."

By our third anniversary those trees
were grown so tall, it was like climbing up
into a tree house when I went to work,
pulling the mind's ladder up behind me
from the absorbing life I was living.
I tried to focus but those branches filled
with songbirds busy at their nest building,
squirrels scampering to the very edges
of blossoming branches buzzing with bees.
How could I write with all this activity?

It took some getting used to but, of course,
life feeds life. Where'd I get the idea
that art and happiness could never jive?
I felt stupid, wasting so many years.
But I took solace from those locust trees,
known for their crooked, seemingly aimless growth.
We have to live our natures out, the seed
we call our soul unfolds over the course
of a lifetime and there's no going back
on who we are—that much I've learned from trees.

Laure-Anne Bosselaar

LATELY,

   when a branch pulls at my sleeve
like a child's tug, or the fog, reticent & thick,
lifts — & strands of it hang like spun sugar
in branches & twigs, or when a phoebe
trills from the hackberry,
        I believe such luck
is meant for me. Does this happen to you?
Do you believe at times that a moment
chooses you to remember it & tell about it—
so that it may live again?

Maggie Smith

FIRST FALL

I'm your guide here. In the evening-dark
morning streets, I point and name.
Look, the sycamores, their mottled,
paint-by-number bark. Look, the leaves
rusting and crisping at the edges.
I walk through Schiller Park with you
on my chest. Stars smolder well
into daylight. Look, the pond, the ducks,
the dogs paddling after their prized sticks.
Fall is when the only things you know
because I've named them
begin to end. Soon I'll have another
season to offer you: frost soft
on the window and a porthole
sighed there, ice sleeving the bare
gray branches. The first time you see
something die, you won't know it might
come back. I'm desperate for you
to love the world because I brought you here.

Nikita Gill

THE FOREST

One day, when you wake up,
you will find that you've become a forest.

You've grown roots and found strength in them
that no one thought you had.

You have become stronger
and full of life-giving qualities.

You have learned to take all the negativity around you
and turn it into oxygen for easy breathing.

A host of wild creatures live inside you
and you call them stories.

A variety of beautiful birds nest inside your mind
and you call them memories.

You have become an incredible
self-sustaining thing of epic proportions.

And you should be so proud of yourself,
of how far you have come from the seeds of who you used to be.

Kai Coggin

ESSENCE

I thinned the seeds already sprouting
in the bamboo garden
the radish beet carrot and bean

pulled each birth
out of the earth
and laid it on my tongue
crushed it with my teeth

and did you know these tiny sprouts
these little leaves and baby greens
already hold the heavy flavors of their final selves?

if only we tasted our own essence from birth
knew the transformations to come
were all part of the becoming—

that we had the imprint all along.

January Gill O'Neil

FOR ELLA

I love a wild daffodil,
the one that grows
where she's planted—
along a wooded highway
left to her own abandon,
but not abandoned.
Her big yellow head
leaning toward or away
from the sun. Not excluded
but exclusive, her trumpet
heralds no one, not even
the Canada geese—
their long-necked honks
announcing their journey.
She'll be here less
than a season, grace us
with green slender stems,
strong enough to withstand
rain and spring's early chill.
And when she goes,
what remains she'll bury
deep inside the bulb of her,
take a part of me with her
until she returns.

Ross Gay

SORROW IS NOT MY NAME

after Gwendolyn Brooks

No matter the pull toward brink. No
matter the florid, deep sleep awaits.
There is a time for everything. Look,
just this morning a vulture
nodded his red, grizzled head at me,
and I looked at him, admiring
the sickle of his beak.
Then the wind kicked up, and,
after arranging that good suit of feathers
he up and took off.
Just like that. And to boot,
there are, on this planet alone, something like two
million naturally occurring sweet things,
some with names so generous as to kick
the steel from my knees: agave, persimmon,
stick ball, the purple okra I bought for two bucks
at the market. Think of that. The long night,
the skeleton in the mirror, the man behind me
on the bus taking notes, yeah, yeah.
But look; my niece is running through a field
calling my name. My neighbor sings like an angel
and at the end of my block is a basketball court.
I remember. My color's green. I'm spring.

REFLECTIVE PAUSE

A Time for Everything

Despite our fears and uncertainties, Ross Gay calls us back to wonder again and again in his poem "Sorrow Is Not My Name." Even the sight of a vulture who "nodded his red, grizzled head at me" can become a source of sudden awe, if we pause long enough to notice the miracle of that creature wearing his "good suit of feathers" then flying off again into the wind. And those "two million naturally occurring sweet things" might make us rapturous as we sing out loud their names: "agave, persimmon, stick ball, the purple okra." In the end, Gay reminds us that the simplest things keep us attached to this difficult yet still praiseworthy world. Our relationships, our home-place, our passions, and the fact that we can still recall them if we wish, give us the resilience to remain "green," to remember that our nature is to keep growing despite the obstacles, and even sometimes because of them.

Invitation for Writing and Reflection

Begin your writing by using the same words that begin Ross Gay's poem, "No matter . . . ," and articulate some of the fearful things that might keep you from delight. See where that repetition leads you, and let your intuition take over as you write from a place of reverence for the simplest things you witness.

Mark Nepo

UNDER THE TEMPLE

The temple hanging over the water is
anchored on pillars that nameless workers
placed in the mud long ago. So never forget
that the mud and the hands of those workers
are part of the temple, too. What frames the
sacred is just as sacred. The dirt that packs
the plant is the beginning of beauty. And
those who haul the piano on stage are the
beginning of music. And those who are
stuck, though they dream of soaring,
are the ancestors of our wings.

Marjorie Saiser

CRANE MIGRATION, PLATTE RIVER

I am in danger of forgetting the cranes,
their black wavering lines in the sky,
how they came as if from the past,
how they came of one mind,
wheeling, swirling over the river.
I am in danger of losing
the purling sound they make,
and the motion of their long wings.
We had stopped the car on the river road
and got out, you and I,
the wind intermittent in our faces
as if it too came from a distant place
and wavered and began again, gusting.
Line after line of cranes
came out of the horizon,
sliding overhead.
The voices of cranes
harsh and exciting.
Something old in me answered.
What did it say? Maybe it said *Kneel*.

I almost forgot the ancient sound,
back in time, back, and back.
The road, the two of us at the guardrail,
low scraggle of weeds flattening and rising
in wind. This is what I must retain:
my knees hit the damp sand of the roadside.
This is what I remember:
you knelt too. We were wordless together
before the birds as they landed on the sandbars
and night came on.

Ellen Rowland

THE WAY THE SKY MIGHT TASTE

The bite of a softened cardamom pod
in a spoonful of Tikka Masala.
Tang of copper, caperberry
other berries, too:
a rasp, a blue, a lingon, elder
lit with lemon, thin slice of moon.
The breath of a first kiss
sweet and deeply surprising.
Dirt on the youngest tongue, the red
flesh of a torn fig eaten
straight from the tree,
the constellation of wings
as champagne leaves the flute.

Lorna Crozier

FIRST KISS

It was like the farm
when it went
electric, remember?

Just like that
you flicked a switch
and it was Genesis.

We saw each other
in our nakedness
though we weren't,

not yet.

Alison Prine

LONG LOVE

blur of years stirs in the room
on a bright February morning

I have studied your face
for ten thousand days

long shadows across the untouched snow
your winter-split fingertips against my spine

tone color of your voice
that has said my name more than any other

ragged with grief, hoarse with desire
warm tenor of dailiness

when our love was illegal
and we were young we promised

not to promise, didn't we
didn't we say we would just begin again

James Crews

HERE WITH YOU

It's too hot on this August afternoon
to move from our places on the couch,
even to slice the peach still waiting
on the counter for the kiss of the knife.

A different kind of hunger keeps me
here with you, rubbing the fine hairs
on your arms that have turned blond
after all those hours in the sun,

and which are just now catching
the light, spinning it into gold I want
to touch over and over, never once
having dreamed I'd ever be this rich.

Alison Luterman

HEAVENLY BODIES

We're falling asleep holding hands.
I can feel his knuckles
rough and dry around the edges.
Hands that work a lathe
five days a week,
cutting, scraping, scouring
the sharp metal.
I've watched them pick their way
up the guitar's neck,
wander over piano keys,
or rub the cat's cheek—
and now, even in sleep
his fingers keep pulsing my palm,
squeezing and releasing
to an inaudible beat.
My own small hand, always cold,
beaches like a starfish
on the reef of his metacarpus.
Twelve years loving and fighting.
How ridiculous
we end up like this—two mis-
matched puzzle pieces,
sanded down to fit.

Clasped and constellated.
There should be
a better name for such
persistence: Stargrit.
Heartlocked. Vowstrung.
Look, love, how we've become
ancient, eternal even,
in our heavenly bodies, wheeling
through the universe without leaving
our bed. Handwoven. Holding on.

Jacqueline Jules

THE HONEYBEE

I almost reacted. Almost
questioned how he could dare
complain about more pots to wash
when I cooked all afternoon.

Then I remembered the honeybee,
how it dies a gruesome death
when its stinger embeds
in human skin. The bee tears
a hole in its belly pulling out
the sac of venom.

A honeybee values peace.
It only stings when threatened,
not over something as petty
as who cooked and who cleaned up.

And certainly not when it could rest,
like I am right now, with feet up
on the couch, while my honey
loads the dishwasher
and scrubs every pot.

REFLECTIVE PAUSE

Choosing Peace

Life presents us with so many moments when we can decide to react or not. Do we choose peace, or move into negativity? In "The Honeybee," the speaker narrowly avoids a fight with her husband over his idle complaint about having to wash so many pots after she cooked all afternoon. How many times has each of us felt threatened like this, angered by some small, offhand comment a loved one made, perhaps not intending to harm us? Yet, to bring herself back from the brink, she remembers the honeybee, "how it dies a gruesome death when its stinger embeds in human skin." As the speaker points out, "A honeybee values peace" above all things because it can literally mean life and death for that tiny creature. We forget that true peace begins at home, in our individual lives, and even if we can't prevent the larger wars and battles for justice that must rage in the outside world, we can do everything in our power to take care of our own corner of the planet, refusing to engage in a fight over such slight things. Our kind and careful intentions ripple out into the larger world whenever we do what we can to keep the peace we know can be so easily shattered between us.

Invitation for Writing and Reflection

Reflect on a moment when you could have chosen to react with anger, but instead decided to practice peace. How did it feel to exist in that sliver of an instant, choosing peace instead of violence? You might begin, as Jacqueline Jules does here, by saying what you "almost" did.

AE Hines

WHAT DID YOU IMAGINE WOULD GROW?

Before you, I never grew anything.
Never looked at the unbroken ground
and imagined what might sprout there,
that I could coax my own sustenance
from the earth.

I never dislodged the pebbles or dry clay,
and the miracle of food appeared on my table
from the downtown Safeway. The flowers,
orchids, all made of silk.

Before you, there was no garden.
No cherry tomatoes, no peonies or roses,
no sweet-smelling melons swelling
on the ground. You had your tricks
for getting the most from the soil,
the way a saint pulls the best
from a soul.

Before you, my dear, no one bothered.
No one had the patience. No one
stood staring at the thin rocky soil
of me, never walked up and down
my barren rows, rubbing dirt
between his fingers, asking himself:
What shall I plant here?
What precisely will grow?

Rachel Michaud

CROSSING OVER

Did I tell you your eyes are mirrors?
I see who I could be.
Did I tell you your eyes are windows?
A world where I could go.

What is it about your smile?
What is it about your laughter?
What is it about you
that shatters me?

You hold me like a newborn,
tell a bedtime story.
When we rock, when we rock,
who is the boat and who is the sea?

Mark Nepo

STOPPED AGAIN BY THE SEA

My early memories are of
motoring out to sea where we
would cut the engine and hoist
the sails. Then, we'd wait for this
unseen force that some called wind
to carry us away from the streets.
Once in the open sea, it was hard
to think, hard to stay with any one
fear. We always left home to drift
near a deeper home. I guess I've
done this my whole life. For what
is poetry but the drift in search of
a deeper home? What is love but
the hoisting of all we hide until
it carries us away from all that is
hidden? What is peace but the
hammock of a wave that
no one can name?

Carolyn Chilton Casas

OCEAN LOVE

Let me not forget to notice
all the seasons of the ocean
with an awe-filled soul—
equally winter's pounding surf
and summer's gentle swells.
Every bay a changing alchemy
of colors—smoke, sapphire,
aqua, slate, and sky.
Let me not forget to search
September's waters
for the curved backs of whales,
their tails breaching toward the sun,
dorsal fins of dolphins undulating
smoothly in and out of waves
just beyond the breaks.
The ocean's briny smell
fills my lungs with longing
for a simpler life.
She urges me to set my cares aside,
float at peace in her salty arms.

Angela Narciso Torres

SELF-PORTRAIT AS WATER

why does the body feel
   most beautiful underwater—
is what goes through me

   when I break the blue
surface, levels rising as I plumb
   the tub's white womb

this second skin thinner,
   slicker, gleaming wet
as a lacquered bowl

   because the simplest
of molecules—two H's
   one O—love

to love each other, cling
   to what they touch
how this universal solvent

   swallows every hill
fills the hollows
   of my surrender

most forgiving of
   substances, I resolve
to live like you—to fill

   and be filled,
to take the shape
   of my vessel

dispensing heat
   displacing matter
lighter than air

George Bilgere

SWIM LESSONS

The pretty lifeguard holds our son to her breast,
counts to three, then plunges him under water
for a full, astonishing second before
lifting him, shocked and sputtering, back
to the sunny morning at the public pool,
and the laughter of his mother and father,
who have betrayed him, who have handed the center
of the universe to a sunburned teenager.

Once again she pulls him to her bosom
and once again the bright young summer,
with its snow cones and beach towels and Coppertone,
closes over his head with a rush, once more
he's far from us, in the drowning element,
until once more a woman brings him gasping
and amazed to the dazzling world,
our little boy, laughing in her arms, beautiful
strangers already laying claim to him.

Rudy Francisco

WATER

When I was six years old,
my brother and my cousins
tried to teach me how to swim.

They did this by throwing me into a pool.
Immediately, my arms became two skinny
brown flailing distress signals.

I think I heard my brother say,
"If he dies, I'm going to be in so much trouble."
I remember them pulling me from the jaws
of the liquid beast before it could devour me whole.
That was the day I almost lost my life.

To anyone brave enough to love me,

Do you know the human body is approximately
sixty percent water? When I walk into a room
full of people, all I see is an ocean.

Rosemerry Wahtola Trommer

BELONGING

And if it's true we are alone,
we are alone together,
the way blades of grass
are alone, but exist as a field.
Sometimes I feel it,
the green fuse that ignites us,
the wild thrum that unites us,
an inner hum that reminds us
of our shared humanity.
Just as thirty-five trillion
red blood cells join in one body
to become one blood.
Just as one hundred thirty-six thousand
notes make up one symphony.
Alone as we are, our small voices
weave into the one big conversation.
Our actions are essential
to the one infinite story of what it is
to be alive. When we feel alone,
we belong to the grand communion
of those who sometimes feel alone—
we are the dust, the dust that hopes,
a rising of dust, a thrill of dust,
the dust that dances in the light
with all other dust, the dust
that makes the world.

Danusha Laméris

DUST

It covers everything, fine powder,
the earth's gold breath falling softly
on the dark wood dresser, blue ceramic bowls,
picture frames on the wall. It wafts up
from canyons, carried on the wind,
on the wings of birds, in the rough fur of animals
as they rise from the ground. Sometimes it's copper,
sometimes dark as ink. In great storms,
it even crosses the sea. Once,
when my grandmother was a girl,
a strong gale lifted red dust from Africa
and took it thousands of miles away
to the Caribbean where people swept it
from their doorsteps, kept it in small jars,
reminder of that other home.
Gandhi said, "The seeker after truth
should be humbler than the dust."
Wherever we go, it follows.
I take a damp cloth, swipe the windowsills,
the lamp's taut shade, run a finger
over the dining room table.
And still, it returns, settling in the gaps
between floorboards, gilding the edges
of unread books. What could be more loyal,
more lonely, and unsung?

Li-Young Lee

TO HOLD

So we're dust. In the meantime, my wife and I
make the bed. Holding opposite edges of the sheet,
we raise it, billowing, then pull it tight,
measuring by eye as it falls into alignment
between us. We tug, fold, tuck. And if I'm lucky,
she'll remember a recent dream and tell me.

One day we'll lie down and not get up.
One day, all we guard will be surrendered.

Until then, we'll go on learning to recognize
what we love, and what it takes
to tend what isn't for our having.
So often, fear has led me
to abandon what I know I must relinquish
in time. But for the moment,
I'll listen to her dream,
and she to mine, our mutual hearing calling
more and more detail into the light
of a joint and fragile keeping.

Holly Wren Spaulding

PRIMITIVE OBJECTS

Sleeping an hour later than usual,
the sweat smell of his neck,

coffee, even the dregs, and brine
as the tide came in. Harbor seals

then whole oceans of gold light,
his illness on the mend, Earth

thawing again, a beginning in the way
we touched each other's bodies.

Like archaeologists, how we dug
and removed by spoonfuls, layer

after layer of dirt. How it was up to us—
with small brushes, bare hands—

to save what we'd found.

Donna Hilbert

RIBOLLITA

I praise the way you save
stale bread left on the shelf too long,
rinds of Parmesan tough to grate,
old greens not crisp enough
for salad, but fine for soup
re-boiled from what's on hand.
I love the way you salvage
bruised tomato, sprouting onion,
imperfect squash, laying no morsel
to mold, nothing to waste,
filling each space with aroma
of soup, saying supper, manga!
come eat, come safely, come home.

Ada Limón

JOINT CUSTODY

Why did I never see it for what it was:
abundance. Two families, two different
kitchen tables, two sets of rules, two
creeks, two highways, two stepparents
with their fish tanks or eight tracks or
cigarette smoke or expertise in recipes or
reading skills. I cannot reverse it, the record
scratched and stopping to that original
chaotic track. But let me say, I was taken
back and forth on Sundays and it was not easy
but I was loved in each place. And so I have
two brains now. Two entirely different brains.
The one that always misses where I'm not,
the one that is so relieved to finally be home.

Lucy Griffith

ATTENTION

Home—the place of attention.
Where you know that swirl in the road
marks the dust bath of a jackrabbit.
Or that a particular Canyon Wren ends
her descending aria with a startling yee-haw.

That on our longest of days,
the sun retires on the breast
of the northwest horizon
and begins a steady southern swing
to the little knoll where we mark its winter twin.

Our lives held in this gentle cup,
palmed within an arc of light.

REFLECTIVE PAUSE

The Place of Attention

Our homes are not always the places where we pay the most attention. We might take care of our house or apartment, but after a while, we can begin to ignore all the things that share space with us. Since coming across "Attention" by Lucy Griffith, I've been feeling much more wonder for all the signs that tell me I'm home—the ruts of our washed-out gravel driveway, certain patches of blackberries ripening, the black-eyed Susan I planted years ago finally blooming. So often we look past such small things, perhaps not thinking our daily lives are worthy of awe. Griffith urges us to bring our attention more deeply into the places we know best and see how we are "held in this gentle cup" of home, no matter what else might be going on in our lives or in the world.

Invitation for Writing and Reflection
What are the images and signs that let you know you are home? What are the daily rituals and encounters that make a place your own?

Peg Edera

HARBORS OF MIRACLE

Once in Quebec
standing on top of a picnic table
I looked out across a valley
and saw only
tree after tree
a marching army of trees
with no space or air
only constancy and
what seemed inevitability.
The lack of welcome for my kind
was a pulse
bigger than mine.
I became weightless,
unbounded,
smaller than a molecule,
untethered.

If I knew to look
for harbors of miracle
I would have found my skin walls
and blood rivers,
the pebbles of fingernails,
the still-working bellows of lungs,
the possibility of eyes
seeing the small thing
like a pinecone,

seed for a tree,
home for a bird,
maker of rain and air—
all in the palm of my hand.

Natalie Goldberg

HOME

I am thinking of the rain in New York
the driving rain over the Metropolitan Museum
and the Guggenheim and the small delicatessen
down in the Village that sells *flanken*
I am thinking of the rain making rivers by the curb
near Ohrbach's and Penn Station
the shop selling pita sandwiches
the grease and char of lamb
rotating slowly in the raining day

I am thinking of the fruit stands now
the five hundred fruit stands all over New York
I'm thinking mostly of the dark celery leaves
above the green stalks and the bright skins of oranges
I am thinking of Macy's meat department
and the Nebraska cows
of the hundred year old air in Macy's
and the green cashmere sweaters on top of the glass counter
I am remembering the way pizza smells in the streets calling
        hunger out of ourselves
I am thinking now of the Hudson River and the rain meeting it
the mist already rising over the George Washington Bridge
and the trees growing wildly on the other shore

Rebecca Baggett

CHESTNUT

I touched a chestnut sapling
in the Georgia mountains.

My friend writes of the great trees
and their vanishing,

but I have seen a young chestnut,
tender and green, rising from its ashes.

I, too, write of loss and grief,
the hollow they carve

in the chest,
but that hollow may shelter

some new thing,
a life I could not

have imagined or wished,
a life I would never

have chosen. I have seen
the chestnut rising,

luminous,
from its own bones,

from the ashes of its first life.

Zeina Azzam

HUGGING THE TREE

It was neither part of a protest
nor a statement to the world.
I simply put my arms around
a tall oak and stood in embrace,
our bodies juxtaposed.
There was no swaying: her
trunk, solid and true, felt like
an ancestor, a pillar thick
with years. Her bark scratched
my skin if I moved, so I stayed
still. It was a time to be calm
and reflect on our presence
together. To look up to the sky
and fathom the height of my
partner. To inhale the earthy
scent. To arc my grateful arms
around this strong matriarch
and whisper into the wood
my wordless secret: I have not
hugged anyone for months,
my dear tree.

Linda Hogan

HOME IN THE WOODS

Oh home in the woods,
I am here as one hungry to eat,
one with no bread
in the garden of trees
in a place where the stone wishes to blossom.
Bullets have gone to sleep
and with effort the water
flows the way it once did.
Here, in winter, there is enough
dry wood for heat
and I enter smiling, forgetting our history.
Can you bring me to the place
where pollen is now the light
and we remember the original song?
Can you keep me
here? Can you unharm me?

Danusha Laméris

NOTHING WANTS TO SUFFER

after Linda Hogan

Nothing wants to suffer. Not the wind
as it scrapes itself against the cliff. Not the cliff

being eaten, slowly, by the sea. The earth does not want
to suffer the rough tread of those who do not notice it.

The trees do not want to suffer the axe, nor see
their sisters felled by root rot, mildew, rust.

The coyote in its den. The puma stalking its prey.
These, too, want ease and a tender animal in the mouth

to take their hunger. An offering, one hopes,
made quickly, and without much suffering.

The chair mourns an angry sitter. The lamp, a scalded moth.
A table, the weight of years of argument.

We know this, though we forget.

Not the shark nor the tiger, fanged as they are.
Nor the worm, content in its windowless world

of soil and stone. Not the stone, resting in its riverbed.
The riverbed, gazing up at the stars.

Least of all, the stars, ensconced in their canopy,
looking down at all of us—their offspring—

scattered so far beyond reach.

REFLECTIVE PAUSE

The Awe of Aliveness

In "Nothing Wants to Suffer," humans don't make an appearance until the very end when the speaker suggests we are the "offspring" of stars. That line alone is enough to generate awe for the smallness and humility we can sometimes feel on this planet. Yet the true source of wonder comes as the poem implies that everything has the potential to feel pain, including those things that we sometimes think of as inanimate objects. A deep sense of compassion seems to unfold as the speaker humanizes the wind, the cliff, and the earth itself: showing us that everything from plants and animals, soil and stones, to the very table at which we sit can feel the "weight of years of argument." If we see all the creatures and objects around us as alive, how can we not feel wonder for them, alongside the tender realization that everything and everyone we encounter is simply seeking the peace of belonging that we can so easily offer them?

Invitation for Writing and Reflection

Begin your own writing with Linda Hogan's words "Nothing wants to suffer," and see where this poignant phrase carries your own imagination. How does your view of the world change if you see everything around you as alive and capable of feeling?

Kimberly Blaeser

THE WAY WE LOVE SOMETHING SMALL

The translucent claws of newborn mice
this pearl cast of color,
the barely perceptible
like a ghosted threshold of being:
here   not here.
The single breath we hold
on the thinnest verge of sight:
not there   there.
A curve nearly naked
an arc of almost,
a wisp of becoming
a wand—
tiny enough to change me.

Brooke McNamara

LISTEN BACK

Stay here at the precipice, quiet.
Quiet as the sun rises
over the rooftops
across the street
and the cats watch, rapt.
Quiet as the coffee deepens
its creamy sweet acidity.
How many mornings
have I woken like this, early
and called to listen
at the window of the unknown?
Sometimes it speaks to me.
Sometimes it listens back.

Michelle Wiegers

SLOW DOWN

This morning I'm so tired
from pushing myself hard,
that as I drive down this country road
I can't bring myself to go

anywhere close to the speed limit.
I feel like a silver haired lady
peeking over my steering wheel
as I creep along, letting

the cars whiz by me.
I always assume the elderly
go slowly because they're cautious,
not wanting to hit anyone

or miss the ambulance
racing down the road with siren blaring.
But maybe they've figured out
a secret that I'm still trying to learn.

What if driving slowly
is the only way
to live my best life,
to keep from running so fast

that I go right past myself?
Running by the small child inside
who seeks to fill herself with wonder,
passing up the chance for rest,

for play, to slow myself
long enough to notice
how pleasant the rain sounds
dripping onto the roof

of the house next door,
tiny wet whispers tapping
those few remaining leaves
clinging to the maple

in my backyard,
an almost silent thrumming
slowing down my weary soul.
The steady chime

of church bells ringing
in the distance, in this moment,
reminding me, I've already
been given all that I need.

Joshua Michael Stewart

NOVEMBER PRAISE

The smell of ferns and understory
after rain. The tick, tick of stove,

flame under kettle. Bing Crosby,
and not just the Christmas records.

Cooking meat slowly off the bone,
and every kind of soup and stew.

To come this close to nostalgia,
but go no further, leaving behind

the boy who wore loneliness
like boots too big for his feet.

That time of evening,
when everything turns blue

in moonlight, when darkness
has yet to consume all for itself.

Susan Varon

THE GENTLE DARK

surrounds the house, meaning no harm.
No sirens, no calls of wolves or coyotes,
no ominous rumbling of thunder.

Nothing at all to remind me
that when I step outside there's
a world waiting. I could be living

at the end, I could be the last human
standing. Hallelujah that this is not so.
Hallelujah for the gradually lightening sky,

in which I see my actual world shining
through the blinds. Not my past world,
of New York neighborhoods and friends,

but this lovely, sun-dappled world
of now, of trees and growing things.
I hold my breath a moment

and then exhale. Yes, I welcome
with open arms another sweet
and necessary day.

Jacqueline Suskin

SUNRISE, SUNSET

Nothing can keep me
from watching first light
rise over eastern mountains.
This is what makes me sit still.
Not sleep. Not a lover.
And nothing can prevent me
from soaking in the final
gift of sun as it bleeds brilliant
over the western mountains.
This is what calls me
to repeatedly walk toward the Pacific.
I have to commit to something
in this life and a flaming circle
in the sky seems right.
The best attempt at ritual
and routine, guided by light.

Joanne Durham

SUNRISE SONNET FOR MY SON

My son unloads the dishwasher first thing
each morning. I think of him, four hundred
miles away, as I stand on tiptoe to shelve
last night's wine glasses, stack my mother's
dessert plates, open the drawer beneath
the oven just deep enough for all the pots
and pans. He says for him, too, it's a kind
of meditation, this routine he and his wife
have shaped into the contours of a shared
life, fluted and spacious as the overflowing
fruit bowl. This is what he possesses, not
Lenox or Waterford, which neither of us owns,
this man I raised, who hums as he sorts
the silverware, noticing how each spoon shines.

Meghan Dunn

ODE TO BUTTER

To its sweetness and salt, to its sunshine
in a stick, spreading in sheets of gold
over a cob of summer corn, a halved
blueberry muffin, to its chameleon nature,
crisping and softening and browning
and caramelizing everything it touches.
To the sound its waxed paper wrapper makes
when a knife is sliced through at the blue line.
Satisfying. To the friend who once answered,
Well, do you want it to be good? when I asked
if this much butter was enough and who watched
without judgment, with motherly approval
as I sliced in more and then more. To the way
it goes "straight to my thighs," themselves butter-
like in their softness, their pleasingly elastic firmness,
the way they too spread, golden, are sweet
and salty. To the sound they make swishing together.
Satisfying. This permission I give myself.

Robbi Nester

ROT

The garbage reeks, full of leftovers
and moldy lemons, mats of dryer lint,
like a skin of algae on the surface
of a pond. I ought to take the full bag
out, but I'm reluctant to engage with
the decay that's at the heart of everything.
And yet, if one could study it impartially,
without a trace of terror or repulsion,
the vivid shades of dissolution rival
the desert after rain, spilled paint
spreading to the far horizon. Even
the odors hover on the edge of almost
beautiful, as full as perfume's ripe musk,
purple as the jacaranda. It can even
be delicious—at least to some. Consider
the fragrant funk of some ripe cheeses,
durian, or kimchi, thousand-year-old eggs,
buried in the yard until the yolk marbles
greenish black. Without rot, none of us
could thrive. Everything that grows
feeds on what went before, ocean reefs
seeded by a wealth of putrid whalefall,
ancient cities stacked one atop another,
rising from the same foundation, fertile
ground for everything to come.

Naomi Shihab Nye

LITTLE FARMER

With love, to Earthdance Farm

She pulled us up the hill in a red wagon.
We rolled home with brown sacks in our laps.
Later I worked at Mueller's Organic Farm,
the rows knew my step.
I plucked berries gently, never bruising.
They paid 5 cents a box, it felt like a lot.
All my life has had that light, square shape.
Such ruddy sunstruck pride
in the farmers named Al and Caroline,
Al loved his mounds of squash, sacks of beans,
with fierce intensity. Caroline said *Nope, I only
love him.* Their okra bore an essence of perfection,
ripe corn whispered inside its perfect sheaves
and drifty web of hair. *You are here,* it said.
You will always be here. Years later Al told me,
Your mother was the most lovely person
who ever walked up my drive, that long shiny
ponytail, those huge eyes. She asked
the best questions. That shows intelligence.
He sang me songs, lost love and lonely stars.
I had never known he played a guitar.
Why didn't I ask more questions?
The lives spun out. He wanted me to stay.

I wish I could harvest his patience
from fifty years away. Al long dead,
his dutiful Caroline dead, their farm still
a farm though, one victory! I'd tell him
how right he was about slowness,
the path of sunlight through leaves,
how dirt has always befriended me,
birdcalls beyond,
how his shy smile, waving goodbye with a hoe,
stayed with me forever, how no tomato
was ever better than the one he held in his hand.

James Crews

TOMATOES

When I bite into the bruise-
colored flesh of this heirloom tomato
known as a Cherokee Purple,
I'm transported back to the dirt road
that ran along the Meramec River
where my father pulled over
at the farm stand, then stepped out
of the truck, brushed for a moment
in gravel dust suspended in the sun.
He came back grinning, gripping
a bag of homegrown Beefsteaks so fat
they were already bursting their juices
through the brown paper, running
down his long-gone hands, which I am
reaching out to touch again before
he turns the key in the ignition,
begging him not to go, not just yet,
as I salt the next slice.

Sarah Wolfson

WHAT I LIKE ABOUT BEANS

That sure way, after they unfurl
from their tiny selves, the plants retain
a flap of former life: the seed relic
sliding down the stalk, lower and
lower, a set of not-quite wings
and not-quite leaves. How even after
the now brown casing has dropped
to earth as compost, the bean itself
remains as two naked curls
of cellulose, a little shriveled,
a lot misshapen, but still
for all the world a set of small
animated hands about to clap
for all the green that outstrips them.

Susan Musgrave

TOMATOES ON THE WINDOWSILL AFTER RAIN

and bread by the woodstove
waiting to be punched down again.
I step out into the dark
morning, find the last white flowers
in a Mason jar by the door
and a note from a friend saying
he would call again later. I go back
into the kitchen, tomatoes
on the windowsill after rain,
small things but vast
if you desire them.

The deep fresh red.
This life rushing towards me.

Mary Jo LoBello Jerome

TOMATO INTUITION

God made me this way, and I don't dispute it. Amen.
—Flannery O'Connor

The cherry tomatoes sprawl and bury every other plant. God, they're tireless. The peppers, chard, eggplants, beets made

into involuntary supports, smothered. New hairy stems daze me each day like Jack's magic stalk. So dizzying, their reach. This

garden, planned in neat rows, now a fecund tangle. The way I've been taught to tie-back or prune branches is useless. And I

finally surrender the need for control. The vines don't hold back. Flower and fruit overflow. Who could dispute

these sweet and acid gifts to the tongue? Such a luscious mess. It is time to give thanks for the persistent, the genuine, amen.

Leah Naomi Green

CARROT

Take all summer,
your ember

from the sun,
its walking meditation.

Store it in small
vaults of light

to keep
the rest of us

when winter seals
around each day.

We'll flicker
to the table.

We'll gather
to your orange flame.

REFLECTIVE PAUSE

Nothing for Granted

I love poems that take the most ordinary things and transform them into something worthy of wonder, using only the power of the writer's close attention. "Carrot" is a short, deceptively simple poem that does just that as it imagines a carrot in the ground, stoking its "ember from the sun" all summer long. Though I'd never thought about how the inside of a carrot looks, Leah Naomi Green shows us up close those "small vaults of light," which still contain summer's brightness and heat. She also imagines the light of the sun as a kind of "walking meditation" passing across the garden, reminding us of the slow yet miraculous process of growth and renewal by which we are all fed.

Invitation for Writing and Reflection

Choose some humble, seemingly ordinary thing and write a poem (perhaps a kind of ode) addressed to it. You might choose as your subject something that you particularly love but that others might find too plain or simple to be worthy of amazement.

Jessica Gigot

AMENDS

It is hard to hold a homegrown
        head of broccoli in your hand
and not feel proud.
Seed to start,

seedling to robust stalk and floret,
I cradle this broccoli like my first born.

The infant I protected from damping-off,
        aphids, club root, and pesky flea beetles
                dotting up all the leaves.

The green gleams and sparkles.
In that one hour on that one day

I made amends with the earth.

Other times, I buy the shipped-in stuff,
        California's wellspring
touched by a thousand hands
        and automated sanitation.

Sweat makes this one something special—
        the give and take of it all,
                my muddied pride.

Lahab Assef Al-Jundi

WHAT THE ROSES SAID TO ME

Don't forget me!
Always remember
my beauty is for your eyes.
My fragrance is for your spirit.
My unfolding
is my invitation to you
to yield to your own.

When your skies seem darkest,
when your heart is gripped by pain,
when uncertainty and fear
creep into your days,
come back to me.
Come into me.
Camp between my scented sheets.
Let me show you
a passageway back
to love.

Rage Hezekiah

LAYERS

after Seamus Heaney

All the lemons lit in the kitchen bowl
seem softened by the sun, whose morning lull

illuminates your hands splayed
open on the butcher block table.

Oh, what you can make with your hands,
and how I ache to witness

your wooden spoon mixing six
simple ingredients in a ceramic vessel.

Bake me a cake again. Place squash blossoms
and nasturtium on the plate,

spread the pastry with sweet cream,
a meditative motion, slow and serene.

Mamma, once you made such gentle things.

Dorianne Laux

MY MOTHER'S COLANDER

Holes in the shape of stars
punched in gray tin, dented,
cheap, beaten by each
of her children with a wooden spoon.

Noodle catcher, spaghetti stopper,
pouring cloudy rain into the sink,
swirling counter clockwise
down the drain, starch slime
on the backside, caught
in the piercings.

Scrubbed for sixty years, packed
and unpacked, the baby's
helmet during the cold war,
a sinking ship in the bathtub,
little boat of holes.

Dirt scooped in with a plastic
shovel, sifted to make cakes
and castles. Wrestled
from each other's hands,
its tin feet bent and re-bent.

Bowl daylight fell through
onto freckled faces, noon stars
on the pavement, the universe
we circled aiming jagged stones,
rung bells it caught and held.

Sue Ann Gleason

ASK ME

Ask me for the measure of starter
and water in a loaf of sourdough bread.
How to gently pull the dough across
the surface of a marble slab, folding
it like an envelope so that the gluten
strengthens slowly and with intention.

Ask me how those loaves of sourdough
kept my hands steady and my mind
occupied on days that fear and anxiety
rose as exponentially as the starter.

Ask me about my grandmother's kitchen.
The sound of onions sizzling in a cast iron skillet,
the smell of garlic, the shape of her hands
chopping vegetables, teasing pie crust over heaps
of cinnamon soaked apples.

Ask me about candles on countertops,
how she lit those candles daily and prayed
to patron saints, the depth of her faith reflected
in the whisper-thin pages of her prayer book
and the seven children she raised in the midst
of The Great Depression.

Ask me about the sound of her voice praying
the rosary in Italian and how that became
a lullaby singing me to sleep. Ask me
about breakfast in her home, thick slabs
of toasted bread slathered
with cinnamon butter and smiles.

Ask me about my grandfather's breakfast—
the crunch of cornflakes, the tap, tap, tap of spoon
on the delicate shell of a soft-boiled egg.
How he swirled the remaining milk in the bowl
with the last drop of thick, dark coffee from his cup.
And, if my memory serves me here, a shot of whiskey
to warm his belly for a day digging ditches,
the price he paid to live in America.

Ask about the garden out back, how in summer months
it resembles the one my grandfather tended—
sun ripened tomatoes, basil and beans.
How every morsel in my kitchen, from sourdough
loaves to the slow simmer of tomato sauce,
is the love language of my grandmother's hands.

Paola Bruni

THE LESSON

On Sundays, Grandmother alight on the altar
of making and I, only old enough to kneel
on a wooden chair beside her, watched.
From the cupboard, she unearthed a dusky
pastry board, flour formed into a heaping crater,
the center hollowed. Eggs, white as doves. Salt.
Cup of milk, fragrant and simple. No spatula.
No bowl or mixer. Just a pastry board
and Grandmother's naked, calcified fingers
proclaiming each ingredient into the next.
She murmured into the composition
until the dough fattened, perspired, grew
under her ravenous eye. A rolling pin
to create a still, quiet surface. Then, the point
of a sharp knife chiseling flags of wide golden noodles.
For days, the fettuccini draped from wooden
clothing racks in her bedroom under the scrutiny
of Jesus and his Mother. Mornings, I slipped
into Grandmother's bed, dreamt about eating noodles
swathed in butter and the sauce of a hundred
ripe tomatoes roasted on the fire.

Meghan Sterling

CHICKADEE

My daughter sang softly this morning,
respecting the sleep of others like a little nun,
whispering her vespers to the dolls she cradled
on a pillow in the middle of the kitchen floor.
I savored her quiet, her voice like wings, delicate
as branch-tips just beginning to crown with buds.
Her song was the black throat of a chickadee,
hopping from limb to limb, crested by blue sky
like all the love that had been waiting
once I stopped searching and started looking.
But that's the way the sky is. Always there,
but still, a revelation on a spring morning
when all is quiet enough to hear it hum.
Suppose I had decided to stay childless?
I'd be listening to the birds on the lines,
desperate to find anything to make me feel
as tender as my daughter so easily does,
singing in hushed tones to her monkey and owl
wrapped in a blanket of old towels.

Faith Shearin

MY DAUGHTER DESCRIBES THE TARANTULA

Her voice is as lovely and delicate as a web.
She describes how fragile they are,
how they can die from a simple fall.
Then she tells me about their burrows
which are tidy and dry and decorated
with silk. They are solitary, she tells me,
and utterly mild, and when they are
threatened they fling their hairs, trying
not to bite. She says they are most
vulnerable when they molt: unable
to eat for days while they change.
They are misunderstood, she explains,
and suddenly her description becomes
personal. She wants to keep one
as a pet, to appreciate it properly,
to build it a place where it belongs.

Laura Foley

LOST AND FOUND

On my sophomore science field trip
to the rocky Maine coast,
I sat captivated by a tidal pool, a little village
of crawling crabs, snails, starfish darting,
a sea anemone appearing to sing.
I stayed so long, I forgot the rising tide,
my teachers, classmates waiting
on the bus. On the exam,
I couldn't calculate the pitch of waves,
or chemical composition of anything,
but I knew how to lose myself
in the world of tiny shifting things.

Joy Harjo

REDBIRD LOVE

We watched her grow up.
She was the urgent chirper,
Fledgling flier.
And when spring rolled
Out its green
She'd grown
Into the most noticeable
Bird-girl.
Long-legged and just
The right amount of blush
Tipping her wings, crest
And tail, and
She knew it
in the bird parade.
We watched her strut.
She owned her stuff.
The males perked their armor, greased their wings,
And flew sky-loop missions
To show off
For her.
In the end
There was only one.
There's that one you circle back to—for home.

This morning
The young couple scavenge seeds
On the patio.
She is thickening with eggs.
Their minds are busy with sticks the perfect size, tufts of fluff
Like dandelion, and other pieces of soft.
He steps aside for her, so she can eat.
Then we watch him fill his beak
Walk tenderly to her and kiss her with seed.
The sacred world lifts up its head
To notice—
We are double, triple blessed.

Kim Stafford

WREN'S NEST IN A SHED NEAR AURORA

Three tiny eggs in thistledown
cupped in a swirl of grass
in the pocket of the tool belt
I hung on the wall of the shed
when it finally stood complete—
will be three songs
offering local dignity for
my country enthralled by war
in distant lands.
                    Stand back
cautiously, close the door
tenderly, let the future
ripen, grow wings,
and build songs.

Sharon Corcoran

ENCOUNTER

The red plastic dish, perforated
with beak-sized holes, decorated
with yellow petals feigning flowers,
dangles from my hand. In it,
sweetened water. As I carry it
toward the stand where it will hang,
some force, invisible at first
but fierce—a delicate wind
against my hand, perhaps—
stops me. I look down
and a small green body hovers,
her beak at the petaled opening,
inches from my hand, my heart.
Her fearlessness and minute fury
overcome me. Every beam in me
is focused on this—the humbling honor
bestowed, being allowed to wait
upon this tiny god.

José A. Alcántara

ARCHILOCHUS COLUBRIS

The hummingbirds have arrived,
beating their invisible wings beyond the window
where buds are beginning to break.

They come bearing the light of Panama,
Colombia, Costa Rica, the red fire of the tropics,
here, to this mountain, still spotted in snow.

I go out among them, in my red coat,
hoping they will mistake me for a flower.
They buzz close, hovering before my face.

If only one of them would touch me, I would
sprout feathers and take to the air, my wings
tracing infinity, my throat turning to rubies.

Emilie Lygren

MEDITATION

Sitting near the window,
I watched a fly stammering
against the glass,
trying to break free
and transcend the
transparent boundary
it could not comprehend.

As I cupped my hands around the fly
then let it out the open door,
I wished that we could trade places—

that someone would gently remove me
from the invisible walls
I have pressed myself up against,
offer an opening I am too small to see.

After sitting longer,
I start to think that maybe I am all parts of the story—

the trembling fly,
the gently cupped hands,
the clear glass window,
the necessary air outside.

Margaret Hasse

ART

As the sun begins to build its house of gold
an artist is called to her window.
Alone in the attic of creation
free to leave her body, lift bird-like
and settle on bare branches,
she can portray what is before,
within or beyond herself.
With pencil, paper, color,
she paints an upside-down bowl
of blue essence some call heaven.
Anne Frank, too, in the bolt-hole
of a tiny annex found her patch
of sky and shared her vision.
She wrote in her diary: *Think*
of all the beauty in yourself and
everything around you and be happy.

Mark Nepo

ART LESSON

The mind moves like a pencil.
The heart moves like a brush.

While the mind can draw
exquisite prints, the heart
with its deep bright colors
will ignore the lines.

If you only follow your mind,
you will never go outside the lines.

If you only follow your heart,
what you touch will never
resemble anything.

We must be
a student of both.

For the mind can build
itself a home, but only
the heart can live in it.

Cristina M. R. Norcross

BREATHING PEACE

If peace was something we could hold
in our hands,
we would mold it like clay.
We would shape it into a circle,
leaving our thumbprint on it,
then carefully pass it into
the knowing hands of the next person,
as if handling a newborn sparrow.

If peace was something we could breathe,
we would close our eyes and savor the precious air
flowing into our lungs—
passing through our lips.
That exhale would be a prayer.
It would be a song in three-part harmony.

If peace was something we could taste,
it would be figs drizzled with honey.
We would arrange it on a plate
with a silk-petaled sunflower
decorating the center.
We would pass the plate around
with reverence, ensuring that every single person
received nourishment.

If peace was something we could walk to,
it would be a sacred labyrinth of circles.
We would greet each other on the meditative path.
We would come together at the center
and admire our cohesive union—
arms raised to the sun,
rejoicing in what we could not see or touch,
but we could feel it.
We have been walking together
for such a long time.
We have always been at peace,
but we become lost in the forgetting.

Caroline Webster

EXPECTING

I wait sometimes
for hours, days, nine months
for an idea,
a first line,
or simply one word.

I wait so long I never start.

The stories, though, are there.
Aren't they?
Gestating, always awaiting birth.

I must prod gently,
nurture,
ease them out.

That is peace,
I think,
delivering
what emerges.

Mark Nepo

THE CLEARING

I had climbed beyond what
I knew, in search of something
lasting, and far away from the
crowd, I found this clearing
from which I glimpsed life
outside of my own story.

And life was never more
revealing, though I couldn't
stay there, any more than a
bird can nest in the sun.

So, I came back into the
world, though I'm never far
from that clearing. I carry it
within like a candle lit from
the great unending fire.

And when exhausted of my
thoughts, I find the clearing in
your quiet breathing as you sleep,
in the song that parts everyone's
trouble, in the moment the old
painter lifts his brush from the
canvas.

Even in these words I leave
on the page like ripples
in the water.

Laura Foley

WHAT STILLNESS

Lily pads ripple in summer breeze,
as if they bloomed for me,
revelation-white clouds float
through a divine blue sky.
No human voices break
the stillness of this hilltop pond
where I come to forget
the foolishness of homo sapiens—
where a trout leaps from the lake,
splashes shining down,
opening a glimpse into
the world below the surface.
My dog, wet from her swim
between the visible and the hidden,
shakes dots of sparkling light
from her dark coat,
forming a watery aura.
What sunlight does to water,
stillness does to us.

REFLECTIVE PAUSE

The Gift of Stillness

As much as I value downtime, especially when spent in nature, I still resist the stillness I most need in order to glimpse, as Laura Foley puts it, "the world below the surface" of our stressful lives. Foley's meditative poem "What Stillness" offers the gift of pointing out what we can do when we start to feel restless or stressed: Find a peaceful place, perhaps like her hilltop pond, where we can go and be quiet, simply reflecting on what's directly around us. Slowly then—and it always takes more time than we'd like—the world opens back up to us, and each cloud turns "revelation-white," as we see the value of a short break from human voices and the "foolishness" of our species, too often bent on harming each other and our planet. Spaces like these, separate from the bustle and noise of crowds and news, are necessary for renewal as they allow our minds and bodies to settle. Only then might we see again the "sparkling light" of water shaken from a dog's coat and be reminded of the small miracles that make life worth living.

Invitation for Writing and Reflection

Find a place like the one Foley describes in the poem, even if it is simply a quiet corner in your home or a bench in a local park. Stay still for a few moments and see what calls to you from that place "between the visible and the hidden."

Lisa Zimmerman

LAKE AT NIGHT

No whales tonight but the moon
sings their music, a net of light
pulling the wind
into blue slopes.

The trees, with their nests
of new leaves, move invisibly
toward shore. The air
is sharp and tangy as seaweed.

Long after dark we hear
fish rise out of the water,
their scales studded
with tiny barnacles,
their joy bigger
than their bodies.

Joseph Bruchac

BIRDFOOT'S GRAMPA

The old man
must have stopped our car
two dozen times to climb out
and gather into his hands
the small toads blinded
by our lights and leaping,
live drops of rain.

The rain was falling,
a mist about his white hair
and I kept saying
you can't save them all
accept it, get back in,
we've got places to go.

But, leathery hands full
of wet brown life
knee deep in the summer
roadside grass
he just smiled and said
they have places to go
too.

Heather Swan

BOY

He burst from the cattails
clutching a bullfrog—
the glabrous body
slick with mud,
thick legs outstretched,
but somehow tranquil.
His hands could easily crush
this creature whose soft belly
is the color of milk,
who can breathe
through her skin,
whose only protections
are a transparent eyelid
and quickness.

This is the child who,
in the darkness, unable
to sleep, curls into
the body he came from
and asks, *But who invented war?*
And, *Can a bullet go through brick?*
Can a bullet go through steel?

Now, at the water's edge,
filled with a wild holiness,
he navigates the balance,
then lets the frog go.

Nikita Gill

YOUR SOFT HEART

You are still the child who gently places
Fallen baby birds back in their nests.
You are still the soft soul that gets
Your heart broken over cruel words
And awful acts when you watch the news.
You are still the gentle heart who once
Tried to heal a flower by attempting to stick
Its petals back on when ignorant feet trampled it.

This is why you are important.
This is why you will always be needed.

Kindness is the greatest endangered thing.
And here you are, existing, your heart so full with it.

Joyce Sutphen

FROM OUT THE CAVE

When you have been
at war with yourself
for so many years that
you have forgotten why,
when you have been driving
for hours and only
gradually begin to realize
that you have lost the way,
when you have cut
hastily into the fabric,
when you have signed
papers in distraction,
when it has been centuries
since you watched the sun set
or the rain fall, and the clouds,
drifting overhead, pass as flat
as anything on a postcard;
when, in the midst of these
everyday nightmares, you
understand that you could
wake up,

you could turn
and go back
to the last thing you
remember doing
with your whole heart:
that passionate kiss,
the brilliant drop of love
rolling along the tongue of a green leaf,
then you wake,
you stumble from your cave,
blinking in the sun,
naming every shadow
as it slips.

Marilyn McCabe

WEB

Lately everything is

astounding me,
miles of phone lines,

garage door openers,

spatulas,
my shoes.

What is the way

to pay tribute to glory?
The aspen knows:

applause with every breeze.

How best to enflame
the holy fire?

Light
is on my face

filtered through glowing leaves.
Around my feet

a tumble of extraordinary
rocks pocked, striated

pink, gold. A frenzy

of riverdrops,
riot of current.

One spider is rapidly

tying me here,
its lines like spokes

to a spinning wheel.

We are silver,
quivering.

Anne Evans

A NEW VARIANT

They say a new variant has been detected.
Have you heard about it?
Wildly contagious, it is believed
to infect the mind's eye.

They say it jams the brain
and may weaken your old opinions.
The machine of your mind
may stop chattering and start to hum.

They say the variant has a side effect—
compassion. Many report tearfulness, a tender heart,
empathy for the stranger with 20 items in the quick check line
or the guy following too close in traffic.

They say it will loosen your grip on your judgments
and create space for curiosity. In fact,
you might be rendered mute by all you do not know.
And, for sure, your immunity to wonder will be broken down.

This variant, they say, will make you dizzy, distract you
with the possibilities for simple kindness. You could
lose your place in line, even forget why you're waiting,
angry and afraid, in the first place.

Barbara Crooker

THIS SUMMER DAY

That sprinkler is at it again,
hissing and spitting its arc
of silver, and the parched
lawn is tickled green. The air
hums with the busy traffic
of butterflies and bees,
who navigate without lane
markers, stop signs, directional
signals. One of my friends
says we're now in the shady
side of the garden, having moved
past pollination, fruition,
and all that bee-buzzed jazz,
into our autumn days. But I say wait.
It's still summer, and the breeze is full
of sweetness spilled from a million petals;
it wraps around your arms, lifts the hair
from the back of your neck.
The salvia, coreopsis, roses
have set the borders on fire,
and the peaches waiting to be picked
are heavy with juice. We are still ripening
into our bodies, still in the act of becoming.
Rejoice in the day's long sugar.
Praise that big fat tomato of a sun.

Ted Kooser

A GLINT

I watched a glint of morning sunlight
climbing a thread of spider's silk
in a gentle breeze. It shinnied up
from the tip of a dewy stalk of grass
to an overhanging branch, then
disappeared into the leaves. But soon
another followed, and then another,
glint after glint, and though they made
no sound, what I could see was music,
not melody but one clear, shining note
plucked over and over, as if the sun
were tuning the day, then handing it
to me so I could be the one to play it.

Derek Sheffield

FOR THOSE WHO WOULD SEE

the swift and ceaseless sprinkler whirling
and flinging its bright globes

drop by drop has filled a blue bowl
left out on the lawn. The little pool
formed by that embrace never stops

breaking and regathering—winks of calm
coming between bouts of splattering—

and in the way the pool accepts
each troubling drop so it becomes
the surface that in the next instant

shatters at the next and so on,
this is also clearly a matter of light

splashed and light
scattered in all directions
for anyone who happens to be watching.

REFLECTIVE PAUSE

Winks of Calm

I can't help but read "For Those Who Would See" as a commentary on the nature of our minds, the way our thoughts and worries come and go with only "winks of calm" in between bouts of distraction and disturbance. At first glance, Derek Sheffield's poem offers something mundane and simple: "a blue bowl left out on the lawn," filled with water from the "swift and ceaseless sprinkler." Yet in Sheffield's masterful hands, this act of truly *seeing* the blue bowl, the "bright globes" of water, and the sprinkler itself becomes an exercise in mindfulness and guided attention. He doesn't simply describe the bowl of water, but instead shows us how its surface (like that of the mind) is always "breaking and regathering." What's different about this "little pool" is that it "accepts each troubling drop" without resistance, adding it to the whole. By watching exactly what happens in this scene and allowing his observations to ripple outward with meaning, the speaker implies that so much of life is not about what we see, but how we *choose* to see whatever crosses our path.

Invitation for Writing and Reflection

What calms you in your world right now, even if it's something very simple? Can you describe the effect of this object or person on you? Can you make a whole list of things that have offered you those "winks of calm" lately?

Sally Bliumis-Dunn

AUBADE

You call it the jeweling hour,
these miniature glistening globes

all over the pines—
like a glass bead necklace

left on a woman's dresser
that cannot possibly tell the tale

of what happened before
the tousled bed lay empty.

With a little wind or sun
the water droplets

will disappear from the trees
and you and I will cut

the peaches for our cereal, read
the paralyzing headlines in the paper,

but for now, their glister
dangles on the branches

from last night's rain that held
the house in its wild pounding

Kim Stafford

ADVICE FROM A RAINDROP

You think you're too small
to make a difference? Tell me
about it. You think you're
helpless, at the mercy of forces
beyond your control? Been there.

Think you're doomed to disappear,
just one small voice among millions?
That's no weakness, trust me. That's
your wild card, your trick, your
implement. They won't see you coming

until you're there, in their faces, shining,
festive, expendable, eternal. Sure you're
small, just one small part of a storm that
changes everything. That's how you win,
my friend, again and again and again.

Danusha Laméris

LET RAIN BE RAIN

Let rain be rain.
      Let wind be wind.
Let the small stone
    be the small stone.

May the bird
   rest on its branch,
the beetle in its burrow.

May the pine tree
   lay down its needles.
The rockrose, its petals.

It's early. Or it's late.
   The answers
to our questions
   lie hidden
in acorn, oyster, the seagull's
   speckled egg.

We've come this far, already.
   Why not let breath
be breath. Salt be salt.

How faithful the tide
   that has carried us—
that carries us now—
      out to sea
   and back.

Nina Bagley

GATHERING

We are gatherers,
the ones who pick up sticks and stones
and old wasp nests fallen by the
door of the barn,
walnuts with holes that look like
eyes of owls,
bits of shell not whole but lovely
in their brokenness,
we are the ones who bring home
empty eggs of birds,
and place them on a small glass shelf,
to keep for what? How long?
It matters not. What matters
is the gathering,
the pockets filled with remnants
of a day evaporated, the traces of
certain memory, a lingering smell,
a smile that came with the shell.

Stuart Kestenbaum

HOLDING THE LIGHT

Gather up whatever is
glittering in the gutter,
whatever has tumbled
in the waves or fallen
in flames out of the sky,

for it's not only our
hearts that are broken,
but the heart
of the world as well.
Stitch it back together.

Make a place where
the day speaks to the night
and the earth speaks to the sky.
Whether we created God
or God created us

it all comes down to this:
In our imperfect world
we are meant to repair
and stitch together
what beauty there is, stitch it

with compassion and wire.
See how everything
we have made gathers
the light inside itself
and overflows? A blessing.

Alberto Ríos

THE BROKEN

Something is always broken.
Nothing is perfect longer than a day—
Every roof has a broken tile,
Every mouth a chipped tooth.
Something is always broken
But the world endures the break:
The broken twig is how we follow the trail.
The broken promise is the one we remember.
Something changed is pushed out the door,
Sad, perhaps, but ready, too ready, for the world.
Something is always broken.
Something is always fixed.

Alfred K. LaMotte

GENTLE

A gentler world begins
in the way you touch your heart.
Be soft with the light inside you.
Caress your body with this breath.
God is nothing else
but the place where the sun comes up
in your chest.
You are the glimmering destination.
You are the golden honey daubed
on the bread of the ordinary.
Whatever is perfect,
whatever is heavenly,
begins here.

Patricia Clark

CREED

I believe in one body, ligaments almighty, skin
wrapping the thankful bones, and the resurrection
of the stomach, waking to hunger each day

with dreams of basil and butter, fennel, old gouda
cheese, and wine poured like sunlight into glass.
I believe in the fretting of shadow and sun

on backyard grass, in the shedding of the oak,
in the temptation of an umbrella on the deck,
a table, a chair, and an opened book.

The ascension into light, especially after lying down
with another, causes us to sit at the right
hand of whatever spirit guides us, called love

by some believers. And I believe in perennials,
bark, moss instead of grass, the pollen stuck
on a stamen, the hyssop turning blue as the night.

Michael Simms

SOMETIMES I WAKE EARLY

Sometimes I wake early and walk through the house
touching doors that swing into darkness
my bare toes searching out
toys and magazines.

Outside it might be raining, a full wind
filling the trees like sails. I sit
in the love seat under the bay window, hugging
myself, letting the children's dreams wash over me
like waves.

Last night we took a friend for a walk along the edge
of our mountain. She looked out
over the city, the rivers, the sultry slopes
crowded with sumac and maple
and said *So you know where you live.*

Yes, in the darkness and rain
our small house stands in a huddle of houses
under the clouds, in a story
we ourselves are telling.

Marjorie Moorhead

HEAD IN THE CLOUDS

The cloud, so distant from me here,
on earth, on this wood of our deck,
on two feet, looking up.
I reel it in, and imagine
droplets misting my face . . .
tears or shower; relief, renewal;
it's all there, in a white fluffy ball
changing semblance in winds
that come from all directions.
Able to morph, adapt.
Can I be the cloud? May I
take it as my cotton-filled pillow,
tuck it under my head,
let muscles relax,
and dream-visions come?
I send thoughts up and away.
Near, and far; supportive, and sieve-like,
I will bring cloud down, wrap it round,
wear it as a shawl, or skirt. I will twirl,
letting cloud take what shapes it may.
I know there are days I laugh aloud,
and in some, feel enveloped by trepidation.
Let me remember, while still free from shroud,
to lift my gaze and not ignore.
In that space and time, of each given day,
whichever season, let me adore,
adore, adore.

Joseph Fasano

LETTER

Tonight, as you walk out
into the stars, or the forest, or the city,
look up
as you must have looked
before love came,
before love went,
before ash was ash.
Look at them: the city's
mists, the winters.
And the moon's glass
you must have held once
in the beginning.
That new moon
you must have touched once
in the waters,
saying *change me, change*
me, change me. All I want
is to be more of what I am.

Penny Harter

JUST GRAPEFRUIT

Carefully, I place half a grapefruit
into the small white bowl that fits it
perfectly, use the brown-handled
serrated knife to cut around the rim,
separate the sections.

The first bite is neither sweet nor bitter,
but I drag a drop or two of honey around
the top, love how it glazes each pink piece,
then seeps between dividing membranes.

Pale seeds pop up from their snug burial
in the center hole, and when I'm finished,
I squeeze sticky juice from the spent rind
and drink it down.

Each grapefruit is an offering, its bright
flesh startling my fasting tongue. When
bitterness spills from the morning news,
I temper it with grapefruit, savor hidden
gifts as I slice it open, free each glistening
segment, and enter honeyed grapefruit time.

Jane Kenyon

IN SEVERAL COLORS

Every morning, cup of coffee
in hand, I look out at the mountain.
Ordinarily, it's blue, but today
it's the color of an eggplant.
And the sky turns
from gray to pale apricot
as the sun rolls up
Main Street in Andover.
I study the cat's face
and find a trace of white
around each eye, as if
he made himself up today
for a part in the opera.

Kathryn Petruccelli

INSTINCT

My cat loves sweat, loves
to tuck the leather patch
of her nose into the space
under my arm, run
her rough-tab tongue along
my neck, flesh glistening
after a brisk walk, craves
nothing more than to taste
salt of exertion,
sometimes even to take
a small bite. What it would be
to have such freedom—
to step into our desires
as if they were owed us,
our faces pressed up against
that which we cannot control.
We'd sniff here and there
for the thing to stir our blood,
and, on finding it, plunge forward
without thought for consequence—
not in wanton greed—
but sure-footed
along trajectories that ignite—
all that surrounds us aglow
in the light of a contented sky.
What kind of world would it be?

Each of us moving to rhythms
passed on by previous purveyors
of stardust, grown in the fat
of our marrow, ancient
knowledge from the whole
of who we are that drives
not toward money,
obligation, fear,
but toward joy and abandon,
instinct, impulse, wonder.

Terri Kirby Erickson

GOLDFINCH

Stunned by an unforgiving
pane of glass, a finch
fell to the ground
like a splash of pale
yellow paint. It sat
shivering in the snow,
its heartbeat faster
than a spinning bobbin
in the aftermath of such
a killing blow. Yet,
this little bird's thimble-
full of life held fast
to its fragile body,
and was soon cradled
by a loving human hand.
There, with splayed
feathers stroked smooth,
belly warmed by
a kind woman's skin,
the goldfinch rallied.
It spread its gilded wings
and flew to a snow-
laden branch, forgetting
before it got there,

the sky's unyielding
reflection—then flew
again—a bird-shaped
star with billions
of years left to burn.

Ada Limón

IT'S THE SEASON I OFTEN MISTAKE

Birds for leaves, and leaves for birds.
The tawny yellow mulberry leaves
are always goldfinches tumbling
across the lawn like extreme elation.
The last of the maroon crabapple
ovates are song sparrows that tremble
all at once. And today, just when I
could not stand myself any longer,
a group of field sparrows, that were
actually field sparrows, flew up into
the bare branches of the hackberry
and I almost collapsed: leaves
reattaching themselves to the tree
like a strong spell for reversal. What
else did I expect? What good
is accuracy amidst the perpetual
scattering that unspools the world.

Katherine J. Williams

LATE AUGUST, LAKE CHAMPLAIN

The longer I sit, the louder they become,
the offerings of this pale morning.
No blare of birdsong, no display of light
to play through night's watery leavings.
Neither chill nor warmth—I'm aware of being
aware of the seamless air.
But the tone of an unknown bird tickles the silence.
Spiderwebs wink in invisible wind.
Beyond the trees, vast lungs of unseen water breathe.
The ferry's wail floats through a muffling cloud.
Almost hidden in the green tangle of maple and beech,
A single red leaf.

Laura Ann Reed

FORTITUDE

Twelve leaves,
all that remains
of the maple's autumn conflagration,
flutter in a chill breeze.
At the tree's base lie the fallen,
shrunken, withered,
their glorious red now the brown of earth
into whose depths they sink and decompose—
their atoms and molecules
the warp and weave
of next spring's flags of victory.
But these dozen leaves,
these flaming angels,
their beauty terrifies.
They spin and turn in wind,
unyielding. I'm consumed
by their magnificence.
I bow to them, sing their praises,
pray to them for courage,
fortitude, protection
from my human uncertainties.

Nathan Spoon

POEM OF THANKFULNESS

Today I am thankful for morning frost
touched by sunlight and sparkling

on lawns and fields   I am thankful too
for you and the warmth provided to my feet

inside ordinary socks and shoes and the way
the music of your voice enters my ears

and warms my heart leaving this planet of ours
spinning (if only slightly) more easily;

and I will consider how the world is good
difficult and good and how a lifetime

is both too short and too long
and how the injured heart cannot heal but

as researchers in Sweden have discovered
the muscle of our disadvantaged organ also can

and does slowly replenish itself   Today
when the bigness of the sky asks whoever

is standing beneath it are you ready
the gray trees drowsing and temporarily losing

the last of their burnt sienna leaves will say yes
and you will say yes and I will say yes too

Annie Lighthart

LET THIS DAY

Let this day born in sackcloth and ashes
shift. Let it change, rearrange. Let it come back
made new and barking, snout pushed to table
with joy. Let it wash us wildly with its tongue
and shake its thick pelt. Let the dust rise off
in waves, in solar clouds, and let our old selves
float up in that haze, particles massed by the window,
motes among a thousand other motes. Now see
our two: we are the two motes laughing as they leave,
the two specks somersaulting right through the screen.

REFLECTIVE PAUSE

Let It Change

If you're anything like me, you have many days that are "born in sackcloth and ashes"—that is, days which at first feel difficult or downright impossible to bear. Yet a feeling or the mood of a moment can always shift toward delight or wonder, and often more completely than we might have expected. In "Let This Day," Annie Lighthart makes the case for not trying to force some immediate change in our outlook, and instead doing our best to give ourselves both time and space. "Let it change, rearrange," she says. I find much reassurance in this—in the way the day transforms into a wild dog, nudging its nose against the table "with joy." And how the past selves of the two people in the poem (no longer needed) turn into dust motes "laughing as they leave," tiny enough now to fly "right through the screen" of the open window.

Invitation for Writing and Reflection

Describe a time when you were able to sit back and stay with a difficult mood or emotion, until it changed into something else. And if you find yourself having one of those days right now, you might see how writing about your mind-state can also bring about a change in mood.

Laura Grace Weldon

COMMON GROUND

What's incomplete in me seeks refuge
in blackberry bramble and beech trees,
where creatures live without dogma
and water moves in patterns
more ancient than philosophy.
I stand still, child eavesdropping on her elders.
I don't speak the language
but my body translates as best it can,
wakening skin and gut, summoning
the long kinship we share with everything.

Rena Priest

TOUR OF A SALMONBERRY

A salmonberry is a
luminous spiral,
a golden basket,
woven of sunshine,
water, and birdsong.

I'm told that the birds
sing so sweet because
of all the berries they eat
and that is how you
can have a sweet voice too.

In my Native language,
the word for salmonberry
is *Alile'*. In Sanskrit, *Lila* means
'God plays.' Salmonberries
sometimes look that way.

Every year, they debut,
spectacular in the landscape,
worthy of their genus name:
Rubus spectabilis, meaning,
red sight worth seeing.

Each drupelet holds a seed
and the shimmering secret
kept by rain, of how to rise,
float above the earth, feel
the sun, and return.

Rosalie Sanara Petrouske

TRUE NORTH

In the woods, my father never needed a compass.
He told time by the sun's position.
When shadows grew long and slanted,
he still knew the way to turn
so we could find home.

We walked for miles, changed paths:
North, South, East, and West,
through golden tamaracks in autumn,
beneath old growth hemlocks, white pines,
and birches in summer.

If nightfall caught up to us, Father took my hand,
admonished me to watch for roots, burrows
tunneled into earth by badgers, woodchucks, or foxes.
At dusk, the Eastern screech owl's eerie trill
filled our ears as it swooped down from its perch
to devour a shrew or bat.

"If you think you are lost," Father told me, "travel downhill,
search for water, read the night sky," and he pointed
at Polaris perched at the tip of the Little Dipper's handle.

In daylight, he taught me why trees have more leaves on
>   one side.
"To find true North," he said, "place a stick straight up in
>   the ground,
mark where the stick's shadow lands with a rock."

But he was my true north, astride his shoulders
when I grew tired, I became taller than his six-foot frame.
His hands were the needle of my compass,
his voice my straight-edged arrow.

Connie Wanek

TALKING TO DAD

It's easier than picking up the phone,
whenever, wherever.
I need only the faintest signal
like a single thread of what used to be
his tennis shirt. Like an empty
chair at our table
into which a grandchild climbs.

After a bee leaves a clover blossom
the buzzing grows faint.
But there are many waves
in the infinite air,
and one of these carries an answer
to the simplest question.
He's fine, everything's fine.

Tyler Mortensen-Hayes

AFTER THE HEARTBREAK

It was summer, so of course the thrushes
were going berserk in the trees, singing
every song that came to them about
how astounding it is to be alive, to be breathing.
I was in the house, alone, my sobs echoing
through the empty rooms. The envelope
was sealed, the fire snubbed, the door
shut and locked. The end had come
and the world felt raw and harsh, like wind
on the inflamed skin that remains after
a sunburn is peeled away. *Don't
touch me*, I said to the wind, and to
the insistent waves of sun. *It's okay*,
I told my cowering little soul. *It's okay.
Take what time you need. Retreat
to the downstairs room, draw the shades.*
Some things, like just-planted seeds,
need isolation and dark. But I won't say
that something was planted. No,
instead, something was torn away—
many branches sliced from the trunk
of an old tree. And yet, something did,
eventually, emerge. What was it? All

I can tell you is that I'm here, writing
this—aren't I? And what would have happened
without the small tenderness I gave
to that wrecked thing I was? Don't the leaves
bloom anyway, on those branches
that are left? Don't they make themselves—
just by being alive, just by breathing—
beautiful again?

Ingrid Goff-Maidoff

THE LISTENING BRIDGE

Listen, heart, to the whispering of the World.
That is how it makes love to you.
—Rabindranath Tagore

When you come to the listening bridge,
you must be still there long enough
for the squirrels to sense you are of no harm;
for the birds to break their silence with singing
and the fluttering of wings; and for you,
and everything around you, to stop holding its breath.
And so, sit. Rest a while.
Give some wonder to the moss and purple violets.

Turn toward the sun and feel it warm your face.
Notice the rippling current of the spring-fed stream.
Allow a sense of softness to splash and filter in.
Trade the weight of all your seriousness
for the lightness of surrender—
by which I mean faith in a Presence
lovingly wiser than your self.
Remain quiet and listen
for what the voice born of stillness
might say· perhaps, simply:
Love. Carry on. Practice kindness.
Have affection for this day.

Brad Peacock

A MORNING IN THAILAND

Waking early, springing from bed
I pull on shorts, lace my running shoes, head out the door.
No thinking required, years of a morning routine,
thousands of miles spent in solitude.
I glide past yellow-robed monks praying in *wats*,
soaking up a culture of color,
listening to the gentle rhythm of motion.
They come out of nowhere,
this group of children laughing and smiling
with such play in their hearts
running beside me,
no language needed
just the sound of their joy, step for step.
I feel my heart unblocking
as dormant tears stream down my face,
their lesson as clear as their aura of innocence,
each one teaching me
how to love the world again.

Julia Fehrenbacher

THE ONLY WAY I KNOW TO LOVE THE WORLD

It is not just a cup of coffee
but the warm hum of hello, an invitation
to wake, to sip, to say *thank you*
for another chance to dance
with another new day.

It's not just a ceramic mug, but the one she
shaped with her own 16-year-old
hands, for me. For *me*.

It is not just one heart held open
to another, or a kiss blown in the mirror,
not just the soft circle of smile,
but a nod of—*I see you. You are not alone.*

Not just life. But *your* life. Your very temporary life.

It isn't just the earth you stand on
but the giver of every single thing, a reason
to get down on humbled, human knees
and say thank you thank you thank you.

It is not just another moment but a door flung open,
a flooded-with-light entrance to every real thing

not just a poem but a prayer whispered
from one listening ear
to another. The only way I know
to love the world.

Jacqueline Suskin

HOW TO FALL IN LOVE WITH YOURSELF

Sit in front of two candles,
one for each eye.
Light them and watch how the fire
takes its time with the wicks, nearly dying,
touching wax and climbing back into air
with a wave of hot yes.
Now, breathe each flame into the crown
of your head. There is a hole there
where elements can enter.
Your skull is a cup hungry for light.
Close your eyes and let
this glowing gift travel throughout
your entire body, take it down
slowly, like a dose of brilliant honey.
See how you overflow?
See how you do magic?
The warmth is red. It's white, orange,
blue and green. It touches every
part of you and when
the tailbone starts snaking,
when you become a tree,
you will love yourself completely
for burning with such ease.

Brad Aaron Modlin

ONE CANDLE NOW, THEN SEVEN MORE

I grew up in a family that did not tell
the story. I am listening to it now:

Even the morning you see a robin
flattened on the street, you hear

another in a tree, the notes
they've taught each other, bird

before bird before we were born.
And elsewhere, the rusty bicycle

carries the doctor all the way
across an island. He arrives in time.

Somewhere his sister adds water
to the soup until payday. And

over the final hill in a Southwestern
desert, a gas station appears. No,

the grief has not forgotten my name,
but this morning I tied

my shoelaces. Outside I can force
a wave at every face who might

need it. We might
spin till we collapse, but we still

have a hub: Even at dusk,
the sun isn't going anywhere.

We have lamps. The story insists
it just *looks* like there's only

enough oil to last one night.

Judith Chalmer

POCKET

Night time. It's quiet.
You're starting to shut down—
a yawn, an empty cup

carried to the sink. Nothing
complex—just a little need
for air. Anyway,

you're out the door.
Did I say February?
It's taken some time

to bundle up. The little park
is white under the lamp—
no one lingers, nor do you.

You walk, you turn home.
Breath, a still cloud.
No matter. A few months

and you'll hear some things
moving. You'll smell
the greening. You have this

for now—the winter
wood and its great
absorbent heart,

the young beech,
its dead leaves tiger bright.
The glitter above, the softness

below. Now you've come
to it. You reach down
in your pocket, step up

to your door. Here
are your cares. Slip off
your coat and be received.

Adele Kenny

SURVIVOR

A jay on the fence preaches to a
squirrel. I watch the squirrel quiver,
the way squirrels do—its whole
body flickers. I'm not sure why this
reminds me of when I was five and

something died in our drain spout.
Feather or fur, I watched my father
dig it out, knowing (as a child knows)
how much life matters. I have seen how
easily autumn shakes the yellow leaves,

how winter razes the shoals of heaven.
I have felt love's thunder and moan, and
had my night on the wild river. I have
heard the cancer diagnosis with my name
in it. I know what mercy is and isn't.

Morning breaks from sparrows' wings
(life's breezy business), and I'm still here,
still in love with the sorrows, the joys—
days like this, measured by memory, the
ticking crickets, the pulse in my wrist.

Lois Lorimer

RESCUE DOG

You came to us
around the time I was healing.
That windy chemo Spring
when I pulled out my hair
in fistfuls and it flew away
to line the nests of birds.
Hope snapped in the air
like prayer flags.

As I was losing my hair
in came yours: dark, abundant
soft for petting,
velcroed to sofas and carpets.
Help mate. Canine healer. You,
the shaggy blackboard
we scrawled our wishes on.

Yvonne Zipter

SEEDS

I brush the dog in the yard, and the wind whips
white wisps of fur airborne like milkweed seeds.
I imagine them taking root and sprouting
tiny greyhounds, the long stems of their legs,
slender heads like whimsical orchid blossoms.

But milkweed seeds themselves are miracle enough
for me, the way the pods part like curtains on a stage,
all the little ballerinas in their white tutus, the little swan
maidens, come gliding out, luminous in the sun's spotlight.
Delicate dancers, twirling out of sight like promises.

Most wondrous of all, though, is globe milkweed, each
pod—the color of a green anole—a prickly orb, an alien
spaceship, a hoop skirt airing on a line. Ripe, the pods
turn the color of unbleached linen, open like lockets,
spill out the milky dreams of seeds.

David Mook

MILKWEED

White folds of silken down
sleep in pods of darkness
until an awakening yawn
exhales its feathered breath,

and each on a silent sigh
carries a lone dark seed
with its own white soul
quietly into the new life.

Bradford Tice

MILKWEED

I tell myself softly, *this is how love begins—*
the air alive with something inconceivable,
seeds of every imaginable possibility
floating across the wet grasses, under
the thin arms of ferns. It drifts like snow
or old ash, settling on the dust of the roadways
as you and I descend into thickets, flanked
by the fragrance of honeysuckle and white
primrose.

I recall how my grandmother imagined
these wanderers were living beings,
some tiny phylum yet to be classified as life.
She would say they reminded her of maidens
decked in white dresses, waltzing through air.
Even after I showed her the pods from which
they sprang, blossoming like tiny spiders,
she refused to believe.

Now, standing beside you in the crowded
autumn haze, I watch them flock, emerge from
brittle stalks, bursting upon the world as
young lovers do—trysting in the tall grasses,
resting fingers lightly in tousled hair.
Listen, and you can hear them whisper
in the rushes, gazing out at us, wondering—
what lives are these?

Jane Hirshfield

SOLSTICE

The Earth today tilts one way, then another.

And yes, though all things change,
this night again will watch its fireflies,
then go in to a bed with sheets,
to lights, a beloved.

To running water cold and hot.

Take nothing for granted,
you who were also opulent, a stung cosmos.

Birds sang, frogs sang, their *sufficient unto*.
The late-night rain-bringing thunder.

And if days grew ordinarily shorter,
the dark's mirror lengthened,

and one's gain was not the other lessened.

Julie Cadwallader Staub

REVERENCE

The air vibrated
with the sound of cicadas
on those hot Missouri nights after sundown
when the grown-ups gathered on the wide back lawn,
sank into their slung-back canvas chairs
tall glasses of iced tea beading in the heat

and we sisters chased fireflies
reaching for them in the dark
admiring their compact black bodies
their orange stripes and seeking antennas
as they crawled to our fingertips
and clicked open into the night air.

In all the days and years that have followed,
I don't know that I've ever experienced
that same utter certainty of the goodness of life
that was as palpable
as the sound of the cicadas on those nights:

my sisters running around with me in the dark,
the murmur of the grown-ups' voices,
the way reverence mixes with amazement
to see such a small body
emit so much light.

Jennifer G. Lai

IN MY MIND'S CORAL, MOTHER STILL CALLS US FROM INSIDE

that summer, we were little chemists, bakers,
storefront merchants hawking our wares. I had never
been to a night market before, but mother told me
they had everything you could ever want. for us,

there were slick mud pies, glossy from the cool shade,
blistering on the raw white concrete.　　sunset-pink
petals from the Big House down the street. warm
daisy chains, holy dandelions, dry whispering grass.

back then, the boy next door was just　　a boy next door.
whatever he said I forgot by morning. whenever we could play,
we played. whenever the leaves were plump, lucky, full
of milk—we collected them.

one day, a rare antidote for deadly poison
and another, a welcome cure for broken arms,
and then a lost currency
and sometimes new shampoo for my dolls.

what we knew then, was　　there was nothing
that could hurt us　　save for scraped knees,
or the fat green Japanese beetle
shimmer-zip buzzing past our ears.

we just rinsed off our dirty heels,
hosed off plastic sandals and that was good enough.
the wasps' nest in the rafters, broken,
too high up to see.

REFLECTIVE PAUSE

Worlds of Wonder

We often call it nostalgia when we look back with joy on those simpler, more innocent times in our lives. "In My Mind's Coral, Mother Still Calls Us from Inside" illustrates certain periods in life truly *are* less complicated—before our culture, families, and peers place their expectations and limitations on us, before a larger awareness of the world seeps in. Here, Jennifer G. Lai transports us back to a summer in childhood when she and her friends made their own worlds to inhabit and found the miraculous in small things like "daisy chains, holy dandelions, dry whispering grass." By the end of the poem, we understand that "the wasps' nest in the rafters" might symbolize all the difficult knowledge that remains too far off, "too high up to see" for now. By admitting us into her private, long-ago world, where the worst worries were "scraped knees, or the fat green Japanese beetle shimmer-zip buzzing past our ears," the speaker reminds us of the wonders that might still be possible, if only we could reclaim that freer, more expansive way of being in our child selves.

Invitation for Writing and Reflection

Can you remember a time from childhood when the world was a place of safety and wonder? Describe some of the private rituals and delights from that time. You might try beginning with Lai's phrase "That summer, we were . . ." and see where it leads you.

Rosemerry Wahtola Trommer

LATENT

Riding our bikes through the warm summer night,
the dark itself parted to let us pass;
wind in our hair, soft whir of the wheels—
and an almost irrational joy grew in me then,
such simple joy, as if joy were always here,
waiting to flourish, needing only to be noticed.

And is joy latent in everything?
I have felt it sometimes in the washing
of dishes, in mowing the lawn,
in peeling the carrots, even washing
the fishtank and scrubbing the floor.

So could it be, too, inside worried pacing?
In envy? In sighing? In the clenching of fists?
Is there joy where I can't imagine it?
Joy—waiting to spin like a wheel,
waiting to rise like laughter
that careens through the deepening dark.

Charles Rossiter

TRANSFORMATION

every heart is its own Buddha
to become a saint, do nothing.
—Shih Shu

The day is warm and cloudless,
the lake a trembling blue

kayakers glide by
seemingly without effort

a light breeze, soft,
like angel's breath.

I read and write, relaxed,
while ever so slowly

like a miracle you can
actually watch happen,

without even trying,
my skin is turning brown.

Tony Hoagland

FIELD GUIDE

Once, in the cool blue middle of a lake,
up to my neck in that most precious element of all,

I found a pale-gray, curled-upwards pigeon feather
floating on the tension of the water

at the very instant when a dragonfly,
like a blue-green iridescent bobby pin,

hovered over it, then lit, and rested.
That's all.

I mention this in the same way
that I fold the corner of a page

in certain library books,
so that the next reader will know

where to look for the good parts.

Rage Hezekiah

LAKE SUNAPEE

for Jess

I rise to find
your face

awash in steam
dark coffee

cupped between
calloused hands

the morning
bathed in sunlight

aspens cloaked
in fresh snow

you look up
from your book

eyes dark-rimmed
jungle cat

thirst-slaked
when we first kissed

years ago
on a dance floor

dimly-lit with
greenish light

I thought you
wore mascara

now I know
your hunger

natural kohl
black lashes

there before & after
you wake

home is where
the kettle whistles

midday we return
from local woods

I watch you
pull a ribbon

of honey into
handmade mugs

sweeten two
cups of tea

we sit quietly
at ease

love
know this

you are who
I asked for

on my knees

January Gill O'Neil

HOW TO LOVE

After stepping into the world again,
there is that question of how to love,
how to bundle yourself against the frosted morning—
the crunch of icy grass underfoot, the scrape
of cold wipers along the windshield—
and convert time into distance.

What song to sing down an empty road
as you begin your morning commute?
And is there enough in you to see, really see,
the three wild turkeys crossing the street
with their featherless heads and stilt-like legs
in search of a morning meal? Nothing to do
but hunker down, wait for them to safely cross.

As they amble away, you wonder if they want
to be startled back into this world. Maybe you do, too,
waiting for all this to give way to love itself,
to look into the eyes of another and feel something—
the pleasure of a new lover in the unbroken night,
your wings folded around him, on the other side
of this ragged January, as if a long sleep has ended.

READING GROUP QUESTIONS AND TOPICS FOR DISCUSSION

"The Grove" by Michael Kleber-Diggs (page 17)
- Michael Kleber-Diggs speaks from the point of view of a grove of trees. How might he also be speaking for all of humanity here? How might we "make vast shelter together" by recognizing how interconnected we all are?
- As this poem indicates, there are many different types of trees, yet the poet says we are "the same the same, not different." How might we make it a practice to turn our wonder toward all the ways we're similar as humans, rather than how we're separate?

INVITATION FOR WRITING AND REFLECTION
- Find a grove of trees and stand or sit among them for as long as you can. Describe what sensory impressions come to you, whether they feel factually true or not.

"Lately" by Laure-Anne Bosselaar (page 22)
- Begin by answering the questions that come in the final lines of this poem. Do you believe that moments sometimes return to us so they might come alive again in the retelling? How do your own moments come back to you?
- Describe a recent time when something seemed to reach for your attention. How did it feel to be called to like that, to notice something out of the blue? Consider the "luck" that Bosselaar mentions in the poem. Why do you think we find such delight in the simple things of nature?

INVITATION FOR WRITING AND REFLECTION
- See if you can re-create a similar moment of "luck" that you experienced when a sense of awe or wonder called you back to the physical world around you.

"Stopped Again by the Sea" by Mark Nepo
(page 42)

- Mark Nepo describes a moment of deep peace he felt while sailing in childhood. What does his description of this memory bring up for you? Why do you think we often find the water of rivers, creeks, lakes, and oceans so calming? What "unseen force" seems to speak to us when we're near water?
- Do you agree with the speaker's description of love at the end of the poem, how by revealing all that we hide, we move beyond our own hidden secrets?

INVITATION FOR WRITING AND REFLECTION

- Keeping in mind the strong images of this poem, what scenes or memories of your own conjure a sense of peace for you? Was there some ritual in childhood that allowed you to escape briefly from the noise of the world?

"To Hold" by Li-Young Lee (page 50)

- This poem begins with the startling statement "So we're dust." What you do think Lee means by this, and why would he start a love poem this way? Lee also says that fear has often led him "to abandon what I know I must relinquish." How does he stay with those difficult feelings in this instance?
- How does this fear show up in your own life, especially with loved ones? Are there ways we might keep it from disrupting the peace we feel in the "joint and fragile keeping" we create together?

INVITATION FOR WRITING AND REFLECTION

- Describe a time when you were able to hold on to a feeling of connection even when you were anxious that you might lose the other person. What allowed you to stay in the wonder of that moment?

"Joint Custody" by Ada Limón (page 53)
- How does Limón immediately reframe the difficulty of her parents' divorce when she was a child? Though she now wishes she could have recognized the "abundance" and wonder of having two families, how does Limón also own the sorrow and challenge of that time?
- Toward the end, she says she now has "Two entirely different brains." What might be the benefits of this, being able to hold both joy and sorrow in the very same instance?

INVITATION FOR WRITING AND REFLECTION
- Write about a difficulty that you've been able to reframe and see differently over time. How has your view of this challenge changed over the years, and why do you see it now in a more positive light?

"Chestnut" by Rebecca Baggett (page 59)
- The speaker acknowledges the distressing disappearance of chestnut trees in the United States yet chooses to focus more on the wonder of having touched "a young chestnut." Why is this scene of rebirth so important? Though she acknowledges her own grief in this poem, how does the speaker also point to the potentially positive aspect of loss?
- Have you ever felt a sense of renewal after grief or tragedy, the "rising" and transformation that Baggett finds in this sapling?

INVITATION FOR WRITING AND REFLECTION
- As you look around, see if you can find small examples, especially in nature, of resilience and renewal that remind us how loss "may shelter some new thing" within us.

"Amends" by Jessica Gigot (page 82)
- Why does the speaker feel such "muddied pride" in holding her "homegrown head of broccoli"? What does it mean to make "amends with the earth," as Gigot describes here. Given the title of the poem, why is the word "amends" so important?

- Toward the end, the speaker says of her homegrown vegetable, "Sweat makes this one something special." How can regular attention and care transform our relationship to the earth, other people, and even ourselves over time?

INVITATION FOR WRITING AND REFLECTION
- Recall a moment when you took pride in something that you had grown or made yourself. Write with a sense of marvel and amazement at your own creation. Did it have any healing effects on you?

"My Mother's Colander" by Dorianne Laux
(page 85)
- What do we learn about the speaker of this poem simply from her descriptions of the old colander once belonging to her mother? Which details stand out to you? Have you ever felt a deep connection to some everyday object that belonged to another person? Why do you think we hold onto the possessions of loved ones, long after they're gone?
- Think about all the ways this colander transforms as the poet's descriptions unfold. What memories or objects from the past does this poem call forth for you?

INVITATION FOR WRITING AND REFLECTION
- Choose some object you have kept over the years that's now become beautiful with use. Describe it in vivid detail as Dorianne Laux does here, letting the images tell the story of this well-loved thing.

"Your Soft Heart" by Nikita Gill (page 109)
- Consider the power of repetition in this poem. Why would the poet choose to use the words "You are still" over and over? Why do we sometimes lose that sense of a "soft heart," armoring up instead of letting ourselves feel empathy for plants and animals, and grief for other people suffering elsewhere in the world?

- How might we bring ourselves back to the wonder that allows us to care for the small things around us, remembering that, although kindness feels "endangered," we are each still "so full with it"?

INVITATION FOR WRITING AND REFLECTION
- What are some of the ways your own "soft heart" showed up in childhood, in the ways that you once cared for the world? How does this essential kindness still guide you in the ways that you cultivate peace and healing for those around you?

"Latent" by Rosemerry Wahtola Trommer (page 166)
- A simple burst of joy felt while riding bikes with a loved one leads the speaker to the question "And is joy latent in everything?" Do you believe that joy always lives inside us, "waiting to flourish"? She also confesses that she has found joy in chores like washing the dishes or mowing the lawn. Have there been times when you felt surprised by a sudden and "irrational joy"? How did you feel it in your body?
- At the end, the speaker takes the question further, wondering if joy might live in "worried pacing" and "envy," "where I can't imagine it." How might we stretch our own definitions of joy so that the word includes every deep feeling that renews us and reminds us we are alive?

INVITATION FOR WRITING AND REFLECTION
- Tell the story of a time when you were doing something ordinary yet felt a burst of joy rising "like laughter" in you. You might also list other times when you felt the renewal of joy while doing some plain and simple task that somehow led you to a new place.

POET BIOGRAPHIES

José A. Alcántara lives in western Colorado. He is the author of *The Bitten World* (Tebot Bach). He has worked as a bookseller, mailman, electrician, commercial fisherman, baker, carpenter, studio photographer, door-to-door salesman, and math teacher. His poems have appeared in *Poetry Daily*, American Life in Poetry, *The Slowdown*, *Ploughshares*, *32 Poems*, the *Southern Review*, and the anthologies *The Path to Kindness: Poems of Connection and Joy* and *America, We Call Your Name: Poems of Resistance and Resilience*. (p. 96)

Lahab Assef Al-Jundi's poetry has appeared in collections such as *In These Latitudes: Ten Contemporary Poets* and *Inclined to Speak: An Anthology of Arab American Poetry*, as well as many other anthologies and literary journals. His most recent poetry collections are *No Faith at All* (Pecan Grove Press) and *This Is It* (Kelsay Books). (p. 83)

Born in New York City in 1950, **Julia Alvarez** has written novels, including *How the García Girls Lost Their Accents*, *In the Time of the Butterflies*, and *Afterlife*, as well as poetry collections, including *Homecoming*, *The Other Side/El Otro Lado*, and *The Woman I Kept to Myself*. Alvarez's awards include the Pura Belpré and Américas Awards for her books for young readers, the Hispanic Heritage Award, and the F. Scott Fitzgerald Award. In 2013, she received the National Medal of Arts from President Obama. (p. 20)

James Armstrong is the author of *Monument in a Summer Hat* (New Issues Press) and *Blue Lash* (Milkweed Editions), and coauthor of *Nature, Culture and Two Friends Talking* (North Star Press). He teaches English at Winona State University in Winona, Minnesota, where he was the city's first poet laureate. He is the cofounder of the Maria W. Faust Sonnet Contest, an international poetry competition. (p. 12)

Zeina Azzam is a Palestinian American poet, editor, and community activist. Her chapbook, *Bayna Bayna: In-Between,* was released in 2021 by The Poetry Box. Zeina's poems are published or are forthcoming in *Pleiades*, *Passager*, *Gyroscope*, *Pensive Journal*, *Streetlight Magazine*, *Mizna*, *Sukoon Magazine*, *Barzakh*, *Making Levantine Cuisine*, *Tales from Six Feet Apart*, *Bettering American Poetry*, *Making Mirrors: Writing/Righting by and for Refugees*, *Gaza Unsilenced*, and others. She holds an MA in Arabic literature from Georgetown University. (p. 60)

Rebecca Baggett is the author of four chapbook collections and *The Woman Who Lives Without Money* (Regal House Publishing), winner of the Terry J. Cox Award. A native of North Carolina, she has lived most of her adult life in Athens, Georgia, where she worked as an academic advisor at UGA. In retirement, she stewards a Little Free Library, gardens, dreams of travel, and chases the two-year-old grandson who reconciles her to staying home. (p. 59)

Nina Bagley is a jewelry designer, mixed media artist, and writer living a quiet life in a small log cabin out in the rural woods of western North Carolina. Inspiration for her work comes from the natural world that surrounds her; creating art with natural findings brings a sweet pleasure, as does hammering words of longing for natural connections into silver or scrawling them across old scraps of weathered paper. (p. 122)

Wendell Berry is a poet, novelist, essayist, environmental activist, and farmer. He is the author of more than fifty books of various genres and has farmed the same ancestral land in Port Royal, Kentucky, for the past forty years. Berry's poetry collections include *This Day: Collected & New Sabbath Poems*, *Given*, and *A Timbered Choir: The Sabbath Poems 1979–1997*. (p. 5)

George Bilgere's seventh book of poems, *Blood Pages*, came out from the University of Pittsburgh Press in 2018. His other collections include

Imperial, *The White Museum*, *Haywire*, *The Good Kiss*, *Big Bang*, and *The Going*. He has received the Midland Authors Prize, the May Swenson Poetry Award, a Pushcart Prize, a grant from the National Endowment for the Arts, a Fulbright Fellowship, a Witter Bynner Fellowship, and the Cleveland Arts Prize. He teaches at John Carroll University in Cleveland, Ohio, where he lives with his wife and two exceptionally fine boys. (p. 46)

Kimberly Blaeser, past Wisconsin poet laureate and founding director of In-Na-Po, Indigenous Nations Poets, is the author of five poetry collections, including *Copper Yearning*, *Apprenticed to Justice*, and *Résister en dansant/Ikwe-niimi: Dancing Resistance*. An enrolled member of the White Earth Nation, Blaeser is an Anishinaabe activist and environmentalist, a professor emerita at University of Wisconsin–Milwaukee, and an MFA faculty member at the Institute of American Indian Arts in Santa Fe. kblaeser.org (p. 64)

Sally Bliumis-Dunn's poems have appeared in *On the Seawall*, *Paris Review*, *Prairie Schooner*, *PLUME*, *Poetry London*, the *New York Times*, PBS NewsHour, *upstreet*, Poem-a-day, and Ted Kooser's column, among others. In 2018, her third book, *Echolocation* (Plume Editions/MadHat Press) was longlisted for the Julie Suk Award, runner-up for the Eric Hoffer Prize, and runner-up for the Poetry by the Sea Prize. (p. 119)

Laure-Anne Bosselaar is the author of *The Hour Between Dog and Wolf*, *Small Gods of Grief* (Isabella Gardner Prize for Poetry), *A New Hunger* (ALA Notable Book), and *These Many Rooms*. A Pushcart Prize recipient, she edited five anthologies. She taught at Sarah Lawrence College and University of California–Santa Barbara. The winner of the 2020 James Dickey Poetry Prize, she served as Santa Barbara's poet laureate (2019–2021). (p. 22)

An enrolled member of the Nulhegan Abenaki nation, **Joseph Bruchac's** work often reflects his Indigenous ancestry and the Adirondack region of New York State where he was raised by his grandparents and has lived throughout his life. The author of over 170 books in many different genres, he's also a traditional Native musician and storyteller. His most recent book, *A Year of Moons*, personal essays about his life and the life around him in the Adirondack foothills, was published by Fulcrum Books. (pp. 14, 107)

Paola Bruni is a two-time Pushcart Prize nominee and a winner of the Morton Marcus Poetry Prize and the Muriel Craft Bailey Poetry Prize, as well as a finalist for the Mudfish Poetry Prize. Her poems have appeared in the *Southern Review*, *Ploughshares*, *Five Points Journal*, *Rattle*, *Massachusetts Review*, *Comstock Review*, and elsewhere. Her debut book of poetry is an epistolary collection titled *How Do You Spell the Sound of Crickets* (Paper Angel Press). (p. 88)

Carolyn Chilton Casas lives on the central coast of California, where she loves hiking and playing beach volleyball. She is a Reiki master and teacher, and often explores ways of healing in her writing. Carolyn's work has appeared in *Braided Way*, *Energy Magazine*, A Network for Grateful Living, *Reiki News Magazine*, and *Touch Magazine*. You can read more of her work online and in her first collection of poems, *Our Shared Breath*. (p. 43)

Judith Chalmer is the author of *Minnow* (Kelsay Books) and *Out of History's Junk Jar* (Time Being Books). She is cotranslator of two books of haiku and tanka with Michiko Oishi, *Red Fish Alphabet* (Honami Syoten) and *Deepening Snow* (Plowboy Press). In 2018, she received the Arthur Williams Award from the Vermont Arts Council for Meritorious Service in the Arts. She lives with her partner, Lisa, in Vermont. (p. 155)

Patricia Clark is the author of six volumes of poetry, including *Sunday Rising*, *The Canopy*, and most recently *Self Portrait with a Million Dollars*. Her work has appeared in *The Atlantic*, *Gettysburg Review*, *Poetry*, and *Slate*, among others. Patricia's awards include a Creative Artist Grant in Michigan, the Mississippi Review Prize, the Gwendolyn Brooks Prize, and cowinner of the Lucille Medwick Prize from the Poetry Society of America. She also received the 2018 Book of the Year Award from the Poetry Society of Virginia for *The Canopy*. (p. 126)

Kai Coggin (she/her) is the author of four collections, most recently *Mining for Stardust* (FlowerSong Press). She is a teaching artist in poetry with the Arkansas Arts Council and the host of the longest-running consecutive weekly open mic series in the country, Wednesday Night Poetry. Her widely published poems have appeared in Poetry, *Prairie Schooner*, *SWWIM*, *Lavender Review*, and elsewhere. She lives with her wife in Hot Springs National Park, Arkansas. (p. 25)

Sharon Corcoran lives in southern Colorado. She translated (from French) the writings of North African explorer Isabelle Eberhardt in the works *In the Shadow of Islam* and *Prisoner of Dunes*, published by Peter Owen Ltd., London. Her poems have appeared in *Braided Way*, *Canary*, *Buddhist Poetry Review*, *One Art*, *Sisyphus*, *Literary North*, and *Bearings Online*, among other journals. She is the author of two books of poetry, *Inventory* (KDP) and *The Two Worlds* (Middle Creek). (p. 95)

James Crews is the editor of several anthologies, including *The Path to Kindness: Poems of Connection and Joy* and the best-selling *How to Love the World*, which has been featured on NPR's *Morning Edition*, in the *Boston Globe*, and in the *Washington Post*. He is the author of four prize-winning collections of poetry: *The Book of What Stays*, *Telling My Father*, *Bluebird*, and *Every Waking Moment*. He lives with his husband in Southern Vermont. jamescrews.net (pp. 9, 35, 76)

Barbara Crooker is the author of nine books of poetry; *Some Glad Morning* (University of Pittsburgh Press) is the latest. Her honors include the W. B. Yeats Society of New York Award, the Thomas Merton Poetry of the Sacred Award, and three Pennsylvania Council on the Arts Fellowships. Her work appears in a variety of literary journals and anthologies and has been read on ABC, the BBC, and The Writer's Almanac and featured on Ted Kooser's American Life in Poetry. (p. 115)

An Officer of the Order of Canada, **Lorna Crozier** has been acknowledged for her contributions to Canadian literature with five honorary doctorates, most recently from McGill and Simon Fraser Universities. Her books have received numerous national awards, including the Governor-General's Award for Poetry. A professor emerita at the University of Victoria, she has performed for Queen Elizabeth II and has read her poetry, which has been translated into several languages, on every continent except Antarctica. She lives on Vancouver Island. (p. 33)

Toi Derricotte was the recipient of the Academy of American Poets' 2021 Wallace Stevens Award and the Poetry Society of America's 2020 Frost Medal for distinguished lifetime achievement in poetry. She is the author of National Book Awards Finalist *I: New & Selected Poems*, *The Undertaker's Daughter*, and four earlier collections of poetry, including *Tender*, winner of the Paterson Poetry Prize. Her literary memoir, *The Black Notebooks*, was a *New York Times* Notable Book of the Year. (p. 18)

Rita Dove published her first book of poems, *The Yellow House on the Corner*, in 1980. She has followed this work with several other collections, including *Museum*, *Thomas and Beulah*, *Grace Notes*, *Selected Poems*, *Mother Love*, *On the Bus with Rosa Parks*, and *American Smooth*. In 1993, Dove became poet laureate of the United States, the first Black poet to receive this honor. (p. 16)

Meghan Dunn is the author of *Curriculum*, winner of the 2020 Barry Spacks Poetry Prize from Gunpowder Press. She lives in Brooklyn, where she teaches high school English. Her work has appeared in *Narrative*, *Poetry Northwest*, and *Four Way Review* and has been featured on *Verse Daily* and *The Slowdown* podcast. She is a recipient of scholarships from the Bread Loaf Writers' Conference and the Sewanee Writers' Conference. (p. 72)

Joanne Durham is the author of *To Drink from a Wider Bowl* (Evening Street Press), winner of the Sinclair Poetry Prize, and *On Shifting Shoals* (Kelsay Books). A retired educator, she lives on the North Carolina coast, with the ocean as her backyard and muse. When not writing poetry, she practices yoga, delights in her grandkids, and works for a better world for them to grow up in. joannedurham.com (p. 71)

Peg Edera is a native of Portland, Maine. She migrated to Portland, Oregon, 35 years ago. She writes in community most days of the week. She is the author of a collection of poetry, *Love Is Deeper Than Distance: Poems of love, death, a little sex, ALS, dementia, and the widow's life thereafter* (Fernwood Press). Her work has also appeared in *Friends Journal, Untold Volumes: Feminist Theology Poetry,* and the OPA anthology *Pandemic*, among others. (p. 56)

Terri Kirby Erickson is the author of six collections, including *A Sun Inside My Chest* (Press 53). Her work has appeared in American Life in Poetry, *Atlanta Review, Healing the Divide: Poems of Kindness and Connection, How to Love the World: Poems of Gratitude and Hope, Christian Century, The Sun,* The Writer's Almanac, and many others. Her awards include the Joy Harjo Poetry Prize, the Atlanta Review International Publication Prize, and a Nautilus Silver Book Award. She lives in North Carolina. (p. 134)

Anne Evans was born and raised on California's central coast. After leaving a long career in secondary education, she joined an AWA group, and her writing practice became more intentional and consistent. During the pandemic, she wrote a poem every day and recently self-published 80 of those poems in a collection called *Peace in the Pandemic*. She continues this healing and enriching daily writing routine, living in Northern California with her husband and her dog, close to her kids and grandkids. (p. 114)

Joseph Fasano is a poet, novelist, and songwriter. His novels include *The Swallows of Lunetto* (Maudlin House) and *The Dark Heart of Every Wild Thing* (Platypus Press). His books of poetry include *The Crossing*, *Vincent*, *Inheritance*, and *Fugue for Other Hands*. His honors include the Cider Press Review Book Award, the Rattle Poetry Prize, seven Pushcart Prize nominations, and a nomination for the Poets' Prize. His debut album, *The Wind That Knows the Way*, is available wherever music is sold or streamed. (p. 129)

Julia Fehrenbacher is a poet, a teacher, a life coach, and a sometimes-painter who is always looking for ways to spread a little good around in this world. She is most at home by the ocean and in the forests of the Pacific Northwest and with pen and paintbrush in hand. She lives in Corvallis, Oregon, with her husband and two beautiful girls. (p. 151)

Laura Foley is the author of seven poetry collections. *Why I Never Finished My Dissertation* received a starred *Kirkus* review and an Eric Hoffer Award. Her collection *It's This* is forthcoming from Fernwood Press. Her poems have won numerous awards and national recognition, been read by Garrison Keillor on The Writer's Almanac, and appeared in Ted Kooser's American Life in Poetry. Laura lives with her wife, Clara Gimenez, among Vermont hills. (pp. 91, 104)

Rudy Francisco is one of the most recognizable names in Spoken Word Poetry. He was born, was raised, and still resides in San Diego, California. As an artist, Rudy Francisco is an amalgamation of social critique, introspection, honesty, and humor. He uses personal narratives to discuss the politics of race, class, gender, and religion while simultaneously pinpointing and reinforcing the interconnected nature of human existence. He is the author of *I'll Fly Away* (Button Poetry). (p. 47)

Albert Garcia is the author of three books of poems, *Rainshadow* (Copper Beech Press), *Skunk Talk* (Bear Star Press), and *A Meal Like That* (Brick Road Poetry Press), as well as a textbook called *Digging In: Literature for Developing Writers* (Prentice Hall). His poems have appeared in journals such as *Prairie Schooner*, *Willow Springs*, *Southern Poetry Review*, and *North American Review*. He has worked most of his career at Sacramento City College both as professor and administrator. (p. 10)

Ross Gay is the author of four books of poetry: *Against Which*; *Bringing the Shovel Down*; *Catalog of Unabashed Gratitude*, winner of the 2015 National Book Critics Circle Award and the 2016 Kingsley Tufts Poetry Award; and *Be Holding* (University of Pittsburgh Press). His best-selling collection of essays, *The Book of Delights*, was released by Algonquin Books, and he is the author most recently of *Inciting Joy* (Algonquin). (p. 27)

Jessica Gigot is a poet, farmer, and coach. She lives on a little sheep farm in the Skagit Valley. Her second book of poems, *Feeding Hour* (Wandering Aengus Press), won a Nautilus Award and was a finalist for the 2021 Washington State Book Award. Jessica's writing and reviews appear in *Orion*, the *New York Times*, the *Seattle Times*, *Ecotone*, *Terrain.org*, *Gastronomica*, *Crab Creek Review*, and *Poetry Northwest*. Her memoir, *A Little Bit of Land*, was published by Oregon State University Press in 2022. (p. 82)

Nikita Gill is a British-Indian poet, playwright, writer, and illustrator based in the south of England. Gill's work was first published when she was 12 years old, and she has since published eight volumes of poetry, including *Your Soul Is a River*; *Wild Embers: Poems of Rebellion, Fire, and Beauty*; *Fierce Fairytales: Poems & Stories to Stir Your Soul*; *Great Goddesses: Life Lessons from Myths and Monsters*; *Your Heart Is the Sea*; *The Girl and the Goddess*; *Where Hope Comes From: Poems of Resilience, Healing, and Light*; and *These Are the Words: Fearless Verse to Find Your Voice*. (pp. 24, 109)

Sue Ann Gleason grew up in the arms of an Italian American immigrant family who shaped her young mind and gave her perspectives and memories that you will see sprinkled throughout her poetry. She is a writer, a teacher, and an activist. Sue Ann holds inspired writing circles and organizes grassroots efforts, nurturing both individuals and agents for change in an increasingly complex world. Her book *in the glint of broken glass* can be found at wellnourishedwoman.com. (p. 86)

Ingrid Goff-Maidoff is the author of more than a dozen books of poetry and inspiration, as well as the creator of a line of cards and gifts. Her books include *What Holds Us*, *Wild Song*, *Befriending the Soul*, *Good Mother Welcome*, and *Simple Graces for Every Meal*. She lives on Martha's Vineyard with her husband and three white cats: Rumi, Hafiz, and Mirabai. Ingrid celebrates poetry, beauty & spirit through her website: tendingjoy.com. (p. 149)

Natalie Goldberg is the author of fourteen books, including *Writing Down the Bones*, which has sold over a million-and-a-half copies and been translated into fourteen languages. Her latest book is *Three Simple Lines: A Writer's Pilgrimage into the Heart and Homeland of Haiku*. Goldberg has been teaching seminars in writing as a practice for the last thirty years. Her lively paintings can be viewed at the Ernesto Mayans Gallery on Canyon Road in

Santa Fe. She currently lives in northern New Mexico. nataliegoldberg.com (p. 58)

Leah Naomi Green is the author of *The More Extravagant Feast* (Graywolf Press), selected by Li-Young Lee for the Walt Whitman Award of the Academy of American Poets. She is the recipient of a 2021 Treehouse Climate Action Poetry Prize, as well as the 2021 Lucille Clifton Legacy Award. Green teaches environmental studies and English at Washington and Lee University. She lives in the mountains of Virginia, where she and her family homestead and grow food. (p. 80)

Lucy Griffith lives beside the Guadalupe River near Comfort, Texas. As a retired psychologist, she explored the imagined life of the Burro Lady of West Texas in her debut collection, *We Make a Tiny Herd*, earning both the Wrangler and Willa Prizes. Her second collection, *Wingbeat Atlas*, pairs her poems with images by wildlife photographer Ken Butler, to celebrate our citizens of the sky. The collection was released in May 2022 by FlowerSong Press. She has been a Bread Loaf scholar, is a Certified Master Naturalist, and is always happiest on a tractor named Mabel. (p. 54)

Joy Harjo served as the 23rd US poet laureate, the first Native American to hold the position, and the only poet to be awarded a third term. Born in Tulsa, Oklahoma, Harjo is an internationally renowned performer and writer of the Muscogee (Creek) Nation. She is the author of nine books of poetry, several plays and children's books, and two memoirs. (p. 92)

Penny Harter's collection of haibun, *Keeping Time: Haibun for the Journey*, is forthcoming from Kelsay Books, joining her recent collections *Still-Water Days* and *A Prayer the Body Makes*. Her work appears in *Persimmon Tree*, *Rattle*, *Tiferet*, and American Life in Poetry, and in many journals, anthologies, and earlier collections. She has won fellowships and awards from the Dodge Foundation, the New Jersey State Council on the Arts, the Poetry Society of America, and the Virginia Center for Creative Arts. pennyharterpoet.com (p. 130)

Margaret Hasse lives in Saint Paul, Minnesota, where she has been active as a teaching poet, among other work in the community. Six of Margaret's full-length poetry collections are in print. During the first year of the COVID-19 pandemic, Margaret collaborated with artist Sharon DeMark on *Shelter*, a collection of poems and paintings about refuge. A chapbook, *The Call of Glacier Park*, is her latest publication. MargaretHasse.com (p. 98)

Rage Hezekiah is a New England–based poet and educator who earned her MFA from Emerson College. She has received fellowships from Cave Canem, MacDowell, and the Ragdale Foundation, and is a recipient of the Saint Botolph Foundation's Emerging Artists Award. Her poems have been anthologized, cotranslated, and published internationally, and her most recent book is *Yearn* (Diode Editions). (pp. 84, 169)

Donna Hilbert's latest book is *Gravity: New & Selected Poems* (Tebot Bach). Her new collection, *Threnody*, is forthcoming from Moon Tide Press. She is a monthly contributing writer to the online journal *Verse-Virtual*. Her work has appeared in the *Los Angeles Times*, *Braided Way*, *Chiron Review*, *Sheila-Na-Gig*, *Rattle*, *Zocalo Public Square*, *One Art*, and numerous anthologies. She writes and leads private workshops in Southern California, where she makes her home. donnahilbert.com (p. 52)

AE Hines grew up in rural North Carolina and now divides his time between Charlotte and Medellín, Colombia. His first poetry collection, *Any Dumb Animal*, was released in 2021, and his work has also appeared in *Southern Review*, *Poet Lore*, *Alaska Quarterly Review*, *Ninth Letter*, *Greensboro Review*, *Missouri Review*, *RHINO Poetry*, and *I-70 Review*, among other places. aehines.net (p. 40)

Jane Hirshfield's ninth, recently published poetry collection is *Ledger* (Knopf). Her work appears in the *New Yorker*, *The Atlantic*, the

Times Literary Supplement, the *New York Review of Books,* and ten editions of The Best American Poetry. A former chancellor of the Academy of American Poets, she was elected to the American Academy of Arts & Sciences in 2019. (p. 162)

Tony Hoagland (1953–2018) was the author of numerous poetry collections, including *Sweet Ruin*; *Donkey Gospel,* winner of the James Laughlin Award; *What Narcissism Means to Me,* a finalist for the National Book Critics Circle Award; *Rain*; and *Unincorporated Persons in the Late Honda Dynasty.* He also published two collections of essays about poetry: *Real Sofistakashun* and *Twenty Poems That Could Save America and Other Essays.* (p. 168)

Linda Hogan is a Chickasaw poet, novelist, essayist, playwright, teacher, and activist who has spent most of her life in Oklahoma and Colorado. Her fiction has garnered many honors, including a Pulitzer Prize nomination, and her poetry collections have received an American Book Award, a Colorado Book Award, and a National Book Critics Circle nomination. Her latest book is *A History of Kindness* (Torrey House Press). (p. 61)

Mary Jo LoBello Jerome is the author of *Torch the Empty Fields* (Finishing Line Press). Her work has appeared in *Paterson Literary Review, Poets Reading the News, Literary North, River Heron Review, Little Patuxent Review,* and the *New York Times,* among others. A poetry editor of Schuylkill Valley Journal and the 2019 poet laureate of Bucks County, Pennsylvania, she led the editing committee of *Fire Up the Poems,* a poetry guidebook for teachers. (p. 79)

Jacqueline Jules is the author of *Manna in the Morning* (Kelsay Books) and *Itzhak Perlman's Broken String,* winner of the 2016 Helen Kay Chapbook Prize from Evening Street Press. Her poetry has appeared in over 100 publications, including the *Sunlight Press, Gyroscope Review,* and *One Art.* She is also the author of a collection for young readers, *Tag Your Dreams:*

Poems of Play and Persistence (Albert Whitman). jacquelinejules.com (p. 38)

Adele Kenny, author of 25 books (poetry and nonfiction), has been widely published in the United States and abroad. Her awards include first prize in the 2021 Allen Ginsberg Poetry Awards, New Jersey State Arts Council poetry fellowships, a Merton Poetry of the Sacred Award, and Kean University's Distinguished Alumni Award. Her book *A Lightness* . . . was a Paterson Poetry Prize finalist. She is poetry editor of *Tiferet* and founding director of the Carriage House Poetry Series. (p. 157)

Jane Kenyon (1947–1995) was an American poet and translator. While a student at the University of Michigan, Kenyon met the poet Donald Hall; though he was more than twenty years her senior, she married him in 1972, and they moved to Eagle Pond Farm, his ancestral home in New Hampshire. Kenyon was New Hampshire's poet laureate when she died in April 1995 from leukemia. When she died, she was working on editing the now-classic *Otherwise: New and Selected Poems*, which was released posthumously in 1996. (p. 131)

Stuart Kestenbaum is the author of six collections of poems: *Pilgrimage* (Coyote Love Press) and *House of Thanksgiving*, *Prayers and Run-on Sentences*, *Only Now*, *How to Start Over*, and *Things Seemed to Be Breaking* (all from Deerbrook Editions). He has also written *The View from Here* (Brynmorgen Press), a book of brief essays on craft and community. He lives in Maine. (p. 123)

Michael Kleber-Diggs is the author of *Worldly Things*, which was awarded the 2020 Max Ritvo Poetry Prize. He was born and raised in Kansas and now lives in St. Paul, Minnesota. His work has appeared in Lit Hub, *The Rumpus*, *Rain Taxi*, McSweeney's Internet Tendency, *Water~Stone Review*, *Midway Review*, and *North Dakota Quarterly*. Michael teaches poetry and creative nonfiction through the Minnesota Prison Writers Workshop. (p. 17)

Thirteenth US Poet Laureate (2004–2006) **Ted Kooser** is a retired life insurance executive who lives on acreage near the village of Garland, Nebraska, with his wife, Kathleen Rutledge. His collection *Delights & Shadows* was awarded the Pulitzer Prize in Poetry in 2005. His poems have appeared in *The Atlantic*, *Hudson Review*, *Antioch Review*, *Kenyon Review*, and dozens of other literary journals. He is the author most recently of *Cotton Candy* (University of Nebraska Press) and *Marshmallow Clouds*, with Connie Wanek (Candlewick Press). (pp. 6, 116)

Jennifer G. Lai is a poet, visual artist, storyteller, and audio producer. Her work has appeared in *Pigeon Pages*, *ANOMALY*, *Canto Cutie*, *The Slowdown*, and *Angry Asian Man*, among others. Her visual work has participated in exhibitions at Jip Gallery and Olympia Gallery (A Place to Visit, V.3) and in Chelsea Market (Futures Ever Arriving). She currently lives in Brooklyn. Find her on Twitter @jenniferglai (p. 164)

Danusha Laméris is the author of two books: *The Moons of August* (Autumn House), which was chosen by Naomi Shihab Nye as the winner of the Autumn House Press Poetry Prize, and *Bonfire Opera* (University of Pittsburgh Press), which won the Northern California Book Award. Winner of the Lucille Clifton Legacy Award, she teaches in the Pacific University low-residency MFA program and co-leads with James Crews the global HearthFire Writing Community. She lives in Santa Cruz County, California. (pp. 49, 62, 121)

Alfred K. LaMotte has authored five books of poetry. A graduate of Yale University and Princeton Theological Seminary, LaMotte is a meditation teacher, interfaith college chaplain, and instructor in world religions. He lives in a small town on Puget Sound with his beloved wife, Anna, and loves to gather circles for meditation and poetry. (p. 125)

Dorianne Laux's sixth collection, *Only as the Day Is Long: New and Selected Poems*, was named a finalist for the 2020 Pulitzer Prize for Poetry. Her fifth collection, *The Book of Men*, was awarded the Paterson Prize, and her fourth book of poems, *Facts About the Moon*, won the Oregon Book Award. Laux is the coauthor of the celebrated *The Poet's Companion: A Guide to the Pleasures of Writing Poetry*. (p. 85)

Li-Young Lee was born in Djakarta, Indonesia, in 1957 to Chinese political exiles. He is the author of *The Undressing*; *Behind My Eyes*; *Book of My Nights*, which won the 2002 William Carlos Williams Award; *The City in Which I Love You*, which was the 1990 Lamont Poetry Selection; and *Rose*, which won the Delmore Schwartz Memorial Poetry Award. (p. 50)

Paula Gordon Lepp lives in South Charleston, West Virginia, with her husband and two almost-grown kids. She grew up in a rural community in the Mississippi Delta, and a childhood spent roaming woods and fields, climbing trees, and playing in the dirt instilled in her a love for nature that is reflected in her poems. Paula's work has been published in the anthologies *How to Love the World: Poems of Gratitude and Hope* and *The Mountain: An Anthology of Mountain Poems* (Middle Creek Publishing). (p. 7)

Annie Lighthart began writing poetry after her first visit to an Oregon old-growth forest and now teaches poetry wherever she can. Poems from her books *Iron String* and *Pax* have been featured on The Writer's Almanac and in many anthologies. Annie's work has been turned into music, used in healing projects, and has traveled farther than she has. She hopes you find a poem to love in this book, even if it is one she didn't write. (p. 140)

Ada Limón is the author of six poetry collections, including *The Hurting Kind* and *The Carrying*, which won the National Book Critics Circle Award. Her fourth book, *Bright Dead Things*, was named a finalist for the National Book Award, the Kingsley Tufts Poetry Award, and the National Book Critics Circle Award. A recipient of a Guggenheim Fellowship for Poetry, she was recently named US poet laureate. (pp. 53, 136)

Lois Lorimer is a Canadian poet, actor, and teacher. Her poems appear in the journals *Arc and Literary Review of Canada*, as well as many anthologies, including *The Bright Well* (Leaf Press) and *Heartwood* (League of Canadian Poets). Her first collection was *Stripmall Subversive* (Variety Crossing Press). A member of the League of Canadian Poets, Lois enjoys writing near water and believes in the power of poetry to heal and delight. (p. 158)

Alison Luterman's four books of poetry are *The Largest Possible Life*, *See How We Almost Fly*, *Desire Zoo*, and *In the Time of Great Fires*. Her poems and stories have appeared in *The Sun*, *Rattle*, *Salon*, *Prairie Schooner*, *Nimrod*, the *Atlanta Review*, *Tattoo Highway*, and elsewhere. She has written an ebook of personal essays, *Feral City*, half a dozen plays, a song cycle, as well as two musicals, *The Chain* and *The Shyest Witch*. (p. 36)

Emilie Lygren is a poet and outdoor educator who holds a bachelor's degree in geology-biology from Brown University. Her poems have been published in *Thimble Literary Magazine*, *English Leadership Quarterly*, *Solo Novo*, and several other literary journals. Her first book of poems, *What We Were Born For* (Blue Light Press), won the Blue Light Book Award. She lives in San Rafael, California. (p. 97)

Marilyn McCabe's work has garnered her an Orlando Prize from A Room of Her Own Foundation; the Hilary Tham Capital Collection contest award from The Word Works, resulting in publication of her book of poems *Perpetual Motion*; and two artist grants from the New York State Council on the Arts. Her second book of poems, *Glass Factory*, was published in 2016. marilynonaroll.wordpress.com (p. 112)

Brooke McNamara is a poet, teacher, and ordained Zen monk and Dharma Holder. She has published two books of poems, *Bury the Seed* and *Feed Your Vow*, and is the recipient of the Charles B. Palmer Prize from the Academy of American Poets. Brooke has taught yoga studies at Naropa University and dance at University of Colorado–Boulder. She lives with her husband and two sons in Boulder. BrookeMcNamara.com (p. 65)

Rachel Michaud is a prize-winning poet and essayist. Her essays have been published in the *Washington Post* and *Hartford Courant* and broadcast on WAMC-Northeast Public Radio. Her poetry has appeared in literary journals and anthologies and been set to music. Michaud has worked on behalf of nonprofit organizations supporting food security, education, and the arts. She divides her time between Washington, DC, and Cambridge, New York. (p. 41)

Brad Aaron Modlin wrote *Everyone at This Party Has Two Names*, which won the Cowles Poetry Prize. *Surviving in Drought* (stories) won the Cupboard Pamphlet contest. His work has been the basis for orchestral scores, an art exhibition, an episode of *The Slowdown* with Ada Limón, and the premier episode of *Poetry Unbound* from On Being Studios. A professor and the Reynolds Endowed Chair of Creative Writing at University of Nebraska–Kearney, he teaches, coordinates the visiting writers' series, and gets chalk all over himself. (p. 153)

David Mook began writing poetry after the sudden death of his eight-year-old daughter, Sarah, a poet who began writing poems in kindergarten. *Each Leaf* (Freewheeling Press) includes poems written by Sarah. The Sarah Mook Poetry Contest honors the work of student poets in grades K–12. David lives in Vermont and teaches at Castleton University. (p. 160)

Marjorie Moorhead writes from the beautiful Connecticut River Valley at the Vermont–New Hampshire border. Having survived AIDS, Marjorie embraced poetry to tell her story and join in community with others. Her collection *Every Small Breeze* is forthcoming from Indolent Books. Marjorie's chapbooks are *Survival: Trees, Tides, Song* (FLP), and *Survival Part 2: Trees, Birds, Ocean, Bees* (Duck Lake Books). She is happy to have poems included in many anthologies and journals. (p. 128)

Tyler Mortensen-Hayes is a poet from Salt Lake City. His work has appeared in *Rattle*, *Frogpond*, and *Weber: The Contemporary West*. He holds an MFA from the University of New Mexico, where he was poetry editor of *Blue Mesa Review*. A student of Insight Meditation and Soto Zen, he hopes to become a teacher of meditation and mindfulness, using poetry as a quintessential practice. (p. 147)

Susan Musgrave lives on Haida Gwaii, islands in the North Pacific that lie equidistant from Luxor, Machu Picchu, Ninevah, and Timbuktu. The high point of her literary career was finding her name in the index of *Montreal's Irish Mafia*. She has published more than 30 books and has received awards in six categories: poetry, novels, nonfiction, food writing, editing, and books for children. Her new book of poetry is *Exculpatory Lilies*. (p. 78)

Mark Nepo has moved and inspired readers and seekers all over the world with his #1 *New York Times* bestseller *The Book of Awakening*. Beloved as a poet, teacher, and storyteller, Mark has been called "one of the finest spiritual guides of our time," "a consummate storyteller," and "an eloquent spiritual teacher." He has published 22 books and recorded 14 audio projects. Recent work includes *The Book of Soul* and *Drinking from the River of Light*, a Nautilus Award winner. marknepo.com and threeintentions.com (pp. 29, 42, 99, 103)

Robbi Nester explores the world from her desk in Southern California. She is the author of four books of poetry and editor of three anthologies. robbinester.net (p. 73)

Cristina M. R. Norcross is the editor of *Blue Heron Review*, the author of nine poetry collections, a multiple Pushcart Prize nominee, and an Eric Hoffer Book Award nominee. Her most recent collection is *The Sound of a Collective Pulse* (Kelsay Books). Cristina's work appears in *Lothlorien*, *Muddy River Poetry Review*, *Verse-Virtual*, the *Ekphrastic Review*, *Visual Verse*, and *Pirene's Fountain*, among others. She is the cofounder of Random Acts of Poetry & Art Day. cristinanorcross.com (p. 100)

Naomi Shihab Nye recently served as the Young People's Poet Laureate of the United States (Poetry Foundation). Her most recent books are *Everything Comes Next: Collected & New Poems*, *Cast Away (Poems about Trash)*, *The Tiny Journalist*, and *Voices in the Air—Poems for Listeners*. She also edited *Dear Vaccine: Global Voices Speak to the Pandemic* with David Hassler and Tyler Meier. She lives in San Antonio, Texas. (p. 74)

January Gill O'Neil is an associate professor of English at Salem State University. She is the author of *Rewilding* (CavanKerry Press), a finalist for the 2019 Paterson Poetry Prize; *Misery Islands* (CavanKerry Press); and *Underlife* (CavanKerry Press). (pp. 26, 172)

Brad Peacock is a veteran and longtime organic farmer from Shaftsbury, Vermont, whose passion is to bring people closer to one another and the natural world. (p. 150)

Rosalie Sanara Petrouske's poem "Eating Corn Soup Under the Strawberry Moon" was one of six finalists in the 2020 Jack Grapes Poetry Prize from *Cultural Weekly*. Recently, she won First Place in the 2022 Poetry Box Chapbook Competition, for *Tracking the Fox*. An English professor at Lansing Community College in Lower Michigan, she has also been a finalist for the distinction of Upper Peninsula poet laureate. (p. 144)

Kathryn Petruccelli holds an MA in teaching English language learners and an obsession around the power of voice. Her work has appeared in places like the *Southern Review*, *Massachusetts Review*, *Hunger Mountain*, *Rattle*, *Tinderbox*, *SWWIM*, and *River Teeth's Beautiful Things*. She's been a Best of the Net nominee and a finalist for the Omnidawn Poetry Broadside Contest. Kathryn tour-guides at the Emily Dickinson Museum and teaches workshops for adults and teens.
poetroar.com (p. 132)

Andrea Potos is the author of *Her Joy Becomes* (Fernwood Press), *Marrow of Summer* and *Mothershell* (both from Kelsay Books), and *A Stone to Carry Home* (Salmon Poetry). Recent poems appear in *Poetry East*, *The Sun*, *Braided Way*, *Potomac Review*, and the anthologies *How to Love the World: Poems of Gratitude and Hope* and *The Path to Kindness: Poems of Connection and Joy*. (p. 11)

Rena Priest is a citizen of the Lhaq'temish (Lummi) Nation. Priest is the author of *Northwest Know-How: Beaches* (Sasquatch Books); *Sublime Subliminal* (Floating Bridge Press); and *Patriarchy Blues* (Moonpath Press), which received an American Book Award. Priest was appointed Washington State Poet Laureate in 2021 and is the 2022 Maxine Cushing Gray Distinguished Writing Fellow. She currently resides near her tribal community in Bellingham, Washington, where she was born and raised. (p. 143)

Alison Prine's debut collection of poems, *Steel* (Cider Press Review) was named a finalist for the 2017 Vermont Book Award. Her poems have appeared in *Ploughshares*, *Virginia Quarterly Review*, *Five Points*, *Harvard Review*, and *Prairie Schooner*, among others. She lives and works in Burlington, Vermont.
alisonprine.com (p. 34)

Laura Ann Reed's work has been anthologized in *How to Love the World: Poems of Gratitude and Hope,* and is forthcoming in the SMEOP anthology *HOT*, in addition to appearing in *Loch Raven*, *One Art*, *MacQueen's Quinterly*,

SWWIM, the *Ekphrastic Review*, *Willawaw*, and *Grey Sparrow Journal*, among other journals. Her chapbook *Shadows Thrown* is slated for publication by SunGold Editions. A San Francisco Bay Area native, Laura currently resides with her husband in western Washington. (p. 138)

Alberto Ríos was named Arizona's first poet laureate in 2013. He is the author of many poetry collections from Copper Canyon Press, including *Not Go Away Is My Name*; *A Small Story About the Sky*; *The Dangerous Shirt*; *The Theater of Night*; and *The Smallest Muscle in the Human Body*, which was nominated for a National Book Award. (p. 124)

Charles Rossiter, a National Endowment for the Arts fellowship recipient, hosts the biweekly podcast at poetryspokenhere.com. His poems are published in *Bennington Review*, *Paterson Literary Review*, *After Hours*, and more. Recent collections include *The Night We Danced with the Raelettes*, a memoir in poetry; *All Over America: Road Poems*; and *Green Mountain Meditations* (all from FootHills Publishing). He has performed at the Nuyorican Poets Café, Green Mill, the Dodge Festival, Detroit Opera House, and Chicago Blues Festival. (p. 167)

Ellen Rowland creates, concocts, and forages when she's not writing. She is the author of *Light, Come Gather Me* and *Blue Seasons*, as well as the book *Everything I Thought I Knew*, essays on living, learning, and parenting. Her writing has appeared in *The Path to Kindness: Poems of Connection and Joy* and *Hope is a Group Project.* Her debut collection of full-length poems, *No Small Thing*, was published by Fernwood Press (2023). She lives off the grid with her family on an island in Greece. (pp. 8, 32)

Marjorie Saiser's seventh collection, *Learning to Swim* (Stephen F. Austin State University Press), contains both poetry and memoir. Her novel-in-poems, *Losing the Ring in the River* (University of New Mexico Press), won the WILLA Award for Poetry in 2014. Saiser's most recent book, *The Track the Whales Make: New & Selected Poems*, is available from University of Nebraska Press. poetmarge.com (p. 30)

Faith Shearin's books of poetry include *The Owl Question* (May Swenson Award); *Moving the Piano*; *Telling the Bees*; *Orpheus, Turning* (Dogfish Poetry Prize); *Darwin's Daughter*; and *Lost Language* (Press 53). She has received awards from Yaddo, the National Endowment for the Arts, and the Fine Arts Work Center in Provincetown. Her poems have been read on The Writer's Almanac and included in American Life in Poetry. She lives in Amherst, Massachusetts. (p. 90)

Derek Sheffield's collection *Not for Luck* was selected by Mark Doty for the 2019 Wheelbarrow Books Poetry Prize. His other books include *Through the Second Skin*, finalist for the Washington State Book Award; *Dear America*; and *Cascadia Field Guide: Art, Ecology, Poetry*. He is the poetry editor of Terrain.org. (p. 117)

Michael Simms's recent books include two collections of poetry, *American Ash* and *Nightjar* (both published by Ragged Sky Press), and a novel, *Bicycles of the Gods: A Divine Comedy* (published by Madville). Simms was the founding editor (1998–2016) of Autumn House Press and currently is the founding editor of *Vox Populi*, an online magazine of poetry, politics, and nature. He lives with his family in the historic neighborhood of Mount Washington overlooking Pittsburgh. (p. 127)

Maggie Smith is the author of the national bestsellers *Goldenrod* and *Keep Moving*, as well as *Good Bones*, *The Well Speaks of Its Own Poison*, and *Lamp of the Body*. Smith's poems and essays have appeared in The Best American Poetry, the *New York Times*, the *New Yorker*, the *Paris Review*, *Ploughshares*, and elsewhere. Smith's latest book is a memoir: *You Could Make This Place Beautiful*. (p. 23)

Holly Wren Spaulding is an interdisciplinary artist, teacher, and author of *Between Us*, *Familiars*, *If August*, and *Pilgrim* (all published by Alice Greene & Co). Spaulding's writing has appeared in *Michigan Quarterly Review*, *Witness*, *Poetry Northwest*, *The Ecologist,* and elsewhere. She is the founder and artistic director of Poetry Forge, where she offers workshops and an annual manuscript intensive. She lives in Maine. hollywrenspaulding.com (p. 51)

Nathan Spoon is an autistic poet with learning disabilities whose poems have appeared or are forthcoming in *American Poetry Review*, *Bennington Review*, *Gulf Coast*, Poem-a-Day, *Poetry*, *Poetry Daily*, and *swamp pink*. He is author of the debut collection *Doomsday Bunker* and the chapbook *Full Better! Feel Great!!* He is editor of *Queerly* and an ally of timemedicine.org. (p. 139)

Kim Stafford directs the Northwest Writing Institute at Lewis & Clark College and is the author of a dozen books, including *The Muses Among Us: Eloquent Listening and Other Pleasures of the Writer's Craft* (University of Georgia Press) and *Singer Come from Afar* (Red Hen Press). He has taught writing in Scotland, Mexico, Italy, and Bhutan. He served as Oregon poet laureate (2018–2020). He teaches and travels to raise the human spirit. (pp. 94, 120)

Julie Cadwallader Staub writes from her home near Burlington, Vermont. Her poems have been published widely in literary and religious journals and anthologies, including *The Path to Kindness: Poems of Connection and Joy* and *Poetry of Presence*. Her poem "Milk" won the 2015 Ruth Stone Award, and the *Potomac Review* nominated "Turning" for a 2019 Pushcart Prize. She has two collections of poems: *Face to Face* (Cascadia Publishing) and *Wing Over Wing* (Paraclete Press). (p. 163)

Meghan Sterling (she/her) lives in Maine. Her work is forthcoming in the *Los Angeles Review*, *RHINO Poetry*, *Nelle*, *Poetry South*, and many others. *These Few Seeds* (Terrapin Books) was an Eric Hoffer Grand Prize finalist. *Self-Portrait with Ghosts of the Diaspora* (Harbor Editions), *Comfort the Mourners* (Everybody Press), and *View from a Borrowed Field* (Lily Poetry Review's Paul Nemser Book Prize) are all forthcoming in 2023. (p. 89)

Joshua Michael Stewart is the author of three poetry collections: *Break Every String*, *The Bastard Children of Dharma Bums*, and *Love Something*. His poems have appeared in the *Massachusetts Review*, *Salamander*, *Plainsongs*, *Brilliant Corners*, *South Dakota Review*, and many other publications. He lives in Ware, Massachusetts. joshuamichaelstewart.com (p. 68)

Jacqueline Suskin is the author of seven books, including *Every Day Is a Poem* (Sounds True) and *Help in the Dark Season* (Write Bloody). With her project Poem Store, Suskin has composed over 40,000 improvisational poems for patrons who chose a topic in exchange for a unique verse. She was honored by Michelle Obama as a Turnaround Artist, and her work has been featured in the *New York Times*, *Los Angeles Times*, *The Atlantic*, and other publications. jacquelinesuskin.com (pp. 70, 152)

Joyce Sutphen grew up on a small farm in Stearns County, Minnesota. Her first collection of poems, *Straight Out of View*, won the Barnard New Women Poets Prize; her recent books are *The Green House* (Salmon Poetry) and *Carrying Water to the Field: New and Selected Poems* (University of Nebraska Press). She is the Minnesota poet laureate and professor emerita of literature and creative writing at Gustavus Adolphus College. (p. 110)

Heather Swan's poems have appeared in such journals as *Terrain*, *The Hopper*, *Poet Lore*, *Phoebe*, and the *Raleigh Review*, and her book of poems, *A Kinship with Ash* (Terrapin Books), was published in 2020. Her nonfiction has appeared in *Aeon*, *Belt*, *Catapult*, *Emergence*, *ISLE*, and *Terrain*. Her book

Where Honeybees Thrive: Stories from the Field (Penn State Press) won the Sigurd F. Olson Nature Writing Award. She teaches environmental literature and writing at the University of Wisconsin–Madison. (p. 108)

Bradford Tice is the author of *Rare Earth* (New Rivers Press), which was named the winner of the 2011 Many Voices Project, and *What the Night Numbered* (Trio House Press), winner of the 2014 Trio Award. His poetry and fiction have appeared in such periodicals as *The Atlantic*, *North American Review*, the *American Scholar*, and *Epoch*, as well as in *The Best American Short Stories 2008*. (p. 161)

Angela Narciso Torres is the author of *Blood Orange*, winner of the Willow Books Literature Award for Poetry. Her recent collections include *To the Bone* (Sundress Publications) and *What Happens Is Neither* (Four Way Books). Her work has appeared in *Poetry*, *Missouri Review*, *Quarterly West*, *Cortland Review*, and *PANK*. Born in Brooklyn and raised in Manila, she serves as a senior and reviews editor for *RHINO Poetry*. (p. 44)

Rosemerry Wahtola Trommer lives on the banks of the San Miguel River in southwest Colorado. She co-hosts the Emerging Form podcast and Secret Agents of Change (a kindness cabal). Her poems have been featured on *A Prairie Home Companion*, American Life in Poetry, and *PBS Newshour*, as well as in *O, The Oprah Magazine*. Her collection *Hush* won the Halcyon Prize. She is also the author of *Naked for Tea* and *All the Honey* (Samara Press). Her one-word mantra: Adjust. (pp. 48, 166)

Susan Varon is a poet, artist, and Interfaith minister. She started writing in 1989 after her life was rearranged by a stroke. Her work has appeared in *Green Mountains Review*, *Notre Dame Review*, *Paterson Literary Review*, and the *Midwest Quarterly*, among many others. After living for 40 years in New York City, she moved to Taos, New Mexico, in April 2007, beckoned there by the Helene Wurlitzer Foundation artists' colony, the mountains, and the sky. (p. 69)

Connie Wanek was born in Wisconsin, raised in New Mexico, and lived for over a quarter century in Duluth. She is the author of *Bonfire* (New Rivers Press), winner of the New Voices Award; *Hartley Field* (Holy Cow! Press); and *On Speaking Terms* (Copper Canyon Press). In 2016, the University of Nebraska Press published Wanek's *Rival Gardens: New and Selected Poems* as part of Ted Kooser's Contemporary Poetry series. (p. 146)

Caroline Webster is a Vermont Artist Development Grant recipient, teacher, and Gateless writer. She has called many places home: Austria, North Carolina, Vermont, Korea, and Oman. The year 2020 brought her back to where she started, Virginia. In her work, she's grateful to support the Teachers in the Movement project and explore how educators' stories add to our understanding of history and influence today. She believes in the power of poetry to provide refuge and promote healing. (p. 102)

Laura Grace Weldon lives on a small ramshackle farm where she works as a book editor, teaches writing workshops, and maxes out her library card each week. Laura served as Ohio's 2019 Poet of the Year and is the author of four books, fifth on the way. lauragraceweldon.com (p. 142)

Diana Whitney writes across the genres in Vermont with a focus on feminism, motherhood, and sexuality. Her work has appeared in the *New York Times*, the *San Francisco Chronicle*, the *Kenyon Review*, *Glamour*, *The Rumpus*, and many more. Diana's poetry debut, *Wanting It* (Harbor Mountain Press, 2014), won the Rubery Book Award, and her inclusive anthology, *You Don't Have to Be Everything: Poems for Girls Becoming Themselves* (Workman, 2021), became a YA bestseller and won the 2022 Claudia Lewis Award. diana-whitney.com (p. 13)

Michelle Wiegers is a poet, creative writer, and mind-body life coach based in southern Vermont. Her poems are inspired by her mind-body recovery from decades of chronic symptoms, the Vermont landscape, and her own backyard. Her work has appeared in *Birchsong*, *How to Love the World: Poems of Gratitude and Hope*, *The Path to Kindness: Poems of Connection and Joy*, and *Third Wednesday*, among others. In her coaching and teaching work, she is a passionate advocate for chronic pain and fatigue sufferers. michellewiegers.com (p. 66)

Katherine J. Williams, art therapist and clinical psychologist, was the director of the art therapy program at George Washington University, where she is now an associate professor emerita. Her poems have been published in journals and anthologies such as *Poet Lore*, the *Broadkill Review*, *3rd Wednesday*, *Delmarva Review*, *The Poet's Cookbook*, *The Widows' Handbook*, and *How to Love the World: Poems of Gratitude and Hope*. She is the author of *Still Life* (Cherry Grove). (p. 137)

Sarah Wolfson is the author of *A Common Name for Everything*, which won the A. M. Klein Prize for Poetry. Her poems have appeared in journals such as *AGNI*, *TriQuarterly*, *The Walrus*, *The Fiddlehead*, and *West Branch*. Her work has also been anthologized in *Rewilding: Poems for the Environment* and received notable mention in *Best Canadian Poetry*. Originally from Vermont, she now lives in Tiohtià:ke/Montreal, where she teaches writing at McGill University. (p. 77)

Lisa Zimmerman's poetry collections include *How the Garden Looks from Here* (Violet Reed Haas Poetry Award winner), *The Light at the Edge of Everything* (Anhinga Press), and *Sainted* (Main Street Rag). Her poetry and fiction have appeared in *Redbook*, *The Sun*, *SWWIM Every Day*, *Cave Wall*, and *Poet Lore*, among other journals. Her poems have been nominated for Best of the Net, five times for the Pushcart Prize, and included in *The Best Small Fictions 2020* anthology. (p. 106)

Yvonne Zipter is author of the poetry collections *The Wordless Lullaby of Crickets*, *Kissing the Long Face of the Greyhound*, *The Patience of Metal* (Lambda Literary Award finalist), and *Like Some Bookie God*; the Russian historical novel *Infraction*; and the nonfiction books *Diamonds Are a Dyke's Best Friend* and *Ransacking the Closet*. Her individual published poems are being sold in two repurposed toy-vending machines in Chicago, the proceeds of which support a local nonprofit organization. (p. 159)

CREDITS

"Archilochus Colubris" by José A. Alcántara, from *The Bitten World* (Tebot Bach, 2022). Reprinted with permission of author.

"What the Roses Said to Me" by Lahab Assef Al-Jundi, from *This Is It* (Kelsay Books, 2021). Reprinted by permission of author.

"Locust" by Julia Alvarez. Copyright © 2004 by Julia Alvarez. From *The Woman I Kept to Myself*, published by Algonquin Books of Chapel Hill. By permission of Susan Bergholz Literary Services, Lamy, NM. All rights reserved.

"First Snow" by James Armstrong, originally published in *Poetry East,* edited by Richard Jones.

"Hugging the Tree" by Zeina Azzam, from *Streetlight Magazine* (Issue no. 39, Fall 2021).

"Chestnut" by Rebecca Baggett from *The Woman Who Lives Without Money* (Regal House Publishing, 2022). Reprinted with permission of author.

"The Peace of Wild Things" by Wendell Berry from *New Collected Poems*. Copyright © 2012 by Wendell Berry. Reprinted with the permission of The Permissions Company, LLC on behalf of Counterpoint Press, counterpointpress.com.

"Swim Lessons" by George Bilgere, from *Blood Pages*. Copyright © 2018 Reprinted by permission of University of Pittsburgh Press

"The Way We Love Something Small" Copyright © 2020 by Kimberly Blaeser. Originally published in Poem-a-Day on April 8, 2020 by the Academy of American Poets.

"Aubade" by Sally Bliumis-Dunn, originally published in *Beltway Poetry Quarterly.*

"Lately," by Laure-Anne Bosselaar, originally published in *Vox Populi.*

"Birdfoot's Grampa" by Joseph Bruchac, from *Entering Onondaga* (Cold Mountain Press, 1978). "Tutuwas" originally appeared in *Gwarlingo Sunday Poem.* Reprinted by permission of author.

"Ocean Love" by Carolyn Chilton Casas, originally published on grateful.org.

"Pocket" by Judith Chalmer, from *Minnow* (Kelsay Books, 2020). Reprinted by permission of author.

"Creed" by Patricia Clark, from *My Father on a Bicycle* (Michigan State University Press, 2005). Reprinted with permission of author.

"Essence" by Kai Coggin, from *Mining for Stardust* (Flower Song Press, 2021). Reprinted by permission of author.

"Encounter" by Sharon Corcoran, from *The Two Worlds* (Middle Creek Publishing & Audio, 2021). Reprinted by permission of author.

"Tomatoes" by James Crews, originally published in *Vox Populi.*

"This Summer Day" by Barbara Crooker, from *A Small Rain* (Purple Flag, 2014). Reprinted by permission of author.

"Cherry Blossoms" by Toi Derricotte, from *The Undertaker's Daughter* Copyright © 2011. Reprinted by permission of University of Pittsburgh Press.

"Horse and Tree" by Rita Dove, from *Grace Notes*. Copyright © 1989 by Rita Dove. Used by permission of W. W. Norton & Company, Inc.

"Ode to Butter" by Meghan Dunn originally appeared in *MUSE: A Journal.*

"Sunrise Sonnet for My Son" by Joanne Durham, from *To Drink from a Wider Bowl* (Evening Street Press, 2022).

"Letter" by Joseph Fasano, from *The Crossing* (Cider Press Review, 2018). Reprinted with permission of the author.

"Lost and Found" by Laura Foley, from *It's This* (Fernwood Press, 2023). "What Stillness" from *Why I Never Finished My Dissertation* (Headmistress Press, 2019). Reprinted with permission of author.

"Water" by Rudy Francisco, from *Helium*. Copyright © 2017 by Rudy Francisco. Courtesy of Button Publishing Inc.

"Ice" by Albert Garcia, from *Skunk Talk* (Bear Star Press, 2005). Reprinted with permission of author.

"Sorrow Is Not My Name" by Ross Gay, from *Bringing the Shovel Down.* Copyright © 2011. Reprinted by permission of University of Pittsburgh Press.

"Amends" by Jessica Gigot originally published in *Silver Birch Press: How to Heal the Earth.*

"The Forest" and "Your Soft Heart" by Nikita Gill, from *Where Hope Comes From.* Copyright © Nikita Gill, 2021, published by Trapeze, reproduced by kind permission by David Higham Associates.

"The Listening Bridge" by Ingrid Goff-Maidoff, from *Wild Song* (2021). Reprinted with permission of the author.

"Carrot" by Leah Naomi Green, from *The More Extravagant Feast*. Copyright © 2020 by Leah Naomi Green. Reprinted with the permission of The Permissions Company, LLC on behalf of Graywolf Press, graywolfpress.org.

"Attention" by Lucy Griffith originally appeared in C*anary Environmental Literary Magazine.*

"Redbird Love" by Joy Harjo, from *An American Sunrise: Poems*. Copyright © 2019 by Joy Harjo. Used by permission of W. W. Norton & Company, Inc. and The Wylie Agency LLC.

"Just Grapefruit" by Penny Harter, from *Still-Water Days* (Kelsay Books, 2021). Reprinted with permission of author.

"Art" by Margaret Hasse, from *Shelter* (Nodin Press, 2020). Reprinted with permission of author.

"Layers" by Rage Hezekiah, from *Stray Harbor*. Copyright © 2019 by Rage Hezekiah. Reprinted with the permission of The Permissions Company, LLC on behalf of Finishing Line Press, finishinglinepress.com.

"Lake Sunapee" by Rage Hezekiah, from *Yearn*. Copyright © 2022 by Rage Hezekiah. Reprinted by permission of Diode Editions and author.

"Ribollita" by Donna Hilbert originally appeared in *One Art.*

"What Did You Imagine Would Grow?" by AE Hines, from *Any Dumb Animal* (Main Street Rag, 2021). Reprinted with permission of author.

"Solstice" by Jane Hirshfield, reprinted with permission of author.

"Field Guide" by Tony Hoagland, from *Unincorporated Persons in the Late Honda Dynasty*. Copyright © 2010 by Tony Hoagland. Reprinted with the permission of The Permissions Company, LLC on behalf of Graywolf Press, graywolfpress.org.

"Home in the Woods" by Linda Hogan, from *Dark. Sweet.: New & Selected Poems*. Copyright © 2014 by Linda Hogan. Reprinted with the permission of The Permissions Company, LLC on behalf of Coffee House Press, coffeehousepress.org.

"The Honeybee" by Jacqueline Jules, originally published in *ONE ART*, edited by Mark Danowsky.

"Survivor" by Adele Kenny from *What Matters* (Welcome Rain Publishers, 2011). Reprinted with permission of author.

"In Several Colors" by Jane Kenyon, from *Collected Poems*. Copyright © 2005 by The Estate of Jane Kenyon. Reprinted with the permission of The Permissions Company, LLC on behalf of Graywolf Press, graywolfpress.org.

"Holding the Light" by Stuart Kestenbaum, from *Only Now* (Deerbrook Editions, 2013). Copyright © 2013 by Stuart Kestenbaum. Used by permission of author.

"The Grove" by Michael Kleber-Diggs, from *Worldly Things*. Copyright © 2021 by Michael Kleber-Diggs. Reprinted with the permission of The Permissions Company, LLC on behalf of Milkweed Editions, milkweed.org.

"In Early April" by Ted Kooser, reprinted by permission of author.

"A Glint," from *A Man with a Rake* (Pulley Press, 2022). Reprinted by permission of author and publisher.

"In My Mind's Coral, Mother Still Calls Us from Inside" by Jennifer G. Lai originally appeared in *Pigeon Pages*.

"Nothing Wants to Suffer" by Danusha Laméris, reprinted by permission of author. "Dust" by Danusha Laméris, from *Bonfire Opera*. Copyright ©2020. Reprinted by permission of University of Pittsburgh Press.

"Gentle" by Alfred K. LaMotte, from *Savor Eternity One Moment at a Time* (St. Julian Press, 2016). Reprinted by permission of the author.

"My Mother's Colander" by Dorianne Laux, from *Only As the Day Is Long: New and Selected Poems*. Copyright © 2019. Used by permission of W. W. Norton & Company, Inc.

"To Hold" by Li-Young Lee, from *Behind My Eyes*. Copyright © 2008 by Li-Young Lee. Used by permission of W. W. Norton & Company, Inc.

"Let This Day" by Annie Lighthart, from *Pax* (Fernwood Press, 2021). Reprinted by permission of the author.

"Joint Custody" and "It's the Season I Often Mistake" by Ada Limón, from *The Hurting Kind*. Copyright © 2022 by Ada Limón. Reprinted with the permission of The Permissions Company, LLC on behalf of Milkweed Editions, milkweed.org.

"Rescue Dog" by Lois Lorimer, from *Stripmall Subversive* (Variety Crossing Press, 2012) and the anthology *The Bright Well* (Leaf Press, 2012). Reprinted by permission of author.

"Heavenly Bodies" by Alison Luterman, from *In the Time of Great Fires* (Catamaran Press, 2020). Reprinted by permission of author.

"Meditation" by Emilie Lygren, from *What We Were Born For* (Blue Light Press, 2021). Reprinted by permission of author.

"Web" by Marilyn McCabe, originally published in *Stone Canoe*.

"One Candle Now, Then Seven More" by Brad Aaron Modlin originally appeared in *Tupelo Quarterly*.

"Tomatoes on the Windowsill After Rain" by Susan Musgrave, from *When the World Is Not Our Home: Selected Poems 1985-2000* (Thistledown, 2009). Reprinted by permission of author.

"Under the Temple," "Stopped Again by the Sea," "Art Lesson," and "The Clearing" by Mark Nepo, from *The Half-Life of Angels* (Freefall Books, 2023). Reprinted by permission of author.

"Rot" by Robbi Nester originally appeared in *Verse-Virtual*.

"Breathing Peace" by Cristina M. R. Norcross, from *The Sound of a Collective Pulse* (Kelsay Books, 2021).

"Little Farmer" by Naomi Shihab Nye. Reprinted by permission of author.

"For Ella" by January Gill O'Neil reprinted by permission of author.

"How to Love" by January Gill O'Neil, from *Rewilding*. Copyright © 2018 by January Gill O'Neil. Reprinted with the permission of The Permissions Company, LLC on behalf of CavanKerry Press, Ltd., cavankerry.org.

"True North" by Rosalie Sanara Petrouske originally appeared in *Tracking the Fox* (The Poetry Box Chapbook Prize, 2022).

"Crocheting in December" by Andrea Potos, from *Her Joy Becomes* (Fernwood Press, 2023). Reprinted with permission of author.

"Tour of a Salmonberry" by Rena Priest, originally published in *A Dozen Nothing* (2021). Reprinted with permission of the author.

"The Broken" by Alberto Ríos, from *A Small Story About the Sky*. Copyright © 2015 by Alberto Ríos. Reprinted with the permission of The Permissions Company, LLC on behalf of Copper Canyon Press, coppercanyonpress.org.

"What Branches Hold" and "The Way the Sky Might Taste" by Ellen Rowland, from *No Small Thing* (Fernwood Press, 2023). Reprinted by permission of author.

"Crane Migration, Platte River" by Marjorie Saiser, from *The Woman in the Moon* (University of Nebraska Press, Backwaters Series, 2018). Reprinted by permission of author.

"My Daughter Describes the Tarantula" by Faith Shearin, from *Telling the Bees* (SFA University Press, 2015). Reprinted by permission of author.

"For Those Who Would See" by Derek Sheffield, from *Not for Luck* (Wheelbarrow Books, 2021). Reprinted by permission of author.

"Sometimes I Wake Early" by Michael Simms, from *Nightjar* (Ragged Sky Press, 2021).

"First Fall" by Maggie Smith, from *Good Bones: Poems*. Copyright © 2017 by Maggie Smith. Reprinted with the permission of The Permissions Company, LLC on behalf of Tupelo Press, tupelopress.org.

"Primitive Objects" by Holly Wren Spaulding, from *Pilgrim* (Alice Greene & Co., 2014). Reprinted with permission of author.

"Poem of Thankfulness" by Nathan Spoon originally published in *Blood Orange Review*.

"Wren's Nest in a Shed near Aurora" and "Advice from a Raindrop" by Kim Stafford, from *Singer Come from Afar*. Copyright © 2021 by

Kim Stafford. Reprinted with the permission of The Permissions Company, LLC on behalf of Red Hen Press, redhen.org.

"Reverence" from *Wing Over Wing* by Julie Cadwallader Staub. Copyright © 2019 by Julie Cadwallader Staub. Used by permission of Paraclete Press, paracletepress.com.

"Chickadee" by Meghan Sterling, originally published in *Literary Mama*.

"November Praise" by Joshua Michael Stewart, from *Love Something* (Main Street Rag, 2022). Reprinted by permission of author.

"Sunrise, Sunset" by Jacqueline Suskin, from *The Edge of the Continent Volume Three—The Desert* (Rare Bird Books, 2020). "How to Fall in Love with Yourself," from *Help in the Dark Season* (Write Bloody, 2019).

"From Out the Cave" by Joyce Sutphen, from *Straight Out of View* (Holy Cow! Books, 2001). Reprinted by permission of author.

"Boy" by Heather Swan, from *A Kinship with Ash* (Terrapin Books, 2020). Reprinted by permission of author and publisher.

"Milkweed" by Bradford Tice, from *Rare Earth* (New Rivers Press, 2013). Reprinted by permission of author.

"Self-Portrait as Water" by Angela Narciso Torres, from *What Happens Is Neither*. Copyright © 2021 by Angela Narciso Torres. Reprinted with the permission of The Permissions Company, LLC on behalf of Four Way Books, fourwaybooks.com

"Common Ground" by Laura Grace Weldon, from *Blackbird* (Grayson Books). Reprinted by permission of author and publisher, Ginny Connors.

"Late August, Lake Champlain" by Katherine J. Williams, from *Still Life* (Cherry Grove, 2022). Reprinted by permission of author.

"What I Like About Beans" by Sarah Wolfson originally appeared in a slightly different form in *Prairie Fire* (Summer 2022, Volume 43, No. 2).

"Lake at Night" by Lisa Zimmerman, from *How the Garden Looks from Here* (Snake Nation Press, 2004). Reprinted by permission of author.

"Seeds" by Yvonne Zipter from *The Wordless Lullaby of Crickets* (Kelsay Books, 2023). Reprinted by permission of author.

All other poems are printed with permission of the authors.

ACKNOWLEDGMENTS

Boundless gratitude once again to the staff at Storey Publishing for believing in these necessary collections of poetry, especially Deborah Balmuth, Liz Bevilacqua, Alee Moncy, Melinda Slaving, Jennifer Travis, Hannah Fries, and everyone else who supported this book. I'm grateful for the community of poets who contributed so generously to this anthology, which would not exist without them. Thanks especially to the following poets for their ongoing inspiration: Ted Kooser, Naomi Shihab Nye, Rosemerry Wahtola Trommer, Jane Hirshfield, Danusha Laméris, Michael Simms, Mark Nepo, Michelle Wiegers, Jacqueline Suskin, Kim Stafford, and Mark Danowsky. One of the greatest gifts of this past year was getting to know the poetry and heart of Nikita Gill, whose beautiful Foreword is a poem in and of itself. I appreciate the ongoing support of my Peacock and Crews families, who finally see what all those years of reading and writing have led to. I also want to thank the readers who have written to me about the lifesaving power of these anthologies, and who use them in hospitals, churches, classrooms, therapy sessions, wellness retreats, and yoga centers: I hold your notes close to my heart, and please don't ever hesitate to reach out. As always, I thank my husband, Brad Peacock, for keeping my wonder for this world alive and well each day.

HOW to LOVE the WORLD

POEMS OF GRATITUDE AND HOPE

Edited by
James Crews

Storey Publishing

The mission of Storey Publishing is to serve our customers by publishing practical information that encourages personal independence in harmony with the environment.

Edited by Liz Bevilacqua
Art direction and book design by Alethea Morrison
Text production by Slavica A. Walzl
Illustrations by © Dinara Mirtalipova

Text © 2021 by James Crews except as shown on pages 187–195

All rights reserved. Hachette Book Group supports the right to free expression and the value of copyright. The purpose of copyright is to encourage writers and artists to produce the creative works that enrich our culture. The scanning, uploading, and distribution of this book without permission is a theft of the author's intellectual property. If you would like permission to use material from the book (other than for review purposes), please contact permissions@hbgusa.com. Thank you for your support of the author's rights.

The information in this book is true and complete to the best of our knowledge. All recommendations are made without guarantee on the part of the author or Storey Publishing. The author and publisher disclaim any liability in connection with the use of this information.

The publisher is not responsible for websites (or their content) that are not owned by the publisher.

Storey books may be purchased in bulk for business, educational, or promotional use. Special editions or book excerpts can also be created to specification. For details, please contact your local bookseller or the Hachette Book Group Special Markets Department at special.markets@hbgusa.com.

Storey Publishing
210 MASS MoCA Way
North Adams, MA 01247
storey.com

Storey Publishing is an imprint of Workman Publishing, a division of Hachette Book Group, Inc., 1290 Avenue of the Americas, New York, NY 10104. The Storey Publishing name and logo are registered trademarks of Hachette Book Group, Inc.

ISBNs: 978-1-63586-386-4 (paperback); 978-1-63586-387-1 (ebook)

Printed in the United States by Lakeside Book Company (interior and bind) and PC (cover) on paper from responsible sources
10 9 8 7

Library of Congress Cataloging-in-Publication Data on file

**Joy is the happiness
that doesn't depend on what happens.**
Brother David Steindl-Rast

**Only the creative mind can make use of hope.
Only a creative people can wield it.**
Jericho Brown

CONTENTS

Acknowledgments x
Foreword, *Ross Gay* xi
The Necessity of Joy, *James Crews* 1
Rosemerry Wahtola Trommer, Hope 5
Ted Kooser, Dandelion 6
Barbara Crooker, Promise 7
Amanda Gorman, At the Age of 18—Ode to Girls of Color . . 8
Dorianne Laux, In Any Event 10
Laura Grace Weldon, Astral Chorus 11
Garret Keizer, My Daughter's Singing 12
David Romtvedt, Surprise Breakfast 13
Ron Wallace, The Facts of Life 15
Rosemerry Wahtola Trommer,
    Fifteen Years Later, I See How It Went 16
Kathryn Hunt, The Newborns 17
Christen Pagett, Shells 18
Laure-Anne Bosselaar, Bus Stop 19
January Gill O'Neil, Hoodie 20
Terri Kirby Erickson, Angel 21
Todd Davis, Thankful for Now 22
Reflective Pause: The Joy of Presence 23

Barbara Crooker, Autism Poem: The Grid..................24
Diana Whitney, Kindergarten Studies the Human Heart...25
Gail Newman, Valentine's Day 27
Abigail Carroll, In Gratitude.............................. 29
Michelle Wiegers, Held Open 32
David Graham, Listening for Your Name 33
Heather Swan, Another Day Filled with Sleeves of Light... 34
Annie Lighthart, A Cure Against Poisonous Thought 35
Mary McCue, Forgiveness 36
Heather Lanier, Two Weeks After a Silent Retreat 37
Reflective Pause: The Kingdom at Hand 39
Jane Hirshfield, Today, When I Could Do Nothing 40
Laura Ann Reed, Red Thyme............................. 42
Laura Foley, The Once Invisible Garden 43
James Crews, Down to Earth.............................. 44
Freya Manfred, Old Friends 45
Brad Peacock, Let It Rain................................. 46
Molly Fisk, Against Panic 47
Naomi Shihab Nye, Over the Weather..................... 48
Paula Gordon Lepp, Notions 49
Ellen Bass, Any Common Desolation 50
Reflective Pause: Returning to the World 51
Mark Nepo, Language, Prayer, and Grace 52

Jane Hirshfield, The Fish 53
Patricia Fargnoli, Reincarnate 54
Linda Hogan, Innocence 55
Farnaz Fatemi, Everything Is Made of Labor 56
Susan Kelly-DeWitt, Apple Blossoms.....................57
Nancy Miller Gomez, Growing Apples.................... 58
Danusha Lamèris, Aspen 59
Margaret Hasse, With Trees 61
Kim Stafford, Shelter in Place 63
Heather Newman, Missing Key 64
Michael Kiesow Moore, Climbing the Golden Mountain ... 65
Laura Foley, To See It 66
Jacqueline Jules, Unclouded Vision.......................67
Danusha Lamèris, Improvement 68
Reflective Pause: Grateful for Small Victories 70
Jack Ridl, After Spending the Morning Baking Bread....... 71
Wally Swist, Radiance....................................72
Kristen Case, Morning....................................73
Ross Gay, Wedding Poem 74
Jehanne Dubrow, Pledge 76
Angela Narciso Torres, Amores Perros....................77
Noah Davis, Mending 79
Penny Harter, In the Dark 80
Nathan Spoon, A Candle in the Night.....................81

Francine Marie Tolf, Praise of Darkness 82
Judith Chalmer, An Essay on Age 83
Ted Kooser, Easter Morning.............................. 84
Andrea Potos, The Cardinal Reminds Me................. 85
Marjorie Saiser, When Life Seems a To-Do List 86
Lahab Assef Al-Jundi, Moon 87
Crystal S. Gibbins, Because the Night You Asked 88
Rob Hunter, September Swim 89
Joyce Sutphen, What to Do...............................91
William Stafford, Any Morning 92
Reflective Pause: Pieces of Heaven 93
Rosemerry Wahtola Trommer, How It Might Continue.... 94
Li-Young Lee, From Blossoms.............................95
Jessica Gigot, Motherhood 96
Sarah Freligh, Wondrous.................................97
Cathryn Essinger, Summer Apples 98
Lynne Knight, Third Year of My Mother's Dementia...... 99
Heather Swan, Rabbit 100
Dale Biron, Laughter 101
January Gill O'Neil, In the Company of Women....... .102
Alice Wolf Gilborn, Leaning to the Light............. ..103
Andrea Potos,
    I Watched an Angel in the Emergency Room......... 104
Alberto Ríos, When Giving Is All We Have 105

Albert Garcia, Offering 106

Alison Luterman, Too Many to Count 108

Marjorie Saiser, If I Carry My Father 110

George Bilgere, Weather 111

Sally Bliumis-Dunn, Work 112

Reflective Pause: The Joy of Making 113

Danusha Laméris, Goldfinches 114

Connie Wanek, The Lesser Goldfinch 116

Tony Hoagland, The Word 117

Barbara Crooker, Tomorrow 119

Cynthia White, Quail Hollow 120

Laura Grace Weldon, Compost Happens 122

Joan Mazza, Part of the Landscape 123

Andrea Potos, Essential Gratitude 124

Reflective Pause: The Gratitude List 125

Laura Foley, Gratitude List 126

Katherine Williams, The Dog Body of My Soul 127

Katie Rubinstein, Scratch, Sniff 129

Mary Elder Jacobsen, Summer Cottage 130

Jane Kenyon, Coming Home at Twilight in Late Summer .. 131

Grace Bauer, Perceptive Prayer 132

Patricia Fontaine, Sap Icicles 133

Lucille Clifton, the lesson of the falling leaves 135

Ted Kooser, A Dervish of Leaves 136

James Crews, Winter Morning..............................137

Tracy K. Smith, The Good Life............................138

Marjorie Saiser, Thanksgiving for Two 139

Reflective Pause: The Feast of Each Moment................. 141

Jeffrey Harrison, Nest...................................142

Ellen Bass, Getting into Bed on a December Night 143

Lisa Coffman, Everybody Made Soups.................... 144

James Crews, Darkest Before Dawn.......................145

Brad Peacock, Rosary....................................146

Julie Murphy, To Ask 147

Tess Taylor, There Doesn't Need to Be a Poem 148

Amy Dryansky, Wingspan 150

Joy Harjo, Eagle Poem.................................... 151

Terri Kirby Erickson, What Matters......................152

Mark Nepo, In Love with the World 153

Reading Group Questions and Topics for Discussion 154

Poet Biographies.. 160

Credits... 187

ACKNOWLEDGMENTS

Deep gratitude to the many people who helped to make this book a reality: the team at Storey Publishing, for agreeing to take a chance on a book of poetry, especially Deborah Balmuth, Liz Bevilacqua, Alee Moncy, Jennifer Travis, and Melinda Slaving, as well as Lauren Moseley at Algonquin Books for publicity support; Katie Rubinstein for making the connection and her beautiful work; everyone at A Network for Grateful Living, especially Kristi Nelson and Saoirse McClory, for their support of poetry; Brother David Steindl-Rast for his teachings on gratefulness, which we need now more than ever; Ted Kooser, for his enduring friendship, inspiration, and example of kindness; the late, great David Clewell, whose exuberant spirit not only made me fall in love with poetry, but also led me to future mentors Ron Wallace and Jesse Lee Kercheval; all of the poets included here for their generosity in sharing their work; Ross Gay for writing a foreword that is both a blessing and a poem in and of itself; Naomi Shihab Nye, Maria Popova, and Elizabeth Berg for their support of writing that makes us all feel more human; Garland Richmond, Diana Whitney, Heather Newman, Heather Swan, and Michelle Wiegers for essential support; my students at SUNY-Albany and Eastern Oregon University for giving me hope and serving as first readers; my husband, Brad Peacock, and our Crews and Peacock families, for reminding me every day why I'm so grateful to be alive.

FOREWORD

I have been spending a lot of time lately thinking about witness, about how witness itself is a kind of poetics, or poesis, which means *making*. By which I mean I have been wondering about how we make the world in our witnessing of it. Or maybe I have come to understand, to believe, *how* we witness makes our world. This is why attending to what we love, what we are astonished by, what flummoxes us with beauty, is such crucial work. Such rigorous work. Likewise, studying how we care, and are cared for, how we tend and are tended to, how we give and are given, is such necessary work. It makes the world. Witnessing how we are loved and how we love makes the world. Witness and study, I should say. Witness as study, I think I mean.

Truth is, we are mostly too acquainted with the opposite, with the wreckage. It commands our attention, and for good reason. We have to survive it. But even if we need to understand the wreckage to survive it, it needn't be the primary object of our study. The survival need be. The reaching and the holding need be. The *here, have this* need be. The *come in, you can stay here* need be. The *let's share it all* need be. The love need be.

The care need be. That which we are made by, held by, need be. Who's taken us in need be. Who's saved the seed need be. Who's planted the milkweed need be. Who's saved the water need be. Who's saved the forest need be. The forest need be. The water. The breathable air. That which witnessed us forth need be. How we have been loved need be. How we are loved need be.

How we need need be, too. Our radiant need. Our luminous and mycelial need. Our need immense and immeasurable. Our need absolute need be. And that study, that practice, that witness, is called gratitude. Our gratitude need be.

This is what I want to study. This is with whom.

Ross Gay

THE NECESSITY OF JOY

One day a few weeks ago, I woke up in a terrible mood. I've always been a morning person, relishing those early hours when the world is still asleep, before emails, texts, and the rest of my distractions take over. I love the ritual of making pour-over coffee for my husband and myself, inhaling the fragrant steam that curls up from the grounds as I pour on the boiling water. Yet this day, I couldn't shake my annoyance as I smashed a pat of cold, hard butter onto my toast, tearing a hole in the bread. I shook my head and scowled, then looked over at my husband who smiled. "What?" I said. He just stared deeply into my eyes and asked, "Are you happy to be alive today?" I glared at him at first, but I also let his question stop my mind. And in that gap, a rush of gratitude swept in. Yes, I was happy to be alive, happy to be standing in the kitchen next to the man I love, about to begin another day together. Happy to have coffee, food, and a warm place to live. Happy even to feel that dark mood swirling through me because it was also evidence of my aliveness.

Are you happy to be alive? The poems gathered in this book each ask, in their own ways, that same question, which has more relevance now than ever. As Brother David Steindl-Rast, the founder of A Network for Grateful Living, has famously pointed out: "In daily life, we must see that it is not happiness that makes us grateful. It is gratefulness that makes us happy." Paying attention to our lives is the first step toward gratitude and hope, and the poems in *How to Love the World* model for us the kind of mindfulness that is the gateway to a fuller, more sustainable happiness that can be called joy. Whether blessing a lawn full of common dandelions, or reminding us, as Tony Hoagland does, to "sit out in the sun and listen," these poets know that hope, no matter how slight it might seem, is as pressing a human need right now as food, water, shelter, or rest. We may survive without it, but we cannot thrive.

During these uncertain and trying times, we tell ourselves that joy is an indulgence we can no longer afford. And we've become all too familiar with the despair filling the airwaves and crowding our social media feeds, leading to what psychologists now call empathy or compassion fatigue, whereby we grow numb and disconnected from the suffering of others. We want to stay informed about what's going on in the world, yet we also know that absorbing so much negativity leaves us drained and hopeless. We know it's robbing us of the ability to be present to our own experience and grateful for something as simple as the moon, which is here, as Lahab Assef Al-Jundi points out, "to illuminate our illusion" of separateness from one another.

For many years, reading and writing poetry has been my personal source of delight, an antidote to the depression that can spring up out of nowhere. I now carve out what I call "soul time" for myself each day, making space for silence and reflection, even if it is just five or ten minutes, even if I have to wake up a little earlier to do it. The time I take to pause and read a favorite poem from a book, or jot down some small kindness from the day before, can utterly transform my mindset for the rest of the day. I invite you to use each poem in *How to Love the World* in a similar way, to make reading (and writing, if you wish) part of your own daily gratitude practice. Throughout the collection, I've also included reflective pauses, with specific suggestions for writing practices based upon the poems. When you encounter one of these, you may simply read that poem and reflection, then move on. Or you might keep a notebook nearby and stop to write, letting the guiding questions lead you more deeply into your own encounters with gratitude, hope, and joy. I encourage you to use any of these poems that spark something as jumping-off points for a journal entry, story, or poem of your own.

I trust in the necessity and pleasure of all kinds of creativity—from cooking a meal to fixing a car to sketching in the margins of a grocery list—but poetry is an art form especially suited to our challenging times. It helps us dive beneath the surface of our lives, and enter a place of wider, wilder, more universal knowing. And because poetry is made of the everyday material of language, we each have access to its ability to hold truths that normal conversation simply can't contain. When you find a poem that speaks to exactly what you've felt but had no way to name, a light bulb flashes in some hidden part of the self that you might have forgotten was there. I'll never forget the first time I read Ellen Bass's poem, "Any Common Desolation," and rushed to share it with my friends and family. "You may have to break your heart," Bass writes, suggesting that we might need to be more open and vulnerable to the world than we feel we can stand at times, but then she reminds us, "it isn't nothing to know even one moment alive." We need poems like the ones gathered here to ground us in our lives, to find in each new moment what Rosemerry Wahtola Trommer describes as, "the chance for joy, whole orchards of amazement."

James Crews, July 2020

Rosemerry Wahtola Trommer

HOPE

Hope has holes
in its pockets.
It leaves little
crumb trails
so that we,
when anxious,
can follow it.
Hope's secret:
it doesn't know
the destination—
it knows only
that all roads
begin with one
foot in front
of the other.

Ted Kooser

DANDELION

The first of a year's abundance of dandelions
is this single kernel of bright yellow
dropped on our path by the sun, sensing
that we might need some marker to help us
find our way through life, to find a path
over the snow-flattened grass that was
blade by blade unbending into green,
on a morning early in April, this happening
just at the moment I thought we were lost
and I'd stopped to look around, hoping
to see something I recognized. And there
it was, a commonplace dandelion, right
at my feet, the first to bloom, especially
yellow, as if pleased to have been the one,
chosen from all the others, to show us the way.

Barbara Crooker

PROMISE

This day is an open road
stretching out before you.
Roll down the windows.
Step into your life, as if it were a fast car.
Even in industrial parks,
trees are covered with white blossoms,
festive as brides, and the air is soft
as a well-washed shirt on your arms.
The grass has turned implausibly green.
Tomorrow, the world will begin again,
another fresh start. The blue sky stretches,
shakes out its tent of light. Even dandelions glitter
in the lawn, a handful of golden change.

Amanda Gorman

AT THE AGE OF 18—ODE TO GIRLS OF COLOR

At the age of 5
I saw how we always pick the flower swelling with
    the most color.
The color distinguishes it from the rest, and tells us:
This flower should not be left behind.
But this does not happen in the case of colored girls.
Our color makes hands pull back, and we, left to grow
    alone,
stretching our petals to a dry sun.
At the age of 12
I blinked in the majesty of the color within myself,
blinded by the knowledge that a skinny black girl, a
    young brown teen,
has the power to light Los Angeles all night,
the radiance to heal all the scars left on this city's
    pavement.
Why had this realization taken so long,
when color pulses in all that is beauty and painting and
    human?
You see, long ago, they told me
that snakes and spiders have spots and vibrant bodies if
    they are poisonous.
In other words, being of color meant danger, warning,
    'do not touch'.
At the age of 18

I know my color is not warning, but a welcome.
A girl of color is a lighthouse, an ultraviolet ray of power,
    potential, and promise
My color does not mean caution, it means courage
my dark does not mean danger, it means daring,
my brown does not mean broken, it means bold backbone
    from working
twice as hard to get half as far.
Being a girl of color means I am key, path, and wonder all
    in one body.
At the age of 18
I am experiencing how black and brown can glow.
And glow I will, glow we will, vibrantly, colorfully;
not as a warning, but as promise,
that we will set the sky alight with our magic.

Dorianne Laux

IN ANY EVENT

If we are fractured
we are fractured
like stars
bred to shine
in every direction,
through any dimension,
billions of years
since and hence.

I shall not lament
the human, not yet.
There is something
more to come, our hearts
a gold mine
not yet plumbed,
an uncharted sea.

Nothing is gone forever.
If we came from dust
and will return to dust
then we can find our way
into anything.

What we are capable of
is not yet known,
and I praise us now,
in advance.

Laura Grace Weldon

ASTRAL CHORUS

Stars resonate like a huge musical instrument.
—*Bill Chaplin, asteroseismologist*

Late for chores after dinner with friends,
I walk up the darkening path,
my mind knitting something warm
out of the evening's words.
The woods are more shadow
than trees, barn a hulking shape on its slope.
I breathe in autumn's leaf-worn air, aware
I am glad to be in this place, this life.
The chickens have come in
from their wanderings. Lined up
like a choir, they croon soft lullabies.
A flock of stars stirs a navy-blue sky.
I can't hear them, but I'm told they
sing of things we have yet to learn.

Garret Keizer

MY DAUGHTER'S SINGING

I will miss the sound of her singing
through the wall that separates
her bathroom from ours, in the morning
before school, how she would harmonize
with the bare-navel angst
of some screaming Ophelia on her stereo,
though she had always seemed a contented kid,
a grower of rare gourds, an aficionado
of salamanders, and a babysitter prized
for her playful, earnest care, her love
of children so pure she seemed to become
a little child whenever she took one by the hand,
entering heaven so handily.
But it reminded me, that singing,
of the soul depths we never know,
even in those we love more than our souls,
so mad we are to anticipate the future,
and already I am talking—
a year to go before she goes
to college, and listen to me talking—
in the past tense as she sings.

David Romtvedt

SURPRISE BREAKFAST

One winter morning I get up early
to clean the ash from the grate
and find my daughter, eight, in the kitchen
thumping around pretending she has a peg leg

while also breaking eggs into a bowl—
separating yolks and whites, mixing oil
and milk. Her hands are smooth,
not from lack of labor but youth.

She's making pancakes for me, a surprise
I have accidentally ruined. "You never
get up early," she says, measuring
the baking powder, beating the egg whites.

It's true. When I wake, I roll to the side
and pull the covers over my head.
"It was too cold to sleep," I say.
"I thought I'd get the kitchen warm."

Aside from the scraping of the small flat shovel
on the iron grate, and the wooden spoon turning
in the bowl, the room is quiet. I lift the gray ash
and lay it carefully into a bucket to take outside.

"How'd you lose your leg?" I ask.
"At sea. I fell overboard in a storm
and a shark attacked me, but I'm fine."
She spins, a little batter flying from the spoon.

I can hear the popping of the oil in the pan.
"Are you ready?" she asks, thumping to the stove.
Fork in hand, I sit down, hoping that yes,
I am ready, or nearly so, or one day will be.

Ron Wallace

THE FACTS OF LIFE

She wonders how people get babies.
Suddenly vague and distracted,
we talk about "making love."
She's six and unsatisfied, finds
our limp answers unpersuasive.
Embarrassed, we stiffen, and try again,
this time exposing the stark naked words:
penis, vagina, sperm, womb, and egg.
She thinks we're pulling her leg.
We decide that it's time
to get passionate and insist.
But she's angry, disgusted.
Why do we always make fun of her?
Why do we lie?
We sigh, try cabbages, storks.
She smiles. That's more like it.
We talk on into the night, trying
magic seeds, good fairies, God . . .

Rosemerry Wahtola Trommer

FIFTEEN YEARS LATER, I SEE HOW IT WENT

They say you fall in love with your child
the moment you first hold them,
still covered in blood and vernix.
I held the strange being
just arrived from the womb and felt curious,
astonished, humble, nervous.
But love didn't come till later.
Came from holding him
while he was screaming. Waking with him
when I wanted to sleep. Bouncing him
when I wanted to be still. Love grew
as my ideas of myself diminished. Love grew
as he came into himself. Love grew
as I learned to let go of what I'd been told
and to trust the emerging form,
falling in love with the flawed beings we are.
Until I couldn't imagine being without him.
Until I was the one being born.

Kathryn Hunt

THE NEWBORNS

All through the night,
all through the long witless hallways of my sleep,
from my hospital bed I heard
the newborn babies cry, bewildered,
between worlds, like new arrivals anywhere,
unacquainted with the names of things.

That afternoon a kind nurse named Laura
had taken me for a stroll to exercise
the red line of my wound.
We stopped by the nursery window
and a flannel-swathed boy in a clear plastic cradle
was pushed to the glass. We peered at him
and said, "Welcome. You've come to Earth."
We laughed and shook our heads.

All through the night, all through the
drug-spangled rapture of my dreams,
I heard the newborn babies sing,
first one, then another. The fierce
beginning of their lament, that bright hiss,
those soft octaves of wonder.

Christen Pagett

SHELLS

The curl of your ear,
A tiny pearl of a shell
That I kiss so gently
You can barely feel it,
Barely hear it.

That pink flushing hot
With sleep,
Nape of your neck damp,
As I tuck the blankets too tight.

Remember when you were three
And held one to your face?
Was it a cockle shell, a conch shell?
Some polished swirl of light.

Wet sand on cheek,
You listened.

Like I listen,
To make sure you are
Still breathing.
Watching for that
Tiny throb of life
Pressing at your throat.

Laure-Anne Bosselaar

BUS STOP

Stubborn sleet. Traffic stuck on Sixth.
We cram the shelter, soaked, strain
to see the bus, except for a man next to me,
dialing his cell-phone. He hunches,
pulls his parka's collar over it, talks slow and low:
"It's daddy, hon. You do? Me too. Ask mom
if I can come see you now. Oh, okay,
Sunday then. Bye. Me too baby. Me too."
He snaps the phone shut, cradles it to his cheek,
holds it there. Dusk stains the sleet, minutes
slush by. When we board the bus,
that phone is still pressed to his cheek.

January Gill O'Neil

HOODIE

A gray hoodie will not protect my son
from rain, from the New England cold.

I see the partial eclipse of his face
as his head sinks into the half-dark

and shades his eyes. Even in our
quiet suburb with its unlocked doors,

I fear for his safety—the darkest child
on our street in the empire of blocks.

Sometimes I don't know who he is anymore
traveling the back roads between boy and man.

He strides a deep stride, pounds a basketball
into wet pavement. Will he take his shot

or is he waiting for the open-mouthed
orange rim to take a chance on him? I sing

his name to the night, ask for safe passage
from this borrowed body into the next

and wonder who could mistake him
for anything but good.

Terri Kirby Erickson

ANGEL

I used to see them walking, a middle-aged
man and his grown son, both wearing brown
trousers and white shirts like boys in a club,
or guys who like to simplify. But anyone
could see the son would never be a man who
walked without a hand to hold, a voice telling
him what to do. So the father held his son's
hand and whispered whatever it was the boy
needed to know, in tones so soft and low it
might have been the sound of wings pressing
together again and again. Maybe it was that
sound, since the father had the look of an angel
about him, or what we imagine angels should
be—a bit solemn-faced, with eyes that view
the world through a lens of kindness—who
sees every man's son as beautiful and whole.

Todd Davis

THANKFUL FOR NOW

Walking the river back home at the end
of May, locust in bloom, an oriole flitting
through dusky crowns, and the early night sky
going peach, day's late glow the color of that fruit's
flesh, dribbling down over everything, christening
my sons, the two of them walking before me
after a day of fishing, one of them placing a hand
on the other's shoulder, pointing toward a planet
that's just appeared, or the swift movement
of that yellow and black bird disappearing
into the growing dark, and now the light, pink
as a crabapple's flower, and my legs tired
from wading the higher water, and the rocks
that keep turning over, nearly spilling me
into the river, but still thankful for now
when I have enough strength to stay
a few yards behind them, loving this time
of day that shows me the breadth
of their backs, their lean, strong legs
striding, how we all go on in this cold water,
heading home to the sound of the last few
trout splashing, as mayflies float
through the shadowed riffles.

REFLECTIVE PAUSE

The Joy of Presence

In "Thankful for Now," we see Todd Davis pausing to appreciate an early evening scene while "walking the river back home" with his two sons. It is one thing to notice and beautifully describe the elements of nature, as Davis does—"the early night sky going peach, day's late glow the color of that fruit's flesh"—but it is another to cultivate the kind of presence that can make us all "thankful for now," no matter our particular circumstances. As Eckhart Tolle has written: "You don't have to wait for something 'meaningful' to come into your life so that you can finally enjoy what you do. There is more meaning in joy than you will ever need."

We often strive to reach for experiences and things beyond what we have in this moment and forget the power of pausing and making space to say thank you for what's right in front of us. Writing of his sons, Davis finds gratitude in simply noticing "the breadth of their backs, their lean, strong legs striding."

Invitation for Writing and Reflection

When was the last time you felt yourself simply "thankful for now," for the present moment that allowed you to notice and appreciate every detail of life as it was just then?

Barbara Crooker

AUTISM POEM: THE GRID

A black and yellow spider hangs motionless in its web,
and my son, who is eleven and doesn't talk, sits
on a patch of grass by the perennial border, watching.
What does he see in his world, where geometry
is more beautiful than a human face?
Given chalk, he draws shapes on the driveway:
pentagons, hexagons, rectangles, squares.
The spider's web is a grid,
transecting the garden in equal parts.

Sometimes he stares through the mesh on a screen.
He loves things that are perforated:
toilet paper, graham crackers, coupons
in magazines, loves the order of the tiny holes,
the way the boundaries are defined. And real life
is messy and vague. He shrinks back to a stare,
switches off his hearing. And my heart,
not cleanly cut like a valentine, but irregular
and many-chambered, expands and contracts,
contracts and expands.

Diana Whitney

KINDERGARTEN STUDIES THE HUMAN HEART

Nothing like a valentine,
pink construction paper
glue-sticked to doilies downstairs
in preschool, the sand table
filled with flour, the Fours
driving trucks through silky powder,
white clouds rising
to dust their round cheeks.
Up here, the Fives are all business:
four chambers on the chalkboard,
four rooms colored hard
in thick-tipped marker, red and red,
blue and blue, oxygen rich
and oxygen poor, the branching vine
of the aorta hanging
its muscled fruit, carmine
blood-flower blooming
in a thick jungle.
My girl squeezes her fist
to show me the size of it.
Pulses it like a live animal.
Taps the double rhythm
that never stops, not a trot
but the echo of a trot, not a drum

but the echo of a drum,
small palms on the art table
laying down the backbeat:
become become become.

Gail Newman

VALENTINE'S DAY

Now that my father is gone,
I send my mother flowers.

She sleeps under a blue blanket
alone on her side of the bed,
fluffing both pillows just so.

She balances as she walks,
one hand skimming the wall.
Sometimes she doesn't know
where her friends are, who is still living.

Einstein was right about time
moving in two directions at once,
how everything that happens
seems to have happened before,

how when I stand before the mirror
combing my hair, I see my mother's eyes,
and happiness wells up like a wave
without warning.

My mother looks forward
to a lunch of bread and cheese,
a glass of apple juice.

She speaks of the weather,
today being only itself.
Her time is reeling in, a line cast
from shore. But how she loves
the sea, the horizon, the flaming sun!

My mother, who knows the brutal world,
who survived while others did not,
says, *Me? I had it easy.*

Abigail Carroll

IN GRATITUDE

For *h*, tiny fire
    in the hollow of the throat,
        opener of every *hey*,

hi, how are you?,
    hello; chums with *c*,
        with *t*, shy lover of *s;*

there and not
    there—never seen,
        hardly heard, yet

real as air
    fluttering the oak,
        holding up the hawk;

the sound
    of a yawn, of sleep, of heat,
        a match, its quivering

orange flame
    turning wood into light,
        light into breath;

the sound
    of stars if stars
        could be heard, perhaps

the sound
>   of space; life speaking life:
>   warm air endowed

to hard clay—
>   a heart, hurt,
>   a desire to be healed—

the work
>   of bees stuck in the nubs
>   of hollyhocks

and columbine, time
>   to the extent that time
>   is light, is bright

as the match,
>   the flame of the sun,
>   real as the muffled hush

of sleep,
>   the fluttering oak,
>   a moth, the silent *oh*

in the throat
>   when a hand is laid
>   upon the shoulder;

hunger—
    the body's empty cry
        for filling, for loving,

for knowing
    the intimacy of breath,
        of half-breathed words

fragile as the stars:
    hollow, hush,
        holy.

Michelle Wiegers

HELD OPEN

After the band concert, we filed out
of the high school auditorium
where the door seemingly stood open
all by itself. As I stepped into the hallway,
there stood one student's grandmother,
smiling as she held the door
for the crowd, her eyes searching
for the grandson she wanted to hug.

The embrace of this night of music
still wrapped its warm arms around me,
as if I'd just been held for over an hour
by the deep tones of the bari sax,
the stunning runs of the flutes, which caught
my breath, my son's steady rhythms
still pulsing in my chest,
as I stepped out into the night air.

David Graham

LISTENING FOR YOUR NAME

As a father steals into his child's half-lit bedroom
slowly, quietly, standing long and long
counting the breaths before finally slipping
back out, taking care not to wake her,

and as that night-lit child is fully awake the whole
time, with closed eyes, measured breathing,
savoring a delicious blessing she couldn't
name but will remember her whole life,

how often we feel we're being watched over,
or that we're secretly looking in on the ones
we love, even when they are far away,
or even as they are lost in the sleep

no one wakes from—what we know
and what we feel can fully coincide, like love
and worry, like taking care in full silence
and secrecy, like darkness and light together.

Heather Swan

ANOTHER DAY FILLED WITH SLEEVES OF LIGHT,

and I carry ripened plums,
waiting to find the one
who is interested in tasting.

How can we ever be known?

Today the lily sends up
a fifth white-tipped tendril, the promise
of another flower opening,
and I think, this must mean this plant
is happy, here, in this house, by this window.
Is this the right deduction?

The taller plant leans and leans toward the light.
I turn it away, and soon its big hands are reaching again
toward what nourishes it,
but which it can never touch.

Couldn't the yellowing leaves of the maple
and their falling also be a sign of joy?
Another kind of leaning into.
A letting go of one thing
to fall into another.
A kind of trust I cannot imagine.

Annie Lighthart

A CURE AGAINST POISONOUS THOUGHT

Believe the world goes on
and this bee bending
in honeysuckle just one
of a mighty nation, golden
beads thrumming
a long invisible thread.

In the green drift of an afternoon,
the body is not root but wick:
the press of light surrounds it.

Mary McCue

FORGIVENESS

How does it creep into arteries,
level blood pressure
and wipe clean
the slate of anger
held close to the chest?

Look long into the mirror,
be tender with the face you see,
then to the blistered past,
the entire landscape,
the smallest detail
as in a Brueghel painting,

then revise and revise
until the story changes shape
and you, no longer the jailor,
have learned to love
what is left.

Heather Lanier

TWO WEEKS AFTER A SILENT RETREAT

How quickly I lose my love
of all things. I nearly flick an ant
off the cliff of an armchair.

But remember, Self,
the week you spent
enveloped in psalms

intoned by monks?
By Wednesday you beheld

a three-balled body
creeping around
the onionskin of your book,

its six teensy toothpick legs
bent into all manner of
delicate angles.

Your chest became
a doorway
to a spacious unmarked

heaven. You loved the ant.
The kingdom,
said Christ,

is at hand, meaning
not ticking above

in a time bomb of gold-
paved streets
but tapping its antennae

along the heart line
of your imperfect palm.

REFLECTIVE PAUSE

The Kingdom at Hand

Stepping outside of life, even for a short while, can help us return with a new perspective on what seemed unworkable before. Though such a wide-open embrace of life never lasts forever, it can be enough to know that it waits within us, accessible when we need it the most. Heather Lanier illustrates this in her poem, as she remembers her own time of reflection while on retreat, when her "chest became a doorway to a spacious unmarked heaven." Such moments often appear after periods of stillness, whether on an actual retreat, at church, or while spending the day outdoors, away from our screens.

Yet our lives do not unfold as a single, unbroken stretch of gratefulness and hope. We are humans living in an imperfectly human world, after all, and so we easily lose our reverence and "love of all things" in the midst of busyness, worry, and strife. We fall out of the practice of patience. But as Lanier points out, we can remind ourselves that the gate to the kingdom at hand remains open anytime we choose to pass through, and the reward for close attention to our lives, even if it is simply to save the life of an ant, is the heaven of a fuller presence in the here and now.

Invitation for Writing and Reflection

Think back to a time when you brought yourself back to the moment at hand and found the world vivid and lovable again. You might begin with Lanier's first line, "How quickly I lose my love," and see where that leads you.

Jane Hirshfield

TODAY, WHEN I COULD DO NOTHING

Today, when I could do nothing,
I saved an ant.

It must have come in with the morning paper,
still being delivered
to those who shelter in place.

A morning paper is still an essential service.

I am not an essential service.

I have coffee and books,
time,
a garden,
silence enough to fill cisterns.

It must have first walked
the morning paper, as if loosened ink
taking the shape of an ant.

Then across the laptop computer—warm—
then onto the back of a cushion.

Small black ant, alone,
crossing a navy cushion,
moving steadily because that is what it could do.

Set outside in the sun,
it could not have found again its nest.
What then did I save?

It did not move as if it was frightened,
even while walking my hand,
which moved it through swiftness and air.

Ant, alone, without companions,
whose ant-heart I could not fathom—
how is your life, I wanted to ask.

I lifted it, took it outside.

This first day when I could do nothing,
contribute nothing
beyond staying distant from my own kind,
I did this.

Laura Ann Reed

RED THYME

In the red thyme
that crawls
languidly
between stepping stones
time stops
as bees
thrust their passion
deep into the promise
of tiny crimson-purple
blooms.

Where blossom
ends
and bee
begins

are the first words
of a lullaby
the world sings
while it rocks you
as you fall
awake
in the later years
of a life
spent mostly
sound
asleep.

Laura Foley

THE ONCE INVISIBLE GARDEN

How did I come to be
this particular version of me,
and not some other, this morning
of purple delphiniums blooming,
like royalty—destined
to meet these three dogs
asleep at my feet, and not others—
this soft summer morning,
sitting on her screened porch
become ours, our wind chime,
singing of wind and time,
yellow-white digitalis
feeding bees and filling me—
and more abundance to come:
basil, tomatoes, zucchini.
What luck or fate, instinct,
or grace brought me here?—
in shade, beneath hidden stars,
a soft, summer morning,
seeing with my whole being,
love made visible.

James Crews

DOWN TO EARTH

The heart of a farmer
is made of muscle
and clay that aches
for return to earth.
And when the sky
releases a steady rain,
massaging each row
of sprouted beans,
my husband leans out
of the car window
and opens his hand
to hold that water
for a single instant,
his heart now beating
in sync with rain
seeping through layers
to kiss the roots
of every plant alive
on this living, breathing
planet on whose back
we were granted
permission to live
for a limited time.

Freya Manfred

OLD FRIENDS

Old friends are a steady spring rain,
or late summer sunshine edging into fall,
or frosted leaves along a snowy path—
a voice for all seasons saying, I know you.
The older I grow, the more I fear I'll lose my old friends,
as if too many years have scrolled by
since the day we sprang forth, seeking each other.

Old friend, I knew you before we met.
I saw you at the window of my soul—
I heard you in the steady millstone of my heart
grinding grain for our daily bread.
You are sedimentary, rock-solid cousin earth,
where I stand firmly, astonished by your grace and truth.
And gratitude comes to me and says:

"Tell me anything and I will listen.
Ask me anything, and I will answer you."

Brad Peacock

LET IT RAIN

I'm not sure why I did my best to outrun you.
Perhaps I had forgotten how your touch
makes me feel alive, like the gentle hands
of my husband reaching out to console me.
I smile, feeling the first drops from the sky
igniting my senses, calling forth the little boy inside
who wants more, to feel it pour. This is not
a shower that will extinguish the light
I've found within. It is a rain that will soak me through,
down to bone, baptizing me again and again,
as I walk these gravel roads that have helped me heal.
Droplets now fall from the brim of my hat,
streaming down my cheeks like the time I cried out,
begging for the shame to subside, wondering
if I had the strength to live this life anymore.

Molly Fisk

AGAINST PANIC

You recall those times, I know you do, when the sun
lifted its weight over a small rise to warm your face,
when a parched day finally broke open, real rain
sluicing down the sidewalk, rattling city maples
and you so sure the end was here, life a house of cards
tipped over, falling, hope's last breath extinguished
in a bitter wind. Oh, friend, search your memory again—
beauty and relief are still there, only sleeping.

Naomi Shihab Nye

OVER THE WEATHER

We forget about the spaciousness
above the clouds

but it's up there. The sun's up there too.

When words we hear don't fit the day,
when we worry
what we did or didn't do,
what if we close our eyes,
say any word we love
that makes us feel calm,
slip it into the atmosphere
and rise?

Creamy miles of quiet.
Giant swoop of blue.

Paula Gordon Lepp

NOTIONS

Look at the silver lining, they say.
But what if, instead,
I pluck it off
and use that tensile strand to bind
myself to those things I do not
want to lose sight of.

Families knit together by evening walks,
board games, laughter.
The filament fixing us to friends
no matter the distance apart.
A braid of gratitude for small kindnesses.
The thin gauge wire of loss.

Let me twist that lining
around my finger,
it's silvery glint a reminder
of just how quickly life can change.
I will remember to love more.
I will remember to give more.

I will remember to be still.

I will knot the string tightly.
So it won't slip away.
So I won't forget.

Ellen Bass

ANY COMMON DESOLATION

can be enough to make you look up
at the yellowed leaves of the apple tree, the few
that survived the rains and frost, shot
with late afternoon sun. They glow a deep
orange-gold against a blue so sheer, a single bird
would rip it like silk. You may have to break
your heart, but it isn't nothing
to know even one moment alive. The sound
of an oar in an oarlock or a ruminant
animal tearing grass. The smell of grated ginger.
The ruby neon of the liquor store sign.
Warm socks. You remember your mother,
her precision a ceremony, as she gathered
the white cotton, slipped it over your toes,
drew up the heel, turned the cuff. A breath
can uncoil as you walk across your own muddy yard,
the big dipper pouring night down over you, and everything
you dread, all you can't bear, dissolves
and, like a needle slipped into your vein—
that sudden rush of the world.

REFLECTIVE PAUSE

Returning to the World

When the world seems incomprehensible and its ills too many, I often retreat to the natural world, looking up "at the yellowed leaves of the apple tree" to calm my mind and try to make sense of our sometimes violent, divided culture. "Any common desolation," as Ellen Bass says, can send us into a frenzy, can glue us to our screens; but it is more healing if we get outside of our minds and commune with "that sudden rush" of the actual world again.

It can be painful to be so open to the world ("You may have to break your heart"), but as Bass points out, it is more than worth it "to know even one moment alive." What truly lifts us back into the flow is noticing each small thing that sparks our senses, whether it be "the sound of an oar," "the smell of grated ginger," or simply "warm socks."

Invitation for Writing and Reflection
What seemingly small joys bring you back to that "sudden rush of the world" even in the midst of worry or fear? How does it feel when gratitude and hope reawaken the heart to what's around you?

Mark Nepo

LANGUAGE, PRAYER, AND GRACE

Language is no more than the impressions
left by birds nesting in snow.

Prayer is the path opened
by a leopard leaping through the brush.

And grace is how the water parts for a fish
letting it break surface.

Jane Hirshfield

THE FISH

There is a fish
that stitches
the inner water
and the outer water together.

Bastes them
with its gold body's flowing.

A heavy thread
follows that transparent river,
secures it—
the broad world we make daily,
daily give ourselves to.

Neither imagined
nor unimagined,
neither winged nor finned,
we walk the luminous seam.
Knot it.
Flow back into the open gills.

Patricia Fargnoli

REINCARNATE

I want to come back as that ordinary
garden snail, carting my brown-striped spiral shell
onto the mushroom which has sprouted
after overnight rain so I can stretch
my tentacles toward the slightly drooping
and pimpled raspberry, sweet and pulsing—
a thumb that bends on its stalk from the crown
of small leaves, weighed down by the almost
translucent shining drop of dew I have
been reaching and reaching toward my whole life.

Linda Hogan

INNOCENCE

There is nothing more innocent
than the still-unformed creature I find beneath soil,
neither of us knowing what it will become
in the abundance of the planet.
It makes a living only by remaining still
in its niche.
One day it may struggle out of its tender
pearl of blind skin
with a wing or with vision
leaving behind the transparent.

I cover it again, keep laboring,
hands in earth, myself a singular body.
Watching things grow,
wondering how
a cut blade of grass knows
how to turn sharp again at the end.

This same growing must be myself,
not aware yet of what I will become
in my own fullness
inside this simple flesh.

Farnaz Fatemi

EVERYTHING IS MADE OF LABOR

The inchworm's trajectory:
pulse of impulse. The worm
is tender. It won't live
long. Its green glows.
It found a place to go.
Arrange us with meaning,
the words plead. Find the thread
through the dark.

Susan Kelly-DeWitt

APPLE BLOSSOMS

One evening in winter
when nothing has been enough,
when the days are too short,

the nights too long
and cheerless, the secret
and docile buds of the apple

blossoms begin their quick
ascent to light. Night
after interminable night

the sugars pucker and swell
into green slips, green
silks. And just as you find

yourself at the end
of winter's long, cold
rope, the blossoms open

like pink thimbles
and that black dollop
of shine called

bumblebee stumbles in.

Nancy Miller Gomez

GROWING APPLES

There is big excitement in C block today.
On the window sill,
in a plastic ice cream cup
a little plant is growing.
This is all the men want to talk about:
how an apple seed germinated
in a crack of damp concrete;
how they tore open tea bags
to collect the leaves, leached them
in water, then laid the sprout onto the bed
made of Lipton. How this finger of spring
dug one delicate root down
into the dark fannings and now
two small sleeves of green
are pushing out from the emerging tip.
The men are tipsy with this miracle.
Each morning, one by one,
they go to the window and check
the progress of the struggling plant.
All through the day they return
to stand over the seedling
and whisper.

Danusha Laméris

ASPEN

They tower above the hilltop,
yellow leaves rustling the air
in a kind of muffled conversation.

And when a breeze bends
their upper branches
they tilt sideways
in the gesture of attentive listeners.

And so, we sit together in silence,
old friends who don't need to speak.

Though sometimes they murmur
amongst themselves,
the kind of banter that once
soothed me as a child
drifting off to sleep

while my parents carried on
upstairs, talking after dinner
with their guests.

Now, a red-winged blackbird
lands on a slender branch
and is lost among shuffling leaves.

Now, a cloud passes overhead—
my mother's silk scarf
trailing on the wind.

Is this what it is to be alone?
This being with my tall,
branched sisters?

Then let me sit
in their lengthening shadow
as the day wanes,
and the hours of my life wane,

and the evening starts to fall,
and the night comes
with its quiet company of stars.

Margaret Hasse

WITH TREES

for Norton Stillman

Something I've forgotten calls me away
from the picnic table to tall trees
at the far end of the clearing.
I remember lying on grass
being still, studying forks of branches
with their thousands of leaves.
While trees accrued their secret rings
life spread a great canopy
of family, work, ordinary activity.
I mislaid what once moved me.

Today I have time to follow
the melody of green wherever it goes,
a tune, maybe hummed
when I was too young
to have the words I wanted
and know how a body returns
to familiar refrains.

Now like a child, I sit down, lie back,
look up at the crowns of maple,
needled spruce and a big-hearted boxwood.
Fugitive birds dart in and out.
In the least little wind, birch leaves turn

and flash silver like a school of minnows.
Clouds range in the blue sky
above earth's great geniuses
of shelter and shade.

Kim Stafford

SHELTER IN PLACE

Long before the pandemic, the trees
knew how to guard one place with
roots and shade. Moss found
how to hug a stone for life.
Every stream works out how
to move in place, staying home
even as it flows generously
outward, sending bounty far.
Now is our time to practice—
singing from balconies, sending
words of comfort by any courier,
kindling our lonesome generosity
to shine in all directions like stars.

Heather Newman

MISSING KEY

The doors are locked and I'm searching for a way in.
I circle my house intent on finding a crack in the system
I painstakingly created, a loose bolt, a faulty window.
It's still light in Vermont but in one hour the sun will dip
behind the mountain, temperatures will fall, and I may still
be stuck outside, cursing. There are friends. There
    are neighbors.
Or I could resolve nothing, sit on the cool grass and wait.
On my iPhone, I view my furious attempts to break in
recorded on the outdoor cameras. There are family
    members
who hold a key, but rescues have never worked for me
    in the past.
I consider places for lost or hidden keys. They say
    gratitude is a key.
Solitude is a mountain. There are pines, cedars and
    hemlocks,
a range against the mango-magenta horizon,
a red-tailed hawk circling its prey.

Michael Kiesow Moore

CLIMBING THE GOLDEN MOUNTAIN

Silence is the golden mountain.
—*Jack Kerouac*

Listen. Turn
everything
off. When
the noise
of our lives
drifts away,
when the
chatter of
our minds
sinks into
that perfect
lake of nothing,
then, oh
then we can
apprehend
that golden
mountain,
always there,
waiting for
us to be
still enough
to hear it.

Laura Foley

TO SEE IT

We need to separate to see
the life we've made.
We need to leave our house
where someone waits for us, patiently,
warm beneath the sheets.
We need to don a sweater, a coat, mittens,
wrap a scarf around our neck,
stride down the road,
a cold winter morning,
and turn our head back,
to see it—perched
on the top of the hill, our life
lit from inside.

Jacqueline Jules

UNCLOUDED VISION

Her lenses, implanted
to uncloud aging eyes,
sparkle now like a bit
of glitter on a card,
rhinestones on a T-shirt.

Twinkle in her eye. An old cliché.
Common long before
surgery was routine, suggesting
joy or affection—intangibles
that lift heels off concrete,
make us notice yellow petals
pushing through sidewalk cracks.

My grandmother
now visits museums again,
marvels at details, stops to read
each acrylic label on the wall.

Danusha Laméris

IMPROVEMENT

The optometrist says my eyes
are getting better each year.
Soon he'll have to lower my prescription.
What's next? The light step I had at six?
All the gray hairs back to brown?
Skin taut as a drum?

My improved eyes and I
walked around town and celebrated.

We took in the letters
of the marquee, the individual leaves
filling out the branches of the sycamore,
an early moon.

So much goes downhill: joints
wearing out with every mile,
the delicate folds of the eardrum
exhausted from years of listening.
I'm grateful for small victories.

The way the heart still beats time
in the cathedral of the ribs.

And the mind, watching its parade
of thoughts, enter and leave,
begins to see them for what they are:
jugglers, fire swallowers, acrobats,
tossing their batons into the air.

REFLECTIVE PAUSE

Grateful for Small Victories

In "Improvement," Danusha Laméris recounts the rare experience of a part of her body actually getting better with age and invites us to celebrate the good news with her. "So much goes downhill," she says, reminding us of the body's fragility and vulnerability. Yet she also urges us to be "grateful for small victories," for the fact that the heart carries on "in the cathedral of the ribs," and that the endlessly busy mind keeps sending out its "parade of thoughts." I love the way the speaker of this poem seems to detach from her own anxieties and intrusive thoughts, even playfully seeing them as "jugglers, fire swallowers, acrobats" meant to entertain, and not to be obeyed. And in her question, "What's next?," I also hear the willingness to have hope that other things in her life, and in the world, might begin to improve as well.

Invitation for Writing and Reflection
Write your own celebration of your "small victories," things you managed to accomplish no matter how slight they might seem. Whatever your list, try to capture that same sense of gratitude and joy for things that went well for you.

Jack Ridl

AFTER SPENDING THE MORNING BAKING BREAD

Our cat lies across the stove's front burners,
right leg hanging over the oven door. He
is looking into the pantry where his bowl
sits full on the counter. His smaller dish,
the one for his splash of cream, sits empty.
Say yes to wanting to be this cat. Say
yes to wanting to lie across the leftover
warmth, letting it rise into your soft belly,
spreading into every twitch of whisker, twist
of fur and cell, through the Mobius strip
of your bloodstream. You won't know
you will die. You won't know the mice
do not exist for you. If a lap is empty and
warm, you will land on it, feel an unsteady
hand along your back, fingers scratching
behind your ear. You will purr.

Wally Swist

RADIANCE

Over your gray and white oval marble-top kitchen table,
the meeting of our eyes makes the room grow brighter.
Our faces, layer after layer, become so vibrant

the light appears to crest in waves.
We have become changed by it, nothing can be
the same after it. When I bend down to touch

the shape of deer tracks in the damp sand, it is in
the same way I place my fingers over your body.
When I stand beside a freshet in a meadow

the sun catches the rings of the water's long ripples
in the wind, that is the same glimmer we hold
when our eyes meet in the kitchen over

your gray and white oval marble-top table.
Every day for the rest of my life, yours is the face
I want to see when I awake in the morning.

Kristen Case

MORNING

Against all probability our bulbs have blossomed,
opened their white rooms, given their assent.
I pull myself from your breathing to take a closer look.
It happened overnight.

Outside a flock of birds folds and unfolds its single body.
I start the coffee. Light comes
from impossible directions.

You are still asleep.
I cup the curve of your skull with my hand.
Alive, sleeping.
Light rises on the flame-colored bricks.

Ross Gay

WEDDING POEM

for Keith and Jen

Friends I am here to modestly report
seeing in an orchard
in my town
a goldfinch kissing
a sunflower
again and again
dangling upside down
by its tiny claws
steadying itself by snapping open
like an old-timey fan
its wings
again and again,
until, swooning, it tumbled off
and swooped back to the very same perch,
where the sunflower curled its giant
swirling of seeds
around the bird and leaned back
to admire the soft wind
nudging the bird's plumage,
and friends I could see
the points on the flower's stately crown
soften and curl inward
as it almost indiscernibly lifted

the food of its body
to the bird's nuzzling mouth
whose fervor
I could hear from
oh 20 or 30 feet away
and see from the tiny hulls
that sailed from their
good racket,
which good racket, I have to say
was making me blush,
and rock up on my tippy-toes,
and just barely purse my lips
with what I realize now
was being, simply, glad,
which such love,
if we let it,
makes us feel.

Jehanne Dubrow

PLEDGE

Now we are here at home, in the little nation
of our marriage, swearing allegiance to the table
we set for lunch or the windchime on the porch,
its easy dissonance. Even in our shared country,
the afternoon allots its golden lines
so that we're seated, both in shadow, on opposite
ends of a couch and two gray dogs between us.
There are acres of opinions in this house.
I make two cups of tea, two bowls of soup,
divide an apple equally. If I were a patriot,
I would call the blanket we spread across our bed
the only flag—some nights we've burned it
with our anger at each other. Some nights
we've welcomed the weight, a woolen scratch
on both our skins. My love, I am pledging
to this republic, for however long we stand,
I'll watch with you the rain's arrival in our yard.
We'll lift our faces, together, toward the glistening.

Angela Narciso Torres

AMORES PERROS

Sometimes I love you
the way my dog loves
his all-beef chew bone,
worrying the knuckled

corners from every angle,
mandibles working
like pistons. His eyes glaze
over with a faraway look

that says he won't quit
till he reaches the soft
marrow. His paws prop
the bone upright,

it slips—he can't clutch it
tight enough, bite hard
enough. A dog's paws
weren't meant for gripping.

And sometimes I love you
the way my dog brushes
his flank nonchalant
against my legs, then flops

on the floor beside me
while I read or watch TV.
His heft warms.
One of us is hungry,

the other needs
to pee. But we sit,
content as wildflowers.
Minutes pass. Hours.

Noah Davis

MENDING

Something there is that doesn't love a wall,
That wants it down.
—*Robert Frost*

When I lie down with your
back against my chest, I think of how
my grandfather stacked river stone,
one upon another, building a wall
along the edge of the meadow.
And as my palm holds your hip,
I imagine the ball of bone
beneath the flesh, resting
like the cat at the foot of the bed.
And just as my grandfather would walk
the walls in April to find where
stones had cracked and crumbled,
I meander your body, placing my lips
along the backs of your legs, the bend
in your back, your neck that strains
under the day's labor. And where lips
cannot reach, words act like the oval rocks
we wedged into crevices, saving the wall
that keeps the world from our bed.

Penny Harter

IN THE DARK

At bedtime, my grandson's breath
rasps in and out of fragile lungs.
Holding the nebulizer mask
over his nose and mouth,
I rock him on my lap and hum
a lullaby to comfort him.

The nebulizer hisses as steroids
stream into his struggling chest,
and suddenly he also starts to hum,
his infant voice rising and falling
on the same few notes—some hymn
he must have learned while in the womb
or carried here from where he was before—
a kind of plainsong, holy and hypnotic
in the dark.

Nathan Spoon

A CANDLE IN THE NIGHT

Stone is tender
to lichen.
Lichen is tender
to the earth and its other
inhabitants. What are
you and I tender to?

When a black hole
swallows a star,
it must do so
tenderly, since
a universe hinges
on tenderness.

At midnight
your candle burns
with tenderness,
dream-like in an amber
votive, its flame
flickering tenderly.

Francine Marie Tolf

PRAISE OF DARKNESS

We touch one another
with defter fingers
at night.

Rain sounds different,
its steady falling
a remembered wisdom.

What if the dark waters
waiting to carry us home
slept inside every one of us?

We were loved
before stars existed.
We are older than light.

Judith Chalmer

AN ESSAY ON AGE

It was a day to sing the praises of fire,
to bow to its purpose,

toes stretched apart, layers peeled,
our bodies gathered

into their warmest folds.
It was a day of mists, of freezing

and love. Now the night
when it returns will be kinder.

Now the moon will dominate
the dogs, sending them wild

into the burdock and we will have them
for hours on their backs.

This is the bright snap of apple, catch
in the throat—you realize how deeply

you have loved. You blow hard
on the flames and each day

is remembered mainly for the brush
of lips, for the way we stand

hip to hip in sheets of rain,
almost covered, enough.

Ted Kooser

EASTER MORNING

A misty rain pushed up against the windows
as if the house were flying through a cloud,
the drops too light, too filled with light to run,
suspended on the glass, each with the same
reflections: barn and yard and garden, grayed.

Then, suddenly appearing, burning in the quince
that soon will bloom, a cardinal, just one
milligram of red allotted to each droplet,
but each a little heavier for picking up
that splash of color, overfilled and spilling,
stumbling headlong down the chilly pane.

Andrea Potos

THE CARDINAL REMINDS ME

It sweeps and arcs across my path
almost every day on my walk to the café,
under sun or cloud, its red
seems lit from inside, a brightness
bold as the lipstick my mother wore
no matter the day or the time,
no matter how near to the end
she got, even two days before the last—
the young dark-haired nurse applying it
for her while I sat near, my own
lips trembling from fear or hope
I could not tell, I could not separate anything,
not now either—the bright flame of this bird
recalling me to loss, or to joy.

Marjorie Saiser

WHEN LIFE SEEMS A TO-DO LIST

When the squares of the week fill
with *musts* and *shoulds*,

when I swim in the heaviness of it,
the headlines, the fear and hate,

then with luck, something like a slice of moon
will arrive clean as a bone

and beside it on that dark slate
a star will lodge near the cusp

and with luck I will have you
to see it with, the two of us,

fools stepping out the backdoor
in our pajamas.

Is that Venus?—I think so—Let's
call it Venus, cuddling up to the moon

and there are stars further away
sending out rays that will not

reach us in our lifetimes
but we are choosing, before the chaos

starts up again,
to stand in this particular light.

Lahab Assef Al-Jundi

MOON

Companion of lonesome hearts.
Dreamy shepherd of starry-eyed lovers.
Cratered dusty-faced rock.

This night you shine through
is just a shadow.
Our smallness makes us believe
the whole universe is immersed in darkness.
Midday sun burns on the other side.
Daylight everywhere!

Moon,
perhaps you are here to illuminate
our illusion?

If all suns are extinguished,
all moons and planets collapsed
into black holes,
what tint would space be?
What are colors without eyes?
How do we sense a vibrating universe?

Go ahead and laugh, hanging moon,
I raise my cup to you—
patient teacher.

Crystal S. Gibbins

BECAUSE THE NIGHT YOU ASKED

for Josh
with first and last line by Linda Pastan

Because the night you asked me
the moon shone like a quarter
in the sky; because the leaves
were the color of wine at our feet;
because, like you, there was a private
sense of absence in my every day;
because in your arms my heart grows
plump as a finch; because we both
pause at the sight of heavy branches
burdened with fruit, the sound
of apples dropping to the ground;
because you hold no secrets;
because I knew what I wanted;
because we both love the snow,
the ice, the feeling of a long deadening
freeze and the mercy of a thaw;
because you gave me an empty
beach on a warm day in fall,
and a feeling that we might stay
for awhile, just the two of us,
looking out across the water,
I said *yes*.

Rob Hunter

SEPTEMBER SWIM

Knee deep just feet from shore
your dive was more of an unhurried fall,

your hands ahead of you,
and then the water closed around your clothes,

your skirt collapsing suddenly
like a flower pulled by its stem through liquid.

You didn't make a sound.
The wind rustled leaves all around us

and corrugated the water.
The sun dipped lower.

I didn't know if you would ever
appear again because in that split second,

standing on the shore of this pond
in the mountains, long afternoon shadows

were black shrouds on the water,
tinges of yellow and orange already

seeping into leaves, I sensed the new season,
felt one season expire and pass on.

And in that moment you were submerged,
swallowed whole; but like a loon,

you bobbed up and shrieked the cold
baptism out of your lungs. You then stood up,

wet clothes clinging to your body,
your hands holding your surprised face.

Joyce Sutphen

WHAT TO DO

Wake up early, before the lights come on
in the houses on a street that was once
a farmer's field at the edge of a marsh.

Wander from room to room, hoping to find
words that could be enough to keep the soul
alive, words that might be useful or kind

in a world that is more wasteful and cruel
every day. Remind us that we are
like grass that fades, fleeting clouds in the sky,

and then give us just one of those moments
when we were paying attention, when we gave
up everything to see the world in

a grain of sand or to behold
a rainbow in the sky, the heart
leaping up.

William Stafford

ANY MORNING

Just lying on the couch and being happy.
Only humming a little, the quiet sound in the head.
Trouble is busy elsewhere at the moment, it has
so much to do in the world.

People who might judge are mostly asleep; they can't
monitor you all the time, and sometimes they forget.
When dawn flows over the hedge you can
get up and act busy.

Little corners like this, pieces of Heaven
left lying around, can be picked up and saved.
People won't even see that you have them,
they are so light and easy to hide.

Later in the day you can act like the others.
You can shake your head. You can frown.

REFLECTIVE PAUSE

Pieces of Heaven

It can be difficult to give yourself permission to do nothing and allow for the space from which a sudden gratefulness can naturally arise. We feel guilty for not tackling the tasks we "should" be doing or we worry that others will judge us if they catch us in the act of indulging what might feel like laziness. "Any Morning" by William Stafford offers a reprieve from the fear of judgment that can keep us from uncovering true joy in a simple moment spent alone. Though we might be busy, though we might be tempted to reach for our phones or some other distraction, this poem invites us to pause and embrace a bit of space before the day begins.

We can always seek out "little corners like this, pieces of Heaven" when we can just be ourselves, and do what makes us happy, even if that means "lying on the couch" and relishing a few minutes of soul time. We're often pressured to put on the frowning faces others wear in order to fit in, to fall in line with finding fault with the world or the people around us. But the more we take time for ourselves throughout each day, the less we feel obliged to act a certain way or complete a list of tasks just to please someone else.

Invitation for Writing and Reflection
What are your own "pieces of Heaven" that you'd like to pick up and save throughout the day? What are those secret things that bring you joy and keep hope alive, but which you worry others might judge?

Rosemerry Wahtola Trommer

HOW IT MIGHT CONTINUE

Wherever we go, the chance for joy,
whole orchards of amazement—

one more reason to always travel
with our pockets full of exclamation marks,

so we might scatter them for others
like apple seeds.

Some will dry out, some will blow away,
but some will take root

and grow exuberant groves
filled with long thin fruits

that resemble one hand clapping—
so much enthusiasm as they flutter back and forth

that although nothing's heard
and though nothing's really changed,

people everywhere for years to come
will swear that the world

is ripe with applause, will fill
their own pockets with new seeds to scatter.

Li-Young Lee

FROM BLOSSOMS

From blossoms comes
this brown paper bag of peaches
we bought from the boy
at the bend in the road where we turned toward
signs painted *Peaches.*

From laden boughs, from hands,
from sweet fellowship in the bins,
comes nectar at the roadside, succulent
peaches we devour, dusty skin and all,
comes the familiar dust of summer, dust we eat.

O, to take what we love inside,
to carry within us an orchard, to eat
not only the skin, but the shade,
not only the sugar, but the days, to hold
the fruit in our hands, adore it, then bite into
the round jubilance of peach.

There are days we live
as if death were nowhere
in the background; from joy
to joy to joy, from wing to wing,
from blossom to blossom to
impossible blossom, to sweet impossible blossom.

Jessica Gigot

MOTHERHOOD

When the lilacs come back
I remember that I was born,
That there was a robin's nest
Outside my mother's window
As she waited to count my toes.
Now her hands rest on her stomach
Tangled in contemplation
As if I am still in there.
Her fingers are woven together
Like a fisherman's net as she tries
One more time to offer advice.

Sarah Freligh

WONDROUS

I'm driving home from school when the radio talk
turns to E. B. White, his birthday, and I exit
the here and now of the freeway at rush hour,

travel back into the past, where my mother is reading
to my sister and me the part about Charlotte laying her eggs
and dying, and though this is the fifth time Charlotte

has died, my mother is crying again, and we're laughing
at her because we know nothing of loss and its sad math,
how every subtraction is exponential, how each grief

multiplies the one preceding it, how the author tried
seventeen times to record the words *She died alone*
without crying, seventeen takes and a short walk during

which he called himself ridiculous, a grown man crying
for a spider he'd spun out of the silk thread of invention—
wondrous how those words would come back and make

him cry, and, yes, wondrous to hear my mother's voice
ten years after the day she died—the catch, the rasp,
the gathering up before she could say to us, *I'm OK*.

Cathryn Essinger

SUMMER APPLES

I planted an apple tree in memory
of my mother, who is not gone,

but whose memory has become
so transparent that she remembers

slicing apples with her grandmother
(yellow apples; blue bowl) better than

the fruit that I hand her today. Still,
she polishes the surface with her thumb,

holds it to the light and says with no
hesitation, *Oh, Yellow Transparent . . .*

*they're so fragile, you can almost see
to the core.* She no longer remembers how

to roll the crust, sweeten the sauce, but
her desire is clear—it is pie that she wants.

And so, I slice as close as I dare to the core—
to that little cathedral to memory—where

the seeds remember everything they need
to know to become yellow and transparent.

Lynne Knight

THIRD YEAR OF MY MOTHER'S DEMENTIA

I looked out the window and it filled with peacocks,
flaring their many eyes at me. I had been waiting
for months for some sign, and now from the high bank
where I was so often afraid to climb blared cries

of the peacocks as they fluttered and dipped
their soft plumules. One lay down to sleep
like a human, positioned on its side, and its fan
folded back into itself, into nothing but a long

dull tail. The others kept moving up and down the bank,
so many eyes I could not count them. They ignored
the sleeping one. Stepped over him, or rushed by
with a swish. As they would rush by me, if I stood

among them in my wonder that beauty is needed
most of all when it is useless, when it fixes nothing.

Heather Swan

RABBIT

After a long numbness, I wake
and suddenly I'm noticing everything,
all of it piercing me with its beautiful,
radical trust: the carpenter bee tonguing
the needles of echinacea believing
in their sweetness, the exuberance
of an orange day lily unfolding itself
at the edge of the street, and the way
the moss knows the stone, and the stone
accepts its trespass, and the way the dog
on his leash turns to see if I'm holding on,
certain I know where to go. And the way
the baby rabbit—whose trembling ears
are the most delicate cups—trusts me,
because I pried the same dogs' jaws
off his hips, and then allows me to feed him
clover when his back legs no longer work,
forcing me to think about forgiveness
and those I need to forgive, and to hope
I am forgiven, and that just maybe
I can forgive myself. This unstoppable,
excruciating tenderness everywhere inviting
us, always inviting. And then later, the firefly
illuminating the lantern of its body,
like us, each time we laugh.

Dale Biron

LAUGHTER

When the
face we wear

grows old and weathered, torn
open by time,

colors
tinted as dawn

like the late
winter mountains

of Sedona
ashen and crimson,

it will no longer
be possible

to distinguish
our deepest scars

from the long
sweet lines left

by laughter.

January Gill O'Neil

IN THE COMPANY OF WOMEN

Make me laugh over coffee,
make it a double, make it frothy
so it seethes in our delight.
Make my cup overflow
with your small happiness.
I want to hoot and snort and cackle and chuckle.
Let your laughter fill me like a bell.
Let me listen to your ringing and singing
as Billie Holiday croons above our heads.
Sorry, the blues are nowhere to be found.
Not tonight. Not here.
No makeup. No tears.
Only contours. Only curves.
Each sip takes back a pound,
each dry-roasted swirl takes our soul.
Can I have a refill, just one more?
Let the bitterness sink to the bottom of our lives.
Let us take this joy to go.

Alice Wolf Gilborn

LEANING TO THE LIGHT

Our neighbor planted twelve
bulbs in the shadow of his barn
in the shadow of the trees
in the shadow of a mountain.
And now a dozen lilies grow
at an angle toward the sun
that touches them only
in the afternoon. Our neighbor
sold his house to strangers
who come for just a week
or two so they never see
their flowers bloom, later
than the rest, their soft pink
petals tinged with white,
curled like shavings, stamen
tuned to the western sky.
Like me since I left the land
where I was born, leaning west,
these laggard lilies with mouths wide
open, drinking in the setting sun.

Andrea Potos

I WATCHED AN ANGEL IN THE EMERGENCY ROOM

Tall in twilit
blue sneakers, feet winged
to the task of holding
my mother's hand as
he explained the source
of the infection, all it will take
to restore her
to the stronghold of
this earth that has known her
eight decades and more, the gate
of her body where my gratitude begins.

Alberto Ríos

WHEN GIVING IS ALL WE HAVE

One river gives
Its journey to the next.

We give because someone gave to us.
We give because nobody gave to us.

We give because giving has changed us.
We give because giving could have changed us.

We have been better for it,
We have been wounded by it—

Giving has many faces: It is loud and quiet,
Big, though small, diamond in wood-nails.

Its story is old, the plot worn and the pages too,
But we read this book, anyway, over and again:

Giving is, first and every time, hand to hand,
Mine to yours, yours to mine.

You gave me blue and I gave you yellow.
Together we are simple green. You gave me

What you did not have, and I gave you
What I had to give—together, we made

Something greater from the difference.

Albert Garcia

OFFERING

Here, take this palmful of raspberries
as my gift. It isn't much

but we've often said our needs
are simple, some quiet

time alone on the patio
in the cool morning, coffee,

a few words over the newspaper.
I've rinsed these berries

so you can tumble them
right into your cereal, one minute

on the vine, the next in your bowl,
my hand to your mouth.

Let's say my words were as simply
sweet as these berries, chosen

as carefully, plucked and held,
then delivered as perfect

morsels of meaning. Not
what you hear, which is never

what I mean to say. Will you take
these berries? Will you feel their weight

on your tongue, taste their tang
as they slide into you, small, bright, honest:

the only gift I have to give?

Alison Luterman

TOO MANY TO COUNT

My father hands me the bucket and scissors
and asks me to go cut peonies: white, pink, magenta.
Tightly balled and slightly unfurled,
they've multiplied like crazy on the slope behind his house.

Long ago, Dad taught himself to garden out of books.
My childhood was fat with exulted-over tomatoes,
blueberry bushes covered with cheesecloth,
and a zillion profligate zucchinis,
which caused an outbreak of zucchini bread,
zucchini muffins, and ill-fated zucchini pizza crust,
inciting both my brothers to go on a zucchini strike
that has lasted to this day.

But these peonies!
God must have been a little stoned when She dreamed
     them up,
not stopping at one petticoat or two,
but piling layer upon layer, until even the exhausted bees
surrender to excessive lingerie.
I stuff the bucket with closed buds
and half-opened blooms showing their lacy knickers
and trudge back up the steep-sloped hill to the house,

leaving behind a glowing field of peonies, too many to
    count,
like my father's many kindnesses over the decades—
pots of soup, loaves of home-baked bread,
hours of earnest listening,
all offered with the same voluptuous generosity
as now when he takes the laden bucket from my arms
and tells me to divide the bounty into smaller bunches
so he can distribute them among the neighbors.

Marjorie Saiser

IF I CARRY MY FATHER

I hope it is a little more
than color of hair
or the dimple or cheekbones
if he's ever here in the space I inhabit
the room I walk in
the boundaries and peripheries
I hope it's some kindness he believed in
living on in cell or bone
maybe some word or action
will float close to the surface
within my reach
some good will rise when I need it
a hard dense insoluble shard
will show up
and carry on.

George Bilgere

WEATHER

My father would lift me
to the ceiling in his big hands
and ask, *How's the weather up there?*
And it was good, the weather
of being in his hands, his breath
of scotch and cigarettes, his face
smiling from the world below.
O daddy, was the lullaby I sang
back down to him as he stood on earth,
my great, white-shirted father, home
from work, his gold wristwatch
and wedding band gleaming
as he held me above him
for as long as he could,
before his strength failed
down there in the world I find myself
standing in tonight, my little boy
looking down from his flight
below the ceiling, cradled in my hands,
his eyes wide and already staring
into the distance beyond the man
asking him again and again,
How's the weather up there?

Sally Bliumis-Dunn

WORK

I could tell they were father and son,
the air between them, slack as though
they hardly noticed one another.

The father sanded the gunwales,
the boy coiled the lines.
And I admired them there, each to his task

in the quiet of the long familiar.
The sawdust coated the father's arms
like dusk coats grass in a field.

The boy worked next on the oarlocks
polishing the brass until it gleamed
as though he could harness the sun.

Who cares what they were thinking,
lucky in their lives
that the spin of the genetic wheel

slowed twice to a stop
and landed each of them here.

REFLECTIVE PAUSE

The Joy of Making

Sally Bliumis-Dunn's "Work" shows two people steeped in the joy of what they're doing. They seem to be beaming, the fullness of their gratitude and good luck suddenly contagious.

We share her relief at watching this father and son build a boat together, disengaged from the technology that can disconnect us from each other. We all crave a creative outlet like this and can deeply enjoy being so involved in the task of making something that we lose all sense of time. In the space of creativity and cooperation, we also lose touch with our *self* for a while and shed those anxious thoughts that can be fed by social media and news.

This poem urges us to bear loving witness to the world as it is, to find beauty in the simple scene of a father and son coming together to accomplish something much larger than themselves. She points to "the spin of the genetic wheel" that led them, and each of us, to this very moment in our lives, and invites us to feel the luck of having become exactly who we are right now.

Invitation for Writing and Reflection

Can you remember a time when you felt so consumed with the act of making something that you lost all sense of time, and your mind seemed to clear? What allowed you to enter this mindful creative space?

Danusha Laméris

GOLDFINCHES

Good luck, they say,
to see one,
its face and breast
pure citrus
against the grey sky.

And today,
I am twice blessed
because two such birds
grace the low boughs
of the persimmon,
eating the soft heart
of winter's fruit—

though they will also
feast on thistles
pulled from the dry flowers
and so are said
to eat the thorns
of Christ's crown,
to lift some small measure
of his suffering.

Whatever your grief,
however long you've carried it—
may something
come to you,
quick and unexpected,
whisk away
the bristled edge
in its sharp
and tender beak.

Connie Wanek

THE LESSER GOLDFINCH

It was hardly bigger than an apricot,
a goldfinch, yes, but smaller and paler,
a little ghost in the lavender
eating seeds too tiny for
my old eyes. Sometimes I think
Heaven needn't measure
even two by two
inches, much less all the sky
above the Vatican;
for peace is lodged deep
within the very
spacious thought of itself.
Quiet bird, your gestures
are vast in such a place
as I dream of.

Tony Hoagland

THE WORD

Down near the bottom
of the crossed-out list
of things you have to do today,

between "green thread"
and "broccoli," you find
that you have penciled "sunlight."

Resting on the page, the word
is beautiful. It touches you
as if you had a friend

and sunlight were a present
he had sent from someplace distant
as this morning—to cheer you up,

and to remind you that,
among your duties, pleasure
is a thing

that also needs accomplishing.
Do you remember?
that time and light are kinds

of love, and love
is no less practical
than a coffee grinder

or a safe spare tire?
Tomorrow you may be utterly
without a clue,

but today you get a telegram
from the heart in exile,
proclaiming that the kingdom

still exists,
the king and queen alive,
still speaking to their children,

—to anyone among them
who can find the time
to sit out in the sun and listen.

Barbara Crooker

TOMORROW

there will be sun, scalloped by clouds,
ushered in by a waterfall of birdsong.
It will be a temperate seventy-five, low
humidity. For twenty-four hours,
all politicians will be silent. Reality
programs will vanish from TV, replaced
by the "snow" that used to decorate
our screens when reception wasn't
working. Soldiers will toss their weapons
in the grass. The oceans will stop
their inexorable rise. No one
will have to sit on a committee.
When twilight falls, the aurora borealis
will cut off cell phones, scramble the internet.
We'll play flashlight tag, hide and seek,
decorate our hair with fireflies, spin
until we're dizzy, collapse
on the dew-decked lawn and look up,
perhaps for the first time, to read the long lines
of cold code written in the stars . . .

Cynthia White

QUAIL HOLLOW

Think of the path as calligraphy—
narrow where it borders
the farm house and horse pens.

Think, how beyond the open gate,
the stroke fattens, traveling
upward into the dark

scrawl of live oak and bay.
See how the light
is a tender wash. Under

your feet, sand that once
cradled a sea. Blue-bellies skitter,
scritching like tiny scribes

among the leaves. Think
how little ink is required to write
three million years.

After the climb, the view,
the final loop. You pass the houses
of sleeping wood rats, the pond,

glassine slashed with cattails.
Now, before getting into your car,
consider with what ease

the rise and fall of robin song
can erase a certain ache,
the day's gathering premonitions.

Laura Grace Weldon

COMPOST HAPPENS

Nature teaches nothing is lost.
It's transmuted.

Spread between rows of beans,
last year's rusty leaves tamp down weeds.
Coffee grounds and banana peels
foster rose blooms. Bread crumbs
scattered for birds become song.
Leftovers offered to chickens come back
as eggs, yolks sunrise orange.
Broccoli stems and bruised apples
fed to cows return as milk steaming in the pail,
as patties steaming in the pasture.

Surely our shame and sorrow
also return,
composted by years
into something generative as wisdom.

Joan Mazza

PART OF THE LANDSCAPE

An old wooden bench, aging gray, colonized
by moss, liverworts, and lichens that drape
the surface, where I rest along my woodland
walks, wear clothes to match the earthy landscape—
grays and greens and browns, a mottled muddle
so I don't stand out. After two weeks, crows
don't scream to warn the neighborhood, but huddle
with their kind to chat. As still as possible,
I am a rock, a tree. Nothing flees from me.
Near my head, a golden crowned kinglet, smaller
than a chickadee or chipping sparrow.
I hold still, photograph this world with just
my eyes, forget the news. My heart is here,
filled with gratitude as I fade and disappear.

Andrea Potos

ESSENTIAL GRATITUDE

Sometimes it just stuns you
like an arrow flung from some angel's wing.
Sometimes it hastily scribbles
a list in the air: black coffee,
thick new books,
your pillow's cool underside,
the quirky family you married into.

It is content with so little really;
even the ink of your pen along
the watery lines of your dimestore notebook
could be a swiftly moving prayer.

REFLECTIVE PAUSE

The Gratitude List

As Andrea Potos's "Essential Gratitude" points out, the sensation of appreciation can come out of nowhere and pierce our hearts until we find ourselves making a whole list "in the air" of those everyday things we might otherwise look past or ignore. One of the most potent practices we can adopt is including a gratitude list as part of our journaling or writing practice, in the morning or at night before bed. Turning the mind toward reverence through our writing can ensure that a grateful attitude becomes a habit and follows us wherever we go.

By regularly listing the elements of this ordinary, miraculous life as concrete lines on the page, we ensure that we move through our days looking for reasons to be happy. Potos also reminds us that saying a simple thank you can be its own kind of prayer, whether it happens out loud or follows "the watery lines of your dimestore notebook."

Invitation for Writing and Reflection

The next time a sudden feeling of appreciation "stuns" you, take the time to write out your own gratitude list as soon as possible. When you pay attention, what specific sensory details about this grateful moment stand out to you as worthy of praise?

Laura Foley

GRATITUDE LIST

Praise be this morning for sleeping late,
the sandy sheets, the ocean air,
the midnight storm that blew its waters in.
Praise be the morning swim, mid-tide,
the clear sands underneath our feet,
the dogs who leap into the waves,
their fur, sticky with salt,
the ball we throw again and again.
Praise be the green tea with honey,
the bread we dip in finest olive oil,
the eggs we fry. Praise be the reeds,
gold and pink in the summer light,
the sand between our toes,
our swimsuits, flapping in the breeze.

Katherine Williams

THE DOG BODY OF MY SOUL

Some days I feel
like a retriever
racing
back and forth
fetching the tired
old balls
the universe
tosses me.

Some days
I'm on a leash
following
someone else's
route,
sensing
I'm supposed
to be grateful.

Some days
I'm waiting
in a darkened
house
bladder insistent
not knowing
when my people
will return.

But some days
I hurl myself
into the sweet
stinging surf,
race wildly back
and roll
in the sand's
warm welcome.

Katie Rubinstein

SCRATCH, SNIFF

It was weeks ago now
that first September I spent here on this island,
still hot and balmy.
I wanted a scratch and sniff for you,
some clever little corner of the screen
so I could share this most perfect thing:
the smell of beach roses, all briney.

They were abundant outside of the cottage,
and each time I passed, I wondered how I'd gotten so lucky—
that they became like dandelions in my life.

Hardy, scrappy and perfectly soft all at the same time,
nestled in their rocky, sandy homes, smelling like heaven—
those round, round hips.
I wanted to eat them, be them,

and I wanted you to smell them
as if sharing them would somehow
exponentially increase the delight
or make the sense more real.

But it was mine alone
and exquisite all the same.

Mary Elder Jacobsen

SUMMER COTTAGE

I'm halfway through a day
that began like a gift
in a blue china eggcup
set on the table before me
by my grandma at the shore
always awake before sunup
always beginning it for me
her soft tap-tap-tapping,
her careful cracking to open
what seemed a rare jewel box
how she raised its little lid
let me peek past the edge
let me see the whole horizon
orbiting the yolk-yellow sun
how brightly it would glisten
hovering there just for me.

Jane Kenyon

COMING HOME AT TWILIGHT IN LATE SUMMER

We turned into the drive,
and gravel flew up from the tires
like sparks from a fire. So much
to be done—the unpacking, the mail
and papers . . . the grass needed mowing . . .
We climbed stiffly out of the car.
The shut-off engine ticked as it cooled.

And then we noticed the pear tree,
the limbs so heavy with fruit
they nearly touched the ground.
We went out to the meadow; our steps
made black holes in the grass;
and we each took a pear,
and ate, and were grateful.

Grace Bauer

PERCEPTIVE PRAYER

The beauty of summer nights
is how they go on—
light lingering so long we can
imagine ourselves immortal.
For moments at a time.

And winter days—
their own kind of beauty.
Any swatch of color:
hint of leaf bud, sway
of dried brown grass, even litter—

a bright yellow bag
light enough for the breeze
to lift and carry,
can render itself as pleasure
to an eye immersed in gray.

May we learn to love
what is both
ordinary and extra.
May our attention be
a kind of praise.
A worship of the all
there really is.

Patricia Fontaine

SAP ICICLES

On the row
of fresh pruned maples
along Bostwick Road
the cold wind
froze sap icicles sideways.
I saw a chickadee
land at an icicle tip,
so I pulled over
and put my tongue
to the cold tears of the tree.
Tasted flint,
tasted maple steam
when it rises off the pan,
tasted the shimmer
pulsing up inside
the cool grey bark
as the sun applies
its long March hands.

The happiest child in me
was tongued to that tree,
while the saddest
grieved the lost limbs.

On the side of the road
we grew up inside
my black coat, became
white-haired,
cared nothing
for the gawping cars.

Lucille Clifton

the lesson of the falling leaves

the leaves believe
such letting go is love
such love is faith
such faith is grace
such grace is god
i agree with the leaves

Ted Kooser

A DERVISH OF LEAVES

Sometimes when I'm sad, the dead leaves
in the bed of my pickup get up on their own
and start dancing. I'll be driving along,
glance up at the mirror and there they'll be,
swirling and bowing, their flying skirts
brushing the back window, not putting a hand
on the top of the cab to steady themselves,
but daringly leaning out over the box,
making fun of the fence posts we're passing
who have never left home, teasing the rocks
rolled away into the ditches, leaves light
in their slippers, dancing around in the back
of my truck, tossing their cares to the wind,
sometimes, when I'm down in my heart.

James Crews

WINTER MORNING

When I can no longer say thank you
for this new day and the waking into it,
for the cold scrape of the kitchen chair
and the ticking of the space heater glowing
orange as it warms the floor near my feet,
I know it is because I've been fooled again
by the selfish, unruly man who lives in me
and believes he deserves only safety
and comfort. But if I pause as I do now,
and watch the streetlights outside winking
off one by one like old men closing their
cloudy eyes, if I listen to my tired neighbors
slamming car doors hard against the morning
and see the steaming coffee in their mugs
kissing their chapped lips as they sip and
exhale each of their worries white into
the icy air around their faces—then I can
remember this one life is a gift each of us
was handed and told to open: Untie the bow
and tear off the paper, look inside
and be grateful for whatever you find
even if it is only the scent of a tangerine
that lingers on the fingers long after
you've finished peeling it.

Tracy K. Smith

THE GOOD LIFE

When some people talk about money
They speak as if it were a mysterious lover
Who went out to buy milk and never
Came back, and it makes me nostalgic
For the years I lived on coffee and bread,
Hungry all the time, walking to work on payday
Like a woman journeying for water
From a village without a well, then living
One or two nights like everyone else
On roast chicken and red wine.

Marjorie Saiser

THANKSGIVING FOR TWO

The adults we call our children will not be arriving
with their children in tow for Thanksgiving.
We must make our feast ourselves,

slice our half-ham, indulge, fill our plates,
potatoes and green beans
carried to our table near the window.

We are the feast, plenty of years,
arguments. I'm thinking the whole bundle of it
rolls out like a white tablecloth. We wanted

to be good company for one another.
Little did we know that first picnic
how this would go. Your hair was thick,

mine long and easy; we climbed a bluff
to look over a storybook plain. We chose
our spot as high as we could, to see

the river and the checkerboard fields.
What we didn't see was this day, in
our pajamas if we want to,

wrinkled hands strong, wine
in juice glasses, toasting
whatever's next,

the decades of side-by-side,
our great good luck.

REFLECTIVE PAUSE

The Feast of Each Moment

It's difficult to resist the social pressure that turns the holidays into an excuse for consumption and a source of stress. Yet in "Thanksgiving for Two," Marjorie Saiser brings love and acceptance to a situation that might anger or disappoint other parents: Her children will not be coming home for the holiday this year. Even in the first line, she acknowledges that they are adults with lives and children of their own, and we sense a hint of relief that she and her husband will get to "indulge" alone and reminisce about "that first picnic" that led them to this day together. Saiser reminds us that when we "make our feast ourselves," we transform the holidays back into holy days that focus on joy and deeper connection; we allow the abundance of our lives to roll out "like a white tablecloth," full of countless blessings laid out for us.

Invitation for Writing and Reflection

Describe a time when you turned what might have been a difficult or disappointing situation into your own feast, making the most of it. What allowed you to generate a thankful, hopeful attitude in those moments, to recognize even the smallest gifts in the midst of a challenge?

Jeffrey Harrison

NEST

It wasn't until we got the Christmas tree
into the house and up on the stand
that our daughter discovered a small bird's nest
tucked among its needled branches.

Amazing, that the nest had made it
all the way from Nova Scotia on a truck
mashed together with hundreds of other trees
without being dislodged or crushed.

And now it made the tree feel wilder,
a balsam fir growing in our living room,
as though at any moment a bird might flutter
through the house and return to the nest.

And yet, because we'd brought the tree indoors,
we'd turned the nest into the first ornament.
So we wound the tree with strings of lights,
draped it with strands of red beads,

and added the other ornaments, then dropped
two small brass bells into the nest, like eggs
containing music, and hung a painted goldfinch
from the branch above, as if to keep them warm.

Ellen Bass

GETTING INTO BED ON A DECEMBER NIGHT

When I slip beneath the quilt and fold into
her warmth, I think we are like the pages
of a love letter written thirty years ago
that some aging god still reads each day
and then tucks back into its envelope.

Lisa Coffman

EVERYBODY MADE SOUPS

After it all, the events of the holidays,
the dinner tables passing like great ships,
everybody made soups for a while.
Cooked and cooked until the broth kept
the story of the onion, the weeping meat.
It was over, the year was spent, the new one
had yet to make its demands on us,
each day lay in the dark like a folded letter.
Then out of it all we made one final thing
out of the bounty that had not always filled us,
out of the ruined cathedral carcass of the turkey,
the limp celery chopped back into plenty,
the fish head, the spine. Out of the rejected,
the passed over, never the object of love.
It was as if all the pageantry had been for this:
the quiet after, the simmered light,
the soothing shapes our mouths made as we tasted.

James Crews

DARKEST BEFORE DAWN

Three days into the new year,
and despite the lack of adequate light,
our white phalaenopsis orchid
has eased open a third delicate bloom.
Perhaps coaxed by the warmth
of the woodstove a few feet away,
the orchid thrives in its tiny pot
shaped like the shell of a nautilus,
sending out new stems and glossy leaves,
its aerial roots—green at the tips—
reaching upward like tentacles
to sip the morning air. These blooms
stir something too long asleep in me,
proving with stillness and slow growth
what I haven't been able to trust
these past few months—that hope
and grace still reign in certain sectors
of the living world, that there are laws
which can never be overturned
by hateful words or the wishes
of power-hungry men. Be patient,
this orchid seems to say, and reveal
your deepest self even in the middle
of winter, even in the darkness
before the coming dawn.

Brad Peacock

ROSARY

for my grandfather

Some say it is darkest before dawn—
they must not be morning dwellers,
those of us who wake
long before the masses
to see the beauty
of a world in transition.
I walk these city streets
stripped of yesterday's worries,
laid bare like the sidewalks in front of me.
A crow calls
stopping me in my tracks,
back to the here and now,
after my mind has taken flight.
I look toward the sky
for the sentinel to sound his alarm again,
and glimpse a sliver of silver light
illuminating the cross
atop a towering cathedral.
I feel my fingers move in my mittens,
as if tracing every detail
of those sacred family beads
you handed me
long before you were gone.

Julie Murphy

TO ASK

To wear your dead husband's sweatshirt
long after his scent has faded,
the cotton soft, wrist and waist bands
frayed, the white *Wrigley Field*
still bright, to pull the hood over your head,
nestle into darkness the way he would on a cold night,
to conjure him, slideshow of your lives
playing in the background, shot by shot,
as if this cloth could incarnate the self
who wore it, day after day, year after year,
or the self who you were, to be that self for an instant,
glimpse whatever it was—joy, sorrow—
that made you whole,
to know yourself forever changed,
glimpse or no glimpse, gone forever.
To not know, in the vast space
of grief, who you ever could become,
and ask who, without despair
to ask with hope—

Tess Taylor

THERE DOESN'T NEED TO BE A POEM

for this sadness. Simply to breathe
next to a stream that slips into the gutter
near your house

would be enough. To see,
next door, in the graveyard,
the brown-and-yellow millipede

bury itself below one granite stone,
joining in the work of making soil,
just as now the faithful oxygen

still turns the copper headstone green,
oxidizing to patina despite all.
By luck, your own feathered alveoli

still redden blood, your fine cell walls
trade oxygen for carbon,
and sift the windy mix we call the air:

This happens, going on invisibly
even if no one remembers how
& even if it seems that pain

is a volatile molecule, grief
bonding unpredictably to things.
Now the late sun rims a cloud.

You, who watch that cloud:
Inhale. Exhale.

Amy Dryansky

WINGSPAN

for Donna

Every day I draw in air you can't
& try to send it to you, alone
in a hospital, a machine breathing
for you, & because we aren't
allowed to see you I'm imagining
wings for you—yes, cynical me
earnestly conjuring an angel
or eagle, golden, wings spread,
alighting immensely gently
on your chest, carrying light & air
from my lungs, from the many
who love you, filling your lungs
with breath, heat, life, a garden.
If I could, I would wake you
with light, believe in anything.

Joy Harjo

EAGLE POEM

To pray you open your whole self
To sky, to earth, to sun, to moon
To one whole voice that is you.
And know there is more
That you can't see, can't hear;
Can't know except in moments
Steadily growing, and in languages
That aren't always sound but other
Circles of motion.
Like eagle that Sunday morning
Over Salt River. Circled in blue sky
In wind, swept our hearts clean
With sacred wings.
We see you, see ourselves and know
That we must take the utmost care
And kindness in all things.
Breathe in, knowing we are made of
All this, and breathe, knowing
We are truly blessed because we
Were born, and die soon within a
True circle of motion,
Like eagle rounding out the morning
Inside us.
We pray that it will be done
In beauty.
In beauty.

Terri Kirby Erickson

WHAT MATTERS

What other people think of you,
what they say, are burdens
no one should carry. Lift a spoon,

a cup, things that fit in your hand.
Carry on a conversation,
pick up a baby. Listen to the wind

when it whispers, nothing else.
There is no one watching you,
no one straining to hear what

you say. The present has arrived
and you are in it. Your heart
is pumping. Your breath moves

in and out of your lungs without
anyone's help or permission.
Let go of everything else. Let

your life, handed to you through
no effort of your own, be all
the proof you need. You are loved.

Mark Nepo

IN LOVE WITH THE WORLD

There is no end to love. We may tear ourselves away, or fall off the cliff we thought sacred, or return one day to find the home we dreamt of burning. But when the rain slows to a slant and the pavement turns cold, that place where I keep you and you and all of you—that place opens, like a fist no longer strong enough to stay closed. And the ache returns. Thank God. The sweet and sudden ache that lets me know I am alive. The rain keeps misting my face. What majesty of cells assembles around this luminous presence that moves around as me? How is it I'm still here? Each thing touched, each breath, each glint of light, each pain in my gut is cause for praise. I pray to keep falling in love with everyone I meet, with every child's eye, with every fallen being getting up. Like a worm cut in two, the heart only grows another heart. When the cut in my mind heals, I grow another mind. Birds migrate and caribou circle the cold top of the world. Perhaps we migrate between love and suffering, making our wounded-joyous cries: alone, then together, alone, then together. Oh praise the soul's migration. I fall. I get up. I run from you. I look for you. I am again in love with the world.

READING GROUP QUESTIONS AND TOPICS FOR DISCUSSION

"In Any Event" by Dorianne Laux (page 10)
- Does this strike you as a hopeful poem, and if so, why?
- What do you think Laux means when she says, "there is something more to come for humanity," and when she refers to the heart as "an uncharted sea"?
- In the end, the poet implies that the praise she applies to humanity will help lift us all up, in spite of our flaws. How might praise of a difficult situation lead to acceptance and gratitude?
- INVITATION FOR WRITING AND REFLECTION: When was the last time you felt a full faith in the goodness and potential of humanity, when you felt truly grateful to be alive? What brought on this feeling?

"Hoodie" by January Gill O'Neil (page 20)
- Why does this mother thinking of her son "fear for his safety," and what is significant about the image of his hoodie in the poem?
- Consider the final lines, when this mother wonders "who could mistake him / for anything but good." How might these words invite us into a sense of greater compassion?
- What are some of the ways that O'Neil's poem urges us to hold on to the basic assumption of goodness and innocence in others, no matter what they might be wearing, no matter the color of their skin?

- **INVITATION FOR WRITING AND REFLECTION**: Describe an instance when you were able to see past your own anxieties and come into a deeper empathy with others in your world. What allowed you to scale the wall of fear, and how did it feel to move toward the hope on the other side?

"A Cure Against Poisonous Thought" by Annie Lighthart (page 35)

- What is the "cure" that Lighthart presents here as she observes a bee bending inside a honeysuckle blossom?
- How can the simple act of observation, especially in nature, lift us out of our minds?
- What do you make of the last lines of the poem? How is the body "not root but wick," always searching for "the press of light" that she mentions?
- **INVITATION FOR WRITING AND REFLECTION**: Describe a time when a moment spent in the natural world helped pause your thoughts and made you feel more fully alive.

"The Fish" by Jane Hirshfield (page 53)

- In this poem, Hirshfield suggests there is some part of us, fishlike, "that stitches / the inner water / and the outer water together." Do you feel there is some part of us that constantly swims between inner and outer worlds to fulfill our needs?
- What do you feel she means when she says, "we walk the luminous seam"? Must we always tread the line between our mind and life as it is around us?

- Do you agree that there's a "broad world we make daily" in our minds, and one we "daily give ourselves to"? Is she implying that we create the world we live in, to a large degree, yet must still surrender to certain aspects of reality that remain out of our control?
- INVITATION FOR WRITING AND REFLECTION: If we take enough time for ourselves (and for our souls), we can sometimes "flow" between self and world, perhaps even enjoying the back and forth. Think back to a time when you walked "the luminous seam" with more ease and consider what allowed you to do so.

"How It Might Continue" by Rosemerry Wahtola Trommer (page 94)

- What does Trommer mean when she suggests that we can go around with "our pockets full of exclamation marks"? Do you know someone like this, who carries the seeds of delight with them wherever they go, giving them freely?
- Do you find that amazement and joy can be contagious? How might you make it a daily practice to "scatter" and spread that joy to others, even knowing that some of the seeds will not grow?
- How can our own joy bring about change in the world, even if it's not "heard," even if the change is not tangible?
- INVITATION FOR WRITING AND REFLECTION: When was the last time you gave yourself permission to fully feel an instance of joy or amazement? Did this feeling catch on with others and carry over into other areas of your life?

"When Giving Is All We Have" by Alberto Ríos
(page 105)

- In this poem, Ríos implies that we give to one another, whether we directly benefit or not. Why is it important to keep giving, even if we end up wounded or feel that there was no point?
- How can giving be both loud and quiet, big and small? What do you think the poet means when he says that generosity can be like "diamond in wood-nails"?
- Toward the poem's end, Ríos says that when we each give what we have to offer, we all come up with something that is "greater from the difference." How so? Does what he's saying here apply to any current political situations?
- INVITATION FOR WRITING AND REFLECTION: What are some of the many small and large ways that you give to others on a daily basis, loved ones and strangers alike?

"Compost Happens" by Laura Grace Weldon
(page 122)

- Weldon describes how kitchen scraps turn back into roses, birdsong, and eggs. How else does nature remind us that everything changes, and "nothing is lost"?
- What are some of the images that stand out to you in this poem, and why?
- Do you think the poet is urging us to embrace difficult emotions like shame or sorrow? How might they eventually come back to us as wisdom or gratitude?
- INVITATION FOR WRITING AND REFLECTION: What experiences (shame, sorrow, anger, regret) would you "compost"

if you could? You might begin each new sentence with the phrase, "I'd compost" and see where that leads as you practice trusting that no feeling is ever wasted.

"Gratitude List" by Laura Foley (page 126)

- In this poem, Foley seems to be describing a family vacation. How does the repeating phrase "praise be" add to the power of the poem?
- The word "praise" is usually associated with religious contexts. How would you define praise?
- Even though the poem unfolds as a gratitude list, how does Foley bring us more deeply into these moments with her choice of specific images?
- **INVITATION FOR WRITING AND REFLECTION:** Describe a particular time in your own life—a vacation perhaps, or just a lazy Sunday—for which you felt deeply grateful. See if you can recreate all the vivid details from that day, and you might start by using the same phrase, "Praise be," to begin each new sentence.

"Everybody Made Soups" by Lisa Coffman (page 144)

- Many of us make soups throughout winter to bring nourishment and warmth to the long days. What brings gratitude and comfort to you during the winter months or during challenging times in your life?
- Which descriptions of food in the poem particularly stand out to you?

- How does Coffman suggest that the act of making a soup is somehow redeeming, making use of all the leftovers to create that "simmered light"?
- INVITATION FOR WRITING AND REFLECTION: This poem seems reminiscent of the Danish word *hygge* (pronounced "hoo-ga"), which refers to something that offers a quality of coziness, comfort, and well-being. What gives you *hygge* in the depths of winter, or on days when you feel especially dull?

"Eagle Poem" by Joy Harjo (page 151)

- How is Harjo, writing from the perspective of a Native American, inviting us to widen our definition of prayer in this poem?
- What are some of the ways her images tie us to the natural world, and those "circles of motion" of which she implies we are all a part?
- What do you think Harjo means when she urges readers to "open your whole self . . . to one whole voice that is you"? How does this poem-prayer ultimately become an expression of gratitude for the blessing of life?
- INVITATION FOR WRITING AND REFLECTION: Toward the middle of the poem, Harjo describes the eagle she saw one Sunday morning above a river and says the vision "swept our hearts clean / with sacred wings." In conversation or in your journal, describe a similar experience you've had with the natural world, which felt sacred and cleansing to you.

POET BIOGRAPHIES

Lahab Assef Al-Jundi was born and raised in Damascus, Syria. After graduating from the University of Texas in Austin with a degree in electrical engineering, he discovered his passion for writing and published his first poetry collection, *A Long Way*, in 1985. His latest collection is *No Faith at All* (Pecan Grove Press, 2014). He lives in San Antonio.

Ellen Bass is a chancellor of the Academy of American Poets and author, most recently, of *Indigo* (Copper Canyon Press, 2020). Her books include *Like a Beggar* (2014), *The Human Line* (2007), and *Mules of Love* (BOA Editions, 2002), which won the Lambda Literary Award. She coedited (with Florence Howe) the first major anthology of women's poetry, *No More Masks!* (Doubleday, 1973), and founded poetry workshops at the Salinas Valley State Prison and the Santa Cruz jails.

Grace Bauer is the author of five collections of poems, plus several chapbooks. *Unholy Heart: New & Selected Poems* is forthcoming from the University of Nebraska Press/ Backwaters.

George Bilgere's collections include *Blood Pages* (University of Pittsburgh Press, 2018), *Imperial, The White Museum, Haywire, The Good Kiss, Big Bang*, and *The Going*. Bilgere has received the *New Ohio Review* Editor's Choice Poetry Award, the Midland Authors Prize, the May Swenson Poetry Award, a Pushcart Prize, a grant from the National Endowment for the Arts, a Fulbright Fellowship, a Witter Bynner Fellowship, and the Cleveland Arts Prize. His work has appeared in *Poetry, Kenyon Review, Ploughshares, Southern Review, Best American Poetry, Georgia Review, Hopkins Quarterly*, and elsewhere. He teaches at John Carroll University in Cleveland, Ohio.

Dale Biron is a poet, an author, a speaker, and a professor. He has presented and taught classes in many venues, including TEDx Marin, Herbst Theatre, Moveon, and OLLI Dominican University. He served on the Marin Poetry Center board and was past poetry editor for A Network for Grateful Living. He is the author of a book of collected poems, *Why We Do Our Daily Practices* (2014), and his latest prose book is *Poetry for the Leader Inside You: A Search and Rescue Mission for the Heart and Soul* (2018).

Sally Bliumis-Dunn teaches modern poetry at Manhattanville College and the Palm Beach Poetry Festival. Her poems have appeared in *New Ohio Review, On the Seawall, The Paris Review, Prairie Schooner, PLUME, Poetry London, New York Times,* and *upstreet,* and on PBS NewsHour, The Writer's Almanac, Academy of American Poets Poem-a-Day, and American Life in Poetry, among others. Her books include *Talking Underwater* (Wind Publications, 2007), *Second Skin* (2010), *Galapagos Poems* (Kattywompus Press, 2016), and *Echolocation* (Madhat Press, 2018).

Laure-Anne Bosselaar is the author of *The Hour Between Dog and Wolf, Small Gods of Grief,* which won the Isabella Gardner Prize for Poetry, and *A New Hunger,* selected as a Notable Book by the American Library Association. Winner of the 2020 James Dickey Prize for Poetry and the recipient of a Pushcart Prize, she is the editor of four anthologies and a member of the founding faculty at the Solstice MFA in Creative Writing. Her latest collection is *These Many Rooms* (Four Way Books). She is Santa Barbara poet laureate (2019-2021).

Abigail Carroll is the author of *Habitation of Wonder; A Gathering of Larks: Letters to Saint Francis from a Modern-Day Pilgrim*; and *Three*

Squares: The Invention of the American Meal. Carroll's poems have appeared in *Crab Orchard Review, Midwest Quarterly, Sojourners, Terrain,* and the anthology *Between Midnight and Dawn: A Literary Guide to Prayer for Lent, Holy Week, and Eastertide* (Paraclete Press, 2016). She serves as pastor of arts and spiritual formation at Church at the Well in Burlington, Vermont, and enjoys weaving, playing Celtic harp, and walking the pastures behind her farmhouse.

Kristen Case's poetry collections include *Little Arias* (New Issues Press, 2015) and *Principles of Economics* (Switchback Books, 2018), which won the Gatewood Prize. She is the recipient of a MacDowell Fellowship and has twice been awarded the Maine Literary Award in poetry. Case is also the author of numerous scholarly essays and is coeditor of the volumes *Thoreau at 200: Essays and Reassessments* (Cambridge, 2016) and *21|19: Contemporary Poets in the 19th Century Archive* (Milkweed Editions). She teaches American literature at the University of Maine at Farmington.

Judith Chalmer is the author of two collections of poems, *Minnow* (Kelsay Books, 2020) and *Out of History's Junk Jar* (Time Being Books, 1995). She is cotranslator of two books of haiku and tanka with Michiko Oishi: *Red Fish Alphabet* (Honami Syoten, 2008) and *Deepening Snow* (Plowboy Press, 2012). She was director of VSA Vermont, a nonprofit in arts and disability. In 2018 she received the Arthur Williams Award from the Vermont Arts Council for Meritorious Service in the Arts. She lives with her partner, Lisa, in Vermont.

Lucille Clifton (1936–2010) authored many collections of poetry, including *Blessing the Boats: New and Selected Poems 1988-2000* (BOA Editions, 2000), which won the National Book Award; *Good Woman: Poems and a Memoir 1969-1980* (BOA Editions,

1987), which was nominated for the Pulitzer Prize; and *Two-Headed Woman* (University of Massachusetts Press, 1980), also a Pulitzer Prize nominee as well as the recipient of the University of Massachusetts Press Juniper Prize. Her honors include an Emmy Award from the American Academy of Television Arts and Sciences, a Lannan Literary Award, two fellowships from the National Endowment for the Arts, and the 2007 Ruth Lilly Prize.

Lisa Coffman's work has been featured on The Writer's Almanac and BBC News, in the *Oxford American*, *Village Voice*, *Philadelphia Inquirer*, and elsewhere. She is the author of *Likely* and *Less Obvious Gods* and has been awarded the Stan and Tom Wick Poetry Prize from Kent State University Press and fellowships from the National Endowment for the Arts, Pew Charitable Trusts, and Bucknell University's Stadler Center for Poetry. She collaborated with composer Timothy Melbinger on the six-poem cycle *Hymns to Less Obvious Gods*, which premiered in spring 2019.

James Crews is the author of four collections of poetry: *The Book of What Stays, Telling My Father, Bluebird,* and *Every Waking Moment*. He is also the editor of the anthology *Healing the Divide: Poems of Kindness and Connection.* He lives with his husband in Shaftsbury, Vermont, and teaches creative writing privately and at the University at Albany. jamescrews.net

Barbara Crooker is a poetry editor for *Italian-Americana*, and the author of nine books of poetry; *Some Glad Morning* (University of Pittsburgh Press, 2019) is the latest. Her awards include the W. B. Yeats Society of New York Award, Thomas Merton Poetry of the Sacred Award, and three Pennsylvania Council on the Arts Creative Writing Fellowships. Her work appears in literary journals and anthologies, including *The Valparaiso Poetry Review, The Chariton Poetry Review, Green Mountains Review,*

Tar River Poetry Review, The Beloit Poetry Journal, The Denver Quarterly, Smartish Pace, Gargoyle, The American Poetry Journal, Dogwood, Passages North, Nimrod, The Bedford Introduction to Literature, Nasty Women: An Unapologetic Anthology of Subversive Verse, and has been read on ABC, the BBC, The Writer's Almanac, and featured in American Life in Poetry.

Noah Davis grew up in Tipton, Pennsylvania, and writes about the Allegheny Front. Davis's manuscript *Of This River* was selected by George Ella Lyon for the 2019 Wheelbarrow Emerging Poet Book Prize from Michigan State University's Center for Poetry. His poems and prose have appeared in *The SUN, Best New Poets, Orion, North American Review, River Teeth, Sou'wester*, and *Chautauqua*, among others. He was awarded a Katharine Bakeless Nason Fellowship at the Bread Loaf Writers' Conference, and the 2018 Jean Ritchie Appalachian Literature Fellowship from Lincoln Memorial University. Davis earned an MFA from Indiana University and now lives with his wife, Nikea, in Missoula, Montana.

Todd Davis is the author of six collections of poetry, most recently *Native Species, Winterkill,* and *In the Kingdom of the Ditch*, all published by Michigan State University Press. He has won Foreword INDIES Book of the Year bronze and silver awards, the Gwendolyn Brooks Poetry Prize, the Chautauqua Editors Prize, and the Bloomsburg University Book Prize. His poems have appeared in *Alaska Quarterly Review, American Poetry Review, Gettysburg Review, Iowa Review, Missouri Review, North American Review, Orion*, and *Poetry Northwest*. He teaches environmental studies, American literature, and creative writing at Pennsylvania State University's Altoona College.

Amy Dryansky has published two poetry collections; *Grass Whistle* (Salmon Poetry) received the Massachusetts Book Award, and *How I Got Lost So Close to Home* won the New England/New York Award from Alice James. Her work is included in several anthologies and in *Barrow Street, Harvard Review, New England Review, Memorious, Orion, The SUN, Tin House*, and other journals. She's received honors from the Massachusetts Cultural Council, MacDowell Colony, and the Bread Loaf Writers' Conference, and is the former poet laureate of Northampton, Massachusetts. She directs the Culture, Brain, and Development Program at Hampshire College and parents two children. amydryansky.com

Jehanne Dubrow is the author of nine poetry collections, including *Wild Kingdom* (Louisiana State University Press, 2021) and *Simple Machines*, winner of the Richard Wilbur Poetry Award, and a book of creative nonfiction, *throughsmoke: an essay in notes*. Her work has appeared in *Poetry, New England Review*, and *The Southern Review*. She is professor of creative writing at the University of North Texas.

Terri Kirby Erickson is the author of six collections, including *Becoming the Blue Heron* (Press 53) and *A Sun Inside My Chest*. Her work has appeared in American Life in Poetry, *Asheville Poetry Review, Atlanta Review, Healing the Divide: Poems of Kindness and Connection, Connotation Press, JAMA, Latin American Literary Review, Plainsongs, Poetry Foundation, Poet's Market, storySouth, The Christian Century, The SUN, Valparaiso Poetry Review, Verse Daily*, and many others. Her awards include the Joy Harjo Poetry Prize, the Atlanta Review International Publication Prize, the Nazim Hikmet Poetry Award, and a Nautilus Silver Book Award. She lives in North Carolina.

Cathryn Essinger is the author of four books of poetry, including *The Apricot and the Moon* (Dos Madres Press, 2020). A

chapbook titled *Wings*, about raising monarch butterflies, is forthcoming. Her poems have appeared in *Poetry, River Styx,* and *PANK* and have been featured on The Writer's Almanac and in American Life in Poetry. She lives in Troy, Ohio, where she raises monarch butterflies and tries to live up to her dog's expectations.
cathrynessinger.com

Patricia Fargnoli was born in Hartford, Connecticut. A retired psychotherapist, she began studying poetry in her mid-thirties. Her first book, *Necessary Light* (Utah State University Press, 1999), was published when she was 62. Fargnoli served as New Hampshire poet laureate from 2006 to 2009 and was associate editor of the *Worcester Review*. Awards include an honorary BFA from the New Hampshire Institute of Arts and a MacDowell fellowship. She resides in Walpole, New Hampshire.

Farnaz Fatemi is an Iranian American writer and editor in Santa Cruz, California. She is a member and cofounder of the Hive Poetry Collective (hivepoetry.org). Her poetry and prose appear in *SWWIM Daily, Grist Journal, Catamaran Literary Reader, Crab Orchard Review, Tahoma Literary Review, Tupelo Quarterly*, and several anthologies, including *My Shadow Is My Skin: Voices from the Iranian Diaspora* and *The BreakBeat Poets Vol. 3: Halal If You Hear Me*. She taught writing at the University of California, Santa Cruz, from 1997–2018. farnazfatemi.com

Molly Fisk, as an Academy of American Poets Laureate Fellow, recently edited *California Fire and Water: A Climate Crisis Anthology*. She's the author of *The More Difficult Beauty, Listening to Winter*, and *Houston, We Have a Possum* among other books, and has won grants from the National Endowment for the Arts, the California Arts Council, and the Corporation for Public Broadcasting. Fisk lives in the Sierra foothills, where she teaches writing to cancer patients, provides weekly commentary to community radio, and works as a radical life coach. patreon.com/mollyfisk

Laura Foley is the author of seven poetry collections, including *Why I Never Finished My Dissertation*, which won an Eric Hoffer Award, and *It's This* (Salmon Press, 2021). Her poems have been read on The Writer's Almanac and appear in American Life in Poetry. She lives with her wife, Clara Gimenez, among the hills of Vermont. laurafoley.net

Patricia Fontaine teaches classes using expressive art and writing as a refuge for those living with illness, and their caregivers. Her self-published book of poems is *Lifting My Shirt: The Cancer Poems*. She lives on a big lake in northwestern Vermont with birds, wind, and a grand collection of friends and family.

Sarah Freligh is the author of *Sad Math*, winner of the 2014 Moon City Press Poetry Prize and the 2015 Whirling Prize from the University of Indianapolis; *A Brief Natural History of an American Girl* (Accents Publishing, 2012); and *Sort of Gone* (Turning Point Books, 2008). Her work has appeared in the *Cincinnati Review*, *SmokeLong Quarterly*, *Diode*, and in the anthologies *New Microfiction* and *Best Microfiction* 2019 and 2020. She received a 2009 poetry fellowship from the National Endowment for the Arts and a grant from the Constance Saltonstall Foundation in 2006.

Albert Garcia is the author of three collections of poetry: *Rainshadow* (Copper Beech Press, 1996), *Skunk Talk* (Bear Starr Press, 2005), and *A Meal Like That* (Brick Road Poetry Press, 2015). His poetry has been published in American Life in Poetry and on The Writer's Almanac, as well as in numerous journals. A former professor and dean at Sacramento Community

College, Garcia lives in Wilton, California.

Ross Gay is the author of four books of poetry: *Against Which; Bringing the Shovel Down; Catalog of Unabashed Gratitude*, winner of the 2015 National Book Critics Circle Award and the 2016 Kingsley Tufts Poetry Award; and *Be Holding* (University of Pittsburgh Press, 2020). His best-selling collection of essays, *The Book of Delights*, was released by Algonquin Books in 2019.

Crystal S. Gibbins is a Canadian American writer, the founder of *Split Rock Review*, the editor of *Rewilding: Poems for the Environment* (Flexible Press), and the author of *Now/Here* (Holy Cow! Press). Her poetry and comics have appeared in *Cincinnati Review, Coffee House Writers Project, Hayden's Ferry Review, Hobart, North American Review, Minnesota Review, Verse Daily,* The Writer's Almanac, and elsewhere. Originally from the Northwest Angle and Islands in Lake of the Woods, she now lives on Lake Superior in northern Wisconsin. crystalgibbins.com

Jessica Gigot is a poet, farmer, teacher, and musician. She is the author of *Flood Patterns* (Antrim House Books, 2015) and *Feeding Hour* (Wandering Aengus Press, 2020). Her work has appeared in *Orion, Taproot, Gastronomica, The Hopper, Mothers Always Write*, and *Poetry Northwest*. She makes artisan sheep cheese and grows organic herbs on her farm in Bow, Washington.

Alice Wolf Gilborn is the founding editor of the literary magazine *Blueline*, published by the English department at SUNY Potsdam. Her poems have appeared in *Healing the Divide* (Green Writers Press) and *After Moby-Dick* (Spinner Publications). She is the author of *Apples and Stones* (Kelsay Books, 2020); the chapbook *Taking Root* (Finishing Line Press); the nonfiction book *What Do You Do With a Kinkajou?* (Lippincott); and an essay collection, *Out of the Blue*. alicewolfgilborn.com

Nancy Miller Gomez lives in Santa Cruz, California. She cofounded Poetry in the Jails, a program that provides poetry workshops to incarcerated men and women. Her work has appeared in *New Ohio Review, The Massachusetts Review, Shenandoah, River Styx, Rattle, Verse Daily*, American Life in Poetry, and elsewhere. Her first chapbook, *Punishment*, was published by Rattle Books. She has worked as a stable hand, an attorney, and a television producer.

Amanda Gorman is the first Youth Poet Laureate of the United States. Her first poetry book is *The One for Whom Food Is Not Enough* (Penmanship Books, 2015). She is founder and executive director of One Pen One Page, which promotes literacy through free creative writing programming for underserved youth. She writes for the *New York Times*'s student newsletter, The Edit.

David Graham is the author of seven collections of poetry, including *The Honey of Earth* (Terrapin Books, 2019), *Stutter Monk* (Flume Press), and *Second Wind* (Texas Tech University Press). He coedited the anthologies *Local News: Poetry About Small Towns* (MWPH Books, 2019) and *After Confession: Poetry as Confession* (Graywolf Press, 2001). He was a faculty member at The Frost Place in Franconia, New Hampshire, where he also served as poet in residence in 1996. He taught and directed the visiting writers series at Ripon College for 28 years. He is a contributing editor and writer at Verse-Virtual, and lives in Glens Falls, New York.
davidgrahampoet.com

Joy Harjo was born in Tulsa, Oklahoma, and is a member of the Mvskoke Nation. Her books of poetry include *How We Became Human: New and Selected Poems, The Woman Who Fell From the Sky,* and *She Had Some Horses*. She has received the New Mexico Governor's Award for Excellence in the Arts, a Lifetime Achievement Award from the Native Writers Circle of the Americas, and the William Carlos Williams Award from the Poetry Society of America. Harjo served as United States poet laureate from 2019–2021, and was the first Native American to serve in the position.

Jeffrey Harrison is the author of five books of poetry: *The Singing Underneath* (1988), selected by James Merrill for the National Poetry Series; *Signs of Arrival* (1996); *Feeding the Fire* (2001); *Incomplete Knowledge* (2006); and *Into Daylight* (2014), winner of Tupelo Press's Dorset Prize. A recipient of fellowships from the Guggenheim Foundation and National Endowment for the Arts, he has published poems in *The New Republic, The New Yorker, The Nation, Poetry, The Yale Review, The Hudson Review, American Poetry Review, The Paris Review, Poets of the New Century, The Twentieth Century in Poetry*, and elsewhere. He lives in Massachusetts.

Penny Harter's poems have appeared in *Persimmon Tree, Rattle, Tiferet,* American Life in Poetry, and the anthologies *Healing the Divide* and *Poetry of Presence*. She has published 22 collections, including *A Prayer the Body Makes* (2020), *The Resonance Around Us* (2013), *One Bowl* (2012), *Recycling Starlight* (2010), and *The Night Marsh* (2008). A featured reader at the 2010 Geraldine R. Dodge Poetry Festival, she has been awarded poetry fellowships from the New Jersey State Council on the Arts; received the Mary Carolyn Davies Award from the Poetry Society of America and the William O. Douglas Nature Writing Award for her work in the anthology *American Nature Writing* 2002; and held two residencies at the Virginia Center for the Creative Arts. pennyharterpoet.com

Margaret Hasse is the author of five books of poems: *Stars*

Above, Stars Below (1985); *In a Sheep's Eye, Darling* (1993); *Milk and Tides* (2008); *Earth's Appetite* (2013); and *Between Us* (2016). She is a recipient of grants and fellowships from the National Endowment for the Arts, McKnight Foundation, Loft Literary Center's Career Initiative Program, Minnesota State Arts Board, and Jerome Foundation. Her work has been published in magazines, broadsides, and anthologies, including *Where One Voice Ends, Another Begins: 150 Years of Minnesota Poetry* and *To Sing Along the Way: Minnesota Women's Voices from Pre-Territorial Day to the Present*, and on The Writer's Almanac. She lives in Minnesota.

Jane Hirshfield's ninth and most recently published collection is *Ledger* (Knopf, 2020). A former chancellor of the Academy of American Poets, her work appears in *The New Yorker, The Atlantic, The Times Literary Supplement, The New York Review of Books*, and ten editions of *The Best American Poetry*. In 2019, she was elected into the American Academy of Arts and Sciences.

Tony Hoagland (1953–2018) was born in Fort Bragg, North Carolina. He is author of the poetry collections *Sweet Ruin* (1992), which was chosen for the Brittingham Prize in Poetry and won the Zacharis Award from Emerson College; *Donkey Gospel* (1998), winner of the James Laughlin Award; *What Narcissism Means to Me* (2003); *Rain* (2005); *Unincorporated Persons in the Late Honda Dynasty* (2010); *Application for Release from the Dream* (2015); *Recent Changes in the Vernacular* (2017); and *Priest Turned Therapist Treats Fear of God* (2018). He also published two collections of essays about poetry: *Real Sofistakashun* (2006) and *Twenty Poems That Could Save America and Other Essays* (2014).

Linda Hogan is the author of several poetry collections, including *Dark. Sweet.: New &*

Selected Poems (Coffee House Press, 2014); *Rounding the Human Corners* (2008); *The Book of Medicines* (1993), which received the Colorado Book Award; and *Seeing Through the Sun* (University of Massachusetts Press, 1985). She is writer in residence for the Chickasaw Nation and was inducted into the Chickasaw Hall of Fame. She has received fellowships from the National Endowment for the Arts and the Guggenheim Foundation, and won the Henry David Thoreau Prize for Nature Writing, a Lannan Literary Award, and a Lifetime Achievement Award from the Native Writers Circle of the Americas. She lives in Colorado.

Kathryn Hunt makes her home on the coast of the Salish Sea. Her poems have appeared in *The SUN, Rattle, Radar, Orion, Missouri Review, Frontier Poetry*, and *Narrative*. Her first collection of poems is *Long Way Through Ruin* (Blue Begonia Press). She's the recipient of residencies and awards from Ucross, Artists Trust, and Joya AIR (Spain). Her documentary film *No Place Like Home* premiered at the Venice Film Festival. Hunt is working on a memoir, *Why I Grieve I Do Not Know*. She's worked as a waitress, ship scaler, short-order cook, bookseller, printer, food bank coordinator, filmmaker, and freelance writer. kathrynhunt.net

Rob Hunter's collection of poems is *September Swim* (Spoon River Poetry Press). His poems have appeared in *Poet Lore, The Oddville Press, The Timberline Review, Sleet, Wild Violet, Straight Forward Poetry, The Blueline Anthology, Foliate Oak, Rat's Ass Review, Gray Sparrow Review*, Sheila-Na-Gig online, and others. He teaches at Burr and Burton Academy in Manchester, Vermont.

Mary Elder Jacobsen's poetry has appeared in *The Greensboro Review, Four Way Review, Green Mountains Review, storySouth, One*, and

Poetry Daily and in anthologies, including *Healing the Divide: Poems of Kindness and Connection*. Born in Washington, D.C., Jacobsen now lives in Vermont. Winner of the Lyric Memorial Prize and recipient of a Vermont Studio Center residency, she is coorganizer of Words Out Loud, an annual reading series of Vermont authors held at a still-unplugged 1823 meetinghouse.

Jacqueline Jules is the author of three chapbooks, including *Itzhak Perlman's Broken String*, winner of the 2016 Helen Kay Chapbook Prize from Evening Street Press. Her poetry has appeared in publications including *The Paterson Literary Review, Potomac Review,* and *Imitation Fruit.* She is the author of a poetry collection for young readers, *Tag Your Dreams: Poems of Play and Persistence* (Albert Whitman, 2020). She lives in Arlington, Virginia. metaphoricaltruths.blogspot.com

Garret Keizer is the author of *The World Pushes Back*, which won the 2018 X. J. Kennedy Poetry Prize, as well as eight books of prose, including *Getting Schooled* (2014), *Privacy* (2012), and *The Unwanted Sound of Everything We Want* (2010). He is a contributing editor at *Harper's* and *Virginia Quarterly Review* and a 2006 Guggenheim fellow. His poems have been published in *AGNI, The Antioch Review, Best American Poetry, Harvard Review, The Hudson Review, Ploughshares, Raritan,* and *The New Yorker*, among others. He was born in Paterson, New Jersey, and lives in Vermont with his wife.

Susan Kelly-DeWitt is a former Wallace Stegner Fellow and the author of *Gravitational Tug* (Main Street Rag, 2020), *Spider Season* (Cold River Press, 2016), *The Fortunate Islands* (Marick Press, 2008), and nine other collections. She has been a reviewer for *Library Journal*, editor in chief of the online journal Perihelion, the program director of the Sacramento Poetry Center and the Women's Wisdom Arts Program, a Poet in the Schools, a Poet in the Prisons, a blogger for Coal Hill Review, and an instructor at UC Davis. She is a member of the National Book Critics Circle and the Northern California Book Reviewers Association, and a contributing editor for Poetry Flash. She is also an exhibiting visual artist. susankelly-dewitt.com

Jane Kenyon (1947–1995) was an American poet and translator. Kenyon met the poet Donald Hall at the University of Michigan; they married in 1972 and moved to Eagle Pond Farm, Hall's ancestral home in New Hampshire. Kenyon was the poet laureate of New Hampshire when she died in April 1995 from leukemia. At the time of her death, she was working on the now-classic *Otherwise: New and Selected Poems*, which was released posthumously in 1996.

Lynne Knight is the author of six poetry collections and six chapbooks. Her work has appeared in journals, including *Poetry* and *Southern Review*. Her awards and honors include publication in *Best American Poetry*, a Prix de l'Alliance Française, a PSA Lucille Medwick Memorial Award, a Rattle Poetry Prize, and a National Endowment for the Arts grant. *I Know (Je sais)*, her translation with the author Ito Naga of his *Je sais*, appeared in 2013. She lives on Vancouver Island.

Ted Kooser, a former US poet laureate and winner of the Pulitzer Prize, has recently retired from teaching poetry in the creative writing program at the University of Nebraska in Lincoln and is now mowing grass and trying to start a weed whacker. His most recent book of poems is *Red Stilts* (Copper Canyon Press, 2020).

Danusha Laméris is the author of *The Moons of August* (Autumn House, 2014), which was chosen by Naomi Shihab Nye as winner of the Autumn House Press poetry prize. Her poems have been published in *Best American Poetry, The New York Times, American Poetry Review, Prairie Schooner, The SUN, Tin House, Gettysburg Review,* and *Ploughshares*. Her second book is *Bonfire Opera* (University of Pittsburgh Press) and she is the 2020 recipient of the Lucille Clifton Legacy Award. She is poet laureate of Santa Cruz County, California.

Heather Lanier is the author of two poetry chapbooks and the memoir *Raising a Rare Girl* (Penguin Press, 2020). Her essays and poems have appeared in *The Atlantic, The SUN, Brevity, Salon, The Southern Review, Threepenny Review,* and elsewhere. She is assistant professor of creative writing at Rowan University, and her TED talk, "Good and Bad Are Incomplete Stories We Tell Ourselves," has been viewed more than two million times.

Dorianne Laux is the author of several collections of poetry, including *What We Carry* (1994); *Smoke* (2000); *Facts about the Moon* (2005), chosen by the poet Ai as winner of the Oregon Book Award; *The Book of Men* (2011), which was awarded the Paterson Prize; and *Only As the Day Is Long: New and Selected Poems* (2018). She has received fellowships from the Guggenheim Foundation and the National Endowment for the Arts and has been a Pushcart Prize winner. She lives with her husband, poet Joseph Millar, in North Carolina.

Li-Young Lee was born in Djakarta in 1957 to Chinese political exiles. Lee's parents came from powerful Chinese families; Lee's great grandfather was the first president of the Republic of China and Lee's father served as personal physician to Mao Zedong. Lee is the author of *The Undressing* (W. W. Norton, 2018); *Behind My Eyes* (2008); *Book of My Nights* (BOA Editions, 2001), which won the 2002 William Carlos Williams Award; *The City in Which I Love You* (1990), the 1990 Lamont Poetry Selection; and *Rose*

(1986), winner of the Delmore Schwartz Memorial Poetry Award. He lives in Chicago with his wife and sons.

Paula Gordon Lepp grew up in a tiny rural community in the Mississippi Delta. A childhood spent roaming woods and fields infuses her poems with imagery from the natural world. As an adult, her lifelong love of poetry has renewed itself, proving the axiom that it's never too late to do what you love. She now lives with her husband and two children in Charleston, West Virginia, where she is working on a collection of poetry. This is her first published work.

Annie Lighthart is a poet and teacher who started writing poetry after her first visit to an Oregon old-growth forest. She is the author of *Pax* (Salmon Poetry, 2020), *Iron String*, and *Lantern*. Her poems have been featured on The Writer's Almanac and in anthologies, including *Poetry of Presence: An Anthology of Mindfulness Poems* and *Healing the Divide*. Her poems have also been turned into choral music, used in healing projects in Ireland, England, and New Zealand, and have traveled farther than she has.

Alison Luterman's four books of poetry are *The Largest Possible Life; See How We Almost Fly; Desire Zoo*; and *In a Time of Great Fires* (Catamaran Press, 2021). Her poems and stories have appeared in *The SUN, Rattle, Salon, Prairie Schooner, Nimrod, The Atlanta Review, Tattoo Highway*, and elsewhere. She has written an ebook of personal essays, *Feral City;* half a dozen plays; and a song cycle, *We Are Not Afraid of the Dark*; as well as two musicals, *The Chain* and *The Shyest Witch*.

Freya Manfred, a longtime Midwesterner who has lived on both coasts, is the author of two memoirs: *Frederick Manfred: A Daughter Remembers* and *Raising Twins: A True-Life Adventure*. Her nine books of poetry include *My Only Home; Swimming with a Hundred-Year-Old Snapping Turtle; Loon in Late November Water;* and *Speak, Mother*. Her poems have appeared in more than 50 anthologies. Her work celebrates the vital lifeline of nature, our fragile mortality, humor, and the passionate arc of long-term relationships. freyamanfredwriter.com

Joan Mazza worked as a microbiologist, a psychotherapist, and, before retiring, taught workshops nationally with a focus on understanding dreams and nightmares. She is the author of six books, including *Dreaming Your Real Self* (Penguin/Putnam), and her poetry has appeared in *Rattle, Valparaiso Poetry Review, Prairie Schooner, Poet Lore, The MacGuffin*, and *The Nation*. She lives in rural central Virginia, where she writes a daily poem. JoanMazza.com

Mary McCue is the author of the chapbook *Raising the Blinds* (Finishing Line Press, 2013). Her poems have appeared in *Southern Review of Poetry, Midwest Poetry Review, Streetlight Magazine, River Oak Review*, and her essays have been published in *Tampa Review, Albemarle Magazine, Chesapeake Bay*, and *Common Boundary*. A former violinist, she lives on eight acres in Albemarle County, Virginia, where deer roam and birds are safe and revered.

Michael Kiesow Moore is the author of the poetry collections *What to Pray For* and *The Song Castle* (Nodin Press). His work has appeared in *Poetry City* and *Water~Stone Review*; the anthologies *Lovejets: Queer Male Poets on 200 Years of Walt Whitman; Among the Leaves: Queer Male Poets on the Midwestern Experience;* and *A Loving Testimony: Losing Loved Ones Lost to AIDS*; and on The Writer's Almanac. He founded the Birchbark Books reading series. When he isn't drinking too much coffee, he can be found in Saint Paul, Minnesota, dancing with the Ramsey's Braggarts Morris Men.

Julie Murphy lives in Santa Cruz, California, surrounded by redwood, pine, and live oak trees. She belongs to the Community of Writers in Squaw Valley, teaches poetry at Salinas Valley State Prison, and is a founding board member of the Right to Write Press. A member of the Hive Poetry Collective, she hosts the Hive radio broadcast on KSQD. Her poems have appeared in *Massachusetts Review, CALYX, Common Ground Review, Red Wheelbarrow, Louisville Review,* and *The Alembic,* among others. She believes there is little better in life than being laid low by a good poem.

Mark Nepo is the author of the #1 *New York Times* bestseller *The Book of Awakening*. He has published 22 books and recorded 14 audio projects. Recent work includes *The Book of Soul* (St. Martin's, 2020) and *Drinking from the River of Light* (Sounds True, 2019), a Nautilus Award winner. marknepo.com and threeintentions.com

Gail Newman was born to survivors of the Polish Holocaust in a displaced persons' camp in Lansberg, Germany. She is the author of *Blood Memory*, chosen by Marge Piercy for the Marsh Hawk Press 2020 Poetry Prize, and *One World* (Moon Tide Press). She has worked as a teacher for CalPoets and as a museum educator at the Contemporary Jewish Museum in San Francisco. Her poems have appeared in *CALYX, Canary, Nimrod, Prairie Schooner,* and *Spillway*; in the anthologies *The Doll Collection* and *Ghosts of the Holocaust*; and in *America, We Call Your Name.* She is the cofounder of *Room, A Women's Literary Journal* and has edited two children's poetry collections: *C is for California* and *Dear Earth.*

Heather Newman's work has appeared in *Barrow Street, Inquisitive Eater, Matter, New Verse News, Two Hawks Quarterly, The Potomac,* and the anthology *Voices from Here.* She is a member of the South Mountain Poets and teaches at The Writers Circle in New Jersey.

Naomi Shihab Nye calls herself a "wandering poet." She has spent 40 years traveling the world to lead writing workshops and inspire students of all ages. Nye was born to a Palestinian father and an American mother and grew up in Saint Louis, Jerusalem, and San Antonio. Her books of poetry include *19 Varieties of Gazelle: Poems of the Middle East*; *A Maze Me: Poems for Girls*; *Red Suitcase*; *Words Under the Words*; *Fuel*; *You & Yours* (a bestseller in 2006); and *The Tiny Journalist* (BOA Editions, 2019).

January Gill O'Neil is author of *Rewilding* (2018), *Misery Islands* (2014), and *Underlife* (CavanKerry Press, 2009). She is assistant professor of English at Salem State University, and is on the board of trustees for the Association of Writers and Writing Programs and Montserrat College of Art. She served as executive director of the Massachusetts Poetry Festival from 2012 to 2018. A Cave Canem fellow, her work has appeared in the *New York Times Magazine*, *American Poetry Review*, *New England Review*, *Ploughshares*, *Ecotone*, and the Academy of American Poets Poem-a-Day series, among others. She was awarded a Massachusetts Cultural Council grant in 2018, and was named the John and Renée Grisham Writer in Residence for 2019–2020 at the University of Mississippi, Oxford. She lives with her two children in Beverly, Massachusetts.

Christen Pagett is most at home in Oregon's Willamette Valley, where she is an educator hoping to inspire teens with her love of language and all the worlds it can open. She currently spends her days pursuing an MFA in poetry at Eastern Oregon University, practicing piano, and trying new recipes on her family.

Brad Peacock is a veteran, longtime organic farmer, and former United States Senate candidate from Shaftsbury, Vermont, whose passion is to bring people closer to one another and the natural world.

Andrea Potos is the author of the poetry collections *Mothershell* (Kelsay Books), *A Stone to Carry Home* (Salmon Poetry), *Arrows of Light* (Iris Press), and *Marrow of Summer* (Kelsay Books/Aldrich Press). Her poems can be found online and in print, most recently in *Spirituality & Health*, *Poetry East*, *Cave Wall*, and *The SUN*. She received the James Hearst Poetry Prize from the *North American Review* and the William Stafford Prize from *Rosebud Magazine*, and several Outstanding Achievement Awards in Poetry from the Wisconsin Library Association. Travelling, art, cafes, and family are her greatest sources of inspiration. She lives in Madison, Wisconsin.

Laura Ann Reed grew up in the hills of Berkeley, California. She holds master's degrees in performing arts, psychology, and career counseling. She has worked as a dancer and dance instructor in the San Francisco Bay Area, and she created and worked in the role of Leadership Development Trainer for scientists and directors at the San Francisco headquarters of the US Environmental Protection Agency. She now lives with her husband in Washington State.

Jack Ridl is poet laureate of Douglas, Michigan, and the author of *Saint Peter and the Goldfinch* (Wayne State University Press); *Practicing to Walk Like a Heron*, winner of the National Gold Medal for poetry by *ForeWord Reviews/Indie Fab*; *Broken Symmetry*, the 2006 Society of Midland Authors best book of poetry; and *Losing Season* (CavanKerry Press), named best sports book of 2009 by the Institute for International Sport. The students at Hope College named him their Outstanding Professor and Favorite Professor, and the Carnegie Foundation (CASE) named him Michigan professor of the year in 1996. ridl.com

Alberto Ríos was named Arizona's first poet laureate in 2013. He is the author of many poetry collections, including *A Small Story About the Sky* (Copper Canyon, 2015), *The Dangerous Shirt* (2009), *The Theater of Night* (2006), and *The Smallest Muscle in the Human Body* (2002), which was nominated for the National Book Award.

David Romtvedt is a writer and musician from Buffalo, Wyoming. His books include *No Way: An American Tao Te Ching*, *Dilemmas of the Angels*, *Some Church*, *Zelestina Urza in Outer Space*, and *The Tree of Gernika*. *A Flower Whose Name I Do Not Know* was a selection of the National Poetry Series. A recipient of the Pushcart Prize and fellowships from the Wyoming Arts Council and the National Endowment for the Arts, Romtvedt is an avid bicyclist. With the band Ospa, he performs traditional and contemporary Basque dance music.

Katie Rubinstein is director of Seven Sisters Community Birth Center, where she has the privilege of serving women and families as a doula and apprentice midwife, and former associate director of A Network for Grateful Living. Fascinated by the many intersections of ecology, health, culture, and social change, she lives in Massachusetts with her husband, three sons, and ever-goofy canine companion, Rainer.

Marjorie Saiser's seventh collection, *Learning to Swim* (Stephen F. Austin Press, 2019), contains both poetry and memoir. Her novel-in-poems, *Losing the Ring in the River* (University of New Mexico Press) won the WILLA Award for Poetry in 2014. Saiser's poems have been published in *Rattle, Poetry East, Nimrod, Fourth River, Alaska Quarterly Review, Poet Lore, Briar Cliff Review, Chattahoochee Review*, and American Life in Poetry. poetmarge.com

Tracy K. Smith is author of the memoir *Ordinary Light* and four books of poetry: *Wade in the Water* (2018); *Life on Mars*, which received the 2012 Pulitzer Prize; *Duende*, recipient of the 2006 James Laughlin Award; and *The Body's Question*, which won the 2002 Cave Canem Poetry Prize. She served as the 22nd US poet laureate, 2017–2019. Smith hosts the popular podcast *The Slowdown*.

Nathan Spoon is an autistic poet whose poems have appeared in *American Poetry Review, Harvard Divinity Bulletin, Mantis, Oxford Poetry, Poetry, Reflections* (Yale Divinity School), *The Scores, South Carolina Review, Western Humanities Review*, and the anthology *What Have You Lost?*. His debut collection, *Doomsday Bunker*, and a chapbook, *My Name Is Gretchen Merryweather*, were both published in 2017. He is editor of Queerly, has been a Tennessee Williams Scholar at the Sewanee Writers' Conference, and has presented papers on poetry and neurodiversity at the University of Pennsylvania and the Association of Literary Scholars, Critics, and Writers conference.

Kim Stafford is the founding director of the Northwest Writing Institute at Lewis & Clark College. He is the author of a dozen books of poetry and prose, including *Singer Come from Afar; The Muses Among Us: Eloquent Listening and Other Pleasures of the Writer's Craft; A Thousand Friends of Rain: New & Selected Poems; 100 Tricks Every Boy Can Do: How My Brother Disappeared; Wind on the Waves: Stories from the Oregon Coast; Having Everything Right: Essays of Place;* and *Wild Honey, Tough Salt*. He was poet laureate of Oregon, 2018–2020. He teaches and travels to raise the human spirit.

William Stafford's (1914–1993) first collection of poems, *West of Your City*, was published when he was in his mid-forties. However, by the time of his death in 1993, Stafford had published hundreds of poems. His collection *Traveling Through the Dark* won the National Book Award in 1963. Stafford also received the Award in Literature from the American Academy and Institute of Arts and Letters, a National Endowment for the Arts Senior Fellowship, and the Western States Book Award Lifetime Achievement in Poetry.

Joyce Sutphen grew up on a small farm in Stearns County, Minnesota. Her first collection of poems, *Straight Out of View*, won the Barnard New Women Poets Prize. Her recent books are *The Green House* (Salmon Poetry, 2017) and *Carrying Water to the Field: New and Selected Poems* (University of Nebraska Press, 2019). She is Minnesota poet laureate and professor emerita of literature and creative writing at Gustavus Adolphus College in Saint Peter, Minnesota.

Heather Swan is the author of *A Kinship with Ash* (Terrapin Books); the chapbook *The Edge of Damage* (Parallel Press); and the nonfiction book *Where Honeybees Thrive: Stories from the Field* (Penn State Press), which won the Sigurd F. Olson Nature Writing Award. Her poems have appeared in *Poet Lore, Cold Mountain, Phoebe, Iris, Midwestern Gothic, The Hopper,* and *Basalt*. Her nonfiction has appeared in *Aeon, Minding Nature, ISLE, Belt Magazine*, and *Edge Effects*. She teaches environmental literature and writing at University of Wisconsin–Madison.

Wally Swist's books include *Huang Po and the Dimensions of Love* (Southern Illinois University Press, 2012); *The Daodejing: A New Interpretation* (Lamar University Literary Press, 2015); and *Invocation* (2015). His poems have appeared in *Appalachia, Commonweal, Miramar, North American Review, Rattle, Sunken Garden Poetry, upstreet,* and on The Writer's Almanac. Swist lives in South Amherst, Massachusetts.

Tess Taylor is the author of *Rift Zone* (Red Hen Press); *The Forage House*; *Work & Days*, named one of the best books of poetry in 2016 by the *New York Times*; and *The Misremembered World*, selected by Eavan Boland for the Poetry Society of America's inaugural chapbook fellowship. She published *Last West* (2020) as part of the exhibition *Dorothea Lange: Words & Pictures* at the Museum of Modern Art in New York. She is a poetry reviewer for NPR's All Things Considered.

Francine Marie Tolf is the author of *Rain, Lilies, Luck* (North Star Press, 2010) as well as a memoir, essay collection, and a number of chapbooks. Her poems and essays have been published in numerous journals. She lives and works in Minneapolis.

Angela Narciso Torres is the author of *Blood Orange*, winner of the Willow Books Literature Award for Poetry; *To the Bone* (Sundress, 2020); and *What Happens Is Neither* (Four Way Books, 2021). Her work has appeared in *Poetry, Missouri Review, Quarterly West, Cortland Review*, and *PANK*. Torres received the 2019 Yeats Poetry Prize (W. B. Yeats Society of New York), and has received fellowships from the Bread Loaf Writers' Conference, Illinois Arts Council, and Ragdale Foundation. Born in Brooklyn and raised in Manila, she is an editor for *RHINO Poetry*.

Rosemerry Wahtola Trommer lives on the banks of the San Miguel River in southwest Colorado. She served as Colorado Western Slope poet laureate (2015–2017) and San Miguel County poet laureate (2007–2011). She cohosts *Emerging Form* (a podcast on creative process), is cofounder of Secret Agents of Change, and codirects Telluride's Talking Gourds Poetry Club. Her poetry has appeared in *O Magazine* and *Rattle*, on A Prairie Home Companion, and on river rocks. She has written 13 poetry collections, most recently *Hush*, winner of the Halcyon Prize for poems of human ecology. She teaches poetry for addiction recovery programs, hospice, mindfulness retreats, women's retreats, scientists, and others. ahundredfallingveils.com and wordwoman.com

Ron Wallace is the author of more than 20 books and chapbooks of poetry, fiction, and criticism, including *For Dear Life*, *For a Limited Time Only*, and *Long for This World: New and Selected Poems*. Founder and director of the University of Wisconsin–Madison's program in creative writing, he is Felix Pollak Professor Emeritus and editor of the University of Wisconsin Press Poetry Series. He divides his time between Madison and a 40-acre farm in Bear Valley, Wisconsin, where he tends a large vegetable garden, helps his wife, Peg, restore prairie, bird-watches, and mows eight miles of grass and sweet clover with his power push mower.

Connie Wanek was born in Wisconsin, raised in New Mexico, and now lives in Duluth, Minnesota. Her first book, *Bonfire* (New Rivers, 1997), won the New Voices Award. She is also the author of *Hartley Field* (Holy Cow!, 2002), *On Speaking Terms* (Copper Canyon, 2010), *Rival Gardens: New and Selected Poems* (University of Nebraska Press, 2016), and the chapbook *Consider the Lilies: Mrs. God Poems* (Will o' the Wisp, 2018). Forthcoming from Candlewick Press is a children's book of poetry cowritten with Ted Kooser.

Laura Grace Weldon is the author of *Blackbird* (Grayson Books, 2019) and *Tending* (Aldrich Press, 2013), as well as a handbook for alternative education, *Free Range Learning* (Hohm Press, 2010). She was named 2019 Ohio Poet of the Year. Her background includes teaching nonviolence classes, facilitating support groups for abuse survivors, and writing collaborative poetry with nursing home residents. lauragraceweldon.com

Cynthia White's poems have appeared in *Massachusetts Review, Narrative, ZYZZYVA, Grist,* and *Catamaran,* among others. She won the Julia Darling Memorial Prize from Kallisto Gaia Press. She lives in Santa Cruz, California.

Diana Whitney writes across genres on feminism, motherhood, and sexuality. Her first book, *Wanting It,* won the Rubery Book Award in poetry. She was the poetry critic for the *San Francisco Chronicle*, where she featured women authors and LGBTQ voices in her column. Her writing has appeared in the *New York Times, Glamour,* the *Washington Post, Kenyon Review*, and elsewhere. A feminist activist, she is a senior contributing editor at HealthyWomen.org. Her latest project is *How to Be Real: Poems for Girls Becoming Themselves* (Workman, 2021). diana-whitney.com

Michelle Wiegers is a poet and life coach based in Southern Vermont. Her work has appeared in *Healing the Divide: Poems of Kindness and Connection, Birchsong Anthology,* and *Third Wednesday,* among other journals. In her mind-body life coaching work, she is a passionate advocate for those in chronic pain.
michellewiegers.com

Katherine Williams's poems have been published in *Poet Lore, The Northern Virginia Review, Voices,* and the anthologies *The Widows' Handbook* and *The Poet's Cookbook*. She is associate professor emerita at George Washington University and works as a psychologist and art therapist in private practice.

CREDITS

"Moon" by Lahab Assef Al-Jundi. Reprinted with permission of the author.

"Any Common Desolation" and "Getting Into Bed on a December Night" from *Indigo*. Copyright © 2016, 2020 by Ellen Bass. Reprinted with the permission of The Permissions Company, LLC on behalf of Copper Canyon Press, coppercanyonpress.org

"Perceptive Prayer" by Grace Bauer from *Nowhere All at Once* (Stephen F. Austin State University Press) Copyright © 2014 Grace Bauer. Reprinted with permission of the author.

"Weather" by George Bilgere, from *Imperial* Copyright © 2014. Reprinted by permission of the University of Pittsburgh Press.

"Laughter" by Dale Biron from *Why We Do Our Daily Practices* Copyright © 2014 Mule Pack Press and published on Gratefulness.org. Reprinted with permission of the author.

"Work" by Sally Bliumis-Dunn, from *Echolocation* (Plume Editions/Mad Hat Press) Copyright © 2018 Sally Bliumis-Dunn. Reprinted with permission of the author.

"Bus Stop" from *A New Hunger*. Copyright © 2007 by Laure-Anne Bosselaar. Reprinted with the permission of The Permissions Company, LLC on behalf of Copper Canyon Press, coppercanyonpress.org

"In Gratitude" by Abigail Carroll, from *Habitation of Wonder* (Cascade Books). Copyright © 2018 Abigail Carroll. Reprinted with permission of the author and used by permission of Wipf and Stock Publishers. wipfandstock.com

"Morning" by Kristen Case, from *Little Arias* (New Issues Poetry & Prose) Copyright © 2015 Kristen Case. Reprinted with permission of author and publisher.

"An Essay on Age" by Judith Chalmer, from *Minnow* (Kelsay Books, 2020) and first published in the DMQ Review (2012). Copyright © 2020 Judith Chalmer. Reprinted with permission of the author.

"the lesson of the falling leaves" by Lucille Clifton, from *The Collected Poems of Lucille Clifton*. Copyright © 1987 by Lucille Clifton. Reprinted with the permission of The Permissions Company, LLC on behalf of BOA Editions Ltd., boaeditions.org

"Everybody Made Soups" by Lisa Coffman, from *Less Obvious Gods* (Iris Press) Copyright © 2013 Lisa Coffman. Reprinted with permission of author and Iris Press.

"Down to Earth" and "Darkest Before Dawn" by James Crews from *Bluebird* (Green Writers Press, 2020) Copyright © 2020 James Crews. "Winter Morning" from *Every Waking Moment* (Lynx House Press, 2020) Copyright © 2020 James Crews, republished on Gratefulness.org and in American Life in Poetry. Reprinted with permission of the author.

"Promise" and "Autism Poem: The Grid" by Barbara Crooker, from *Radiance* (Word Press, 2005) Copyright © 2005 Barbara Crooker. "Tomorrow" by Barbara Crooker from *Some Glad Morning* Copyright © 2019. Reprinted by permission of the University of Pittsburgh Press.

"Mending" by Noah Davis, from *Of This River* (Michigan State University Press) Copyright © 2020 by Noah Davis. Reprinted with permission of the author.

"Thankful for Now" by Todd Davis, from *Native Species* Copyright © 2019 Todd Davis (Michigan State University Press, 2019). Reprinted with permission of the author.

"Apple Blossoms" by Susan Kelly-DeWitt, from *Gravitational Tug* (Main Street Rag) Copyright © 2020 Susan Kelly-DeWitt. Reprinted with permission of the author.

"Wingspan" by Amy Dryansky, originally published in *The SUN*. Reprinted with permission of the author.

"Pledge" by Jehanne Dubrow. Reprinted with permission of the author.

"Angel" by Terri Kirby Erickson, from *Becoming the Blue Heron* (Press 53) Copyright © 2017 Terri Kirby Erickson. "What Matters" by Terri Kirby Erickson, from *A Sun Inside My Chest* (Press 53) Copyright © 2020 Terri Kirby Erickson. Reprinted by permission of the author and publisher.

"Summer Apples" by Catherine Essinger, from *The Apricot and the Moon* (Dos Madres Press) Copyright © 2020 Catherine Essinger. Reprinted with permission of the author.

"Reincarnate" by Patricia Fargnoli from *Hallowed: New and Selected Poems*. Copyright © 2017 by Patricia Fargnoli. Reprinted with the permission of The Permissions Company, LLC on behalf of Tupelo Press, tupelopress.org

"Everything Is Made of Labor" by Farnaz Fatemi. Reprinted by permission of the author.

"Against Panic" by Molly Fisk. Reprinted with permission of the author.

"The Once Invisible Garden" by Laura Foley, originally published in *Sheila-Na-Gig*. "To See It" by Laura Foley, from *It's This* (Salmon Poetry, 2021). "Gratitude List," from *Why I Never Finished My Dissertation* (Headmistress Press) Copyright © 2019. All reprinted with permission of author.

"Sap Icicles" by Patricia Fontaine. Reprinted by permission of the author.

"Wondrous" by Sarah Freligh, from *Sad Math* (Moon City Press) Copyright © 2015 Sarah Freligh. Reprinted with permission of the author.

"Offering" by Albert Garcia. Originally published in Catamaran Literary Reader, Summer 2018. Reprinted by permission of the author.

"Wedding Poem" by Ross Gay, from *Catalog of Unabashed Gratitude* by Ross Gay Copyright © 2015. Reprinted with permission of University of Pittsburgh Press.

"Because the Night You Asked" by Crystal S. Gibbins, from *Now/Here*, Holy Cow! Press. Copyright © 2017 by Crystal S. Gibbins. Reprinted with permission of the author and publisher. holycowpress.org

"Motherhood" Jessica Gigot, from *Flood Patterns* (Antrim House Press) Copyright © 2015 by Jessica Gigot. Reprinted with permission of author and publisher.

"Leaning to the Light" by Alice Wolf Gilborn, from *Apples & Stones* Copyright © 2020 Kelsay Books. Reprinted with permission of the author and publisher.

"Growing Apples" Nancy Miller Gomez, from *Punishment* (Rattle) Copyright © 2014 Nancy Miller Gomez. Reprinted with permission of the author.

"At the Age of 18—Ode to Girls of Color" by Amanda Gorman. Text copyright © 2016 by Amanda Gorman. Reprinted by permission of Writers House LLC acting as agent for the author.

"Listening for Your Name" by David Graham, from *The Honey of Earth*. Copyright © 2019 by David Graham. Reprinted by permission of Terrapin Books.

"Eagle Poem" by Joy Harjo, from *In Mad Love and War.* Copyright © 1990 by Joy Harjo. Published by Wesleyan University Press. Reprinted with permission.

"Nest" by Jeffrey Harrison from *Into Daylight*. Copyright © 2014 by Jeffrey Harrison. Reprinted with the permission of The Permissions Company, LLC on behalf of Tupelo Press, tupelopress.org

"In the Dark" by Penny Harter, from *The Resonance Around Us* (Mountains and Rivers Press) Copyright © 2013 Penny Harter. Reprinted with permission of the author.

"With Trees" by Margaret Hasse, from *Between Us* (Nodin Press) Copyright © 2016 Margaret Hasse. Reprinted with permission of the author.

"The Fish" by Jane Hirshfield and "Today, When I Could Do Nothing" by Jane Hirshfield, originally published in *The San Francisco Chronicle* (March 23, 2020 edition). Reprinted with permission of the author.

"The Word" by Tony Hoagland, from *Sweet Ruin*. Copyright © 1992 by the Board of Regents of the University of Wisconsin System. Reprinted by permission of the University of Wisconsin Press.

"Innocence" by Linda Hogan, from *Dark. Sweet.: New & Selected Poems*. Copyright © 2014 by Linda Hogan. Reprinted with the permission of The Permissions Company, LLC on behalf of Coffee House Press, coffeehousepress.org

"The Newborns" by Kathryn Hunt, from *Long Way Through Ruin* (Blue Begonia Press) Copyright © 2013. Reprinted with permission of the author.

"September Swim" by Rob Hunter, from *September Swim* (Spoon River Poetry Press). Copyright © 2005 by Rob Hunter. Reprinted by permission of the author.

"Summer Cottage" by Mary Elder Jacobsen. Reprinted with permission of the author.

"Unclouded Vision" by Jacqueline Jules, previously published in *The Healing Muse* (October 2017). Reprinted with permission of the author.

"My Daughter's Singing" by Garret Keizer, from *The World Pushes Back*. Copyright © 2019 Garret Keizer. Reprinted with permission of Texas Review Press and author.

"Coming Home at Twilight in Late Summer" by Jane Kenyon, from *Collected Poems*. Copyright © 2005 by The Estate of Jane Kenyon. Reprinted with the permission of The Permissions Company, LLC on behalf of Graywolf Press, Minneapolis, graywolfpress.org

"Third Year of My Mother's Dementia" by Lynne Knight, from *Night in the Shape of a Mirror* (WordTech) Copyright © 2006 Lynne Knight. Reprinted with permission of the author

"Dandelion," "Easter Morning," and "A Dervish of Leaves" by Ted Kooser Copyright © 2020 Ted Kooser. Reprinted with permission of the author.

"Improvement" by Danusha Laméris, from *Bonfire Opera* by Danusha Laméris Copyright © 2020. Reprinted by permission of University of Pittsburgh Press. "Goldfinches" and "Aspen" by Danusha Laméris Copyright © 2020 Danusha Laméris. Reprinted by permission of the author.

"Two Weeks After a Silent Retreat" by Heather Lanier Copyright © 2020 Heather Lanier, originally published in *The SUN*. Reprinted with permission of the author.

"In Any Event" by Dorianne Laux, originally published in *Raleigh Review*. Reprinted with permission of the author.

"From Blossoms" by Li-Young Lee, from *Rose*. Copyright © 1986 by Li-Young Lee. Reprinted with the permission of The Permissions Company, LLC on behalf of BOA Editions Ltd., boaeditions.org

"Notions" by Paula Gordon Lepp. Reprinted with permission of the author.

"A Cure Against Poisonous Thought" by Annie Lighthart, from *Iron String* (Airlie Press). Copyright © 2013 Annie Lighthart. Reprinted with permission of the author.

"Too Many to Count" by Alison Luterman. Reprinted with permission of the author.

"Old Friends" by Freya Manfred, from *Loon in Late November Water*, Copyright © 2018 by Freya Manfred (Red Dragonfly Press). Reprinted with permission of the author.

"Part of the Landscape" by Joan Mazza. Reprinted with permission of the author.

"Forgiveness" by Mary McCue. Reprinted with permission of the author.

"Climbing the Golden Mountain" by Michael Kiesow Moore, from *The Song Castle* (Nodin Press) Copyright © 2018 by Michael Kiesow Moore. Reprinted with permission of the author.

"To Ask" by Julie Murphy. Reprinted with permission of the author.

"Language, Prayer, and Grace" by Mark Nepo Copyright © 2020 Mark Nepo. Reprinted with permission of the author. "In Love with the World" from *Things That Join the Sea and the Sky* Copyright © 2017 Mark Nepo and used with permission of author and publisher, Sounds True, Inc.

"Valentine's Day" by Gail Newman, from *Blood Memory* Copyright © 2020 Gail Newman, published by Marsh Hawk Press. Reprinted with permission of the author.

"Missing Key" by Heather Newman. Reprinted with permission of the author.

"Over the Weather" from *A Maze Me* by Naomi Shihab Nye; Illustrated by Terre Maher. Text copyright © 2005 by Naomi Shihab Nye. Used by permission of HarperCollins Publishers.

"Hoodie" from *Rewilding*. Copyright © 2018 by January Gill O'Neil "In the Company of Women" from *Misery Islands*. Copyright © 2014 by January Gill O'Neil. Both reprinted with the permission of The Permissions Company, LLC on behalf of CavanKerry Press, Ltd., cavankerrypress.org

"Shells" by Christen Pagett. Reprinted with permission of the author.

"Let It Rain" and "Rosary" by Brad Peacock. Reprinted with permission of the author.

"Essential Gratitude" by Andrea Potos, first appeared on Gratefulness.org; and "I Watched an Angel in the Emergency Room" from *Arrows of Light* (Iris Press) Copyright © 2017 Andrea Potos. "The Cardinal Reminds Me" originally published in *Cave Wall* No. 16. Reprinted with permission of the author.

"Red Thyme" by Laura Ann Reed. Reprinted by permission of the author.

"After Spending the Morning Baking Bread" by Jack Ridl from *Practicing to Walk Like a Heron*. Copyright © 2013 Wayne State University Press, with the permission of Wayne State University Press.

"When Giving Is All We Have" by Alberto Ríos, from *A Small Story About the Sky*. Copyright © 2015 by Alberto Ríos. Reprinted with the permission of The Permissions Company, LLC on behalf of Copper Canyon Press, coppercanyonpress.org

"Surprise Breakfast" by David Romtvedt, from *Dilemmas of the Angels* (LSU Press) Copyright © 2017 David Romtvedt. Reprinted with permission of the publisher and the author.

"Scratch, Sniff" by Katie Rubinstein, originally published on Gratefulness.org. Reprinted with permission of the author.

"When Life Seems a To-Do List" and "If I Carry My Father" by Marjorie Saiser, from *The Woman in the Moon* (Backwaters Press) Copyright © 2018 Marjorie Saiser. "Thanksgiving for Two," first published in American Life in Poetry and then in *I Have Nothing to Say About Fire* (Backwaters Press) Copyright © 2016 Marjorie Saiser. Reprinted by permission of the author.

"The Good Life" by Tracy K. Smith, from *Life on Mars*. Copyright © 2011 by Tracy K. Smith. Reprinted with the permission of The Permissions Company, LLC on behalf of Graywolf Press, Minneapolis, Minnesota, graywolfpress.org

"A Candle in the Night" by Nathan Spoon, originally published in *American Poetry Review*. Reprinted by permission of the author.

"Shelter in Place" by Kim Stafford, originally published in *Stone Gathering*, edited by Deborah Jacobs. Reprinted with permission of the author.

"Any Morning" by William Stafford, from *Ohio Review* #50 (1993). Copyright © 1993 by William Stafford. Reprinted with the permission of The Permissions Company, LLC on behalf of Kim Stafford.

"What to Do" by Joyce Sutphen, originally published on The Writer's Almanac. Reprinted with permission of the author.

"Another Day Filled with Sleeves of Light" and "Rabbit" by Heather Swan, from *A Kinship with Ash*. Copyright © 2020 by Heather Swan. Reprinted by permission of Terrapin Books.

"Radiance" by Wally Swist, from *Huang Po and the Dimensions of Love* by Wally Swist. Copyright © 2012 Wally Swist. Reprinted by permission.

"There Doesn't Need to Be a Poem" by Tess Taylor. Reprinted by permission of the author.

"Praise of Darkness" by Francine Marie Tolf, from *Rain, Lilies, Luck* (North Star Press) Copyright © 2010 Francine Marie Tolf. Reprinted with permission of the author.

"Amores Perros" by Angela Narciso Torres, originally published in *Spoon River Poetry Review*. Reprinted with permission of the author.

"Hope" and "Fifteen Years Later, I See How It Went" by Rosemerry Wahtola Trommer, first published on A Hundred Falling Veils (ahundredfallingveils.com). "How It Might Continue" Copyright © 2018 by Rosemerry Wahtola Trommer, from *Naked for Tea* (Able Muse Press, 2018). Reprinted with permission of the author.

"The Facts of Life" by Ron Wallace, from *Long for This World: New and Selected Poems* Copyright © 2003. Reprinted by permission of the University of Pittsburgh Press.

"The Lesser Goldfinch" by Connie Wanek, originally published in *Freshwater Review* (Duluth, MN). Reprinted with permission of the author.

"Astral Chorus" and "Compost Happens" by Laura Grace Weldon Copyright © 2020 Laura Grace Weldon, from *Blackbird* (Grayson Books, 2019). Reprinted with permission of the author and the publisher.

"Quail Hollow" by Cynthia White. Reprinted by permission of the poet.

"Kindergarten Studies the Human Heart" by Diana Whitney. Originally published in *Bloodroot* Literary Magazine Copyright © 2016. Reprinted with permission of the author.

"I Held Open" by Michelle Wiegers. Reprinted with permission of author.

"The Dog Body of My Soul" by Katherine Williams. Reprinted with permission of the author.

TRANSFORM YOUR LIFE
WITH MORE BOOKS FROM STOREY

Wake Up Grateful by Kristi Nelson

Learn to see the abundance and opportunity in every moment. With daily exercises and prompts for deep reflection, this book offers profound personal change through the practice of taking nothing for granted.

Everyday Gratitude by A Network for Grateful Living

Invite joy with this beautiful hand-lettered collection of uplifting quotes from Maya Angelou, Confucius, Anne Frank, and dozens of other thoughtful writers. Reflections and practices help you consciously appreciate life's abundance, every day.

Forest Bathing Retreat by Hannah Fries

This inspiring volume of stunning nature photography, evocative text, and mindfulness exercises is your guide to the healing peace and restorative power of trees and nature.

---

*From Our Sister Company, **Algonquin Books***

The Book of Delights by Ross Gay

This spirited collection of short lyric essays, written daily over a tumultuous year, reminds us of the pleasure of celebrating ordinary wonders.

Join the conversation. Share your experience with this book, learn more about Storey Publishing's authors, and read original essays and book excerpts at storey.com.
Look for our books wherever quality books are sold or call 800-441-5700.

The Path to Kindness

POEMS OF CONNECTION AND JOY

Edited by
James Crews

Foreword by
Danusha Lamèris

Storey Publishing

The mission of Storey Publishing is to serve our customers by publishing practical information that encourages personal independence in harmony with the environment.

Edited by Liz Bevilacqua
Art direction and book design by Alethea Morrison
Text production by Slavica A. Walzl
Cover art and illustrations by © Dinara Mirtalipova

Text © 2022 by James Crews except as shown on pages 207–211

All rights reserved. Hachette Book Group supports the right to free expression and the value of copyright. The purpose of copyright is to encourage writers and artists to produce the creative works that enrich our culture. The scanning, uploading, and distribution of this book without permission is a theft of the author's intellectual property. If you would like permission to use material from the book (other than for review purposes), please contact permissions@hbgusa.com. Thank you for your support of the author's rights.

The information in this book is true and complete to the best of our knowledge. All recommendations are made without guarantee on the part of the author or Storey Publishing. The author and publisher disclaim any liability in connection with the use of this information.

The publisher is not responsible for websites (or their content) that are not owned by the publisher.

Storey books may be purchased in bulk for business, educational, or promotional use. Special editions or book excerpts can also be created to specification. For details, please contact your local bookseller or the Hachette Book Group Special Markets Department at special.markets@hbgusa.com.

Storey Publishing
210 MASS MoCA Way
North Adams, MA 01247
storey.com

Storey Publishing is an imprint of Workman Publishing, a division of Hachette Book Group, Inc., 1290 Avenue of the Americas, New York, NY 10104. The Storey Publishing name and logo are registered trademarks of Hachette Book Group, Inc.

ISBNs: 978-1-63586-533-2 (paperback); 978-1-63586-534-9 (ebook)

Printed in the United States by Lakeside Book Company (interior and bind) and PC (cover) on paper from responsible sources
10 9 8 7 6 5 4 3 2

Library of Congress Cataloging-in-Publication Data on file

Your legacy is every life you touch.
Maya Angelou

CONTENTS

Foreword, Danusha Laméris	xi
The Practice of Connection, James Crews	1
Danusha Laméris, Small Kindnesses	5
Naomi Shihab Nye, Red Brocade	6
Shari Altman, Worry Stone for My Grandfather	7
Rosemerry Wahtola Trommer, Kindness	8
Reflective Pause: The Soil That Is You	10
Kai Coggin, Into Wildflower Into Field	11
Laura Budofsky Wisniewski, A Beginner's Guide to Gardening Alone	13
Heather Lanier, The Heartbeat of My Unborn Child	14
Mary Elder Jacobsen, Sponge Bath	15
Laura Grace Weldon, Most Important Word	16
James Crews, Only Love	17
David Van Houten, Breathe	18
January Gill O'Neil, Elation	19
Tricia Knoll, My Daughter Meets My White Pine	20
Julie Cadwallader Staub, Turning	21
Ingrid Goff-Maidoff, Peace Came Today	22
Kim Stafford, A Chair by the Creek	23
Danny Dover, Floodwood Pond	24

Ted Kooser, Filling the Candles 25

Mary Ray Goehring, Pinch Pot 26

Margaret Hasse, Clothing 27

Angela Narciso Torres, Chore........................... 28

Reflective Pause: The Sacred Everyday 29

Twyla M. Hansen, Trying to Pray 30

Joy Harjo, For Keeps 31

Barbara Crooker, Sustenance 32

Ruth Arnison, Twenty Years of Longing 33

Danusha Laméris, The Heart Is Not 34

Laura Foley, Learning by Heart......................... 35

Jacqueline Jules, Billowing Overhead 36

Penny Harter, Two Meteors 37

Tom Hennen, Made Visible............................. 38

Cornelius Eady, A Small Moment 39

Zoe Higgins, Ode...................................... 40

Donna Hilbert, Credo 41

James Crews, Self-Care 42

Reflective Pause: Reassembling the Parts 43

January Gill O'Neil, Sunday 44

Laura Grace Weldon, Thursday Morning 45

Joy Gaines-Friedler, Touch............................. 46

Heather Swan, On Lightness 47

José A. Alcantara, Divorce 48

Susan Moorhead, Shift................................ 49

Tracy K. Smith, Song................................. 50

Mark Nepo, Drinking There 51

Susan Musgrave, More Than Seeing 52

Julia Fehrenbacher, The Most Important Thing 53

Julia Alvarez, Vain Doubts............................ 54

Molly Fisk, Before I gained all this weight 56

Ross Gay, Thank You 57

Lorna Crozier, Small Lesson........................... 58

Leah Naomi Green, The Age of Affection............... 59

Barbara Crooker, Forsythia............................ 60

Karen Craigo, Last Scraps of Color in Missouri........... 61

Ted Kooser, It Doesn't Take Much 62

Reflective Pause: Part of It All Again 64

Ellen Bass, The Thing Is............................... 65

James Crews, Self-Compassion 66

Kelli Russell Agodon, Praise........................... 68

Dorianne Laux, Joy 69

Jack Ridl, Take Love for Granted....................... 71

Terri Kirby Erickson, Free Breakfast 73

Annie Lighthart, Passenger 74

Christine Stewart-Nuñez, Site Planning 75

Laura Foley, A Perfect Arc	76
Michael Simms, The Summer You Learned to Swim	77
James Crews, The Pool	78
Joyce Sutphen, Carrying Water to the Field	79
David Romtvedt, At the Creek	80
Reflective Pause: Would That Be Heaven?	81
Michael Kleber-Diggs, Coniferous Fathers	82
Zeina Azzam, My Father's Hands	84
Li-Young Lee, Early in the Morning	85
Terri Kirby Erickson, Night Talks	87
Julia Alvarez, Love Portions	88
Kate Duignan, Grandmother	90
Todd Davis, Heliotropic	92
Marjorie Saiser, Everybody in the Same House	93
Lahab Assef Al-Jundi, Hot Tea	94
Gregory Orr, Morning Song	95
Annie Lighthart, How to Wake	96
Alice Wolf Gilborn, Wake Up	97
Alberto Ríos, Dawn Callers	98
Reflective Pause: A Welcoming World	99
Susan Moorhead, First Light	100
Faith Shearin, My Mother's Van	101
Ada Limón, The Raincoat	103
Marjorie Saiser, I Save My Love	104

Lailah Dainin Shima, In Praise of Dirty Socks 105

Carolee Bennett, Exactly 299,792,458 Meters Per Second 106

Kimberly Blaeser, About Standing (in Kinship) 107

Rebecca Foust, Kinship of Flesh 108

Chana Bloch, The Joins 109

Heather Swan, Bowl 111

Reflective Pause: Where Beauty Is Honed 112

Natasha Trethewey, Housekeeping 113

Ted Kooser, Round Robin Letter 114

Sally Bliumis-Dunn, Mailman 115

Joseph Millar, Telephone Repairman 117

David Graham, The News of Love 118

Linda Hogan, Arctic Night, Lights Across the Sky 119

Alicia Ostriker, The Dogs at Live Oak Beach, Santa Cruz . . 120

Nancy Gordon, Rescue Dog 121

Dan Butler, New York Downpour 122

Richard Jones, After Work 123

Andrea Potos, Abundance to Share with the Birds 124

Fady Joudah, Mimesis 125

Rudy Francisco, Mercy 126

Naomi Shihab Nye, Kindness 127

Christine Kitano,
     For the Korean Grandmother on Sunset Boulevard 129

Reflective Pause: So You Are Here 130

Paula Gordon Lepp, Gas Station Communion............ 131

Annie Lighthart, A Great Wild Goodness 133

Ellen Rowland, No Small Thing........................134

Jane Hirshfield, I Would Like..........................135

Peter Pereira, A Pot of Red Lentils......................137

William Stafford, You Reading This, Be Ready 138

Connie Wanek, Come In!...............................139

Susan Rich, Still Life with Ladder 140

Alison Luterman, Braiding His Hair.....................142

Judith Sornberger, Love in Our Sixties...................143

Susan Rothbard, That New 145

Susan Zimmerman, Get Close 146

David Axelrod,
   The Innermost Chamber of My Home Is Yours 147

Dave Baldwin, Summer Romance 148

Anya Silver, Late Summer..............................149

Judith Sornberger, Assisted Living......................150

Patricia McKernon Runkle,
   When You Meet Someone Deep in Grief.............151

Reflective Pause: Here to Listen 152

Megan Buchanan, Dream Visitation 153

Phyllis Cole Dai, Ladder................................154

Michelle Mandolia, The Thing She Loves Most 156

Marjorie Saiser, Last Day of Kindergarten 157

Gillian Wegener, Juvie Kid 159

Emilie Lygren, Make Believe 161

Brad Aaron Modlin, What You Missed
    That Day You Were Absent from Fourth Grade....... 162

Reflective Pause: What You Missed 164

Dorianne Laux, On the Back Porch 165

Suzanne Nussey, Lullaby for an Empty Nester............166

Michelle Wiegers, Moving...............................167

Marie Howe, Delivery...................................169

Ray Hudson, Unbreakable Clarities 170

Danusha Laméris, Insha'Allah.......................... 171

Andrea Potos, Where I Might Find Her 172

Rosemerry Wahtola Trommer, The Question 173

Jacqueline Suskin, Future...............................174

Reading Group Questions and Topics for Discussion 175

Poet Biographies..181

Credits... 207

Acknowledgments 212

FOREWORD

Most of us spend a lot of time waiting for the right moment, by which I mean the moment when everything is as we want it to be: the laundry done, the faucet fixed, the kids all getting along with each other. We wait for it to rain, or for it to stop raining. For the pandemic to be over. For a baby to be born, or for the kids to leave the house. Wait until we get the promotion, the car, the partner. The conditions we place on our experience of life are endless.

And when I'm struck by a moment of sanity, I notice those conditions falling away, if only for an instant. The house is a mess, and yet, here I am, as I was earlier today, accepting a rose from a woman I don't even know, who, on the small country road where I walk with my husband, ran after me to extend her hand and offer a flower the most brilliant shades of pink and apricot, the petals ruffled like petticoats. "Here!" she said. "For you!" And I don't know what was more beautiful: the rose, or the effort she made to deliver it. For the whole walk, it glowed, a presence, between us.

Meanwhile, wars waged on, the hospital wards remained full, many went to bed hungry. How do we live in the gap between the hoped-for and the real?

We want the world to be less broken. Ourselves to be less broken. To love an unbroken person. But here we are. So many days, it's difficult to carry on. The simple, mammalian pleasure of touch can be the anchor we need. Or witnessing a beloved engaged in an everyday task—like washing dishes, or braiding a child's hair—and there it is, the breath of the sacred.

What we really want to know is, "Am I welcome here? Am I part of the tribe? Do I have a place?" And so, when a stranger offers a flower, it seems possible. Possible that we are meant to be exactly where—and who—we are. That we are meant.

The most memorable moments of my life are often the smallest. Not my college graduation (a blur), but the moment a little girl took the ends of my scarf when I was walking through a crowd at the farmer's market, and began to twirl, inviting me into an impromptu *pas de deux*. It seemed no one else saw it, and so it felt as if we'd stepped outside of time.

Kindness is not sugar, but salt. A dash of it gives the whole dish flavor. I want to keep remembering, to keep living into these moments and the worlds they contain. To know they are where the world I want to live in is made. That it is made right here, in the heart of the broken, the ordinary. These poems remind me. These voices give shape to that world. They show a way.

Danusha Laméris

THE PRACTICE OF CONNECTION

When my husband, Brad, was nineteen years old, he joined the military, hoping to follow in the footsteps of his uncle and grandfather. During his first few weeks at the assigned Air Force base, however, he fell into a deep depression. After a few sessions with the on-base psychologist, he finally realized he was gay and came out. "You know what this means," the psychologist said. It meant that under the Don't Ask, Don't Tell policy, he was soon discharged from the military and sent home. I can only imagine the shame that followed him to the small town in Vermont where he grew up, and where he told no one for years the real reason he'd left the Air Force.

Brad first shared this story with me not long after we moved in together. "Suicide was a daily option," he said. The idea that this gentle farmer, who uplifts everyone he meets and cares so much for the land, might have ended his life still seems inconceivable to me. Yet what kept him pushing through those dark days, he says, were the small kindnesses offered by neighbors, friends, and customers at the organic farm where he began to work. He would be out for a run or walk, certain that this would be the day he could bear his secret no longer, and someone passing by in their pickup truck would wave, or a friend of the family would stop to ask how he was doing. The weight of his shame became lighter, and he knew he could keep going for another day.

As a lifelong city dweller, I struggled at first with receiving all the caring attention from friends and family in our small community. But after Brad shared his story with me, and then with the whole state of Vermont during his campaign for the US Senate, I soon saw how the daily kindnesses were saving me as well. I felt it when my mother-in-law called if she saw an unfamiliar car in our driveway; when our neighbor Christy would leave mason jars of fresh-pressed apple cider on our side porch; or when my father-in-law would wake early after a nor'easter to plow our driveway. I began to see too that we can create a beloved community like this no matter where we live.

Many of us have faced times when life felt impossible to bear—until a friend texted, or the barista at our favorite coffee shop started chatting with us. Because the sparks of connections like this last for just a few minutes, we might lose heart, believing that what little we can give to each other will have no lasting effect on a world that feels so broken and divided. But my hope is that, as you read through the poems gathered here, you will see kindness not just as a spontaneous act that happens on its own, but as a *practice* of noticing and naming the many moments of tenderness we witness, give, and receive throughout our days. Over the past year, as I shared these poems with students, family, and friends, I felt profoundly moved by the goodness they seem to prove is our basic human nature. It has become a daily, conscious ritual for me to hold on to as many of my own small kindnesses as possible in what social psychologist Barbara Fredrickson calls "moments of positive resonance."

These poems retrained me to seek out and find connection at a time when so many of us have grown more isolated. Sometimes a simple hello from someone I passed on the trail in the park or a glimmer in the eyes of a grocery-store cashier was enough to restore my faith in humanity for another day. I began to find ways to be kinder to the people in my own life, too, welcoming the task of helping my elderly mother order groceries online, or sending care packages to friends I hadn't seen in months. By showing us all the ways we can still practice being together, these poems encourage us to capture and hold on to the moments that matter the most to us in life. Many of the poems included here also model for us the ways that we might let ourselves surrender more fully to joy, especially in service of self-care. In "Ode," Zoe Higgins uncovers the pleasure of leaving "everything undone" and relieving herself of the constant pressure of the to-do list. And in "Before I gained all this weight," Molly Fisk shares the desire to go back and shake the girl she once was, awakening her to all the beauty she couldn't see around her because of shame and fear.

Because a poem contains just a dose of the author's experience, including the sorrows, pleasures, and struggles all at the same time, it offers us the truest expression of the human condition. If we let it, each poem here can become an invitation to step deeper into our own lives and relationships with others, too. We might read a poem like Christine Kitano's "For the Korean Grandmother on Sunset Boulevard" and remember that we can find pleasure and kinship even in the simplest observation of a stranger to whom we never speak. Or we might take in the motherly sacrifice at the heart of Ada Limón's "The Raincoat" and Faith Shearin's "My Mother's Van," and recall the sacrifices our own loved ones made for us, or that we made for others. These poems also urge us toward a deeper relationship with the natural world so that we notice, as January Gill O'Neil does in "Elation," the way a grove of trees will "claim this space as their own, making the most of what's given them," just like we do. I encourage you to use these poems, Reflective Pauses, and Discussion Questions at the end of the book as companions on your own path. Let a poem bring some memory to the surface or follow the call of an opening line or image to some truth of your own, whether you write it down or share it with someone you trust.

Poetry is an ideal tool in times of uncertainty and change in our lives because it grounds us in the now, opening our hearts and minds to the worlds outside and within. Please feel free to share the poems that move you with family and friends, allowing these deeply felt pieces to bring us all closer together until we see, as Dr. Martin Luther King Jr. put it so well, that we are all "caught in an inescapable network of mutuality, tied in a single garment of destiny." Perhaps that's why, when my husband and I take our daily walks on the roads around our house, we make a point of waving and smiling at every person and every car we pass. We both know all too well that a simple gesture of welcome might change someone's day and might even save their life.

James Crews

Danusha Laméris

SMALL KINDNESSES

I've been thinking about the way, when you walk
down a crowded aisle, people pull in their legs
to let you by. Or how strangers still say "bless you"
when someone sneezes, a leftover
from the Bubonic plague. "Don't die," we are saying.
And sometimes, when you spill lemons
from your grocery bag, someone else will help you
pick them up. Mostly, we don't want to harm each other.
We want to be handed our cup of coffee hot,
and to say thank you to the person handing it. To smile
at them and for them to smile back. For the waitress
to call us honey when she sets down the bowl of clam
    chowder,
and for the driver in the red pick-up truck to let us pass.
We have so little of each other, now. So far
from tribe and fire. Only these brief moments of exchange.
What if they are the true dwelling of the holy, these
fleeting temples we make together when we say, "Here,
have my seat," "Go ahead—you first," "I like your hat."

Naomi Shihab Nye

RED BROCADE

The Arabs used to say,
When a stranger appears at your door,
feed him for three days
before asking who he is,
where he's come from,
where he's headed.
That way, he'll have strength
enough to answer.
Or, by then you'll be
such good friends
you don't care.

Let's go back to that.
Rice? Pine nuts?
Here, take the red brocade pillow.
My child will serve water
to your horse.

No, I was not busy when you came!
I was not preparing to be busy.
That's the armor everyone put on
to pretend they had a purpose
in the world.

I refuse to be claimed.
Your plate is waiting.
We will snip fresh mint
into your tea.

Shari Altman

WORRY STONE FOR MY GRANDFATHER

You let me cut the mint,
put me in charge of taming the kittens.
We picked tomatoes and beans
in a bushel basket, collected
water from the healing springs.
For years you saved me with action,
the beauty and relief of work.

When you became sick,
who knows how our thoughts collided?

A worry stone passed from young to old,
smoothed down by a thumbprint.
I had nothing else to give.
When you gave it back to me,
I did not expect it, found it hard
to witness your acceptance.

On the day you died
I brought you a poinsettia,
the same red as your favorite sweater
that lives in my closet now.
I still believed
in invincibility.

My limp wrist, the tilt
of the pot brushing the ground.

Rosemerry Wahtola Trommer

KINDNESS

Consider the tulip,
how long ago
someone's hands planted a bulb
and gave to this place
a living scrap of beauty,
how it rises every spring
out of the same soil,
which is, of course,
not at all the same soil,
but new.

Consider the six red petals,
the yellow at the center,
the soft green rubber of the stem,
how it bows to the world.
How, the longer you sit beside the tulip,
the more you want to bow, too.

It is this way with kindness:
someone plants in someone else
a bit of beauty—
a kind word, perhaps, or a touch,
the gift of their time or their smile.
And years later, in that inner soil,
that beauty emerges again,
pushing aside the dead leaves,
insisting on loveliness,

a celebration of the one who planted it,
the one who perceives it, and
the fertile place where it has grown.

REFLECTIVE PAUSE

The Soil That Is You

Our bodies and minds often hold on to memories of past wrongs and ways that others have harmed us more strongly than anything else. This makes sense; after all, we don't want to be hurt again. Yet we sometimes forget to hold on to the beauty and good that's been planted in us as well, remembering all the positive ways we have been touched by strangers and loved ones alike. In "Kindness," Rosemerry Wahtola Trommer invites us to see how these kindnesses might rise up again in us later on like tulips—"a bit of beauty" that has blossomed from the root of "a kind word, perhaps, or a touch, the gift of their time or their smile." The smallest gifts can transform the ground that we are into something new, until some long-ago tenderness "emerges again, pushing aside the dead leaves, insisting on loveliness," perhaps when someone else needs it the most. The final lines of the poem remind us that when we can notice the fruits of some past kindness in ourselves, this becomes "a celebration of the one who planted it" as well as "the one who perceives it." We can rejoice in recognizing how we have "grown" like those tulips because of the caring attention of the many who came before us.

Invitation for Writing and Reflection
Consider all the ways that others have planted "a bit of beauty" in you, and all the many kindnesses you have offered others. How has your own life changed as a result of such simple, caring actions?

Kai Coggin

INTO WILDFLOWER INTO FIELD

it's dusk and I watch you
water our newly-planted garden,
the radish and arugula
are first to push up through the soil,
green hands in prayer
unfolding toward sun and sky
and I sit on the side and write
as you coax them
toward you

it's like you're singing
invisibly to the sleeping bed of seeds
like I can see the vibration of
your gentle harvest hope

my own fingers
begin searching the earth
my body bends toward the light
of you
I green into a personal spring
my seeds
break open again
and again
searching for sun and sky *(your eyes)*

constant gardener—
you water the drought of me

into wildflower
into royal meadow
into fields and fields and fields

did you ever think our lives
would bloom into this?

on the ridge-line
the setting day paints
us in an impermanent gold
but even now in the darkest dark of night
everything around us is aglow

Laura Budofsky Wisniewski

A BEGINNER'S GUIDE TO GARDENING ALONE

Because a hummingbird perched
on a high branch of the alder,
because I raised my eyes
from the ground of my obsessions
I saw her linger.
Because a green tinged feather causes this world
with its fools' winds, with its flawed light
with its thrusts, its false fledges,
a red hibiscus opened.
Its petals were like palms parting,
like the lips of the world parting.
Because a teardrop of nectar ran
from the deep mine of the flower
onto its trembling stamen,
onto its stigma, its muteness,
onto its speckled rubies,
I brought my hands together.
Between my palms, there formed
a dark cave of prayer. Between my lips,
there slipped a faint breath of flight.

Heather Lanier

THE HEARTBEAT OF MY UNBORN CHILD

used to be a flutter, a hummingbird's
blurry wing buzzing
a half-inch of spring,

is now a runner
barefoot through a wet forest.

Determined. Compelled
by what, I wonder?
Chasing nothing but another
and another and another beat?
The chance to be

in a new now?
The want, my barely baby, as simple as that
single grass blade being,
in this new season of green,
its thin bendable self in the sun?

Mary Elder Jacobsen

SPONGE BATH

At first, to let him know I'm here,
I start with song, a kind of coo,
or croon. My voice breaks,
morning waking into lullaby.
I test the water at my wrist,
here, the bare pulse point.
Not hot. Not cold. Just warm.
I dip the soft infant cloth into
the wash basin, swish, and squeeze.
Damp, not dripping. I bring
some order to our routine, begin
with crown, brow, temples.
Traveling the topography
of the face—ears, eyes,
mouth, nose—all our animal
pathways, I grow humbled
by the whole of us, this space
I find myself within, caring for
another being, my newborn
at home, only a few days old,
a kind of gift that overwhelms,
to know we've only just begun
to say hello.

Laura Grace Weldon

MOST IMPORTANT WORD

Before teaching my first child
all eight letters of his name,
I showed him how to write
the most important word.

Tongue tucked against upper lip,
pencil tight in soft four-year-old fingers,
he copied my letters. Drew
a chairback with wobbly seat,
tippy egg, empty ice cream cone,
pitchfork without a handle.

That spells *LOVE*, I told him.
He wrote it on crayoned pictures,
breath-fogged windows,
chalked sidewalks.
He wrote it alongside the next words
he learned—*love mom, love dad, love tree,
love* squeezed next to his own name.

Shapes unlocked into symbols,
soon he read aloud stories
to go with pictures he drew.
Now I teach his daughter
that first magical word.
She concentrates,
lines rollicking onto the paper,
tongue curled against her lip.

James Crews

ONLY LOVE

Only love is big enough to hold all the pain of this world.
—*Sharon Salzberg*

And so I imagine the entire earth
as one beating heart held in the space
of this universe, inside a larger body
we can't fathom, filling with enough
love to lead each of us out of the cave
of our personal pain and into the light—
enough love to lead all humans as one
out of collective fear, rage, and hate
into a place of peace that is found only
within our own hearts, beating in sync
with the pulse of this planet we were
born to inhabit, despite the daily storms
which overtake us and make us forget
we are the lifeblood pumped into these
veins, every particle of love we generate
running into rivers, lakes, and creeks,
evaporating into the air we breathe,
give back, and breathe again.

David Van Houten

BREATHE

beside a dry river wash
stands a grove of desert pines

steadfast trunks rise from roots
braided deep within the earth

branches stretch overhead
arc in full canopy

offer shelter from relentless heat
amid streams of filtered sunlight

ground dense with needlework
no footstep is heard

boughs beckon in the breeze
move me to pause

ease into their embrace
accept their generosity

surrender
to shaded sanctuary

January Gill O'Neil

ELATION

In the city's center is an unwalled forest:
a dense plot of cedars so thick their canopy
keeps light from reaching the ground.

We gaze at the stretched-out stalks—
Etiolation, you say, pointing skyward,
but all I hear is *elation*.

It's the elongation of stems,
the branches growing up, not out,
their long trunks turned white

from too little light. Tolerant trees.
They claim this space as their own,
making the most of what's given them.

Their back and forth sway moves us.
We listen to spindly trees creaking—
rocking chairs on a wooden porch,

the sound of a cello's drawn breath,
the clatter of branches like the chatter
between old, coupled voices

when no one is around.

Tricia Knoll

MY DAUGHTER MEETS MY WHITE PINE

That was my woodlot; that was my lot in the woods. The silvery needles of the pine straining the light.
—*Henry David Thoreau*

If we added together your age
and mine, this pine is older,
destined to outlive us both.
Touch its bark,
trace the puzzle pieces.
A thin maple twines beside
and up inside the pine:
maple's red-gold flaunting
its place within wind-blown silver.

You study the bowing-to-earth gnarled
branching of this wolf tree, an old one spared
to leave shade for grazers when the woods
was cleared for pasture, a century older
than other trees in the forest.

You see my sacred tree as a scientist does;
I see this as a mother.

We are not so different—
years from now, return,
to sit under one limb or the other
to remember me,
after the crickets stop singing.

Julie Cadwallader Staub

TURNING

There comes a time in every fall
before the leaves begin to turn
when blackbirds group and flock and gather
choosing a tree, a branch, together
to click and call and chorus and clamor
announcing the season has come for travel.

Then comes a time when all those birds
without a sound or backward glance
pour from every branch and limb
into the air, as if on a whim
but it's a dynamic, choreographed mass
a swoop, a swerve, a mystery, a dance

and now the tree stands breathless, amazed
at how it was chosen, how it was changed.

Ingrid Goff-Maidoff

PEACE CAME TODAY

Peace came today
through a slender breeze.
Stopping for a moment in the field,
I felt the clouds of my mind
gently lift and move along.
Some days it happens like this—
with simplicity, lightness, ease.

Others, I must haul my complaints
to the ocean's edge,
look out across the blue water,
out beyond I know not what,
somewhere past the horizon,
and beseech, and invoke, and beg,
and breathe the salt air in
until, quieted again, I am opened
with no words to pour in between
this life and the life I am living.

Nothing left to long for.
Nothing left to say.

Kim Stafford

A CHAIR BY THE CREEK

Someone spoke twisted words to hurt you,
control you, tarnish your name. Good thing
you have this chair out under the cottonwoods
where leaves swivel trouble away.

A nosey neighbor shouts across the property line—
something about your right to be. Good thing those
words were swallowed by the friendly rattle
and chuckle of the creek.

Settled in your chair, enchanted by moving water,
your thoughts turn green, your heart fills with
slanted sunlight, whisper of aspen. You put all
words of envy, anger, and greed into the sound

of moving water, and listen as they flow away.

Danny Dover

FLOODWOOD POND

Before a shattered world
can begin to heal
it might first float here
amid moss and minnows
in the shimmering mist
of an approaching dawn.

We have only this body
and only one earth
made from flesh and blood
of porous mountains
where a doubtful heart
may soak in warm
uncertainty.

You could stay awhile
with breath and gravity
your only guides
a primal sound
pooling and rising
from somewhere deep
within your belly.

And if you pray to stars
then here is the infinite
dance of light
upon a shrine
of rippling water.

Ted Kooser

FILLING THE CANDLES

The eight candles that stand at the altar
aren't candles at all, but oil lamps
in the waxy white raiment of candles.

A woman has come, through snow, alone
on Saturday, to fill them, a plastic jug
in one hand, a funnel and rag in the other.

From a high window, soft hands of light,
in reds, blues and greens, pat snow
from the sleeves of her winter parka,

brush flakes from her silvery hair
as she moves from wick to wick to wick,
lifting the brass caps, trickling the oil.

The church is otherwise empty, dark
and cold, but now those eight flames burn
within her as she caps and tilts the jug

into the light to see how much is gone,
the day, too, halfway gone, not spilled
but used, a little warmth within it.

Mary Ray Goehring

PINCH POT

It fits perfectly
into the cup of my hands
when they are pressed together as if holding
precious water gathered fresh
from a clear ice-capped mountain stream

A pinch pot
made by my son in high school
terra cotta colored clay
carefully smoothed by his hands
rounded on the bottom like a bowl
or an ancient Anasazi vessel

Inside
an indigo blue glazed line
spirals away from the center
as if this opening
this empty space
can be forever filled
to overflowing

Into the cradle of my hands
it conjoins
like a prayer
finally answered

Margaret Hasse

CLOTHING

Clothes press against
the glass window
of a washing machine
like faces in the rain.

After they've spun
in the big dryer, I fold
my baby's plush onesies,
my son's favorite jeans,
and t-shirts my husband
taught me to roll
like window shades
when it's my turn
to do the laundry.

I stack up the items
then hug everything
to my chest, smelling
warm clean cotton
that covers the ones I love.

Angela Narciso Torres

CHORE

My friend turns anything into
prayer. Sweeping the leaves, shaving
his beard, washing dishes—

every act a purging
of what doesn't serve. Today
I'm folding laundry. I start with jeans,

crisp from the dryer, smoothing the creases
then draping them on wooden hangers.
Shaking wrinkles from the sheets, I square

the corners the way Mother taught.
White T-shirts stacked flat on a shelf,
sundresses on felt hangers, sweaters

nestled in drawers. I find a place
for every blouse, every scarf, until
it feels inevitable. *Order our days—*

the remnant floats up from decades
of Sundays like words of a forgotten
song—*in Your peace.* My mantra:

fold, hang, repeat, the hamper
half-empty, the bureau warm
with balled-up socks.

REFLECTIVE PAUSE

The Sacred Everyday

By describing how a friend can turn any chore into a form of prayer, and then showing us how she does this simply by folding laundry, Angela Narciso Torres teaches us to transform ordinary tasks of our lives into acts of generosity. She writes so carefully and lovingly of how she smoothes, folds, stacks, and drapes all of her family's clothing, we can't help but feel a sense of calm and order emanating from this simple scene. The gateway to a mindful poem that stays with the reader is often strong sensory details; and the sense that stands out in this poem is that of touch and texture. Notice how those creased jeans, felt hangers, and "sweaters nestled in drawers" all come to physical life, until we reach the final, vivid lines describing the bureau now "warm with balled-up socks." That warmth passes not only to the dresser she's filling with folded clothing but also to the reader as we feel those socks fresh from the dryer, each one blessed for a moment by the heat of her attentive touch, turning what could have been an unpleasant chore into a kindness that she offers her family.

Invitation for Writing and Reflection
How might you bring a sense of the sacred and reverence to the repetitive tasks you have to complete each day? Is there some chore that has been transformed for you into an act of generosity or devotion, a kind of offering?

Twyla M. Hansen

TRYING TO PRAY

With my arms raised in a vee,
I gather the heavens and bring
my hands down slow together,
press palms and bow my head.

I try to forget the suffering,
the wars, the ravage of land
that threatens songbirds,
butterflies, and pollinators.

The ghosts of their wings flutter
past my closed eyes as I breathe
the spirit of seasons, the stirrings
in soil, trees moving with sap.

With my third eye, I conjure
the red fox, its healthy tail, recount
the good of this world, the farmer
tending her tomatoes, the beans

dazzled green *al dente* in butter,
salt and pepper, cows munching
on grass. The orb of sun-gold
from which all bounty flows.

Joy Harjo

FOR KEEPS

Sun makes the day new.
Tiny green plants emerge from earth.
Birds are singing the sky into place.
There is nowhere else I want to be but here.
I lean into the rhythm of your heart to see where it will
    take us.
We gallop into a warm, southern wind.
I link my legs to yours and we ride together,
Toward the ancient encampment of our relatives.
Where have you been? they ask.
And what has taken you so long?
That night after eating, singing, and dancing
We lay together under the stars.
We know ourselves to be part of mystery.
It is unspeakable.
It is everlasting.
It is for keeps.

Barbara Crooker

SUSTENANCE

The sky hangs up its starry pictures: a swan,
a crab, a horse. And even though you're
three hundred miles away, I know you see
them, too. Right now, my side
of the bed is empty, a clear blue lake
of flannel. The distance yawns and stretches.
It's hard to remember we swim in an ocean
of great love, so easy to fall into bickering
like little birds at the feeder fighting over proso
and millet, unaware of how large the bag of grain is,
a river of golden seeds, that the harvest was plentiful,
the corn is in the barn, and whenever we're hungry,
a dipperful of just what we need will be spilled . . .

Ruth Arnison

TWENTY YEARS OF LONGING

She leans back.
His arms curl around
holding her against him.

She releases twenty years
of longing to the wind and grabs from it
a new breath.

His face nuzzles into her hair,
fingertips surfing over the waves of connection.
She turns, molding her face into his.

Bare feet sinking into the wet sand,
tangled talkative toes expressing love
as they breathe into each other's bloodstream.

Curtained by windblown hair
their mouths merge, eyes blinded as tongues braille
each other's senses, finding their way home.

Danusha Laméris

THE HEART IS NOT

A pocket. A thing that
can be turned inside out
by anybody's hand. Not
a place for pebbles or loose
change. Not to carry old
receipts. It does not tear
at the seam. It doesn't have
a seam. It cannot be torn.

Laura Foley

LEARNING BY HEART

I was seven, couldn't sleep,
fearing my French teacher,
afraid I couldn't learn
a line I had to memorize.

Mom, trilling the night's
loneliest hour, at the piano,
made up a lilting song,
to help me remember—

I did, and still do,
her voice etched in tenderness,
fingers running over the keys,
somewhere deep inside me.

Jacqueline Jules

BILLOWING OVERHEAD

Her absence is like the sky, spread over everything.
—*C.S. Lewis*

It's not your absence I feel,
but your presence, palpable,
still snoring on the sofa
after chemo.

You are not missing
from any moment I breathe.

You exist.

In the painting you bought on a trip to Spain.
The chipped blue mug from your alma mater.
Broadway tickets I found in a drawer.

You are with me.

On the grocery shelf
beside those square orange crackers
you ate by the box.

In the sky,
billowing overhead,
declaring your existence
as someone still loved
on this earth.

Penny Harter

TWO METEORS

Two meteors flared last night, flamed above
the twilit trees, their arcing signatures dropping
so quickly they sputtered out and died.

Driving on, I thought that we must burn through
whatever sorrows ride our shoulders, or learn to
carry them like that young turtle I saw today

crossing the road before me, bearing his shell.
I did not stop to help, only swerved to avoid him,
then looked in the rear-view mirror, hoping that

he was still on his way. And I wrapped a prayer
around his fragile back, blessing his stumpy legs
and plodding faith on that slowly darkening road.

Tom Hennen

MADE VISIBLE

The world is full of bodies. It's a happy thing and they should all be loved. Human bodies, raccoon bodies, blueberry and limestone bodies are the shapes we take when we want to be seen. How curious we are when we wake up and find ourselves in one of these new homes. The feel of snow, which we faintly remember, also the smell of wind, the sunshine's sweet taste. Sometimes I forget which body I'm in, like now, as I rest on my favorite log, an old aspen near Muddy Creek. The log, warm in the spring day, seems to lose more weight each year. It is dissolving as it dries. Before long it will be light enough to lift off the ground, rise past the treetops and into the sky, leaving behind the reminder that we are meant to spend our whole lives trembling in anticipation of the next instant.

Cornelius Eady

A SMALL MOMENT

I walk into the bakery next door
To my apartment. They are about
To pull some sort of toast with cheese
From the oven. When I ask:
What's that smell? I am being
A poet, I am asking

What everyone else in the shop
Wanted to ask, but somehow couldn't;
I am speaking on behalf of two other
Customers who wanted to buy the
Name of it. I ask the woman
Behind the counter for a percentage
Of her sale. Am I flirting?
Am I happy because the days
Are longer? Here's what

She does: She takes her time
Choosing the slices. "I am picking
Out the good ones," she tells me. It's
April 14th. Spring, with five to ten
Degrees to go. Some days, I feel my duty;
Some days, I love my work.

Zoe Higgins

ODE

Here's to everything undone today:
laundry left damp in the machine,
the relatives unrung, the kitchen
drawer not sorted; here's to jeans
unpatched and buttons missing,
the dirty dishes, the novel
not yet started. To Christmas
cards unsent in March, to emails
marked unread. To friends unmet
and deadlines unaddressed;
to every item not crossed off the list;
to everything still left, ignored, put off:
it is enough.

Donna Hilbert

CREDO

I believe in the Tuesdays
and Wednesdays of life,
the tuna sandwich lunches
and TV after dinner.
I believe in coffee with hot milk
and peanut butter toast,
Rosé wine in summer
and Burgundy in winter.
I am not in love with holidays,
birthdays—nothing special—
and weekends are just days
numbered six and seven,
though my love
dozing over TV golf
while I work the Sunday puzzle
might be all I need of life
and all I ask of heaven.

James Crews

SELF-CARE

Some days it feels like a foreign language
I'm asked to practice, with new words
for happiness, work, and love. I'm still learning
how to say: a cup of tea for no reason,
what to call the extra honey I drizzle in,
how to label the relentless urge to do more
and more as *useless*. And how to translate
the heart's pounding message when it comes:
enough, enough. This morning, I search for words
to capture the glimmering sun as it lifts
above the mountains, clouds already closing in
as fat droplets of rain darken the deck.
I'm learning to call this stillness self-care too,
just standing here, as goldfinches scatter up
from around the feeder like broken pieces
of bright yellow stained-glass, reassembling
in the sheltering arms of a maple.

REFLECTIVE PAUSE

Reassembling the Parts

In my poem "Self-Care," I am thinking about the habits of busyness and how self-care is a new language I have to learn again and again. Often, after a stressful time, I need space and stillness to let go of the frenetic energy coursing through my body. This takes hours of gentle living and what can feel like indulgence to the logical mind, even when the heart tells me I've had enough. But if I sit on the back porch with a cup of tea, just watching chipmunks and squirrels scurry through the yard—if I hit the pause button—I always return to life and work refreshed, less driven by pressure and fear. If I take a moment to appreciate the sunrise, a new one every day, or stop at the kitchen window to note the comings and goings of birds at the feeder, I punctuate my endless stream of thinking with a little space outside of time. During these slower moments of what I call "soul time," gratitude often slips in. My problems don't disappear, but are right-sized in the container of a mind that takes in the vastness of the world around me. The parts that feel shattered and scattered slowly reassemble, clicking back into place like the pieces of a jigsaw puzzle that reveals a fuller picture of life.

Invitation for Writing and Reflection
Can you recall an instance when you were especially kind to yourself, perhaps taking the time and making space for more gratitude in your days?

January Gill O'Neil

SUNDAY

You are the start of the week
or the end of it, and according
to The Beatles you creep in
like a nun. You're the second
full day the kids have been
away with their father, the second
full day of an empty house.
Sunday, I've missed you. I've been
sitting in the backyard with a glass
of Pinot waiting for your arrival.
Did you know the first Sweet 100s
are turning red in the garden,
but the lettuce has grown
too bitter to eat. I am looking
up at the bluest sky I have ever seen,
cerulean blue, a heaven sky
no one would believe I was under.
You are my witness. No day
is promised. You are absolution.
You are my unwritten to-do list,
my dishes in the sink, my brownie
breakfast, my braless day.

Laura Grace Weldon

THURSDAY MORNING

Darkness frees me to stand nightgowned
on the porch, watch
the dogs merge into shadow,
snuffle, pee, reappear.

I stretch, inhale summer's warm weight,
imagine staying in this spot
while what has to be done
swirls by undone.

I imagine a taproot growing down my spine,
out my feet, through the porch floor
and deep underground,
rootlets reaching all directions.

Imagine remaining here so long
I fade from sight, although
everyone crossing this portal
pauses as they pass through my arms.

Joy Gaines-Friedler

TOUCH

A chickadee lands in your hand
its body a buoy.

It grips your finger. You
don't hold it. It holds you.

It is a kiss, both hard & soft,
both lip & bone.

On your way about your life,
at the mailbox or a stop light,

your body remembers
those feathers. That touch & others.

Heather Swan

ON LIGHTNESS

Outside my window,
a wren alights
on a fiddlehead fern,
and the plant is forced
to bend its green spine.
As he rests there,
the air never leaves
the bird's body—
the way he floats
through trees. And then
he takes to the sky again,
and the fern sways
upright, opening its arms,
once again, to the sun.
If only it could always
be like this:
the burden of one
never breaking another.

José A. Alcantara

DIVORCE

He has flown headfirst against the glass
and now lies stunned on the stone patio,
nothing moving but his quick beating heart.
So you go to him, pick up his delicate
body and hold him in the cupped palms
of your hands. You have always known
he was beautiful, but it's only now, in his stillness,
in his vulnerability, that you see the miracle
of his being, how so much life fits in so small
a space. And so you wait, keeping him warm
against the unseasonable cold, trusting that
when the time is right, when he has recovered
both his strength and his sense of up and down,
he will gather himself, flutter once or twice,
and then rise, a streak of dazzling
color against a slowly lifting sky.

Susan Moorhead

SHIFT

If you hold a sparrow
in the cup of your hand,
a found one, stunned
by the smash of glass
that was window not sky,
forever after
when you see a sparrow,
you'll remember
the feel of the feather-soft body,
the tiny heart beating against
your fingers.

Tracy K. Smith

SONG

I think of your hands all those years ago
Learning to maneuver a pencil, or struggling
To fasten a coat. The hands you'd sit on in class,
The nails you chewed absently. The clumsy authority
With which they'd sail to the air when they knew
You knew the answer. I think of them lying empty
At night, of the fingers wrangling something
From your nose, or buried in the cave of your ear.
All the things they did cautiously, pointedly,
Obedient to the suddenest whim. Their shames.
How they failed. What they won't forget year after year.
Or now. Resting on the wheel or the edge of your knee.
I am trying to decide what they feel when they wake up
And discover my body is near. Before touch.
Pushing off the ledge of the easy quiet dancing between us.

Mark Nepo

DRINKING THERE

No matter how many conversations I
start, they all end with me kneeling at
the same deep well. And drinking there,
I remember who I am. I rise from that
drinking able to see, again, that we are
at heart the same. And the secret wound
you show me there is my wound which I
have hidden for so long. And the secret
joy you bring into the open is my joy
which I thought I had lost. Experience
has us meet in the most unexpected ways.
Until we're forced to show the soft center
that never dies. Until our soul appears in
the world like a pearl before it hardens.
Until the gift of life stirs in our hand
like a tuft of feathers that needs to
be loved into a wing.

Susan Musgrave

MORE THAN SEEING

There is a moment before the kingfisher dives,
the eagle swoops, the small green ducks disappear
like the breeze in the low hanging cedar branches
over the river; there is a moment before I name
the kingfisher, the eagle, the ducks when I am not
the observer, I am the dart of light, rush of wings,
the trusting wind; I am grace: an end of living
in awe of things, a beginning of living with them.

Julia Fehrenbacher

THE MOST IMPORTANT THING

I am making a home inside myself. A shelter
of kindness where everything
is forgiven, everything allowed—a quiet patch
of sunlight to stretch out without hurry,
where all that has been banished and buried
is welcomed, spoken, listened to—released.

A fiercely friendly place I can claim as my very own.

I am throwing arms open
to the whole of myself—especially the fearful,
fault-finding, falling apart, unfinished parts, knowing
every seed and weed, every drop
of rain, has made the soil richer.

I will light a candle, pour a hot cup of tea, gather
around the warmth of my own blazing fire. I will howl
if I want to, knowing this flame can burn through
any perceived problem, any prescribed perfectionism,
any lying limitation, every heavy thing.

I am making a home inside myself
where grace blooms in grand and glorious
abundance, a shelter of kindness that grows
all the truest things.

I whisper hallelujah to the friendly
sky. Watch now as I burst into blossom.

Julia Alvarez

VAIN DOUBTS

Years ago now—a breezy, bygone day,
walking a city street, my hair tossing,
feeling the beauty of my young body,
that animal friskiness triggered by spring,
I glanced admiringly at my reflection
in a storefront window, tossing my head
to watch that mirrored waving of a mane
I thought my best feature—when a young man
coming in my direction barred my way.
Glaring at me, he uttered, "Vanity!"

And I was stopped in my mindless moment
of physical joy, shamed to associate
that deadly sin with the upsurge of life
and self-love I'd been feeling, never doubting
my urban prophet had been right. Vanity—
so this was what that ugly sin felt like!
In his disgust, I heard the click of keys
in convents, harems, attics, marriages,
down the generations, doors closing on
bodies that could give both pleasure and life.

Now that the years have granted me release
from such vain doubts, I'd like to post myself
at slumber parties, bathrooms, dressing rooms,
wherever young girls gather, frowning at
their wrong-size figures, blah hair, blemished skin—
already taught to find fault or disguise
joy in their bodies. I'd like to be the voice
that drowns out their self-doubt, singing in praise
of what I couldn't see when I was young:
we're simply beautiful, just as we are.

Molly Fisk

BEFORE I GAINED ALL THIS WEIGHT

I was so self-conscious I could barely
walk into town for fear people
would stare. I thought I was hideous,
unlovable. Now I want to shake
that poor girl, even though it wasn't
her fault, so afraid to be human—
rattle her cage of good grades, self-
tanning lotion and green eye-liner,
fast-acting depilatory cream, tell her
to smile for God's sake and kiss
the next boy she sees, life is shorter
than anyone imagines. Silver planes
plummet from clean skies, cancer gnaws
the marrow of even younger bones
than yours, wake up! There's still time!
Everything around you is unbelievably
beautiful.

Ross Gay

THANK YOU

If you find yourself half naked
and barefoot in the frosty grass, hearing,
again, the earth's great, sonorous moan that says
you are the air of the now and gone, that says
all you love will turn to dust,
and will meet you there, do not
raise your fist. Do not raise
your small voice against it. And do not
take cover. Instead, curl your toes
into the grass, watch the cloud
ascending from your lips. Walk
through the garden's dormant splendor.
Say only, thank you.
Thank you.

Lorna Crozier

SMALL LESSON

Hoarfrost
feathering the window
and behind that

a high cloud
and behind that
the winter moon.

Three things without
their own light
yet how they shine.

Leah Naomi Green

THE AGE OF AFFECTION

Thank you, moon, for following
across the pond

while I walked,
for bringing me

to the shore
to say goodnight.

The affection
of your speech

is inside me.
That is exactly where I want it.

Has anyone I've loved
ever been

anywhere else?
You followed over the field too,

and into the house,
though the grass

did not reflect you,
or the milky way rising,

as I can sometimes witness
even from inside it.

Barbara Crooker

FORSYTHIA

What must it feel like
after months of existing
as bare brown sticks,
all reasonable hope
of blossoming lost,
to suddenly, one warm
April morning, burst
into wild yellow song,
hundreds of tiny prayer
flags rippling in the still-
cold wind, the only flash
of color in the dull yard,
these small scraps of light,
something we might
hold on to.

Karen Craigo

LAST SCRAPS OF COLOR IN MISSOURI

Today I passed a stand
of trees: tall, closely packed,
bare and almost black
from rain. But underneath,
I saw smaller trees, just
getting started on their slow
snatch-and-grab of sky,
and I saw these were golden
still, and they glowed
like campfires in the dark.
Lately I'd been wanting
a little light — and there it was,
and all I had to do was turn
my gaze a few degrees
from center. Some blessings
find us when we move to them —
they're waiting only to be seen.
Near the end of a difficult year,
may we spot the light,
as we breathe in prayer
or supplication: *Show me,
show me, show me.*

Ted Kooser

IT DOESN'T TAKE MUCH

Maybe an hour before sunrise, driving alone
on the way to reach somewhere, seeing,
set back from the highway, the dark shape
of a farmhouse up against deeper darkness,
a light in one window. Or farther along

into a gray, watery dawn, passing
a McDonald's, lighted bright as a city,
and seeing one man, in ball cap, alone
in a booth, not looking down at his table
but ahead, over the empty booths. Or

maybe an hour farther, in full daylight,
at a place where a bus stops, seeing
a woman somewhere in her forties,
dressed for cold, wearing white ear muffs,
a red and white team jacket, blue jeans

and Muk Luks, one knit mitten holding
a slack empty mitten, her bare hand
extended, pinching a lit cigarette,
dry leaves—the whole deck of a new day—
fanned out face-down in the gutter, but

she's not stooping to turn over a card,
but instead watching a long ash grow
even longer at the ends of her fingers.
Just that much might be enough for one
morning to make you feel part of it all.

REFLECTIVE PAUSE

Part of It All Again

In "It Doesn't Take Much," Ted Kooser shows us how simply noticing the people we encounter, and seeing them in all their uniqueness and humanity, can become a form of kindness. The speaker of this poem at first seems lonely as he drives aimlessly "into a gray, watery dawn," yet even the "bright city" of a fast-food restaurant, and the man at a booth inside, can remind him he's not entirely alone in the world. When we're feeling disconnected, we often forget that one of the surest ways to lift ourselves out of despair is to give our attention to the people around us. Instead of just speeding past the woman he sees waiting at a bus stop, for instance, he takes in all of her details, from how she's dressed to the way she's "pinching a lit cigarette." Though he has not spoken to the man and woman he describes, by the end of the poem, he nevertheless feels more connected to the larger world, "part of it all" again, having shifted his focus away from himself and his own troubles to what's around him, remembering that there are countless stories contained in each person we meet, even if we do only briefly glimpse them as we move through our lives.

Invitation for Writing and Reflection
The next time you find yourself struggling or distracted, absorbed in your own thoughts and worries, take a notebook or laptop out into the world, and truly notice the people who cross your path. Who stands out to you, and what details might give you a glimpse into their story?

Ellen Bass

THE THING IS

to love life, to love it even
when you have no stomach for it
and everything you've held dear
crumbles like burnt paper in your hands,
your throat filled with the silt of it.
When grief sits with you, its tropical heat
thickening the air, heavy as water
more fit for gills than lungs;
when grief weights you down like your own flesh
only more of it, an obesity of grief,
you think, *How can a body withstand this?*
Then you hold life like a face
between your palms, a plain face,
no charming smile, no violet eyes,
and you say, yes, I will take you
I will love you, again.

James Crews

SELF-COMPASSION

My friend and I snickered the first time
we heard the meditation teacher, a grown man,
call himself *honey*, with a hand placed
over his heart to illustrate how we too
might become more gentle with ourselves
and our runaway minds. It's been years
since we sat with legs twisted on cushions,
holding back our laughter, but today
I found myself crouched on the floor again,
not meditating exactly, just agreeing
to be still, saying *honey* to myself each time
I thought about my husband splayed
on the couch with aching joints and fever
from a tick bite—what if he never gets better?—
or considered the threat of more wildfires,
the possible collapse of the Gulf Stream,
then remembered that in a few more minutes,
I'd have to climb down to the cellar and empty
the bucket I placed beneath a leaky pipe
that can't be fixed until next week. How long
does any of us really have before the body
begins to break down and empty its mysteries
into the air? Oh *honey*, I said—for once

without a trace of irony or blush of shame—
the touch of my own hand on my chest
like that of a stranger, oddly comforting
in spite of the facts.

Kelli Russell Agodon

PRAISE

Find me wild about stir-fry, about red velvet
sofas and the people who sleep inside books
and dream about commas. We are flooded
with forgetfulness, with fallen plum blossoms
misspelling our names on the driveway. Praise
our too many expectations, how we overestimate
the weather, each other, overestimate how deer
will appear if we arrive with food. Because reality
can be a knife, we sometimes ache to tear open
the tea bag, the ketchup packet, because wine
arrives ready to be poured, we are foolish
and happy—though our clothes do not fit,
we return to being alive and living
between roadblocks and detours, driving
our fingers into the edge of each other's
pockets. Praise the bare trees that tried
to spell our names for their belief
they could—spells and misspellings,
fail and fail better, how lucky we are
just to be here, both of us touching each other
through these words, with all this exasperating joy.

Dorianne Laux

JOY

Even when the gods have driven you
from your home, your friends, the tree
you planted brought down by storm,
drought, chain saw, beetles, even

when you've been scrubbed
hollow by confusion, loss,
accept joy, those unbidden
moments of surcease—

the quiet unfolding
around your shoulders
like a shawl, the warmth
that doesn't turn to burning.

When the itch has stopped, the cough,
the throb, the heart's steady beat
resumed, the barn door

open to the shade, the horse inside
waiting for your touch, apple
in your pocket pocked, riddled

the last to fall, the season
done. As you would accept
air into your lungs, without
thinking, not counting

each breath. As you accepted
the earth the first time you stood
up on it and it held you, how it was

just there, a solid miracle,
gravity something you would
learn about only later
and still be amazed.

Jack Ridl

TAKE LOVE FOR GRANTED

Assume it's in the kitchen,
under the couch, high
in the pine tree out back,
behind the paint cans
in the garage. Don't try
proving your love
is bigger than the Grand
Canyon, the Milky Way,
the urban sprawl of L.A.
Take it for granted. Take it
out with the garbage. Bring
it in with the takeout. Take
it for a walk with the dog.
Wake it every day, say,
"Good morning." Then
make the coffee. Warm
the cups. Don't expect much
of the day. Be glad when
you make it back to bed.
Be glad he threw out that
box of old hats. Be glad
she leaves her shoes
in the hall. Snow will
come. Spring will show up.
Summer will be humid.
The leaves will fall

in the fall. That's more
than you need. We can
love anybody, even
everybody. But *you*
can love the silence,
sighing and saying to
yourself, "That' s her."
"That's him." Then to
each other, "I know!
Let's go out for breakfast!"

Terri Kirby Erickson

FREE BREAKFAST

The Springhill Suites free breakfast area
was filling up fast when a man carrying his
disabled young son lowered him into his
chair, the same way an expert pilot's airplane
kisses the runway when it lands. And all the
while, the man whispered into his boy's ear,
perhaps telling him about the waffle maker
that was such a hit with the children gathered
around it, or sharing the family's plans for the
day as they traveled to wherever they were
going. Whatever was said, the boy's face was
alight with some anticipated happiness. And
the father, soon joined by the mother, seemed
intent on providing it. So beautiful they all
were, it was hard to concentrate on our eggs
and buttered toast, to look away when his
parents placed their hands on the little boy's
shoulders and smiled at one another, as if
they were the luckiest people in the room.

Annie Lighthart

PASSENGER

This child between us here in our dark bed asks nothing
but to be held all night, to burrow, to stay wedged
and warmed by our bodies until day.
Tomorrow he will demand more jam, will need
new shoes, will drop the toast and plate to the floor.
But just now, here, breathing softly between us,
he is a small Venetian gondolier refusing pay,
taking us back and forth all night singing
underneath the Bridge of Sighs.

Christine Stewart-Nuñez

SITE PLANNING

As I cross this network of interstates
driving toward home, I'm dried out
of words until I hear *neural network*
on the radio, and I picture a lake
with streams that branch and taper.
Net. Work. My mother-made nets
for my oldest son: family, stories,
photos, arms reaching, reaching.
Across chasms, I've woven lifelines
to schools, doctors, and specialists
so he won't fall through. And as I drive
past fields so flooded I can't see
where they thin or end, I recall
the pervasiveness of his seizures—
one per minute when he slept.
They're receding now, but what
will they leave when they've dried up?
Some say new knowledge and new
memories; I imagine sunflower fields.
What work will my nets do then?
Perhaps he'll make his own trawls
weave into mine. Either way, each day
brings a facet of him to the surface,
polished and gleaming.

Laura Foley

A PERFECT ARC

I remember the first time he dove.
He was five and we were at a swimming pool
and I said: you tip your head down as you are going in,
while your feet go up.

And then his lithe little body did it exactly right,
a perfect dive, sliding downward, arcing without a wave,
and I just stood
amazed and without words
as his blond head came up again
and today

I watched him for the longest time as he walked
firm and upright along the street,
with backpack, guitar, all he needs,
blossoming outward in a perfect arc,
a graceful turning
away from me.

Michael Simms

THE SUMMER YOU LEARNED TO SWIM

for Lea

The summer you learned to swim
was the summer I learned to be at peace with myself.
In May you were afraid to put your face in the water
but by August, I was standing in the pool once more
when you dove in, then retreated to the wall saying,
You forgot to say Sugar! So I said Come on Sugar, you can
    do it,
and you pushed off and swam to me and held on
laughing, your hair stuck to your cheeks—
you hiccuped with joy and swam off again.
And I dove in too, trying new things.
I tried not giving advice. I tried waking early to pray. I tried
not rising in anger. Watching you I grew stronger—
your courage washed away my fear.
All day I worked hard thinking of you.
In the evening I walked the long hill home.
You were at the top, waving your small arms,
pittering down the slope to me and I lifted you high,
so high to the moon. That summer all the world
was soul and water, light glancing off peaks.
You learned the turtle, the cannonball, the froggy, and the
    flutter
and I learned to stand and wait for you to swim to me.

James Crews

THE POOL

Because he couldn't afford
the kidney-shaped, in-ground pool
we all wanted, my father went out
and bought a used galvanized pool
whose rusted rim I refused to touch.

As usual, he had a solution:
he split a length of black rubber hose
down the middle with his pocketknife
then stretched it over the rough sides,
inch by inch, until no rust showed.

Back then, I never thought such gestures
were selfless, evidence of what we call
unconditional love. But now I feel
my small hands gripping soft rubber,
and I see my father on the back porch,

cigarette hanging from his smiling lips
as he watches me lift myself
out of the pool, flinging cold water
from my goose-pimpled skin
as if I'd been reborn again.

Joyce Sutphen

CARRYING WATER TO THE FIELD

And on those hot afternoons in July,
when my father was out on the tractor
cultivating rows of corn, my mother
would send us out with a Mason jar
filled with ice and water, a dish towel
wrapped around it for insulation.

Like a rocket launched to an orbiting
planet, we would cut across the fields
in a trajectory calculated to intercept—
or, perhaps, even—surprise him
in his absorption with the row and the
turning always over earth beneath the blade.

He would look up and see us, throttle
down, stop, and step from the tractor
with the grace of a cowboy dismounting
his horse, and receive gratefully the jar
of water, ice cubes now melted into tiny
shards, drinking it down in a single gulp,
while we watched, mission accomplished.

David Romtvedt

AT THE CREEK

I go to the creek with my daughter.
We squat at the water's edge
and look around. Some pebbles,
a few sticks, a cottonwood leaf.
With these we make a tiny world
in which nothing moves.

Would that be heaven then
where all things come to rest?

It's as if I stand
once again by my desk
on the first day of school
and the teacher calls my name,
and I say, "Here."

She looks up and smiles
at me and I at her. "Here,"
I say again, "Here."

REFLECTIVE PAUSE

Would That Be Heaven?

David Romtvedt's poem begins with a father and daughter as they "squat at the water's edge," doing nothing but looking around at the seemingly plainer things of nature: "Some pebbles, a few sticks, a cottonwood leaf." And yet with these, they manage to create "a tiny world" of their own, separate from the often crowded, noisy environment many of us inhabit daily, our minds and bodies moving at speeds that leave us drained and disconnected. The speaker goes on to ask the question "Would that be heaven then where all things come to rest?" Yet he seems to know the answer, that this instant of shared time with his daughter is indeed a heaven that can never be re-created. The poem's gentle, careful touch, like that of a father leading his daughter by the hand through the woods, offers an unexpected but welcome peace to readers. The poet's question also reminds me of what St. Catherine of Siena once said: "All the way to heaven is heaven." So often, we think of paradise as some place other than where we are, even though the most lasting versions of heaven on Earth tend to be found in our own backyards, in our ordinary lives, when we pause long enough to say "Here" and "Here," over and over, calling our attention back to the now.

Invitation for Writing and Reflection

Think about a time when you discovered your own heaven embedded in a moment of togetherness with someone you cared about. What simple elements allowed you to build "a tiny world" of your own, even for just a few minutes?

Michael Kleber-Diggs

CONIFEROUS FATHERS

Let's fashion gentle fathers, expressive—holding us
how we wanted to be held before we could ask.

Singing off-key lullabies, written for us—songs
every evening, like possibilities. Fathers who say,

this is how you hold a baby, but never mention
a football. Say nothing in that moment, just bring

us to their chests naturally, without shyness.
Let's grow fathers from pine, not oak, coniferous

fathers raising us in their shade, fathers soft enough
to bend—fathers who love us like their fathers

couldn't. Fathers who can talk about menstruation
while playing a game of pepper in the front yard.

No, take baseball out. Let's discover a new sort—
fathers as varied and vast as the Superior Forest.

Let's kill off sternness and play down wisdom;
give us fathers of laughter and fathers who cry,

fathers who say *Check this out,* or *I'm scared,* or *I'm sorry,*
or *I don't know*. Give us fathers strong enough

to admit they want to be near us; they've always
wanted to be near us. Give us fathers desperate

for something different, not Johnny Appleseed,
not even Atticus Finch. No more rolling stones.

No more La-Z-Boy dads reading newspapers in
some other room. Let's create folklore side-by-side

in a garden singing psalms about abiding—just that,
abiding: being steadfast, present, evergreen, and

ethereal—let's make the old needles soft enough
for us to rest on, dream on, next to them.

Zeina Azzam

MY FATHER'S HANDS

They were not large, but thick
fleshy workers in the garden
nursing eggplants and fennel,
okra and chard,
digging and tilling and weeding,
making the soil an obliging host.

Maybe that's what made
his fingers rough in spots,
or maybe it was the constant leafing
through books: a loving lick
and a flip-flap of the page
in search of nuggets
that would be turned over and over
in his mind.

After he died
I found bookmarks between pages
carefully pointing
like tags next to seedlings in the earth:
These are the plants I hoped for.
These are the ideas that made me grow.

Li-Young Lee

EARLY IN THE MORNING

While the long grain is softening
in the water, gurgling
over a low stove flame, before
the salted Winter Vegetable is sliced
for breakfast, before the birds,
my mother glides an ivory comb
through her hair, heavy
and black as calligrapher's ink.

She sits at the foot of the bed.
My father watches, listens for
the music of comb
against hair.

My mother combs,
pulls her hair back
tight, rolls it
around two fingers, pins it
in a bun to the back of her head.
For half a hundred years she has done this.
My father likes to see it like this.
He says it is kempt.

But I know
it is because of the way

my mother's hair falls
when he pulls the pins out.
Easily, like the curtains
when they untie them in the evening.

Terri Kirby Erickson

NIGHT TALKS

When one would wake in the night, the other
followed. Then, in their bed, next to their window
that was always open, my mother and father
would talk to the sound of cars going by,
the hum of streetlights, the occasional bark
of a neighbor's dog. They spoke of high school
dances, family vacations, raising children,
being grandparents. And their faces, soft
with age and sleep, were hidden in the dark,
so they could speak at last of their lost son,
without any need to shield each other from
that pain. It must have been a relief to unpack
the shared sadness they courageously carried,
to put it down, if only for an hour. It was like
I could hear them from my own bed
across town, as I slipped into a deeper sleep,
reassured and comforted by their beloved
familiar voices echoing among the stars.

Julia Alvarez

LOVE PORTIONS

We're always fighting about household chores
but with this twist: we fight to do the work:
both wanting to fix dinner, mow the lawn,
haul the recycling boxes to the truck,
or wash the dishes when our guests depart.
I don't mean little spats, I mean real fights,
banged doors and harsh words over the soapsuds.
You did it last night! No fair, you shopped!
The feast spoils while we argue portions—
both so afraid of taking advantage.

But love should be unbalanced, a circus clown
carrying a tower of cups and saucers
who slips on a banana peel and lands
with every cup still full of hot coffee—
well, almost every cup. A field of seeds
pushing their green hopes through the frozen earth
to what might be spring or a springlike day
midwinter. Love ignores neat measures,
the waves leave ragged wet marks on the shore,
autumn lights one more fire in the maples.

Tonight, you say you're making our dinner
and won't let me so much as stir the sauce.
I march up to my study in a huff.
The oven buzzer sounds, the smells waft up
of something good I try hard to ignore

while I cook up my paper concoction.
Finally, you call me down to your chef d'oeuvre:
a three-course meal! I hand you mine, this poem.
Briefly, the scales balance between us:
food for the body, nurture for the soul.

Kate Duignan

GRANDMOTHER

When I was five
you taught me how to separate an egg.

I watched you tap it on the rim
of the bowl,
press your thumbs to the spot
and crack it clean in two.

You let me take the speckled shell
in my own hands
and rock the yolk back and forth,
quivering
as it slid from one half to the other,
a tiny yellow sun.

We put the splintered pieces
in the brown bin
for the compost

and the empty carton
in the red bin
for the incinerator.

In the garden,
the light went out of the golden elm.
We stood at the window.
The moon was a white cup.

The birds had gone to their nests, you said
and tomorrow would be a good day.

I spread my fingers on the dark glass.
Our cake, you said, would rise.

Todd Davis

HELIOTROPIC

In the evening light the dove's undersides
look yellow, and the bush that grows along
the porch has flowers red as a tanager's back.

At dinner, hummingbirds come to press needle-
beaks into trumpet-blossoms, the music
of their work drowning our conversation.

Why would anyone forsake this gospel of beauty?
Consider the bees covering the heads of sunflowers,
the sunflowers turning to follow the light.

When the world is pink, and the sun has begun
to sink to the other side of the earth, we walk
into fields tall with goldenrod to pick the daisies

my grandmother called moon-pennies, until the dark
makes it hard to see, and we must search for the light
glowing in the windows of the house to guide us home.

Marjorie Saiser

EVERYBODY IN THE SAME HOUSE

It was after someone's graduation
and even though some did
not want their picture taken,
I engineered the photo,
set up the tripod,
cajoled, insisted, got it:
faces in a jagged line,
the dog a blur,
and some of my love shining
(like now?) old-fashioned in my face.
That night everybody sleeping
under the same roof
in various cots and cubbyholes,
makeshift,
camping out.
This could be the occasion
we'll calculate from:
Remember that time
when we were all together?
That hour perhaps adjacent
to what the sacred might be:
a cave we have found, a temporary
stay, and the children
in their niches, full of sleep,
full of daring, full of risk,
turning over to other poses,
one by one, in safety.

Lahab Assef Al-Jundi

HOT TEA

Many years ago
my grandmother showed me
how to stir the sugar in my glass of hot tea.
She held the small spoon in her fingers
as if it were a feather,
lowered it until it rested on the bottom
then gently moved it from side to side.
Sugar swirled like a hazy cloud in amber sky,
then slowly faded away.
I had been spinning the spoon round and round
turning the hot liquid into a whirl,
spilling some of it over the rim.
Why is it every time I scoop a spoonful of sugar
to put in my tea
I go back to that sunny morning in Salamiyeh
sitting on colorful rugs under the big pine trees
in my grandparents' backyard?
I start to move the spoon in circles
then change,
side to side,
and momentarily get lost
in the turbulent sweet cloud
inside . . .

Gregory Orr

MORNING SONG

Sun on his face wakes him.
The boy makes his way down
through the spidery dark
of stairs to his breakfast
of cereal in a blue bowl.
He carries to the barn
a pie plate heaped
with vegetable scraps
for the three-legged deer.
As a fawn it stood still
and alone in high hay
while the red tractor
spiraled steadily inward,
mowing its precise swaths.
"I lived" is the song
the boy hears as the deer
hobbles toward him.
In the barn's huge gloom
light falls through the cracks
the way sword blades
pierce a magician's box.

Annie Lighthart

HOW TO WAKE

Wake your brother with a soft voice by his pillow.
He has been very afraid.
Wake your mother with a kiss before calling her
      name.
Wake your grandfather with a touch on his knee,
      then wait—
he has far to come from the places he's been.
Wake the young dog with an open door, wake the
      old dog
with an outstretched hand. And yourself?
How will you wake that stubborn sleeper to life?
Look for a line let down through the water.
The silver hook is baited with a word.
Bite and awaken to that wild, clear sound.

Alice Wolf Gilborn

WAKE UP

On the radio this morning
they played something truly
remarkable—the sound of unknown

birds around the world awakening
to first light, starting in the east at dawn,
going west—hoots, howls, warbles,

then riffs and trills as another
contingent, another continent woke
up, until I could feel earth itself

turning with its brocade and bristle
of trees and music, that strange
and lovely communion of birds.

I wished and failed to name them.
Miffed, I let other thoughts jump in—
What were they doing? Why were they

singing? For mates, for space, for joy?
I heard only myself, my mind a darting
squirrel making a din, while the dawning

music slowly died. Maybe it's time to listen.
To think sunrise, birds, trees, earthturn.
To sing a little song at daybreak.

Alberto Ríos

DAWN CALLERS

The dawn callers and morning bringers,
I hear them as they intend themselves to be heard,

Quick sonic sparks in the morning dark,
Hard at the first work of building the great fire.

The soloist rooster in the distance,
The cheeping wrens, the stirring, gargling pigeons

Getting ready for the work of a difficult lifetime,
The first screet of the peahen in the far field,

All of it a great tag-of-sounds game engaging even the owls,
The owls with their turned heads and everything else that is animal.

Then, too, the distant thunder of the garbage truck,
That lumbering urban whale.

Through it all, the mourning doves say
There, there—which is to say, everything is all right.

I believe them. They have said this to me ever since childhood.
I hear them. I hear them and I get up.

REFLECTIVE PAUSE

A Welcoming World

It can be useful and centering to meditate on the sounds that begin our days, becoming attuned to certain birdsongs or noises of the human-made world. In "Dawn Callers," Alberto Ríos employs a playfulness with language to convey what brings forth the morning. The speaker describes the calls of birds as "Quick sonic sparks in the morning dark" that help to awaken him. He also hears what's going on around him as "a great tag-of-sounds game," perhaps suggesting that this is a practice for him each morning, waking and naming all of the things and people that "intend themselves to be heard." He invites us to make this a habit for ourselves as well, to sense in the presence of these things that announce themselves each morning a promise that, as the mourning doves suggest, "everything is all right." Rituals like this can provide comfort, especially when our minds run away with overwhelming worry or fear. We might have to look hard in a world that is constantly changing to find such routines, to take solace in what remains the same each day. Yet we can simply pause and return to the moment, allowing the sounds of this world, whether we label them as pleasant or unpleasant, to welcome us back on the path to kindness.

Invitation for Writing and Reflection

Take some time out of the morning to notice the sounds around you that announce the new day. What can you name? What brings you comfort as you listen and identify the source of all those ritual noises?

Susan Moorhead

FIRST LIGHT

I know this sound, first birds of morning.
As a child, I waited for hours for the drape
of night to roll up again. Leaning into the first
hint of the fresh day, the fragile lace of hesitant
light, the receding darkness dappled with bird song,
able at last to close my eyes.

I know this sound, some kind of redemption,
waking me from scattered sleep, a healing fragment
even as the work of the previous day marks my bones
in notches. Night leaves its small fur as the dawn
pushes, as the birds persist, and morning unfurls
like a promise you hoped someone would keep.

Faith Shearin

MY MOTHER'S VAN

Even now it idles outside the houses
where we failed to get better at piano lessons,
visits the parking lot of the ballet school

where my sister and I stood awkwardly
at the back. My mother's van was orange
with a door we slid open to reveal
beheaded plastic dragons and bunches

of black, half-eaten bananas; it was where
her sketchbooks tarried among
abandoned coffee cups and

science projects. She meant to go places
in it: camp in its back seat
and cook on its stove while

painting the coast of Nova Scotia,
or capturing the cold beauty of the Blue Ridge
mountains at dawn. Instead, she waited
behind its wheel while we scraped violins,

made digestive sounds
with trumpets, danced badly at recitals
where grandmothers recorded us

with unsteady cameras. Sometimes, now,
I look out a window and believe I see it,
see her, waiting for me beside a curb,

under a tree, and I think I could open the door,
clear off a seat, look at the drawing in her lap,
which she began, but never seemed to finish.

Ada Limón

THE RAINCOAT

When the doctor suggested surgery
and a brace for all my youngest years,
my parents scrambled to take me
to massage therapy, deep tissue work,
osteopathy, and soon my crooked spine
unspooled a bit, I could breathe again,
and move more in a body unclouded
by pain. My mom would tell me to sing
songs to her the whole forty-five minute
drive to Middle Two Rock Road and forty-
five minutes back from physical therapy.
She'd say, even my voice sounded unfettered
by my spine afterward. So I sang and sang,
because I thought she liked it. I never
asked her what she gave up to drive me,
or how her day was before this chore. Today,
at her age, I was driving myself home from yet
another spine appointment, singing along
to some maudlin but solid song on the radio,
and I saw a mom take her raincoat off
and give it to her young daughter when
a storm took over the afternoon. My god,
I thought, my whole life I've been under her
raincoat thinking it was somehow a marvel
that I never got wet.

Marjorie Saiser

I SAVE MY LOVE

I save my love for what is close,
for the dog's eyes, the depths of brown
when I take a wet cloth to them
to remove the gunk. I save my love
for the smell of coffee at the Mill,
the roasted near-burn of it, especially
the remnant that stays later
in the fibers of my coat. I save my love
for what stays. The white puff
my breath makes when I stand
at night on my doorstep.
That mist doesn't last, gone
like your car turning the corner,
you at the wheel, waving.
Your hand a quick tremble in a
brief illumination. Palm and fingers.
Your face toward me. You had
turned on the overhead light so I would
see you for an instant, see you waving,
see you gone.

Lailah Dainin Shima

IN PRAISE OF DIRTY SOCKS

Say what you want
to stay and never fade.
Choose.

I consider my daughter's socks,
strewn on the sofa. Thick cotton.
Pink with gold-threaded hearts.
Dingy soles. Rank.

Long-ago weeks, when chemo
pinned me like a butterfly,
too nauseous to nag,
she cleaned her things
like saying a spell,
like making a wish.

How she forgets.
How I strain to remember.

How if illness or violence
should still her, the empty arms
of this charcoal couch would ache.

Now the socks draped here
quiet my mind, as morning wind
churns, ferrying amber leaves.

Carolee Bennett

EXACTLY 299,792,458 METERS PER SECOND

On the screen, shadows and bones. My son's
right arm. Radius in two. Displaced. Separated.
In the ER bed, he curls around the misshapen
limb, his skeleton a tiny crescent. Someone's
cranium is projected on the wall in another
room, glaring at us just like the full moon does.
Has it been a skull up above all along? And was
anyone cradling that child until he found his mother?
These questions haunt us, but there is within a secret
glow, exposed by x-ray like a telescope aimed down at
night sky. I don't know where luminosity comes
from, but I've watched a brilliant mechanism
heal the body. Brightness fuses to brightness. Beams
reach for one another across the space between.

Kimberly Blaeser

ABOUT STANDING (IN KINSHIP)

We all have the same little bones in our foot
twenty-six with funny names like *navicular*.
Together they build something strong—
our foot arch a pyramid holding us up.
The bones don't get casts when they break.
We tape them—one *phalange* to its neighbor for support.
(Other things like sorrow work that way, too—
find healing in the leaning, the closeness.)
Our feet have one quarter of all the bones in our body.
Maybe we should give more honor to feet
and to all those tiny but blessed cogs in the world—
communities, the forgotten architecture of friendship.

Rebecca Foust

KINSHIP OF FLESH

I swung my legs up to the table
as I always like to do
and saw another pair
swing up, identical
gesture, length and curve.

I saw your taper-finger,
knot-vein, walnut knuckle
hand just like Mom's
and mine, somehow
knitting together years
miles, dollars, cultures
of division.

Visits, letters, calls, e-mails
dwindled
until it seemed we had less
in common than people I met
on line at the post office.

Then you sat down next me,
sister, and I saw
what I'd forgotten.

Chana Bloch

THE JOINS

Kintsugi is the Japanese art of mending
precious pottery with gold.

What's between us
seems flexible as the webbing
between forefinger and thumb.

Seems flexible but isn't;
what's between us
is made of clay

like any cup on the shelf.
It shatters easily. Repair
becomes the task.

We glue the wounded edges
with tentative fingers.
Scar tissue is visible history

and the cup is precious to us
because
we saved it.

In the art of kintsugi
a potter repairing a broken cup
would sprinkle the resin

with powdered gold.
Sometimes the joins
are so exquisite

they say the potter
may have broken the cup
just so he could mend it.

Heather Swan

BOWL

for my mother

From the mud in her hands,
the bowl was born.
Opening like a flower
in an arch of petals,
then becoming a vessel
both empty and full.

Later, in the kiln
it was ravaged by fire,
its surface etched and vitrified,
searing the glaze into glass
as its body turned
to stone.

It is at the edge of damage
that beauty is honed.
And in Japan,
the potter tells me,
when a tea bowl
cracks in the fire,
that crack is filled
with gold.

REFLECTIVE PAUSE

Where Beauty Is Honed

The practice Heather Swan refers to in the last stanza of "Bowl" is called *kintsugi*, which in Japanese means, literally, "golden joinery." Yet this drive to highlight the cracks in something—what some might call its failures—goes against the message most of us receive throughout our lives, that we should be striving for perfection. We are each born of such humble materials, "From the mud," as it were, and are then sent into the fires of life with little protection, often to be "ravaged ... etched and vitrified." We are then (oddly enough) encouraged to hide all evidence of past pain, to conceal our scars and the markings that can render us kinder and more compassionate people. Eventually, we come to see, as Swan puts it so well: "It is at the edge of damage that beauty is honed." It is by risking brokenness that we grow stronger, "a vessel both empty and full," made more true by its so-called flaws. Instead of covering up our "cracks" or pretending they don't exist, this poem implies, we can flaunt them like gold for all the world to see.

Invitation for Writing and Reflection
Think back to some supposed flaw or failure in your past, which you have come to see as a source of beauty and strength. How have you learned to highlight your own "cracks," and embrace imperfection as evidence of authenticity and beauty?

Natasha Trethewey

HOUSEKEEPING

We mourn the broken things, chair legs
wrenched from their seats, chipped plates,
the threadbare clothes. We work the magic
of glue, drive the nails, mend the holes.
We save what we can, melt small pieces
of soap, gather fallen pecans, keep neck bones
for soup. Beating rugs against the house,
we watch dust, lit like stars, spreading
across the yard. Late afternoon, we draw
the blinds to cool the rooms, drive the bugs
out. My mother irons, singing, lost in reverie.
I mark the pages of a mail-order catalog,
listen for passing cars. All day we watch
for the mail, some news from a distant place.

Ted Kooser

ROUND ROBIN LETTER

They've all spun down, wobbled, and fallen still
in this digital age, those lost merry-go-rounds
of a whole family's news, each recipient—brother
and sister, cousin or aunt—adding a page or two
written in ballpoint, addressing a fresh envelope,
licking the stamps and mailing it on, plenty of time
between stops to collect something to say, then to
carefully offer it up in school-blackboard cursive—
a nephew who liked his new job, a chestnut foal
born with a diamond-shaped patch on its nose,
a good neighbor who'd been found in his barn
and been buried in rain—each envelope fattened
on gossip and family news, then sent on its way,
an event for the next addressee, something special
to find in the box by the road, then to carry back,
place on the table, and wait, not to be opened
till part of your part of the family was there.

Sally Bliumis-Dunn

MAILMAN

Each day the mailman rides
to a dutiful stop, slides his hand

into the small aluminum tunnel
of our mailbox.

I wonder if the air feels differently
than it did a few years back —
all the emails zipping past him
like no-see-ums.

Sometimes I miss
seeing someone's script

make its way across the envelope
with the sure sense
of the steady straight line,

and then unfolding the letter,
the slight shadows from
the creases as I read it,

reminding me
for a moment of who
had folded and tucked the letter

into the envelope,
sealed it with their tongue,
and carried it to a mailbox

where it sat with all
the other letters in a long silence
that could've lasted for days.

Joseph Millar

TELEPHONE REPAIRMAN

All morning in the February light
he has been mending cable,
splicing the pairs of wires together
according to their colors,
white-blue to white-blue
violet-slate to violet-slate,
in the warehouse attic by the river.
When he is finished
the messages will flow along the line:
thank you for the gift,
please come to the baptism,
the bill is now past due:
voices that flicker and gleam back and forth
across the tracer-colored wires.
We live so much of our lives
without telling anyone,
going out before dawn,
working all day by ourselves,
shaking our heads in silence
at the news on the radio.
He thinks of the many signals
flying in the air around him,
the syllables fluttering,
saying please love me,
from continent to continent
over the curve of the earth.

David Graham

THE NEWS OF LOVE

How old the News of Love must be . . .
—*Emily Dickinson*

The squirrel on our maple flicks
its tail, our dog at his window
watching steadily.

Love is steady, too, and sturdy,
like a thousand year old tree—
they built the house around it.

But dumb love's fun, too,
like the baby laughing nonstop
whenever you rip some paper.

You feel love more than see it,
like the wind on your face.
But don't take my word for it.

Look instead at shoreline pines,
how they all lean one direction,
even when there's no wind.

Linda Hogan

ARCTIC NIGHT, LIGHTS ACROSS THE SKY

We are curved together,
body to body, cell to cell,
arm over another.
The world is the bed for the cold night,
one cat curled in the bend of a knee,
dog at the feet,
my hand in yours, we are embraced
in animal presence, warmth,
the sea outside sounding
winter waves, one arriving after another
from the mystery far out
where in the depths of the sea
are other beings
that create their own light,
this world all one heartbeat.

Alicia Ostriker

THE DOGS AT LIVE OAK BEACH, SANTA CRUZ

As if there could be a world
Of absolute innocence
In which we forget ourselves

The owners throw sticks
And half-bald tennis balls
Toward the surf
And the happy dogs leap after them
As if catapulted—

Black dogs, tan dogs,
Tubes of glorious muscle—

Pursuing pleasure
More than obedience
They race, skid to a halt in the wet sand,
Sometimes they'll plunge straight into
The foaming breakers

Like diving birds, letting the green turbulence
Toss them, until they snap and sink

Teeth into floating wood
Then bound back to their owners
Shining wet, with passionate speed
For nothing,
For absolutely nothing but joy.

Nancy Gordon

RESCUE DOG

Jake comes into sight—ten pounds
of whirling golden fur, legs and feet a blur,
released from his leash to greet me,
racing toward me.
Eyes dark pools, shining, ears flapping
with his running and jumping—
up into my arms, onto my shoulder,
his body close to my chest—my heart.
Tongue lapping everywhere—"doggy kisses,"
says my friend who lets me share walks with him.
Quick breaths, his heart pounding, his body
warm and flexible as a gymnast's.

He drinks water from my hands.
He walks us. He explores the scents, the grass,
all that he can reach from his reattached leash.
He and my friend debate the boundaries.

When I have to leave, I turn to watch them go.
And Jake turns, looks back, looks back again,
crooks his head—
where are you going? aren't you coming with us?

Dan Butler

NEW YORK DOWNPOUR

The night sky cracked open on us full force,
a deluge, a drench, and laughing, arms around
one another, we soaked it up like a couple
of Gene Kellys, stomping, singing, not even
a twinge of an urge to run, just pure revel,
hummingbird joy, as lightning flashed
capturing the moment. Soon the storm
grew tired of scaring us off the streets
and subsided into grumpy rumblings,
while we splashed our way through puddles
from West End Avenue through Riverside Park
all the way to the edge of the Hudson.

Richard Jones

AFTER WORK

Coming up from the subway
into the cool Manhattan evening,
I feel rough hands on my heart—
women in the market yelling
over rows of tomatoes and peppers,
old men sitting on a stoop playing cards,
cabbies cursing each other with fists
while the music of church bells
sails over the street,
and the father, angry and tired
after working all day,
embracing his little girl,
kissing her,
mi vida, mi corazón,
brushing the hair out of her eyes
so she can see.

Andrea Potos

ABUNDANCE TO SHARE WITH THE BIRDS

Another early morning
in front of the bathroom mirror—
my daughter making faces
at herself while I pull
back her long brown hair,
gathering the breadth and shine
in my hands, brushing
and smoothing before weaving
the braid she will wear
to school for the day.
Afterwards, stray strands
nestle in the brush, and because
nothing of beauty is ever wasted,
I pull them out,
stand on the front porch and let them fly.

Fady Joudah

MIMESIS

My daughter
                 wouldn't hurt a spider
That had nested
Between her bicycle handles
For two weeks
She waited
Until it left of its own accord

If you tear down the web I said
It will simply know
This isn't a place to call home
And you'd get to go biking

She said that's how others
Become refugees isn't it?

Rudy Francisco

MERCY

after Nikki Giovanni

She asks me to kill the spider.
Instead, I get the most
peaceful weapons I can find.

I take a cup and a napkin.
I catch the spider, put it outside
and allow it to walk away.

If I am ever caught in the wrong place
at the wrong time, just being alive
and not bothering anyone,

I hope I am greeted
with the same kind
of mercy.

Naomi Shihab Nye

KINDNESS

Before you know what kindness really is
you must lose things,
feel the future dissolve in a moment
like salt in a weakened broth.
What you held in your hand,
what you counted and carefully saved,
all this must go so you know
how desolate the landscape can be
between the regions of kindness.
How you ride and ride
thinking the bus will never stop,
the passengers eating maize and chicken
will stare out the window forever.

Before you learn the tender gravity of kindness,
you must travel where the Indian in a white poncho
lies dead by the side of the road.
You must see how this could be you,
how he too was someone
who journeyed through the night with plans
and the simple breath that kept him alive.

Before you know kindness as the deepest thing inside,
you must know sorrow as the other deepest thing.
You must wake up with sorrow.
You must speak to it till your voice
catches the thread of all sorrows

and you see the size of the cloth.
Then it is only kindness that makes sense anymore,
only kindness that ties your shoes
and sends you out into the day to mail letters and purchase
    bread,
only kindness that raises its head
from the crowd of the world to say
it is I you have been looking for,
and then goes with you everywhere
like a shadow or a friend.

Christine Kitano

FOR THE KOREAN GRANDMOTHER ON SUNSET BOULEVARD

So you are here. Night comes as it does
elsewhere: light pulls slowly away
from telephone posts, shadows of buildings
darken the pavement like something
spilled. Even the broken moon
seems to turn its face.
And again you find yourself
on this dark riverbed, this asphalt
miracle, holding your end of a rope
that goes slack when you tug it.
Such grief you bear alone.
But wait. Just now a light
approaches, its rich band draws
you forward, out of shadow.
It is here, the bus that will ferry
you home. Go ahead,
grandmother, go on.

REFLECTIVE PAUSE

So You Are Here

As Christine Kitano shows in her moving poem, if we're present enough to another person, we can sometimes become attuned to what they're feeling. In fact, even the act of paying attention to a stranger can create a sense of connection, no matter how fleeting. The speaker in this poem watches the Korean grandmother at a bus stop so closely that she seems to feel her way into the grief that this older woman must bear alone. Yet that sadness soon lifts as "a light approaches" and "its rich band draws you forward, out of shadow." Both strangers seem brought out of the shadows by their momentary brush with each other, reminding me of what June Jordan once wrote: "I am a stranger learning to worship the strangers around me." If we can learn to see even the people we don't know in our lives as worthy of reverence and attention, perhaps we can treat ourselves with that same kindness and regard. Ultimately, this poem serves as a blessing for the grandmother who, through the act of the speaker's close observation, becomes a stranger no longer.

Invitation for Writing and Reflection

Have you had a moment like the one Christine Kitano describes here, of almost being able to see into someone else's life? See if you can re-create that moment and capture the connection you felt.

Paula Gordon Lepp

GAS STATION COMMUNION

It was a little thing, really,
this offer to fill my tire.
I was unscrewing the valve cap
and heard a voice behind me,
"Here, I'll get that for you."

"Oh that's okay, I've got it," is what
I normally say to such overtures,
this knee-jerk reaction to refuse.
I am the one who offers to help,
I am the one who serves.

Perhaps it was the eager spirit
in his face or his brown eyes
full of hopeful connection that
caused me to say okay.

I felt the vibration of
his unspoken benediction:
I can't do much for you,
fellow weary traveler,
but I can do this. Lay
down your burden and
I will carry it for a bit.

And I couldn't help but wonder
how many times I have denied
someone the blessing of serving

because I have been too stubborn
to accept their gift.

As I was standing there
in the sun-drenched gas station
parking lot, the hiss and tick of
the air pump sounded very much
like a psalm. I watched his hands
filling more than just my tire with air,
while goodness and grace
swirled around us.

Annie Lighthart

A GREAT WILD GOODNESS

One morning I was looking out the window
when a great wild goodness came over me:
I wanted to be kind to everything. I promised
not to kill the big spider on the wall; in the cold
I took the dog for the long walk she'd been wanting;
I fetched a trash can lid for an ornery neighbor
and did not, just then, add a single adjective to his name.
I went back inside to the laundry and dishes
with a clean heart such as I have never had.

Before dinner the wild goodness shouted, "Too tame!
Too tame!" so I went outside without my coat
and shouted poems up to the stars
until my children came home with their small
warm hands. Then we ate bread
in the kitchen, unafraid to be happy.
The stars in wild darkness were right over our heads.

Ellen Rowland

NO SMALL THING

The smell of baking bread, smooth floured hands,
butter waiting to be spread with blackberry jam
and I realize, this is no small thing.
These days spent confined,
I am drawn to life's ordinary details,
the largeness of all we can do
alongside what we cannot.
The list of allowances far outweighs my complaints.
I am fortunate to have flour and yeast, a source of heat
not to mention soft butter, the tartness of blackberries
harvested on a cold back road.
A kitchen, a home, two working
hands to stir and knead,
a clear enough head to gather it all.
Even the big toothy knife feels miraculous
as it grabs hold and cracks the crust.

Jane Hirshfield

I WOULD LIKE

I would like
my living to inhabit me
the way
rain, sun, and their wanting
inhabit a fig or apple.

I would like to meet it
also in pieces,
scattered:
a conversation set down
on a long hallway table;

a disappointment
pocketed inside a jacket;
some long-ago longing glimpsed,
half-recognized,
in the corner of a thrift store painting.

To discover my happiness,
walking first
toward
then away from me
down a stairwell,
on two strong legs all its own.

Also,
the uncountable
wheat stalks,

how many times broken,
beaten, sent
between grindstones,
before entering
the marriage
of oven and bread—

Let me find my life in that, too.

In my moments
of clumsiness, solitude;
in days of vertigo and hesitation;
in the many year-ends
that found me
standing on top of a stovetop
to take down a track light.

In my nights' asked,
sometimes answered, questions.

I would like
to add to my life,
while we are still living,
a little salt and butter,
one more slice of the edible apple,
a teaspoon of jam
from the long-simmered fig.

To taste
as if something tasted for the first time
what we will have become then.

Peter Pereira

A POT OF RED LENTILS

simmers on the kitchen stove.
All afternoon dense kernels
surrender to the fertile
juices, their tender bellies
swelling with delight.

In the yard we plant
rhubarb, cauliflower, and artichokes,
cupping wet earth over tubers,
our labor the germ
of later sustenance and renewal.

Across the field the sound of a baby crying
as we carry in the last carrots,
whorls of butter lettuce,
a basket of red potatoes.

I want to remember us this way—
late September sun streaming through
the window, bread loaves and golden
bunches of grapes on the table,
spoonfuls of hot soup rising
to our lips, filling us
with what endures.

William Stafford

YOU READING THIS, BE READY

Starting here, what do you want to remember?
How sunlight creeps along a shining floor?
What scent of old wood hovers, what softened
sound from outside fills the air?

Will you ever bring a better gift for the world
than the breathing respect that you carry
wherever you go right now? Are you waiting
for time to show you some better thoughts?

When you turn around, starting here, lift this
new glimpse that you found; carry into evening
all that you want from this day. This interval you spent
reading or hearing this, keep it for life—

What can anyone give you greater than now,
starting here, right in this room, when you turn around?

Connie Wanek

COME IN!

for Marsha

It was the neighbor at the back door
with a Vidalia onion in each hand,
straight from the ten-pound sack
the Shriners were selling, or the Rotarians
or Odd Fellows or one of those
antique civic organizations of great uncles
atoning for their sins on a just-in-time basis.

"Come in!" And she did, smiling.
The fifteen months of Covid had given
those simple words a radical new meaning,
an assertiveness. I felt I was
tearing up a contract I never wanted to sign,
membership in an HOA maybe.

Pale yellow onions, too clean
to have come from the soil, surely,
too sweet to make you cry.

Susan Rich

STILL LIFE WITH LADDER

Today, the sky saved my life
caught between smoked rum and cornflower.
Today, there is a color I can't name cruising past

the backdoor—it is the idea of color.
Cloudscapes evaporate like love songs
across lost islands, each a small bitcoin of thought.

Today, I am alive and this is a good thing—

clams in the half shell, a lemon rosemary tart.
I live in the day and the day lives past me.
If I could draw a map of the hours, a long

horizon would travel on indefinitely—a green, backlit
  thread.

The sky? It is never the same—it is sour milk
and whipped cream, a sketchbook and flour-dusted jeans.
Today, I am in love with the sky.

It doesn't care if my father is dead,
or that I live by myself with his Masonic watch.
I sew time with my mother's button jar.

I've improvised my life —let the sky pull the strings.

Tonight, I will borrow the golden ladder from the orchard,
travel from this sphere into the next and expunge
the leftover sadness of the hemispheres, to move beyond

the beyond which is here, present, alive in this hyacinth
    room;

time leaps over itself, after and out of the tangled past
over shadows of weather falling across a back window—
to forgive one another; to try once more to live it right.

Alison Luterman

BRAIDING HIS HAIR

Here we are each morning:
my husband on our old kitchen chair, its upholstery
mended with duct tape, his head bent forward
while I comb out his long
wheat-colored hair. Not what I thought
we'd be doing in our sixties,
me dividing the wet silk of it, still stubbornly
reddish-gold, only a little
white at the sideburns. Three thick hanks
in hand, I begin to plait: *over, under, over, under.*
I don't remember when he stopped
cutting his hair and decided
to let it grow long as a girl's —
and he was mistaken for a girl once,
a tall, stoop-shouldered man-girl,
when he stood on the sidewalk, back to the street,
and a car drove by, honking and catcalling.
At him, not me. We laughed,
but I had to wonder: When did his tresses, now
halfway to his waist, first spill
over his shoulders? It must have happened while we slept,
as most things do. And how did he come to sit
before me so patiently now, head bowed while I braid,
as if he were the daughter I never had
and this my one chance
to weave my care into each *over, under,
over, under*?

Judith Sornberger

LOVE IN OUR SIXTIES

For Karl

You lead me, hand in hand,
through your apple orchard
like the one where I was
married half a life ago.
Although we met when old,
I once thought we might wed,
become partners as we were
with our former, longtime loves.

You're showing me the once-wild
apple tree onto whose boughs
you grafted other varieties—
Priscilla, Fameuse, Ida Red—
like the names of children
we will never have.

I once hoped that we—potter
and poet, man and woman—
might graft our lives in such a way
that they couldn't be divided,
though we're as white-haired
as crowns of apple trees in May.

You point out the raised place
where old met new and melded
right down to the heartwood,

where separateness has almost
been erased. I trace the scar
as you reach up to pick a few
apples for us to taste.
Oh, the scarlet kiss of skin,
the sweetness of today.

Susan Rothbard

THAT NEW

At the market today, I look for Piñata
apples, their soft-blush-yellow. My husband
brought them home last week, made me guess at
the name of this new strain, held one in his hand
like a gift and laughed as I tried all
the names I knew: Gala, Fuji, Honey
Crisp—watched his face for clues—what to call
something new? It's winter, only tawny
hues and frozen ground, but that apple bride
was sweet, and I want to bring it back to him,
that new. When he cut it, the star inside
held seeds of other stars, the way within
a life are all the lives you might live,
each unnamed, until you name it.

Susan Zimmerman

GET CLOSE

So close you see something you thought you knew
as if for the first time, then closer, beyond seeing—
lost, mystified.

Like the time I photographed
the grey shadow on the side of a tree, magnifying
until I realized it was not a shadow but growing moss.

Until I realized the white dots were not dots
but tiny flowers blooming in the moss,
until I was so close I disappeared.

In the whole universe there was nothing
and no one but the tree and me,
and we were only one thing.

David Axelrod

THE INNERMOST CHAMBER OF MY HOME IS YOURS

Until now, I hadn't looked up all day—

it's already late October
and this last month of the campaign
the rains returned,

the Earth soft underfoot,
lawns in town, fescue, wildrye
and bunchgrass in the foothills,
winter wheat in the valley,

all bled together into a green film.

And for no reason at all
I glanced up the slopes
at Glass Hill, where forests
burned forty years ago

and caught a glimpse of it—
a future world
where a young aspen grove

yields back all of summer's light into air.

Dave Baldwin

SUMMER ROMANCE

Of all my days to middle age,
you gave me less than ten;
so little time

from moon to rising moon.
A meteor flared and fell
on an August night

now thirty winters dead.
The lingering light:
for that, I give you thanks.

Anya Silver

LATE SUMMER

August evening, church bells,
light shattered on the quick
creek as in a Seurat painting,
grass thick with Queen Anne's lace,
the summer sun still so late
in setting that bedtime comes late
for the children scattered in a garden
to catch the slugs eating their plants.
Late summer, and the roses in second
bloom know what's coming.
But for now, bells, water, laughter,
my mother and I walking together
arm in arm, because happiness
is a decision each of us has made,
without even discussing it.

Judith Sornberger

ASSISTED LIVING

This time, Mom, I'd stay overnight
at Assisted Living when you asked.
Borrow a pair of your satin pajamas,
paint your fingernails pearly white.
Finish off a box of Russell Stover
chocolates with you. I wouldn't
even complain when you pinched
each piece to reveal its center,
avoiding the dreaded marshmallow.

Forgive me. I was trying to avoid
sleeping on the sofa too narrow
for my body, staying up later
than I like while you filled ashtrays
with cigarette butts and my eyes
burned and watered from your smoke.

This time I'd visit the past
for as long as you wanted.
Sit with you, hip to hip,
looking at pictures of me
and my sisters, the ones with
scalloped white edges like
the lace on our Easter anklets.
I'd watch as many classic black
and white flicks as you wished,
and weep beside you at their endings.

Patricia McKernon Runkle

WHEN YOU MEET SOMEONE DEEP IN GRIEF

Slip off your needs
and set them by the door.

Enter barefoot
this darkened chapel

hollowed by loss
hallowed by sorrow

its gray stone walls
and floor.

You, congregation
of one

are here to listen
not to sing.

Kneel in the back pew.
Make no sound,

let the candles
speak.

REFLECTIVE PAUSE

Here to Listen

Patricia McKernon Runkle's words call us to be as present as possible with another person, to recognize the sanctity of the space we share with someone who has recently endured a loss of any kind. She asks us to see the "hollowing" of grief as a "hallowing" as well, deserving of reverence. With its short lines and many pauses, the poem makes us feel as if we too are entering the "darkened chapel," step by slow step, toward the person who needs us, and she reminds us, most importantly, that we are "here to listen not to sing." When sitting with someone in mourning, we might think it's our job to fix things for them, to make the other person feel better. Yet often what we most need from a companion is their deep presence, their willingness to enter the place of mystery, confusion, and pain with us. That's the greatest gift we can give to another during a trying time, and it's essential to point out that Runkle's poem also works in another way: We can just as easily take her advice when we meet *ourselves* in the depths of loss. At that time too, all we can do is listen deeply to the self and its needs, leaving all expectations for outcome or a quick recovery at the door.

Invitation for Writing and Reflection
Is there a time when someone showed up for you, or you showed up for someone else during a difficult loss in their lives? How were you able to offer compassion, and how were you changed by that experience?

Megan Buchanan

DREAM VISITATION

This morning before dawn,
my dad visited me in my dream.
He was here, where I live now
in a house he never did see.
I came down the wide staircase
with a lost dog
that had spent the night,
to find my dad
sitting in a chair near the kitchen.

As I walked into the lamp-lit room,
he rose up and hugged me.
He was wearing a red plaid shirt
and his navy blue blazer,
signifying important business.
He was warm; it was him.
He held me tightly in his arms,
my tears streamed.

With a gasp, I asked, *Dad!*
Where are you now? Where did you go?
And he answered:
I am in the pixels
of the pictures you are looking at
by which I think he meant:
I am here
and everywhere.

Phyllis Cole-Dai

LADDER

for my father

The night before you died
I dreamed a wooden ladder
rose straight into the sky,
propped against only a wall of air
yet sturdy on its feet, like you
in that faded old photo, tall and lean,
knee-high in a field of ripening beans.

I wasn't with you at the end
but I know that when you left your bed
you mounted that ladder, young again,
body light and nimble, clambering up
the rungs worn smooth by shoes
and stained from use like wooden spoons.
After a few uncertain steps,
your long legs took them two at a time,
a rapturous climb to glory,
up past the crowns of maples and oaks,
up past the tops of barns and silos,
up past the soaring vultures and hawks,
up through the thin cool veil of clouds.
Now and then on your way to the stars
I see you pause upon that ladder,
look down from the heavens,

not to gauge how far you've come
but to gaze with love on what you loved.

Michelle Mandolia

THE THING SHE LOVES MOST

I hear my daughter introduce
her favorite stuffed animal to her kindergarten class.
The school year is more than half over
and she has spent it in this house
peering into this one screen.
Her first name is Reeree, I hear my daughter say,
*and her last name is Hillary. She doesn't have a middle
    name.*
I picture the audience, squares on her screen,
her teacher's broad smile of interest, the alert posture
of the boy who signs in first every morning,
the foreheads of children looking down to doodle,
as my daughter often does, the unoccupied desk
of someone who is using the potty.
These five and six year olds have met Reeree
at least ten times, maybe twenty.
I am grateful for whatever instructional philosophy
keeps the teacher from suggesting a new share.
On these days, my daughter gets a few extra moments
with the thing she loves most.
Her turn over, her fingertips skim Reeree's coat, settling
on the mane, felted from so much washing.

Marjorie Saiser

LAST DAY OF KINDERGARTEN

In the photograph
the boy is ecstatic,
set free, a young king,
everything ahead of him.
There is nothing he can't have
if he wants it and he wants it,
as does his friend beside him.
They are ready now to ride off
together and slay dragons,
rescue the world. It's all here
in the park after the last bell;
it's here in the green summer
they have been released to.
It's here in their manhood.
They've only finished kindergarten
but they understand freedom
and friendship. They're on top
of the picnic table, they're on top
of the world in their tennis shoes,
they have raised their arms,
they are such men as could
raise continents; they have
survived. Look how their
fingers reach the sky

and their legs are sure as
horses. Their bodies
will forever do anything they ask.

Gillian Wegener

JUVIE KID

for Gus

Again, we meet in the hallway.
As usual, he's sweeping the floor.

Look at all the bugs, he says, leaning in
to examine his pile of dust and flies.

Hey, he says, *when are you going
to write poetry with us?*

His hair a wild halo, his eyes intense,
his shoulders not yet as wide as mine.

He means, when will I matter to you?

I've been in here four whole months,
he says. *But I'm getting out soon.*

*I'm going to a group home, far away.
They gave me a choice, but I don't care where.*

Far away from here.

Regulations say no handshakes, no touching.
We aren't supposed to be talking, but

we say good luck, good luck. We say
something about second chances
something about taking the right path.

We aren't supposed to be talking to him,
this boy, excited at what's ahead.

We turn and pause at another door.
We know his slim chances.

Pray for me, he calls. *Pray for me, okay?*

Emilie Lygren

MAKE BELIEVE

Mr. Rogers, what would you say to us now?
I miss your soft voice and slow smile.

Somehow you would remind us of what it means to share a neighborhood—
how our breath travels farther than we think,
but so can our care.

You would've made the puppets tiny cloth masks,
had them ask all the questions children need to ask like,
Why? and *How Long?* and *Can't we . . . ?*
Let Daniel Tiger feel sad and antsy, itchy under the ear straps.

You would have explained it all patiently and truthfully:
   No, we don't know how long.
   Yes, it's OK to feel afraid.
   This is how we care for everyone right now.

Maybe the adults would have listened, too.

Brad Aaron Modlin

WHAT YOU MISSED THAT DAY YOU WERE ABSENT FROM FOURTH GRADE

Mrs. Nelson explained how to stand still and listen
to the wind, how to find meaning in pumping gas,

how peeling potatoes can be a form of prayer. She took
questions on how not to feel lost in the dark

After lunch she distributed worksheets
that covered ways to remember your grandfather's

voice. Then the class discussed falling asleep
without feeling you had forgotten to do something else—

something important—and how to believe
the house you wake in is your home. This prompted

Mrs. Nelson to draw a chalkboard diagram detailing
how to chant the Psalms during cigarette breaks,

and how not to squirm for sound when your own thoughts
are all you hear; also, that you have enough.

The English lesson was that *I am*
is a complete sentence.

And just before the afternoon bell, she made the math equation
look easy. The one that proves that hundreds of questions,

and feeling cold, and all those nights spent looking
for whatever it was you lost, and one person

add up to something.

REFLECTIVE PAUSE

What You Missed

At times, we might feel that we missed out on some necessary information for life handed out to everyone else long ago. It's a natural human response to compare ourselves to others, to look around and wonder why they seem to have it together, possessing some secret knowledge that we don't. Brad Aaron Modlin offers a playful yet sincere take on this idea as he explores what we all might have missed that day in fourth grade when we were absent, unraveling a list of the kinder, wiser things we might wish our teachers would have taught us. It could have been useful, for instance, to be told that "*I am* is a complete sentence," to stop feeling that we have to be someone other than who we are to feel worthy. Or we might have been shown "how to find meaning in pumping gas," or turn an act as ordinary as peeling potatoes into "a form of prayer." This poem longs for some deeper knowledge that would have matched the tender needs of a child, like "worksheets that covered ways to remember your grandfather's voice," or "how to believe the house you wake in is your home." Perhaps we might all have felt more at home if we had been given the freedom and kindness as kids simply to be ourselves.

Invitation for Writing and Reflection
What do you wish your teachers and grown-ups would have taught you? And what might be more helpful to know now in everyday life? Feel free to be both playful and profound as you work with this idea.

Dorianne Laux

ON THE BACK PORCH

The cat calls for her dinner.
On the porch I bend and pour
brown soy stars into her bowl,
stroke her dark fur.
It's not quite night.
Pinpricks of light in the eastern sky.
Above my neighbor's roof, a transparent
moon, a pink rag of cloud.
Inside my house are those who love me.
My daughter dusts biscuit dough.
And there's a man who will lift my hair
in his hands, brush it
until it throws sparks.
Everything is just as I've left it.
Dinner simmers on the stove.
Glass bowls wait to be filled
with gold broth. Sprigs of parsley
on the cutting board.
I want to smell this rich soup, the air
around me going dark, as stars press
their simple shapes into the sky.
I want to stay on the back porch
while the world tilts
toward sleep, until what I love
misses me, and calls me in.

Suzanne Nussey

LULLABY FOR AN EMPTY NESTER

You have a bed that loves your bones.
The dog snores softly at your feet,
partnering your partner's drone.
Hermit thrush and tree frog sing
the creeping dark to sleep.
Make a cradle of the night,
a cradle for what's gone.
Nothing to fear
in your twilight.
You are here.
You are home.

Michelle Wiegers

MOVING

I find myself jealous of those who rest
quarantined inside their homes,
while I have to pack every last item I own
in order to carry it just a few blocks away.

And now as I reach around inside
this new house, I keep looking
for the things I know, certainties to hold
me up, cushion me on all sides.

How do I know that all will be well?

Because the morning sun still
warms my cheek, illuminating
small flecks of dust on my glasses
that look like layered circles of modern art.

Because the red squirrel still comes to raid
the feeders I hang, not intended for him
while the chickadee sings
his same vibrant song.

Because the ferns in my garden
I feared had not survived the move
are finally unfurling
their bright green bodies.

Because spring doesn't know
the anxiety of uncertainty,
but declares, through her gentle unwrapping
of the world, life will come again.

Marie Howe

DELIVERY

The delivery man slowly climbs
the five steep flights of stairs
as I lean down to watch him walking up

as he's talking on the phone
and now he pauses
on the third-floor landing

to touch a little Christmas light
the girl had wrapped around the banister—
speaking to someone in a language
so melodic I ask him what—
when he hands the package up to me,
and he says Patois—from Jamaica—
smiling up at me from where he's standing
on the landing

a smile so radiant that
re-entering the apartment I'm
a young woman again, and
the sweetness of the men I've loved walks in,
through the closed door

one of them right now,
kicking the snow off his boots,
turning to take my face in his cold hands,
kissing me now with his cold mouth.

Ray Hudson

UNBREAKABLE CLARITIES

Across America
curtains are pulled open
and delivery trucks back up
ever so carefully with the sun

in their rearview mirrors.
The coffee is almost
ready. On a pad beside
the telephone is the number

you left when you called.
It is too early to call you back
and to tell you how
it began snowing

last night after I had gone
to bed and how
outside, beneath the window,
a few leaves are still green

and how the barbed wire
between me and the field
glistens with frost.
I am blinded by unfamiliar

possibilities. I count myself
lucky to live in such times
as I hit the replay button
just to hear your voice.

Danusha Laméris

INSHA'ALLAH

I don't know when it slipped into my speech
that soft word meaning, "if God wills it."
Insha'Allah I will see you next summer.
The baby will come in spring insha'Allah.
Insha'Allah this year we will have enough rain.

So many plans I've laid have unraveled
easily as braids beneath my mother's quick fingers.

Every language must have a word for this. A word
our grandmothers uttered under their breath
as they pinned the whites, soaked in lemon,
hung them to dry in the sun, or peeled potatoes,
dropping the discarded skins into a bowl.

Our sons will return next month, insha'Allah.
Insha'Allah this war will end, soon. Insha'Allah
the rice will be enough to last through the winter.

How lightly we learn to hold hope,
as if it were an animal that could turn around
and bite your hand. And still we carry it
the way a mother would, carefully,
from one day to the next.

Andrea Potos

WHERE I MIGHT FIND HER

for Mom

Overnight it seems, the pink vaults
of the peonies open;
in an iridescent second, a hummingbird
twirls inches from my face.

Pennies spot the sidewalk—so bright,
I believe they would smile if they could.

And if kindness were air, the rooms of my house
expand with it.
Breathing deeply is simple, and hope
is the natural choice.

Rosemerry Wahtola Trommer

THE QUESTION

for Jude Janett

All day, I replay these words:
Is this the path of love?
I think of them as I rise, as
I wake my children, as I wash dishes,
as I drive too close behind the slow
blue Subaru, *Is this the path of love?*
Think of them as I stand in line
at the grocery store,
think of them as I sit on the couch
with my daughter. Amazing how
quickly six words become compass,
the new lens through which to see myself
in the world. I notice what the question is not.
Not, "Is this right?" Not,
"Is this wrong?" It just longs to know
how the action of existence
links us to the path to love.
And is it *this*? Is it *this*? All day
I let myself be led by the question.
All day I let myself not be too certain
of the answer. *Is it this?* I ask as I
argue with my son. *Is it this?* I ask
as I wait for the next word to come.

Jacqueline Suskin

FUTURE

I can't see my future clearly.
It's a wash of color and light.
Maybe a glimpse of a house
with wood floors, the death
of a parent, a dog, a cat, a love,
but nothing certain. I like its fog.
Inevitably something will happen, pieces
will fall into place if I keep breathing
and I'll eat, I'll work, I'll learn
and know and forget. There'll be
another bowl full of berries, a hot cup
of tea, additional travel and sorrow.
There'll be a clean pair of pants,
the sun's good glow, a cut and blood,
a hole to dig, a bath to take, a mistake to mend.
What lies ahead is a promise
standing in shadow, one second
pasted to the next. I don't need to call it
by name. A riddle ensues, a song of guessing,
a vow of risk. The road becomes itself
single stone after single stone
made of limitless possibility,
endless awe.

READING GROUP QUESTIONS AND TOPICS FOR DISCUSSION

"Small Kindnesses" by Danusha Lamèris (Page 5)
- How would you define *kindness*? What does the word mean to you?
- In this poem, Lamèris meditates on all the small ways we take care of each other, pointing out: "Mostly, we don't want to harm each other." Do you agree that kindness is our basic nature as humans?
- The speaker wonders if the "moments of exchange" between us are the "true dwelling of the holy," yet goes on to call them "fleeting temples." Why do you think negative experiences often stay with us longer than the positive? How might we train ourselves to hold on to kindness and joy?
- **INVITATION FOR WRITING AND REFLECTION:** Write a list of the small kindnesses you have received or given recently, those "moments of exchange" that we might ignore or take for granted. You might also make this a regular part of your writing practice, keeping a kindness journal to capture such moments of connection.

"Elation" by January Gill O'Neil (Page 19)
- We forget how deeply we can connect with the natural world when we make the time to go outside. How does this poem make these "Tolerant trees" come more alive for the reader?

- The next time you happen to be among trees, listen to the sounds they make in the wind. The speaker here describes them as being like "rocking chairs," "a cello's drawn breath," and "the chatter between old, coupled voices." How would you describe that sound yourself?
- Why does the speaker come to see these trees as such resilient beings? What lessons might we humans learn from the trees?
- **INVITATION FOR WRITING AND REFLECTION:** Think back to a time when you had a similar sense of "elation" while in nature. What did you notice that you had never paid attention to before?

"Coniferous Fathers" by Michael Kleber-Diggs
(Page 82)
- How does Michael Kleber-Diggs challenge our typical ideas about how fathers and men in general should behave?
- Why do you think he chose the metaphor of "coniferous" trees like pines to describe the kind of father he would prefer, "soft enough to bend"?
- How does this poem imagine a new type of intimacy between fathers and their children? What images of connection stand out to you?
- **INVITATION FOR WRITING AND REFLECTION:** Write a wish list for your own ideal father. What qualities would he embody for you, and what images spring to mind as you consider those perhaps more loving, gentler, and softer traits?

"Mimesis" by Fady Joudah (Page 125)
- Young people have the uncanny ability to distill what we believe are complex concepts into the simplest, most

relatable human terms. How does the speaker's daughter help him to understand the plight of refugees more clearly?
- Why is the daughter's argument for kindness so moving and convincing?
- How is the father's initial justification for destroying the spider's home similar to justifications we often hear from governments, including our own, especially during times of war?
- INVITATION FOR WRITING AND REFLECTION: What living things in your own daily life do you often look past or brush away, which you might work to include more fully in your own sense of compassion and empathy?

"The Raincoat" by Ada Limón (Page 103)
- What kinds of sacrifices do the speaker's parents make in this poem to correct her "crooked spine," and to help her finally "breathe again"?
- What do you think of the speaker's revelation when she says of her mother, "I never asked her what she gave up to drive me." What do you think she means in that final image when she realizes she's been "under her raincoat" for her whole life?
- Do you see similarities between Ada Limón's poem and "My Mother's Van" by Faith Shearin (page 101), both of which focus on the sacrifice of mothers? How have those sacrifices followed each of these speakers into their present lives?
- INVITATION FOR WRITING AND REFLECTION: Think about a time when a parental figure or mentor made sacrifices for your well-being. Did you recognize what they were doing for you and what they were giving up at the time? How did those past sacrifices help you to become who you are?

"About Standing (in Kinship)" by Kimberly Blaeser (Page 107)

- This poem begins with one way we are similar as humans: "We all have the same little bones in our foot." How does the poet use this image to capture the idea of community and connection among us?
- When she discusses how we tape together broken toes for support and healing, she points out that "Other things like sorrow work that way, too." What are the ways we can "find healing in the leaning, the closeness," especially when someone is struggling?
- Why does the poet suggest we ought to "give more honor to feet," even going so far as to call them "blessed cogs in the world"? What are some other "blessed cogs" we might work to honor in our lives and society?
- **INVITATION FOR WRITING AND REFLECTION:** Think back to a time when you found "healing in the leaning, the closeness," and reached out to others for help with a difficult situation. How did you manage to move beyond your isolation, and remember the "kinship" that allows us all to thrive?

"Kinship of Flesh" by Rebecca Foust (Page 108)

- When we disagree fundamentally with others, it can be easy to forget their humanity. How does this poem call us back to our essential connection with each other, especially with other family members?
- What allows the speaker of this poem to see what she had forgotten about how "knitt[ed] together" she is with her sister?
- What do you make of the title of the poem, especially the word *kinship*? How does Foust encourage us to see ourselves in others from whom we feel so separate?

- **INVITATION FOR WRITING AND REFLECTION:** Describe a time when you were able to see and feel your way past a disagreement or division with someone else. What brought you back to the fact of your connectedness? How can you practice seeing the humanity and kinship in others who seem so different from you?

"Filling the Candles" by Ted Kooser (Page 25)
- How does the speaker's close observation of the church volunteer who has come to fill the candles bring "a little warmth" to this otherwise chilly day?
- Shared ritual and routine often steady us during challenging times and give us a sense of purpose. Based on Kooser's intricate descriptions of this woman, how would you describe her devotion to this act? Do you think she finds pleasure in what she's doing?
- How does the woman filling the candles, and the speaker who's watching her, encourage us to bring mindfulness and deep attention to the seemingly ordinary acts of our lives?
- **INVITATION FOR WRITING AND REFLECTION:** Consider some ritual that's become an important part of your life. What do you do to fulfill this task, paying close attention to every detail, as the poet does here? How does this routine ground you in the moment and connect you with others?

"Late Summer" by Anya Silver (Page 149)
- How does the poet capture the beauty and joy of a late summer evening? What sensory details stand out to you?
- What do you think Silver means when she says, "the roses in second bloom know what's coming," given the fact that autumn is just around the corner?

- In the final lines of the poem, we see the speaker and her mother, "walking together arm in arm, because happiness is a decision each of us has made." Do you feel that happiness is a choice or decision we can each make, no matter the circumstances?
- **INVITATION FOR WRITING AND REFLECTION:** Was there a time when you felt yourself immersed in the joy of a moment that you knew would end but that you decided to savor anyway? What images come back from that time, and what makes them so vivid to you?

"On the Back Porch" by Dorianne Laux (Page 165)

- The speaker re-creates a moment of joy and completeness that might seem plain to some. As she stands out on her back porch, how does she convey the gratefulness she feels for this simple moment when, as she says, "Inside my house are those who love me"?
- How do Dorianne Laux's word choices ("sparks," "gold," and "rich") affect the way we read this poem? What are some of the concrete descriptions that bring us into the scene?
- She ends by saying, "I want to stay on the back porch . . . until what I love misses me, and calls me in." Why is it necessary for us to step out of our lives in order to fully appreciate what we have right now?
- **INVITATION FOR WRITING AND REFLECTION:** As you move through the next few days, stay on the lookout for moments of sudden connection and joy, and see if you can drop into them fully. With a notebook, or just in your mind, pause and take stock of what's around you. What calls to you as you savor the gift of the moment?

POET BIOGRAPHIES

Kelli Russell Agodon's fourth collection of poems, *Dialogues with Rising Tides*, was published by Copper Canyon Press. She's the cofounder of Two Sylvias Press and serves on the poetry faculty at the Rainier Writing Workshop, a low-residency MFA program at Pacific Lutheran University. Agodon lives in Washington State on traditional lands of the Chimacum, Coast Salish, S'Klallam, and Suquamish people. Write to her at kelli@agodon.com or visit her website: www.agodon.com.

José A. Alcantara is a former construction worker, baker, commercial fisherman, math teacher, and studio photographer. His poems have appeared or are forthcoming in *Poetry Daily*, *The Southern Review*, *Spillway*, *Rattle*, and *Beloit Poetry Journal*, and have been shared on gratefulness.org.

Shari Altman grew up in the South but now lives in rural Vermont with her husband, three cats, eleven chickens, and several beehives. She is the cofounder of Literary North, a literary arts organization based in the Upper Valley of Vermont. Her work has been featured in *Amirisu*, *Taproot*, and *Bloodroot Literary Magazine*.

Born in New York City in 1950, **Julia Alvarez** has written novels, including *How the García Girls Lost Their Accents*, *In the Time of the Butterflies*, and *Afterlife*, as well as poetry collections, including *Homecoming*, *The Other Side/El Otro Lado*, and *The Woman I Kept to Myself*. Alvarez's awards include the Pura Belpré and Américas Awards for her books for young readers, the Hispanic Heritage Award, and the F. Scott Fitzgerald Award. In 2013, she received the National Medal of Arts from President Obama.

Ruth Arnison loves playing with words whether it be haiku, poetry, or short stories. She was the editor of Poems in the Waiting Room (NZ) for 13 years. She is the instigator of Lilliput Libraries—New

Zealand's little neighborhood libraries—and every summer paints poems on steps and seats around her hometown, Dunedin. In 2018 she was awarded the QSM (Queen's Service Medal) for services to poetry and literature.

Lahab Assef Al-Jundi was born and raised in Damascus, Syria. He attended The University of Texas at Austin, where he graduated with a degree in electrical engineering. Not long after graduation, he discovered his passion for writing and published his first poetry collection, *A Long Way*, in 1985. His latest poetry collection, *No Faith At All*, was published in 2014 by Pecan Grove Press. He lives in San Antonio, Texas.

David Axelrod's new collection of poems, *Years Beyond the River*, appeared in 2021 from Terrapin Books. His second collection of nonfiction, *The Eclipse I Call Father: Essays on Absence,* was published by Oregon State University Press in the spring of 2019. Axelrod directs the low-residency MFA and Wilderness, Ecology, and Community program at Eastern Oregon University. He makes his home in Missoula, Montana.

Zeina Azzam is a Palestinian American poet, editor, and community activist. Her chapbook, *Bayna Bayna, In-Between*, was released in 2021 by The Poetry Box. Zeina's poems are published or are forthcoming in *Pleiades, Passager, Gyroscope, Pensive Journal, Streetlight Magazine, Mizna, Sukoon Magazine, Barzakh, Making Levantine Cuisine, Tales from Six Feet Apart, Bettering American Poetry, Making Mirrors: Writing/Righting by and for Refugees, Gaza Unsilenced*, and others. She holds an MA in Arabic literature from Georgetown University.

Dave Baldwin retired from the Walt Disney Company (Technology Division) in 2017 after 40+ years as a technical writer and editor. In his career, he also worked for Boeing, Microsoft, Hewlett-Packard, and Amazon. He has been a naval officer, college teacher, and masters track and field athlete. In 2009, he served as the national secretary for the Haiku Society of America. Dave lives in Lake Stevens, Washington, a few miles north of Seattle.

Ellen Bass is a chancellor of the Academy of American Poets and author most recently of *Indigo* (Copper Canyon Press, 2020). Her book *Like a Beggar* (Copper Canyon Press, 2014) was a finalist for the Paterson Poetry Prize, the Publishing Triangle Award, the Milt Kessler Poetry Award, the Lambda Literary Award, and the Northern California Book Award. Previous books include *The Human Line* (Copper Canyon Press, 2007) and *Mules of Love* (BOA Editions, 2002).

Carolee Bennett is a writer and artist living in Upstate New York, where—after a local poetry competition—she has fun saying she's been the "almost" poet laureate of Smitty's Tavern. Her work has received recognition from Sundress Best of the Net, the Crab Creek Review Poetry Prize (semi-finalist), and the Tupelo Quarterly Poetry Prize (finalist). She has an MFA in poetry from Ashland University and works full-time as a writer in social media marketing.

Kimberly Blaeser, former Wisconsin poet laureate, is the author of five poetry collections, including *Copper Yearning, Apprenticed to Justice,* and *Résister en dansant/Ikwe-niimi: Dancing Resistance.* An Anishinaabe activist and environmentalist from White Earth Reservation, Blaeser is a professor of English and Indigenous Studies at University of Wisconsin–Milwaukee, an MFA faculty member for the Institute of American Indian Arts in Santa Fe, and founding director of the literary organization In-Na-Po—Indigenous Nations Poets.

Sally Bliumis-Dunn's poems have appeared in *On the Seawall, Paris Review, Prairie Schooner, PLUME, Poetry London,* the *New York Times,* PBS NewsHour, *upstreet,* Poem-a-day, and Ted Kooser's column, among others. In 2018, her third book, *Echolocation* (Plume Editions/MadHat Press), was long-listed for the Julie Suk Award, runner-up for the Eric Hoffer Prize, and runner-up for the Poetry by the Sea Prize.

Chana Bloch was the author of several collections of poetry, including *The Secrets of the Tribe, The Past Keeps Changing, Mrs. Dumpty, Blood Honey,* and *Swimming in the Rain: New & Selected Poems* (Autumn House Press, 2015). She was cotranslator of the biblical *Song of Songs* as well as contemporary Israeli poetry. Her awards included the Poetry Society of America's Di Castagnola Award, the Felix Pollak Prize in Poetry, and the 2012 Meringoff Poetry Award.

Megan Buchanan is a teaching artist, a poet, a performer, a collaborative dancemaker, and an English teacher to students with language-based exceptionalities. Her collection *Clothesline Religion* (Green Writers Press, 2017) was nominated for the 2018 Vermont Book Award. Her work appears in numerous journals and anthologies, including *The Sun Magazine, make/shift,* and *A Woman's Thing*. She's grateful for support from the Arizona Commission on the Arts, Vermont Arts Council, Vermont Performance Lab, and the Vermont Studio Center. www.meganbuchanan.net

Dan Butler is known primarily as an actor whose credits include major roles on and off Broadway, on television, and in film, where he has also written, directed, and produced. In 2011, Dan adapted and directed a screen version of Poet Laureate Ted Kooser's verse poem "Pearl" starring Francis Sternhagen and himself, which had a great life on the film festival circuit. "New York Downpour" marks Dan's first published poem.

Kai Coggin is the author of *Mining for Stardust* (FlowerSong Press, 2021), *Incandescent* (Sibling Rivalry Press, 2019), *Wingspan* (Golden Dragonfly Press, 2016), and *Periscope Heart* (Swimming with Elephants Publications, 2014). She is a teaching artist in poetry with the Arkansas Arts Council, and the host of the longest-running consecutive weekly open mic series in the country, Wednesday Night Poetry. Her widely published poems have appeared in *Poetry, Cultural Weekly, SWWIM, Lavender Review*, and elsewhere.

Phyllis Cole-Dai began pecking away on an old manual typewriter in childhood and never stopped. She has authored or edited 11 books in multiple genres, "writing across what divides us." Her latest title is *Staying Power: Writings from a Pandemic Year* (Bell Sound Books, 2021). Originally from Ohio, she now resides with her scientist husband, college-bound son, and two cats in a 130-year-old house in Brookings, South Dakota. Learn more at phylliscoledai.com.

Karen Craigo is Missouri's fifth poet laureate, as well as the author of two books, *Passing Through Humansville* (Sundress, 2018) and *No More Milk* (Sundress, 2016). She is a freelance writer and editor and is based in Springfield, Missouri.

James Crews is the editor of the best-selling anthology *How to Love the World*, which has been featured on NPR's Morning Edition, in the *Boston Globe*, and the *Washington Post*, and is the author of four prize-winning collections of poetry: *The Book of What Stays, Telling My Father, Bluebird,* and *Every Waking Moment*. He lives with his husband in Shaftsbury, Vermont. jamescrews.net

Barbara Crooker is the author of nine books of poetry; *Some Glad Morning* (University of Pittsburgh, 2019) is the latest. Her honors include the WB Yeats Society of New York Award, the Thomas Merton Poetry of the Sacred Award, and three Pennsylvania Council on the Arts Fellowships. Her work appears in a variety of literary journals and anthologies, and has been read on ABC, the BBC, and The Writer's Almanac, and featured on Ted Kooser's American Life in Poetry.

An Officer of the Order of Canada, **Lorna Crozier** has been acknowledged for her contributions to Canadian literature with five honorary doctorates, most recently from McGill and Simon Fraser Universities. Her books have received numerous national awards, including the Governor-General's Award for Poetry. A professor emerita at the University of Victoria, she has performed for Queen Elizabeth II and has read her poetry, which has been translated into several languages, on every continent except Antarctica. Crozier lives on Vancouver Island.

Todd Davis is the author of seven books of poetry, most recently *Coffin Honey* (2022) and *Native Species* (2019), both published by Michigan State University Press. His writing has won the Foreword INDIES Book of the Year Bronze and Silver Awards, the Midwest Book Award, the Gwendolyn Brooks Poetry Prize, the Chautauqua Editors Prize, and the Bloomsburg University Book Prize. He teaches environmental studies at Pennsylvania State University's Altoona College.

Danny Dover is a retired piano technician living in Bethel, Vermont. He has two books of poetry: *Tasting Precious Metal* (published by Antrim House and available at norwichbookstore.com), and a chapbook, *Kindness Soup, Thankful Tea*. His poems have appeared in *Oberon, Himalayan Journal, Birchsong, Bloodroot,* and others, and also on two CDs of original music by Aaron Marcus of Montpelier, Vermont.

Kate Duignan is a New Zealand novelist and occasional poet. Her most recent novel, *The New Ships*, was short-listed in 2019 for the Acorn Prize, New Zealand's premier fiction prize. Kate is currently working on a collection of short stories. She teaches fiction at the IIML, Victoria University of Wellington. She lives in Wellington with her partner and children.

Cornelius Eady's poetry collections include *Victims of the Latest Dance Craze*, winner of the 1985 Lamont Prize; *The Gathering of My Name*, nominated for a 1992 Pulitzer Prize; and *Hardheaded Weather*. He teaches at the University of Tennessee, Knoxville and is cofounder of the Cave Canem Foundation.

Terri Kirby Erickson is the author of six collections, including *A Sun Inside My Chest* (Press 53). Her work has appeared in American Life in Poetry, *Atlanta Review, Healing the Divide: Poems of Kindness & Connection, How to Love the World: Poems of Gratitude and Hope, The Christian Century, The SUN*, on The Writer's Almanac, and many others. Her awards include the Joy Harjo Poetry Prize, the Atlanta Review International Publication Prize, and a Nautilus Silver Book Award. She lives in North Carolina.

Julia Fehrenbacher is a poet, a teacher, a life coach, and a sometimes-painter who is always looking for ways to spread a little good around in this world. She is most at home by the ocean and in the forests of the Pacific Northwest and with pen and paintbrush in hand. She lives in Corvallis, Oregon, with her husband and two beautiful girls.

Molly Fisk edited *California Fire & Water: A Climate Crisis Anthology*, with a Poets Laureate Fellowship from the Academy of American Poets when she was poet laureate of Nevada County, California. She's also won grants from the NEA, the California Arts Council, and the Corporation for Public Broadcasting. Her most recent poetry collection is *The More Difficult Beauty*; her latest book of radio commentary is *Naming Your Teeth*. Fisk lives in the Sierra foothills.
mollyfisk.com

Laura Foley is the author of seven poetry collections. *Why I Never Finished My Dissertation* received a starred Kirkus Review and an Eric Hoffer Award. Her collection *It's This* is forthcoming from Salmon Press. Her poems have won numerous awards and national recognition, been read by Garrison Keillor on The Writers' Almanac, and appeared in Ted Kooser's American Life in Poetry. Laura lives with her wife, Clara Gimenez, among Vermont hills.

Rebecca Foust is the author of three chapbooks and four books, including *Only*, forthcoming from Four Way Books in 2022, with poems in *The Hudson Review, Narrative, Ploughshares, Poetry, Southern Review,* and elsewhere. Recognitions include the 2020 Pablo Neruda Prize for Poetry, judged by Kaveh Akbar; the CP Cavafy and James Hearst poetry prizes; a Marin Poet Laureateship; and fellowships from The Frost Place, Hedgebrook, MacDowell, and Sewanee.

Rudy Francisco is one of the most recognizable names in spoken word poetry. He was born, raised, and still resides in San Diego, California. As an artist, Rudy Francisco is an amalgamation of social critique, introspection, honesty, and humor. He uses personal narratives to discuss the politics of race, class, gender, and religion while simultaneously pinpointing and reinforcing the interconnected nature of human existence. He is the author of *I'll Fly Away* (Button Poetry, 2020).

Joy Gaines-Friedler is the author of three books of poetry, including the award-winning *Capture Theory*. Joy teaches for nonprofits in the Detroit area, including Freedom House Detroit, where she offers the art of poetry to asylum seekers from western and northern Africa. She's also taught for the University of Michigan Prison Creative Arts Project (PCAP), where she worked with male lifers. Widely published, Joy has numerous awards and multiple Pushcart Prize nominations.

Ross Gay is the author of four books of poetry: *Against Which*; *Bringing the Shovel Down*; *Catalog of Unabashed Gratitude*, winner of the 2015 National Book Critics Circle Award and the 2016 Kingsley Tufts Poetry Award; and *Be Holding* (University of Pittsburgh Press, 2020).

His best-selling collection of essays, *The Book of Delights*, was released by Algonquin Books in 2019.

Alice Wolf Gilborn, a native of Colorado, is the founding editor of the literary magazine *Blueline*, published by the English department, SUNY Potsdam. Her poems have appeared in various journals and anthologies, most recently *Healing the Divide* (Green Writers Press) and *After Moby-Dick* (Spinner Publications). She is also author of a chapbook, *Taking Root* (Finishing Line Press), as well as a full-length book of poetry, *Apples and Stones* (Kelsay Books, 2020). alicewolfgilborn.com

Mary Ray Goehring, a snowbird, migrates between her central Wisconsin prairie and the pine forests of East Texas. She has been published in *Steam Ticket Review, Blue Heron Review, Ariel Anthology, Brick Street Poetry, Your Daily Poem, Texas Poetry Calendar, Bramble,* and several Wisconsin Fellowship of Poets poetry calendars. A retired landscape designer turned naturalist, she loves to write about family, friends, and nature.

Ingrid Goff-Maidoff is the author of more than a dozen books of poetry and inspiration, as well as a beautiful line of cards and gifts. Her books include *What Holds Us, Wild Song, Befriending the Soul, Good Mother Welcome,* and *Simple Graces for Every Meal.* She lives on the island of Martha's Vineyard with her husband and three white cats: Rumi, Hafiz, and Mirabai. Ingrid celebrates poetry, beauty, and spirit through her website, www.tendingjoy.com.

Nancy Gordon grew up in the Adirondacks, her true home, then taught English in New Jersey for years, including a year on exchange in New Zealand. A midlife marriage and move were followed by law school and years of law practice. She and her husband have returned home to the Adirondacks, and she now has more time for poetry, always an important part of her life.

Most recent of **David Graham's** seven collections of poetry is *The Honey of Earth* (Terrapin

Books, 2019). Others include *Stutter Monk* (Flume Press) and *Second Wind* (Texas Tech University Press). He coedited (with Tom Montag) the poetry anthology *Local News: Poetry About Small Towns* (MWPH Books, 2019) and with Kate Sontag the essay anthology *After Confession: Poetry as Confession* (Graywolf Press, 2001). He lives in Glens Falls, New York. www.davidgrahampoet.com

Leah Naomi Green is the author of *The More Extravagant Feast* (Graywolf Press, 2020), selected by Li-Young Lee for the Walt Whitman Award of the Academy of American Poets. She is the recipient of a 2021 Treehouse Climate Action Poetry Prize from the AAP, as well as the 2021 Lucille Clifton Legacy Award. Green teaches environmental studies and English at Washington and Lee University. Green lives in the mountains of Virginia, where she and her family homestead and grow food.

Twyla M. Hansen, Nebraska's state poet 2013–2018, codirects Poetry from the Plains, and conducts readings/workshops through Humanities Nebraska. Her book *Rock • Tree • Bird* won the 2018 WILLA Literary Award and Nebraska Book Award. Previous books won Nebraska Book Awards and a 2017 Notable Nebraska 150 Book. Recent publications: *Briar Cliff Review, Prairie Schooner, South Dakota Review, More in Time: A Tribute to Ted Kooser, Nebraska Poetry: A Sesquicentennial Anthology 1867–2017*, poets.org, poetryfoundation.org, poetryoutloud.org, and more.

Joy Harjo is an internationally renowned performer and writer of the Muscogee (Creek) Nation. She is serving her second term as the 23rd poet laureate of the United States. The author of nine books of poetry, including the highly acclaimed *An American Sunrise*, she has also written several plays and children's books, and two memoirs, *Crazy Brave* and *Poet Warrior*.

Penny Harter's most recent collections are *Still-Water Days* (2021) and *A Prayer the Body Makes* (2020). Her work has appeared in *Persimmon Tree, Rattle, Tiferet*, and American Life in Poetry, as well as in many journals, anthologies, and earlier collections. An invited reader at the 2010 Dodge Festival, she has won fellowships and awards from the New Jersey State Council on the Arts, VCCA, and the Poetry Society of America. For more information visit pennyharterpoet.com.

Margaret Hasse lives in Saint Paul, Minnesota, where she has been active as a teaching poet, among other work in the community. Six of Margaret's full-length poetry collections are in print. During the first year of the COVID-19 pandemic, Margaret collaborated with artist Sharon DeMark on *Shelter*, a collection of poems and paintings about refuge. A chapbook, *The Call of Glacier Park* (2022), is her latest publication. To learn more, visit her website: MargaretHasse.com.

Tom Hennen is the author of six books of poetry, including *Darkness Sticks to Everything: Collected and New Poems* (Copper Canyon Press, 2013), and was born and raised in rural Minnesota. After abandoning college, he married and began work as a letterpress and offset printer. He helped found the Minnesota Writer's Publishing House, then worked for the Department of Natural Resources wildlife section, and later at the Sand Lake National Wildlife Refuge in South Dakota. Now retired, he lives in Minnesota.

Zoe Higgins is a Pākehā poet and theatre-maker living in Te Whanganui-a-Tara in Aotearoa. Her work can be found in journals such as *Landfall, Sport, Starling*, and *Sweet Mammalian*.

Donna Hilbert's latest book is *Gravity: New & Selected Poems* (Tebot Bach, 2018). Her new collection, *Threnody*, is forthcoming from Moon Tide Press. She is a monthly contributing writer to the online journal *Verse-Virtual*. Her work has appeared in the

Los Angeles Times, Braided Way, Chiron Review, Sheila-Na-Gig, Rattle, Zocalo Public Square, One Art, and numerous anthologies. She writes and leads private workshops in Southern California, where she makes her home. Learn more at www.donnahilbert.com.

Jane Hirshfield's ninth, recently published poetry collection is *Ledger* (Knopf, 2020). A former chancellor of the Academy of American Poets, her work appears in *The New Yorker, The Atlantic, The Times Literary Supplement, The New York Review of Books,* and 10 editions of The Best American Poetry series. In 2019, she was elected to the American Academy of Arts and Sciences.

Linda Hogan is a Chickasaw poet, novelist, essayist, playwright, teacher, and activist who has spent most of her life in Oklahoma and Colorado. Her fiction has garnered many honors, including a Pulitzer Prize nomination, and her poetry collections have received the American Book Award, the Colorado Book Award, and a National Book Critics Circle nomination. Her latest book is *A History of Kindness* (Torrey House Press, 2020).

Marie Howe is the author of four books of poetry, the most recent of which is *Magdalene* (Norton). She was New York state poet from 2012 to 2014, is a chancellor of the Academy of American Poets, and teaches at Sarah Lawrence College. She is also the poet in residence at the Cathedral Church of Saint John the Divine in New York City.

After teaching public school in Alaska for about 30 years, **Ray Hudson** moved to Vermont. He is the author of *Moments Rightly Placed: An Aleutian Memoir*, along with several works on Aleutian history and ethnography. His most recent publication is a YA novel, *Ivory and Paper: Adventures In and Out of Time* (University of Alaska Press).

Mary Elder Jacobsen's poetry has appeared in *The Greensboro Review, Four Way Review, Green Mountains Review, storySouth, One,*

Poetry Daily, and anthologies, including *Healing the Divide: Poems of Kindness & Connection* (edited by James Crews). Winner of the Lyric Memorial Prize and recipient of a Vermont Studio Center residency, Jacobsen is co-organizer of Words Out Loud, an annual reading series of Vermont authors held at a still-unplugged 1823 meetinghouse.

Richard Jones's sixteen books include *Apropos of Nothing* (Copper Canyon, 2006), *The Correct Spelling & Exact Meaning* (Copper Canyon, 2010), and *Stranger on Earth* (Copper Canyon, 2018). He has two new books forthcoming, *Paris* and *Avalon*. For 40 years he has edited the literary journal *Poetry East* and curated its many anthologies, including *Origins, The Last Believer in Words,* and *Bliss*. He is professor of English at DePaul University in Chicago.

Fady Joudah is a Palestinian American physician, poet, and translator. He was born in Austin, Texas, but grew up in Libya and Saudi Arabia. Joudah's debut collection of poetry, *The Earth in the Attic* (2008), won the 2007 Yale Series of Younger Poets competition, chosen by Louise Glück. Joudah lives with his family in Houston, where he serves as a physician of internal medicine.

Jacqueline Jules is the author of *Manna in the Morning* (Kelsay Books, 2021), *Itzhak Perlman's Broken String* (Evening Street Press, 2017), *Field Trip to the Museum* (Finishing Line Press, 2014), and *Stronger Than Cleopatra* (ELJ Publications, 2014). She is also the author of 50 books for young readers, including the poetry collection *Tag Your Dreams: Poems of Play and Persistence* (Albert Whitman, 2020). Visit her online at www.jacquelinejules.com.

Christine Kitano is the author of two collections of poetry, *Birds of Paradise* (Lynx House Press) and *Sky Country* (BOA Editions), which won the Central New York Book Award and was a finalist for the Paterson Poetry Prize. She is coeditor of the forthcoming *They Rise Like a Wave* (Blue Oak Press), an anthology of

Asian American women and nonbinary poets. In addition to teaching at Ithaca College, she serves as Tompkins County poet laureate. christinekitano.com

Michael Kleber-Diggs is the author of *Worldly Things*, which was awarded the 2020 Max Ritvo Poetry Prize. He was born and raised in Kansas and now lives in St. Paul, Minnesota. His work has appeared in *Lit Hub, The Rumpus, Rain Taxi, McSweeney's Internet Tendency, Water~Stone Review, Midway Review,* and *North Dakota Quarterly*. Michael teaches poetry and creative nonfiction through the Minnesota Prison Writers Workshop.

Tricia Knoll lives in a Vermont woods. Her work appears widely in journals and anthologies, and has received nine Pushcart nominations and one Best of Net. Her collected poems include *Ocean's Laughter, Urban Wild, Broadfork Farm, How I Learned to Be White,* and *Checkered Mates. How I Learned to Be White* received the 2018 Indie Human Rights Award for Motivational Poetry. She is a contributing editor to *Verse-Virtual*. triciaknoll.com

The 13th US poet laureate (2004–2006), **Ted Kooser** is a retired life insurance executive who lives on acreage near the village of Garland, Nebraska, with his wife, Kathleen Rutledge. His collection *Delights & Shadows* was awarded the Pulitzer Prize in Poetry in 2005. His poems have appeared in *The Atlantic, The Hudson Review, The Antioch Review, The Kenyon Review,* and dozens of other literary journals. He is the author most recently of *Kindest Regards: New and Selected Poems* (2018) and *Red Stilts* (2020), both from Copper Canyon Press.

Danusha Laméris is the author of two books: *The Moons of August* (Autumn House, 2014), which was chosen by Naomi Shihab Nye as the winner of the Autumn House Press Poetry Prize, and *Bonfire Opera* (University of Pittsburgh, 2020), which won the Northern California

Book Award. Winner of the Lucille Clifton Legacy Award, she teaches in the Pacific University low-residency MFA program and cohosts with James Crews the Poetry of Resilience online seminars. She lives in Santa Cruz County, California.

Heather Lanier's memoir *Raising a Rare Girl* was a *New York Times Book Review* Editors' Choice. She is also the author of two award-winning poetry chapbooks. She is an assistant professor of creative writing at Rowan University, and her TED talk has been viewed over two million times. You can sign up for her newsletter, *The Slow Take*, by visiting her website, heatherlanierwriter.com.

Dorianne Laux's sixth collection, *Only as the Day Is Long: New and Selected Poems,* was named a finalist for the 2020 Pulitzer Prize for Poetry. Her fifth collection, *The Book of Men*, was awarded the Paterson Poetry Prize, and her fourth book of poems, *Facts About the Moon*, won the Oregon Book Award. Laux is the coauthor of the celebrated *The Poet's Companion: A Guide to the Pleasures of Writing Poetry.*

Li-Young Lee was born in Djakarta, Indonesia, in 1957 to Chinese political exiles. He is the author of *The Undressing* (W. W. Norton, 2018); *Behind My Eyes* (W. W. Norton, 2008); *Book of My Nights* (BOA Editions, 2001), which won the 2002 William Carlos Williams Award; *The City in Which I Love You* (BOA Editions, 1990), which was the 1990 Lamont Poetry Selection; and *Rose* (BOA Editions, 1986), which won the Delmore Schwartz Memorial Poetry Award.

Paula Gordon Lepp lives in South Charleston, West Virginia, with her husband and two almost-grown kids. She grew up in a rural community in the Mississippi Delta, and a childhood spent roaming woods and fields, climbing trees, and playing in the dirt instilled in her a love for nature that is reflected in her poems. Paula's work has been published in the anthologies *How to Love the World:*

Poems of Gratitude and Hope and *The Mountain* (Middle Creek Publishing).

Annie Lighthart began writing poetry after her first visit to an Oregon old-growth forest and now teaches poetry wherever she can. Poems from her books *Iron String* and *Pax* have been featured on The Writer's Almanac and in many anthologies. Annie's work has been turned into music, been used in healing projects, and traveled farther than she has. She hopes you find a poem to love in this book, even if it is one she didn't write.

Ada Limón is the author of five poetry collections, including *The Carrying*, which won the National Book Critics Circle Award for Poetry. Her fourth book, *Bright Dead Things*, was named a finalist for the National Book Award, the Kingsley Tufts Poetry Award, and the National Book Critics Circle Award. A recipient of a Guggenheim Fellowship for Poetry, she serves on the faculty of the Queens University of Charlotte's low-residency MFA program and lives in Lexington, Kentucky.

Alison Luterman's four books of poetry are *The Largest Possible Life, See How We Almost Fly, Desire Zoo,* and *In the Time of Great Fires* (Catamaran Press, 2020). Her poems and stories have appeared in *The Sun, Rattle, Salon, Prairie Schooner, Nimrod, The Atlanta Review, Tattoo Highway,* and elsewhere. She has written an e-book of personal essays, *Feral City*; half a dozen plays; and a song cycle, as well as two musicals, *The Chain* and *The Shyest Witch*.

Emilie Lygren is a poet and an outdoor educator who holds a bachelor's degree in geology-biology from Brown University. Her poems have been published in *Thimble Literary Magazine, The English Leadership Quarterly, Solo Novo,* and several other literary journals. Her first book of poems, *What We Were Born For* (Blue Light Press, 2021), won the Blue Light Book Award. She lives in San Rafael, California.

Michelle Mandolia works as an analyst at the US Environmental Protection

Agency. She lives with her husband and two children in Reston, Virginia.

Joseph Millar is the author of six books of poetry, including *Dark Harvest: New and Selected Poems* (Carnegie Mellon University Press, 2021) and *Overtime* (Eastern Washington University Press, 2001), which was a finalist for the Oregon Book Award. He is the recipient of fellowships from the Guggenheim Foundation and the National Endowment for the Arts, and teaches in the MFA programs at North Carolina State and Pacific University.

Brad Aaron Modlin wrote *Everyone at This Party Has Two Names*, which won the Cowles Poetry Prize. *Surviving in Drought* (stories) won the Cupboard contest. His work has been the basis for orchestral scores, an art exhibition in New York City, and the premier episode of *Poetry Unbound* from On Being Studios. A professor and the Reynolds Endowed Chair of Creative Writing at the University of Nebraska at Kearney, he teaches (under)graduates, coordinates the visiting writers' series, and gets chalk all over himself.

Susan Moorhead writes poetry and stories in New York. Her work has appeared in many journals and anthologies. She's received four Pushcart Prize nominations for fiction, nonfiction, and poetry, and first prize in the Greenburgh, New York, poetry contest. Her poetry collections are *The Night Ghost* and *Carry Darkness, Carry Light*. Daytimes find her working as a librarian, where she is happy to be surrounded by books.

Susan Musgrave lives on Haida Gwaii, a group of islands in the North Pacific that lie equidistant from Luxor, Machu Picchu, Ninevah, and Timbuktu. The high point of her literary career was finding her name in the index of *Montreal's Irish Mafia*. She has published more than 30 books and has received awards in six categories: poetry, novels, nonfiction, food writing, editing, and books for children. Her new book of poetry, *Exculpatory Lilies,* will be published by M&S in 2022.

With over a million copies sold, **Mark Nepo** has moved and inspired readers and seekers all over the world with his #1 *New York Times* bestseller *The Book of Awakening*. Beloved as a poet, teacher, and storyteller, Mark has been called "one of the finest spiritual guides of our time," "a consummate storyteller," and "an eloquent spiritual teacher." A best-selling author, he has published 22 books and recorded 14 audio projects. Recent work includes *The Book of Soul* (St. Martin's Essentials, 2020) and *Drinking from the River of Light* (Sounds True, 2019), a Nautilus Award winner. marknepo.com and threeintentions.com

Suzanne Nussey has worked as an editor, writer, memoir coach, and writing instructor in Ottawa, Canada. Her poetry, creative nonfiction, and essays have been published in *The New Quarterly, EVENT, The Fiddlehead, Prairie Fire,* and *Spark and Echo*, among others, and have won several national Canadian literary competitions. Suzanne has also developed and facilitated creative writing workshops for women living in shelters. She holds master's degrees in creative writing (Syracuse University) and pastoral counseling (St. Paul University).

Naomi Shihab Nye is the Young People's Poet Laureate of the United States (Poetry Foundation). Her most recent books are *Everything Comes Next, Collected & New Poems, Cast Away: Poems for Our Time* (poems about trash), *The Tiny Journalist,* and *Voices in the Air: Poems for Listeners*. She lives in San Antonio, Texas.

January Gill O'Neil is an associate professor of English at Salem State University. She is the author of *Rewilding* (CavanKerry Press, 2018), a finalist for the 2019 Paterson Poetry Prize; *Misery Islands* (CavanKerry Press, 2014); and *Underlife* (CavanKerry Press, 2009).

Gregory Orr is the author of two books about poetry, *Poetry as Survival* and *A Primer for Poets and Readers of Poetry*; a memoir, *The Blessing*; and 12 collections of poetry, including *How Beautiful the Beloved* and *The Last Love Poem I Will Ever Write*. He taught at the University of Virginia from 1975 to 2019, where he founded the university's MFA program in creative writing.

Alicia Ostriker is professor emerita of English at Rutgers University and a faculty member of Drew University's low-residency poetry MFA program. In 2018, she was named New York state poet by Governor Andrew Cuomo. Ostriker served as chancellor of the Academy of American Poets from 2015 to 2021. She lives in New York City.

Peter Pereira is a family physician in Seattle whose poems have appeared in *Poetry, Prairie Schooner, New England Review, Virginia Quarterly Review,* and *Journal of the American Medical Association*. His books include *What's Written on the Body* (Copper Canyon Press, 2007), which was a finalist for the Washington State Book Award; *Saying the World* (Copper Canyon Press, 2003), which won the 2002 Hayden Carruth Award; and the limited-edition chapbook *The Lost Twin* (Grey Spider Press, 2000).

Andrea Potos is the author of several poetry collections, including *Marrow of Summer* (Kelsay Books), *Mothershell* (Kelsay Books), and *Yaya's Cloth* (Iris Press). Her poems most recently appeared in *Spirituality & Health Magazine, Poetry East, The Sun, Braided Way,* and *How to Love the World: Poems of Gratitude and Hope.* Andrea lives in Madison, Wisconsin.

Susan Rich is an award-winning poet, editor, and essayist. She is the author of *Cloud Pharmacy, The Alchemist's Kitchen, Cures Include Travel,* and *The Cartographer's Tongue.* She coedited the anthology *The Strangest of Theatres* (McSweeney's Books) and has received awards from PEN America and the Fulbright

Foundation. *Gallery of Postcards and Maps: New and Collected Poems* is forthcoming from Salmon Press, and *Blue Atlas* from Red Hen Press in 2024.

Jack Ridl, poet laureate of Douglas, Michigan, recently released *Saint Peter and the Goldfinch* (Wayne State University Press). His *Practicing to Walk Like a Heron* (WSU Press, 2013) was awarded the National Gold Medal for poetry by ForeWord Reviews/Indie Fab. His collection *Broken Symmetry* (WSU Press) was corecipient of the Society of Midland Authors Best Book of Poetry Award for 2006. For more information about Jack, visit: www.ridl.com.

Alberto Ríos was named Arizona's first poet laureate in 2013. He is the author of many poetry collections from Copper Canyon Press, including *Not Go Away Is My Name* (2020); *A Small Story About the Sky* (2015); *The Dangerous Shirt* (2009); *The Theater of Night* (2006); and *The Smallest Muscle in the Human Body* (2002), which was nominated for the National Book Award.

David Romtvedt is a writer and musician from Buffalo, Wyoming. His books include *Dilemmas of the Angels; Some Church;* the novel *Zelestina Urza in Outer Space*; and *The Tree of Gernika,* translations of the nineteenth-century Basque poet Joxe Mari Iparragirre. A recipient of the Pushcart Prize and of fellowships from the Wyoming Arts Council and the National Endowment for the Arts, Romtvedt also performs older and more contemporary Basque dance music with the band Ospa.

Susan Rothbard's poems have appeared in *Paterson Literary Review, The Comstock Review, English Journal, Dogwood,* and *Spindrift*. She earned her MFA in creative writing at Fairleigh Dickinson University, and her recent book, *Birds of New Jersey* (Broadkill River Press), was awarded the Dogfish Head Poetry Prize.

Ellen Rowland creates, concocts, and forages when she's not writing. She is the author of *Light Come Gather Me*, a selection of mindfulness haiku, and *Everything I Thought I Knew*, a collection of essays about living, learning, and parenting outside the status quo. Her writing has appeared in various literary journals and in several poetry anthologies. She lives off the grid on a tiny island in Greece. Connect with her at ellenrowland.com.

Patricia McKernon Runkle values the quiet work of listening to one another and building community. She has volunteered at a peer-support center for grieving children and their families, worked as a writer and editor, and directed a choir. She has published poems, songs and collaborative choral pieces, and an award-winning memoir on grief. She and her husband cherish their two grown children. griefscompass.com

Marjorie Saiser's seventh collection, *Learning to Swim* (Stephen F. Austin State University Press, 2019), contains both poetry and memoir. Her novel-in-poems, *Losing the Ring in the River* (University of New Mexico Press), won the WILLA Award for Poetry in 2014. Saiser's most recent book, *The Track the Whales Make: New & Selected Poems*, is available from University of Nebraska Press. Her website is www.poetmarge.com.

Lailah Dainin Shima walks and writes on the shores of Lake Wingra. She loves folding poems into envelopes she drops into mailboxes and forgets. Some of them have shown up in *One Art Poetry, Buddhist Poetry Review*, and *CALYX Journal*.

Faith Shearin is the author of six books of poetry: *The Owl Question, The Empty House, Moving the Piano, Telling the Bees, Orpheus Turning*, and *Lost Language*. Recent work has appeared in *Alaska Quarterly Review* and *Poetry East*, and has been read aloud by Garrison Keillor on The Writers' Almanac.

Michael Simms is an American poet and literary publisher. His most recent books are

American Ash and *Nightjar*. His poems have been published in literary journals and magazines, including *5 A.M.*, *Poetry*, *Black Warrior Review*, *Mid-American Review*, *Pittsburgh Quarterly*, *Southwest Review*, and *West Branch*. He is the founder and editor of *Vox Populi*.

Anya Silver (1968–2018) won a Guggenheim Fellowship and the Georgia Author of the Year Award. She was the author of five books of poetry: *The Ninety-Third Name of God* (2010), *I Watched You Disappear* (2014), *From Nothing* (2016), and *Saint Agnostica* (2021), all published by the Louisiana State University Press, as well as *Second Bloom*, which was published in 2017 by Cascade Books. Until her death, she taught English at Mercer University in Macon, Georgia.

Tracy K. Smith is the author of the memoir *Ordinary Light* and four books of poetry: *Wade in the Water* (2018); *Life on Mars*, which received the 2012 Pulitzer Prize; *Duende*, recipient of the 2006 James Laughlin Award; and *The Body's Question*, which won the 2002 Cave Canem Poetry Prize. In 2017 she was named the 22nd US poet laureate by the Library of Congress, 2017–2019.

Judith Sornberger is the author of four poetry collections: *Angel Chimes: Poems of Advent and Christmas* (Shanti Arts), *I Call to You from Time* (Wipf and Stock), *Practicing the World* (CavanKerry), and *Open Heart* (Calyx Books). Her prose memoir, *The Accidental Pilgrim: Finding God and His Mother in Tuscany*, is published by Shanti Arts. She is professor emerita of Mansfield University, where she taught English and women's studies. She lives on the side of a mountain in the northern Appalachians of Pennsylvania.

Kim Stafford directs the Northwest Writing Institute at Lewis & Clark College, and is the author of a dozen books, including *The Muses Among Us: Eloquent Listening and Other Pleasures of the Writer's Craft* (University of Georgia Press, 2003) and *Singer Come from Afar* (Red Hen Press,

2021). He has taught writing in Scotland, Mexico, Italy, and Bhutan. He served as Oregon poet laureate, 2018–2020. He teaches and travels to raise the human spirit.

William Stafford's (1914–1993) first collection of poems, *West of Your City*, wasn't published until he was in his mid-forties. However, by the time of his death, Stafford had published hundreds of poems, and was said to have written at least one new poem a day. His collection *Traveling Through the Dark* won the National Book Award for Poetry in 1963. Stafford also received the Award in Literature from the American Academy and Institute of Arts and Letters and a National Endowment for the Arts Senior Fellowship.

Julie Cadwallader Staub grew up with five sisters beside one of Minnesota's lakes. Her favorite words to hear were "Now you girls go outside and play." She now lives and writes from her home near Burlington, Vermont. Her poems have been published in literary journals and anthologies, including in *Poetry of Presence: An Anthology of Mindfulness Poems*. Her two collections of poems are *Face to Face* (Cascadia Publishing, 2010) and *Wing Over Wing* (Paraclete Press, 2019).

Christine Stewart-Nuñez, South Dakota's poet laureate, is the author of seven books of poetry, most recently *The Poet & The Architect*, *Untrussed*, and *Bluewords Greening*, winner of the 2018 Whirling Prize. She's also the founder of the Women Poets Collective, a regional group focused on advancing its members' writing through peer critique and support.

Jacqueline Suskin is a poet and educator based in Northern California, where she is currently the artist in residence at Folklife Farm. Suskin is the author of seven books, including *Every Day Is a Poem* (Sounds True, 2020) and *Help in the Dark Season* (Write Bloody, 2019). With her project Poem Store, Suskin has composed over 40,000 improvisational poems for patrons who chose a topic in exchange for a unique verse. She was honored by Michelle Obama as a Turnaround Artist, and her work has been featured in the *New York Times*, the *Los Angeles Times*, *The Atlantic*, and other publications. For more, see jacquelinesuskin.com.

Joyce Sutphen grew up on a small farm in Stearns County, Minnesota. Her first collection of poems, *Straight Out of View*, won the Barnard New Women Poets Prize; her recent books are *The Green House* (Salmon Poetry, 2017) and *Carrying Water to the Field: New and Selected Poems* (University of Nebraska Press, 2019). She is the Minnesota poet laureate and professor emerita of literature and creative writing at Gustavus Adolphus College.

Heather Swan's poems have appeared in such journals as *Terrain*, *The Hopper*, *Poet Lore*, *Phoebe*, and *The Raleigh Review*, and her book of poems, *A Kinship with Ash* (Terrapin Books), was published in 2020. Her nonfiction has appeared in *Aeon*, *Belt*, *Catapult*, *Emergence*, *ISLE*, and *Terrain*. Her book *Where Honeybees Thrive: Stories from the Field* (Penn State Press) won the Sigurd F. Olson Nature Writing Award. She teaches environmental literature and writing at the University of Wisconsin–Madison.

Angela Narciso Torres is the author of *Blood Orange*, winner of the Willow Books Literature Award for Poetry. Her recent collections include *To the Bone* (Sundress, 2020) and *What Happens Is Neither* (Four Way Books, 2021). Her work has appeared in *Poetry*, *Missouri Review*, *Quarterly West*, *Cortland Review*, and *PANK*. Born in Brooklyn and raised in Manila, she serves as a senior and reviews editor for *RHINO Poetry*.

Natasha Trethewey's first collection of poetry, *Domestic Work* (Graywolf Press, 2000), was selected by Rita Dove as the winner of the inaugural Cave Canem Poetry Prize. She is also the author of *Monument: Poems New and Selected* (Houghton Mifflin, 2018). In 2012, Trethewey was named both the State Poet Laureate of Mississippi and the 19th US poet laureate by the Library of Congress. Trethewey is the Board of Trustees Professor of English at Northwestern University in Evanston, Illinois.

Rosemerry Wahtola Trommer lives on the banks of the San Miguel River in southwest Colorado. She cohosts the *Emerging Form* podcast, the Stubborn Praise poetry series, and Secret Agents of Change (a kindness cabal). Her poems have been featured on A Prairie Home Companion, American Life in Poetry, and PBS News Hour, and in *Oprah Magazine*. Her most recent book, *Hush*, won the Halcyon Prize. One-word mantra: Adjust.

A retired educator of young children, **David Van Houten** moved from Michigan to Tucson, Arizona, with his husband in 2010. His interest in writing was cultivated by instructor Dan Gilmore at the Osher Lifelong Learning Institute at the University of Arizona. David is a docent at the University of Arizona Poetry Center and participates in their "Free Time" workshop, corresponding with writers who are incarcerated. David's poems were published in the *Oasis Journal* in 2017.

Connie Wanek was born in Wisconsin, was raised in New Mexico, and lived for over a quarter century in Duluth, Minnesota. She is the author of *Bonfire* (New Rivers Press), winner of the New Voices Award; *Hartley Field* (Holy Cow! Press); and *On Speaking Terms* (Copper Canyon Press). In 2016, the University of Nebraska Press published Wanek's *Rival Gardens: New and Selected Poems* as part of their Ted Kooser Contemporary Poetry series.

Gillian Wegener lives in central California. She is the author of *The Opposite of Clairvoyance* (2008) and *This Sweet Haphazard* (2017), both from Sixteen Rivers Press. She is the founding president of Modesto-Stanislaus Poetry Center, a past poet laureate for the City of Modesto and, as a volunteer, taught creative writing to teens in juvenile detention for five years.

Laura Grace Weldon has published three poetry collections—*Portals* (Middle Creek,

2021), *Blackbird* (Grayson, 2019), and *Tending* (Aldrich, 2013)—as well as a handbook of alternative education titled *Free Range Learning* (Hohm Press, 2010). She served as Ohio Poet of the Year and recently won the Halcyon Poetry Prize. She works as a book editor, teaches writing workshops, and maxes out her library card each week. Connect with her on Twitter, Facebook, and at lauragraceweldon.com.

Michelle Wiegers is a poet and mind-body life coach based in southern Vermont. Her work has appeared in *Healing the Divide, How to Love the World, Birchsong Anthology,* and *Third Wednesday*, among other journals. In her coaching work, she is a passionate advocate for those who suffer with chronic pain and fatigue. michellewiegers.com

Laura Budofsky Wisniewski is the author of the collection *Sanctuary, Vermont* (Orison Books) and the chapbook *How to Prepare Bear* (Redbird Chapbooks). Her work has appeared in *Image, Hunger Mountain Review, American Journal of Poetry, Passengers Journal, Confrontation,* and others. She is winner of the 2020 Orison Poetry Prize, *Ruminate Magazine*'s 2020 Janet B. McCabe Poetry Prize, the 2019 Poetry International Prize, and the 2014 Passager Poetry Prize. Laura lives in a small town in Vermont.

Susan Zimmerman is a retired lawyer who lives and writes in Toronto. Her poetry chapbook, *Nothing Is Lost*, was published by Caitlin Press, and her poems are published in periodicals such as *Room, Fiddlehead, The Ontario Review, Fireweed, Matrix,* and *Calyx*. She has taught a creative writing course called Writing like Breathing at a healing center, and since her retirement in 2015, she has returned to participating regularly in poetry retreats and workshops.

CREDITS

"Praise" by Kelli Russell Agodon originally published in *Redivider*.

"Hot Tea" by Lahab Assef Al-Jundi originally published in *KNOT Literary Magazine* and *San Antonio Express-News*.

"Vain Doubts" and "Love Portions" Copyright © 2004 by Julia Alvarez. From *The Woman I Kept to Myself*, published by Algonquin Books of Chapel Hill. By permission of Susan Bergholz Literary Services, New York, NY, and Lamy, NM. All rights reserved.

"The Innermost Chamber of My Home Is Yours" by David Axelrod from *Years Beyond the River* Copyright © 2021 David Axelrod. Reprinted with permission of Terrapin Books.

"My Father's Hands" by Zeina Azzam, originally published in *Heartwood Literary Magazine* (2017) and in *Bayna Bayna, In-Between* (The Poetry Box) © 2021 by Zeina Azzam. Reprinted with permission of the author.

Ellen Bass, "The Thing Is" from *Mules of Love*. Copyright © 2002 by Ellen Bass. Reprinted with the permission of The Permissions Company, LLC on behalf of BOA Editions Ltd., boaeditions.org.

"Exactly 299,792,458 Meters Per Second" by Carolee Bennett originally published in *Contrary Magazine* (2017) and *Sundress Best of the Net Anthology* (2018).

"About Standing (in Kinship)" by Kimberly Blaeser originally published in *Poetry Magazine* (March 2021).

"Mailman" by Sally Bliumis-Dunn from *Second Skin* (Wind Publications, 2010). Reprinted with permission of the author.

"The Joins" by Chana Bloch from *Swimming in the Rain: New & Selected Poems* (Autumn House Press, 2015). Copyright © 2015 by Chana Bloch. Reprinted with permission of the publisher.

"Into Wildflower Into Field" by Kai Coggin from *Mining for Stardust* (FlowerSong Press, 2021). Reprinted with permission of the author.

"Ladder" by Phyllis Cole-Dai from *Staying Power: Writings from a Pandemic Year* (Bell Sound Books, 2021). Reprinted with permission of the author.

"Last Scraps of Color in Missouri" by Karen Craigo originally published in *The New York Times*. Reprinted with permission of the author.

"Self-Compassion" by James Crews originally appeared as part of the Academy of American Poets Poem-a-Day, edited by Kimberly Blaeser. "The Pool" by James Crews from *Every Waking Moment* (Lynx House Press, 2021). James Crews, "Self-Care," originally appeared in One Art edited by Mark Danowsky.

"Sustenance" by Barbara Crooker from *Small Rain* (Purple Flag, 2014), and "Forsythia" in *More In Time: A Tribute to Ted Kooser* (University of Nebraska Press, 2021). Reprinted with permission of the author.

"Heliotropic" by Todd Davis from *In the Kingdom of the Ditch* Copyright © 2013 Todd Davis (Michigan State University Press, 2013). Reprinted with permission of the author.

"Grandmother" by Kate Duignan originally published in *Sport 36, New Zealand New Writing*, Winter 2008, Victoria University Press, Wellington, NZ.

"A Small Moment" by Cornelius Eady from *Hardheaded Weather: New & Selected Poems* (Putnam, 2008). Reprinted with permission of the author.

"Free Breakfast" by Terri Kirby Erickson from *A Sun Inside My Chest* (Press 53, 2020). Reprinted by permission of the author and the publisher. "Night Talks" originally published in *ONE ART: a journal of poetry* (2020).

"Before I gained all this weight" by Molly Fisk originally published in *Cultural Weekly* and *Stone Gathering*, edited by Deborah Jacobs.

"A Perfect Arc" by Laura Foley from *Syringa*. © StarMeadow Press, 2007. Reprinted with permission. "Learning by Heart" from *Panoply Zine*.

"Kinship of Flesh" by Rebecca Foust from *Mom's Canoe* (Texas Review Press, 2009).

"Mercy" by Rudy Francisco from *Helium*. Copyright © 2017 by Rudy Francisco. Courtesy of Button Publishing Inc.

Ross Gay, "Thank You" from *Against Which*. Copyright © 2006 by Ross Gay. Reprinted with the permission of The Permissions Company, LLC on behalf of CavanKerry Press, Ltd., cavankerrypress.org.

"Wake Up" by Alice Gilborn from *Apples & Stones* (Kelsay Books, 2020). Reprinted with permission of the author.

"Peace Came Today" by Ingrid Goff-Maidoff from *Wild Song* (Sarah's Circle, 2021). Reprinted with permission of the author.

"The Age of Affection" by Leah Naomi Green, forthcoming in *Orion Magazine*.

"Trying to Pray" by Twyla M. Hansen from *Rock • Tree • Bird* (Backwaters Press, 2017). Reprinted with permission of the author.

"For Keeps," from *Conflict Resolution for Holy Beings: Poems* by Joy Harjo. Copyright © 2015 by Joy Harjo. Used by permission of W. W. Norton & Company, Inc.

"Two Meteors" by Penny Harter from *A Prayer the Body Makes* (Kelsay Books, 2020). Reprinted with permission of the author.

"Clothing" by Margaret Hasse from *Shelter* (Nodin Press, 2020). Reprinted with permission of author and publisher.

Tom Hennen, "Made Visible" from *Darkness Sticks to Everything: Collected and New Poems*. Copyright © 1997 by Tom Hennen. Reprinted with the permission of The Permissions Company, LLC on behalf of Copper Canyon Press, coppercanyonpress.org.

"Ode" by Zoe Higgins originally published in *Poems in the Waiting Room* (NZ), edited by Ruth Arnison.

"Credo" by Donna Hilbert from *Gravity: New & Selected Poems* (Tebot Bach, 2018). Reprinted with permission of the author.

"Arctic Night, Lights Across the Sky" by Linda Hogan from *A History of Kindness* (Torrey House Press, 2020). Reprinted with permission of the publisher.

"Delivery" by Marie Howe Copyright © 2017 by Marie Howe.

"Sponge Bath" by Mary Elder Jacobsen is part I of a two-part poem first published in *storySouth*. Copyright

© 2020 by Mary Elder Jacobsen. Excerpt reprinted with permission of the author.

Richard Jones, "After Work" from *The Blessing: New and Selected Poems.* Copyright © 2000 by Richard Jones. Reprinted with the permission of The Permissions Company, LLC on behalf of Copper Canyon Press, coppercanyonpress.org.

Fady Joudah, "Mimesis" from *Alight.* Copyright © 2013 by Fady Joudah. Reprinted with the permission of The Permissions Company, LLC on behalf of Copper Canyon Press, coppercanyonpress.org.

"Billowing Overhead" by Jacqueline Jules originally published in *K'in Literary Journal* (November 2019).

Christine Kitano, "For the Korean Grandmother on Sunset Boulevard" from *Sky Country.* Copyright © 2017 by Christine Kitano. Reprinted with the permission of The Permissions Company, LLC on behalf of BOA Editions Ltd., boaeditions.org.

Michael Kleber-Diggs, "Coniferous Fathers" from Worldly Things. Copyright © 2012 by Michael Kleber-Diggs. Reprinted with the permission of The Permissions Company LLC on behalf of Milkweed Editions, milkweed.org.

"Small Kindnesses" by Danusha Laméris from *Bonfire Opera.* Reprinted by permission of the University of Pittsburgh Press. "Insha'Allah" by Danusha Laméris from *The Moons of August* Copyright © 2014 by Danusha Laméris and reprinted with permission of Autumn House Press.

"Joy" by Dorianne Laux originally published in *Salt* (The Field Office, 2020). "On the Back Porch" from *Awake* (Carnegie Mellon University Press, 2013). Reprinted with permission of the author.

Li-Young Lee, "Early in the Morning" from *Rose.* Copyright © 1986 by Li-Young Lee. Reprinted with the permission of The Permissions Company, LLC on behalf of BOA Editions, Ltd., boaeditions.org.

"Gas Station Communion" by Paula Gordon Lepp originally published (as "Communion at the BP") in *Braided Way: Faces and Voices of Spiritual Practice.*

"Passenger," "A Great Wild Goodness," and "How to Wake" by Annie Lighthart from *PAX* (Fernwood Press, 2021). Reprinted with permission of the author and publisher.

Ada Limón, "The Raincoat" from *The Carrying.* Copyright © 2018 by Ada Limón. Reprinted with the permission of The Permissions Company LLC on behalf of Milkweed Editions, milkweed.org.

"Braiding His Hair" by Alison Luterman originally published in *The Sun Magazine* and *In the Time of Great Fires* (Catamaran, 2020). Reprinted with permission of the author.

"Make Believe" by Emilie Lygren from *What We Were Born For* (Blue Light Press, 2021). Reprinted with permission of the author.

"Telephone Repairman" by Joseph Millar from *Overtime* (Carnegie Mellon University Press, 2013). Reprinted with permission of the author

"What You Missed That Day You Were Absent from Fourth Grade" by Brad Aaron Modlin from *Everyone at This Party Has Two Names* (Southeast Missouri State University Press, 2016). Reprinted with permission of the author.

"Shift" and "First Light" by Susan Moorhead from *Carry Darkness, Carry Light* (Kelsay Books, 2021). Reprinted with permission of the author.

"Drinking There" by Mark Nepo forthcoming in *The Fifth Season*. Reprinted with permission of the author.

"Red Brocade" and "Kindness" from *Everything Comes Next: Collected and New Poems* by Naomi Shihab Nye. Text copyright © 2020 by Naomi Shihab Nye. Used by permission of HarperCollins Publishers.

"Sunday" by January Gill O'Neil from *Rewilding*. Copyright © 2018 by January Gill O'Neil. Reprinted with the permission of The Permissions Company, LLC on behalf of CavanKerry Press, Ltd., cavankerry.org. "Elation" originally published in *Kenyon Review* Online.

Gregory Orr, "Morning Song" from *The Caged Owl: New and Selected Poems*. Copyright © 1980 by Gregory Orr. Reprinted with the permission of The Permissions Company, LLC on behalf of Copper Canyon Press, coppercanyonpress.org.

Alicia Ostriker, "The Dogs at Live Oak Beach, Santa Cruz" from *The Little Space: Poems Selected and New, 1968-1998*. Copyright © 1998 by Alicia Ostriker. Reprinted by permission of the University of Pittsburgh Press.

Peter Pereira, "A Pot of Red Lentils" from *Saying the World*. Copyright © 2003 by Peter Pereira. Reprinted with the permission of The Permissions Company, LLC on behalf of Copper Canyon Press, coppercanyonpress.org.

"Abundance to Share with the Birds" by Andrea Potos first appeared in *Poetry East* and the chapbook *Abundance to Share With the Birds* (Finishing Line Press). "Where I Might Find Her" first appeared in *The Sunlight Press*. Reprinted with permission of the author.

"Still Life with Ladder" by Susan Rich is forthcoming in *Blue Atlas* (Red Hen Press, 2024). Reprinted with permission of the author.

"Take Love for Granted" by Jack Ridl, from *Practicing to Walk Like a Heron*. © Wayne State University Press, 2013. Reprinted with permission of the author.

Alberto Ríos, "Dawn Callers" from *Not Go Away Is My Name*. Copyright © 2020 by Alberto Ríos. Reprinted with the permission of The Permissions Company, LLC on behalf of Copper Canyon Press, coppercanyonpress.org.

"At the Creek" by David Romtvedt, from *No Way: An American Tao Te Ching* (LSU Press) Copyright © 2019 David Romtvedt. Reprinted with permission of the publisher and the author.

Susan Rothbard, "That New," from *Birds of New Jersey*. Broadkill River Press, 2021. Reprinted with permission of the author.

"I Save My Love" by Marjorie Saiser from *Learning to Swim* (Stephen F. Austin State University Press, 2019) and "Last Day of Kindergarten" from *I Have Nothing to Say About Fire* (University of Nebraska Press, 2016). Reprinted with permission of the author.

"My Mother's Van" by Faith Shearin Copyright © 2018 Faith Shearin, from *Darwin's Daughter* (Stephen F. Austin State University Press, 2018). Poem reprinted by permission of the author.

"In Praise of Dirty Socks" by Lailah Dainin Shima, originally published in *The Buddhist Poetry Review*.

"Late Summer" by Anya Silver from *Second Bloom* (Cascade Books, 2017). Used by permission of Wipf and Stock Publishers, www.wipfandstock.com.

"The Summer You Learned to Swim" by Michael Simms originally published in *Poetry* (March 2021).

Tracy K. Smith, "Song" from *Life on Mars*. Copyright © 2011 by Tracy K. Smith. Reprinted with the permission of The Permissions Company, LLC on behalf of Graywolf Press, Minneapolis, MN, graywolfpress.org.

"Assisted Living" by Judith Sornberger originally published in *Third Wednesday*.

William Stafford, "You Reading This, Be Ready" from *Ask Me: 100 Essential Poems*. Copyright © 1977, 2014 by William Stafford and the Estate of William Stafford. Reprinted with the permission of The Permissions Company, LLC on behalf of Graywolf Press, Minneapolis, MN, graywolfpress.org.

"Turning" from *Wing Over Wing* by Julie Cadwallader Staub Copyright © 2019 by Julie Cadwallader Staub. Used by permission of Paraclete Press, www.paracletepress.com.

"Site Planning" by Christine Stewart-Nuñez from *The Poet & the Architect* Copyright © 2021 Christine Stewart-Nuñez. Reprinted with permission of Terrapin Books.

"Future" by Jacqueline Suskin from *Help in the Dark Season* (Write Bloody, 2019). Reprinted with permission of the author.

"Carrying Water to the Field" by Joyce Sutphen from *Carrying Water to the Field: New and Selected Poems* (University of Nebraska Press, 2019). Reprinted with permission of the author.

"On Lightness" and "Bowl" by Heather Swan from *A Kinship with Ash*. Copyright © 2020 Heather Swan. Reprinted with permission of Terrapin Books.

"Chore" by Angela Narciso Torres from *What Happens Is Neither*. Copyright © 2021 by Angela Narciso Torres. Reprinted with the permission of The Permissions Company, LLC, on behalf of Four Way Books, fourwaybooks.com.

Natasha Trethewey, "Housekeeping" from *Domestic Work*. Copyright © 2000 by Natasha Trethewey. Reprinted with the permission of The Permissions Company, LLC on behalf of Graywolf Press, graywolfpress.org.

"Kindness" and "The Question" by Rosemerry Wahtola Trommer, originally published on her blog, A Hundred Falling Veils.

"Breathe" by David Van Houten from *2020 Visions* (2021).

"Most Important Word" and "Thursday Morning" by Laura Grace Weldon from *Portals* (Middlecreek Publishing, 2021). Reprinted with permission of the author.

"Moving" by Michelle Wiegers originally published as part of The Gatherings Project.

"A Beginner's Guide to Gardening Alone" by Laura Budofsky Wisniewski first appeared in the 2020 *Mizmor Anthology* as "Suddenly While Gardening," and is forthcoming in *Sanctuary, Vermont* (Orison Books, 2022). Reprinted with permission of the author.

All other poems reprinted with permission of the author.

ACKNOWLEDGMENTS

My deepest thanks to the amazing team at Storey Publishing, who once again brought such a beautiful book into being, especially Deborah Balmuth, Liz Bevilacqua, Alethea Morrison, Alee Moncy, Jennifer Travis, and Melinda Slaving. I'm grateful for the community of poets who contributed to this book, too, some of whom I first met in Zoom workshops: These anthologies would not be possible without your generosity. Special thanks to my mentors and friends, especially Ted Kooser and Naomi Shihab Nye: You are both my North Stars in poetry as well as in life. Deepest appreciation to Danusha Laméris for her generous and beautiful foreword, and for the anchor of her timeless poems: I can't believe we get to be coworkers. Thank you to my family and friends, and to all the poetry readers out there (you are the best). Thanks to Dinara Mirtalipova for another gorgeous cover and for her own beautiful work. I couldn't do any of this without the essential support of my husband and best friend, Brad Peacock, who has taught me more about kindness than I ever thought possible, and who still asks me, when I need to hear it: "Are you happy to be alive?"